WOLFESWORD

A MEDIEVAL ROMANCE

BY KATHRYN LE VEQUE

DE WOLFE PACK GENERATIONS

KATHRYN LE VEQUE
NOVELS

ARE YOU SIGNED UP FOR KATHRYN'S BLOG?

You'll get the latest news and information on exclusive giveaways, exclusive excerpts, coming releases, sales, free books, cover reveals and more.

Kathryn's blog followers get it all first. No spam, no junk.

Get the latest info from the reigning Queen of English Medieval Romance!

Sign Up Here
kathrynleveque.com

AUTHOR'S NOTES

Welcome to Cassius' story!

We first met Cassius in *WolfeHeart*, as the second-eldest son of Patrick de Wolfe and the younger brother of Markus de Wolfe. I never really intended to give Cassius his own story, but I liked him so much in *WolfeHeart*, I thought – why not?

So now, we have Cassius a few years after *WolfeHeart*, and he's becoming something of a rock star purely based on his looks. To put it mildly, he's a comely lad. To put it not so mildly, imagine if Henry Cavill and Tom Welling had a baby. Yes, Cassius is *that* gorgeous.

And all of England's women know it.

Surprisingly, Cassius is not full of himself about it. Not too full, anyway. He's more interested in his career at this point in his life because he's the king's *Lord Protector*, a highly prestigious post. Sure, he loves women and doesn't shy away from one who interests him, but they're secondary to his ambition at this point in his life.

Enter Dacia of Doncaster.

Dacia, you'll find, is an interesting character. She's a beautiful girl and more than a match for Cassius in that department, except for one thing – she's got a fairly heavy dusting of freckles on her nose and cheeks. Since clear, pale skin was a prized beauty attribute to a Medieval woman, freckles are worse than pimples. She might as well have scars all over her face because freckles were about the worst physical trait one could have. Freckles were definitely a trait for the red-haired, Celtic crowd and not so frowned upon in their culture, but for the Normanancestry, Anglo-Saxon women, freckles were a problem.

We're in the early fourteenth century at this point and about a hundred years before witches were burned in earnest. But even so, witchcraft was a terrifying thing and women with moles or freckles were considered by some to be marked by the devil.

And that's what we're dealing with – lots of freckles.

This book also deals with something interesting that I've had in other books, but I'm revisiting it again – Medieval medicine. There is something called "Rotten Tea" I've used in several books and it actually does exist. It's the forerunner of penicillin and there are recipes for it on the internet (like, on survivalist websites). So, can you make penicillin? You can. But it's uncontrolled and dicey. Not really recommended unless you're in an apocalypse and have no other choice.

But in Medieval times, they really didn't have a choice, especially if you're going to lose a limb or die of an infection, so Rotten Tea was a thing. So was a formula called "Bald's potion" that called for wine, garlic, onions, and bile salts – literally, salts produced from the human liver. How do you get bile salts in Medieval times? From corpses. These days, they are artificially manufactured, but not in the 14th century. Medieval medicine makes for interesting reading.

Also of note – remember that the grandsons of William de Wolfe have the de Wolfe standard tattoo somewhere on their torsos, but in Medieval times, tattoos were referred to as a stigmata – it's the closest word I can come to that means tattoo, so when you see that word, that's what we're referring to.

And one final thing – Magnus the Law-Mender, Cassius' grandfather and Patrick "Atty" de Wolfe's father-in-law, really did exist. He was a great king of Norway, known for restoring law and order to his country. Hence, the nickname "Law-Mender". However, he died about twenty years before this story is set, but I really like Magnus and what he brings to the House of de Wolfe, so I have taken the liberty of expanding his lifespan just a little. We need the pushy Norwegian king who demands to name all of his grandsons and great-grandsons.

Now, with all that said, the usual pronunciation guide:

- The heroine's name is the interesting part here. I've heard it pronounced three ways – DAY-cee-uh, DAY-sha, and DAH-cee-uh. For our purposes, we're going with DAH-cee-uh.
- Cassius – basically, Cash-us
- Amata – Uh-MAH-tuh

I hope you enjoy this truly romantic tale – it has some very, very sweet moments and Cassius is a very charismatic hero. That is something we really didn't see from him in his brother's tale, but here, it comes out fully. He has quickly become one of my favorites!

Happy Reading!

Hugs,

Kathryn

DE WOLFE PACK GENERATIONS

The grandsons of William de Wolfe are referred to as "The de Wolfe Cubs". There are more than forty of them, both biological and adopted, and each young man is sworn to his powerful and rich legacy. When each grandson comes of age and is knighted, he tattoos the de Wolfe standard onto some part of his body. It is a rite of passage and it is that mark that links these young men together more than blood.

More than brotherhood.

It is the de Wolfe birthright.

The de Wolfe Pack standard is meant to be worn with honor, with pride, and with resilience, for there is no more recognizable standard in Medieval England. To shame the Pack is to have the tattoo removed, never to be regained.

This is their world.

Welcome to the Cub Generation.

De Wolfe Motto: *Fortis in arduis*

Strength in times of trouble

PROLOGUE

Spring, 1303 A.D.
Hagg Crag
Six miles northwest of Doncaster

"YOU HAVE SEEN the fortress?"

"I have. And it will cost you more to take it."

There was a pause. In a small, cluttered solar that smelled of urine and dog feces, a man with bad teeth and even worse hair was facing off against a well-dressed, well-armed man of Flemish origins.

It was a business meeting.

The man from Flanders wore a yellow tunic with a black lion, the claws bloodied and a big, red tongue lashing out from the mouth. His standard was recognizable to most warlords in England, France, and Scotland because it was his calling card. It was a walking advertisement.

Marcil Clabecq advertised his services through that distinguishable standard.

But those services were pricey.

That was something Catesby Hagg was discovering. He'd

already paid the man twenty pounds sterling to bring him and his eighty-one man army from Flanders to the inlet in Grimsby. From Grimsby, they'd taken the land route to Doncaster, which is where they found themselves now. Even if he didn't hire this small army of some of the best fighters in the world, it had still cost him plenty to bring them to England.

Now, they wanted more.

He felt as if they were trying to fleece him.

"How *much* more?" Catesby asked, trying not to sound annoyed in the face of a man who was paid to kill people. "I told you that Edenthorpe Castle was a substantial bastion. That was never kept from you, so you knew when you came what you would be facing. I fail to see why it is going to cost me more for you to do the job I want you to do."

Marcil Clabecq could hear the frustration in the man's voice. But he could also hear his desperation. "Because you failed to mention just how big Edenthorpe was," he said in his thick Flemish accent. "My men have seen the place and tell me it is massive. There are enormous walls and massive earth-works, which make it more difficult to breach. You also failed to mention that Doncaster has more than a thousand men inside that castle."

Catesby eyed him. "Who told you that?"

Marcil snorted. A tall man with shoulder-length black hair, a trim mustache and beard, and black eyes that were as black as his mercenary soul, he had been a soldier for hire for many years. So had his father. The Lords of Clabecq were quite rich and well-known mercenaries, hired by barons and kings alike.

Marcil saw great potential in this particular job.

"My men were in Doncaster for several days before we went to the castle," he said, moving to the sideboard that contained a rock crystal decanter of wine and fine crystal cups. "They asked questions and received answers. It is necessary in my line of work to know exactly what I am dealing with."

Catesby was a little miffed that Marcil had gone off on his own fact-finding exhibition. "And what are you dealing with?"

Marcil poured himself some wine, ruby-red liquid trickling out of the decanter. "I am dealing with a spoiled lord," he said pointedly. "I am dealing with a man who was not completely truthful when he summoned me. You want me to destroy Edenthorpe Castle but I am telling you now that it will be impossible with only eighty-one men and a big army inside her walls. Therefore, I must be clever about this."

"What do you mean?"

Marcil drank the wine, smacking his lips to savor the tart flavor. "You have stated that the Duke of Doncaster is not a great warlord."

Catesby shook his head. "He does not go to war constantly if that's what you mean," he said. "Edenthorpe is quite peaceful."

"Good. That makes my job easier."

"Then you will accept the terms?"

"Explain them again to me so there is no mistake."

Catesby had gone from frustrated to eager. "If you manage to capture Edenthorpe, we will split her spoils," he said. "I will get the fortress and I will split her wealth with you."

"I will have first pick."

"Very well," Catesby said, somewhat unhappily. "But Doncaster has a granddaughter. She belongs to me. I have a son, you know. He will make an excellent Duke of Doncaster."

Marcil cocked an eyebrow, a smile on his lips. "Ah," he said. "So there is more behind this than a land dispute. You want something more."

Catesby nodded without regret. "I want Doncaster and Edenthorpe," he said. "When I marry my son to the heiress, the land dispute becomes null. All of it shall be mine."

Marcil thought on those words for a few moments before downing the entire glass of wine and setting the cup back on the table.

"Then I must make plans," he said. "I will need to inspect the castle myself and see what I am truly up against."

Catesby looked at him warily. "You cannot simply walk up to the castle," he said. "There are guards everywhere. They will want to know why you are there."

But Marcil waved him off. "Do not worry so much," he said. "There are other ways of inspecting the castle."

"What ways?"

Marcil grinned, revealing yellowed teeth in a gesture that was innately evil. "There are ways," he said evasively. "That is why I have come, *n'est pas?*"

He was gone before Catesby could question him any further, out of the solar and into the yard of the small fortress where his well-dressed, well-fed mercenaries waited. Catesby made his way to the window overlooking the bailey, watching Marcil speak with his men.

He was starting to think he'd made a deal with the devil.

In truth, he had.

Hell was coming.

CHAPTER ONE

T HERE WERE PEOPLE everywhere.

In the midst of a bright spring day, upon the cusp of noon, Cassius de Wolfe and his men had entered the outskirts of the village of Doncaster and proceeded into a crowd of people, the mass of which Cassius had not seen outside of London.

But it wasn't just any crowd.

It was a *very* happy crowd.

It didn't take very long for Cassius to figure out that there was some kind of festival going on, for the women had flowers in their hair and the men were drinking from big, wooden cups overflowing with cheap and frothy ale. Children ran about, chasing one another, with garlands hanging around their necks. Even the dogs had flower collars.

It was a joyful place.

Intrigued, Cassius and his men continued towards the center of town.

"What in the world do you suppose is going on?"

The question came from Sir Rhori du Bois, a massive knight with black hair and blazing blue eyes. He was part of the du

5

Bois-de Lohr family, his father being one Macsen du Bois, son of Maddoc, and his great-great-grandfather had been the Earl of Canterbury, David de Lohr. Rhori had the du Bois looks but the de Lohr personality, all fire and brilliance. The product of two great bloodlines, his prowess in battle was unmatched.

Cassius shook his head to the man's question.

"I do not know," he said, eyeing a group of wild boys running in their direction. "A feast some kind, clearly. Or a festival. Or mayhap even an execution because you know how quickly those can turn into a festive occasion. Especially if the man to be executed is hated enough."

Rhori grunted in disapproval. "Entertainment."

"Exactly."

The third knight in their group was bringing up the rear and happened to be in the path of the wild boys. The children zipped past Cassius and Rhori, but when they came to the third knight, they began throwing something at each other. It could have been pebbles because a couple pinged the warhorse, who swung his big head unhappily. The big, ugly dog who followed Cassius around barked when the children ran by. One of the objects landed in the knight's black hair and stuck.

Cassius and Rhori watched him curiously.

"Something is in your hair, Bose," Cassius pointed out the obvious.

Sir Bose de Shera wasn't one to get worked up about anything, not even children throwing projectiles into his hair. He was calm and cool like his legendary grandfather, Bose de Moray, and he reached up to pluck whatever it was out of his hair. He looked at it, sniffed it, and promptly popped it into his mouth.

Cassius and Rhori recoiled in disgust.

"Bose," Cassius scolded. "How many times have I told you not to put things in your mouth when you do not know where they have come from? For Christ's sake, you're like a child who sits in the dirt and shoves pebbles in his mouth."

Bose was chewing on whatever it was. "It is a sweet," he said. "Cinnamon and honey, I think. It is delicious."

Cassius stared at him for a long moment before breaking down into snorts. Rhori simply shook his head.

"God," he muttered. "The man puts anything in his mouth."

"Of course I do," Bose said seductively. "Ask the ladies."

Cassius' laughter grew. The rapport between Rhori, a serious knight, and Bose, a sometimes irreverent one, was truly hilarious at times. It could also be grating and they were known to throw punches at each other from time to time. But the two were utterly devoted to one another and would kill for each other, so most of the grumbling was for show. Even the fist fights turned into hugs, and Cassius had been listening to all of it for the past three years, ever since he took command of the king's personal guard.

The king's Lord Protector.

Cassius de Wolfe was from the great northern House of de Wolfe, a massive family that had all started with one man, William de Wolfe, a knight called the greatest of his generation. He'd served at Northwood Castle, an enormous fortress along the Scottish border, until the king had awarded him his own lands and title for meritorious service.

William de Wolfe went on to become the Earl of Warenton and his seat of Castle Questing was one of the greatest in the north. He and his Scottish bride, Jordan Scott, had eight children, including five sons, all of whom had procreated prodigiously. Cassius was the second son of William's third son,

Patrick de Wolfe, who was also the Earl of Berwick. De Wolfe knights were in high demand, including from the king himself, and it had been quite by chance that Cassius had been offered the role of Lord Protector to King Edward when his eldest brother had passed on the position.

That had been three years ago and Cassius had found himself in a world that was leaps and bounds more complicated and dangerous than anything he'd ever experienced to date. As the king's personal bodyguard, he went where Edward went, and for an active and battle-seasoned king, Cassius had found himself in some hairy situations.

Three years of politics, battle, and being on his guard every day and every night.

And now... *this*.

This was some well-deserved time away from Edward to return home to see his family. Cassius hadn't been home since he'd accepted the prestigious position and he'd performed so well that it was with great reluctance that Edward allowed him to return home to visit. Cassius' reason for wanting to return home was very simple – he wanted to see his grandmother.

That was the truth.

Of course, he wanted to see his parents, too, but his grandmother was more time sensitive. In her ninth decade, the Dowager Countess of Warenton, Lady Jordan, was very precious to her family, and very precious to Cassius. The woman wasn't going to live forever. Edward understood that, and since he and his father owed a great deal to the House of de Wolfe, he'd permitted Cassius to return home for a short time.

Cassius couldn't wait to get there.

However, on his way home, he was stopping in Doncaster on the king's official business which included a visit to the Duke of Doncaster, Vincent Rossington de Ryes. Edward was seeking financial support from Doncaster, or Old Cuffy as he was known, a man who was wildly rich from not only his English lands but his French lands as well, and Edward was always looking for financial support. Cassius happened to be a very good emissary, so he sent the man to flatter the duke, reiterate the king's affection for him, and then beg for money.

That was the gist of it.

Cassius couldn't wait to get it over with.

After a swift journey north from London, Cassius, his dog, and his men found themselves in Doncaster. The truth was that Cassius was so valuable to Edward that the man had sent two of his elite knights along with him to ensure Cassius made it home safely. Rhori and Bose came from some of the finest families England had to offer and also happened to be Cassius' best friends, so here they were, traveling as a trio, in a leisure situation.

Therefore, the festivities around them were alluring.

Perhaps coming to Doncaster was a good thing, after all.

With Bose chewing the last of the cinnamon sweet, the trio entered the center of town. Now, the full glory of the festivities were upon them and it seemed as if the whole of Doncaster was enjoying the merriment. There was laughing and music and food, and gaily colored banners flying in the breeze.

The entire village was undulating in mass celebration.

Cassius reined his horse to a halt.

"We seemed to have arrived on a day of days," he said. As a couple passed near, both man and woman in garlands, he grabbed the man by the neck. "You, there! What is this celebration?"

The man was forced to pause. Not that he had a choice with

an enormous hand around his neck. Worse still, there was an enormous gray dog with a head as large as a pig's standing up against him. The dog's hand-sized paws were on his shoulders.

Nay, he had no choice.

"'Tis the Lords of Misrule," the man said fearfully. "'Tis the first of April, my lord. The Lords of Misrule command this day with their fun and mischief."

Cassius let go of the man and looked around. He noted that there were several men running about, each wearing a jester's cap and red tunic.

Now, it was starting to make some sense.

"Ah," he said, waving the man on as he turned to Rhori and Bose. "The Lords of Misrule rule the day, then. This should be interesting."

The celebration of the Lords of Misrule wasn't an unusual celebration, in fact. It was a day of pranks and mischief and frivolity, and they could hear screams as young women were pinched or poked, or even boldly kissed. Those in the jester's caps were doing a good deal of teasing and pranking as dancing and laughter went on around them.

Cassius looked at his men.

"Well?" he said. "We could spend an hour or two here eating and drinking before moving on to Old Cuffy of Edenthorpe Castle. It seems as if there is plenty to go around."

Rhori's blue eyes glimmered. "What you mean to say is that *you* want to spend an hour or two here eating and drinking."

Cassius flashed that seductive smile that had every woman between the ages of eighteen and eighty falling at his feet. "Well and why not?" said the man whose male beauty made him something of a celebrity among the nobility of England. "It has been a long time since we've engaged in such leisure. We deserve it."

Rhori laughed softly. "As you wish," he said, throwing a leg over the saddle and sliding to the ground. "Come along, my Adonis. Let us go find some women to fawn over you."

And fawn, they did. After they took the horses over to the livery and left the dog there to guard both the horses and their possessions, the famous knight that was Cassius de Wolfe entered the crowd and, predictably, the women gravitated towards him. Cassius had a head full of dark, curly hair, pale blue eyes, and a square jaw. He was built like a god, as Rhori had suggested, with broad shoulders, enormous arms, and a narrow waist. But it was his smile that could melt even the hardest heart – big, bright, and devilish. He smiled, women swooned, and all was right in the world.

And he attracted the opposite sex like flies to honey.

The king would laugh at the way Cassius drew women to him. Edward would joke that all the women were concerned with when he traveled or held court was that Cassius de Wolfe was somewhere in his midst. The king was quite certain he would be trampled to death someday by women anxious to get a glimpse of Cassius, an ignoble death to a noble monarch. But the truth was that Cassius had the skill to match all of that beauty, which is why Edward kept the man close.

Now that they were in the midst of a festival with many maidens, Rhori and Bose were hoping for Cassius' leavings. He would probably select one lass to keep company with, leaving a horde of disappointed women just looking for a broad shoulder to cry on. There were tables set out with food and drink in the town center, and the knights collected cups of a free frothy ale even though a better, more flavorful one could be bought for a pence or two.

Unwilling to spend their money if they didn't have to, however, they took the free stuff, wandering to the food tables where bread and cheese and all manner of pies were laid out – fruit pies, meat pies, pies made into the shape of chickens. Each man collected a couple of the pies and wolfed them down as a dance commenced in the middle of the square. It was a big, open area, now filled with hundreds of revelers. A large group of minstrels played a lively tune as women were lifted into the air by their strong partners, spun around to the sounds of their delighted screams.

Cassius had just finished his second pie when a lovely lass with flowers wound into her blonde hair grasped him by the arm.

"Come!" she said happily, pulling him towards the festivities. "Dance with me, my lord!"

Cassius' lips curled into that lazy, sexy smile. "Me?" he said. "I am not much for dancing."

The girl was pretty and she knew it. She batted her eyes at him. "Please?" she begged. "It would only take a moment and would make me so very happy."

Cassius was a pushover. Plus, she was lovely, so it was no hardship to dance with her. He shrugged weakly and she took that as consent, pulling him into the dancing crowd as Rhori and Bose were abducted by maidens for the very same purpose. Soon, all of them were dancing gaily, lifting their partners into the air and listening to them squeal.

It was delightful.

The dance seemed to go on for quite some time, enough to work Cassius into a sweat. It was exertion, that was true, but it was mostly the fact that he was wearing chain mail and heavy tunics. He was dressed for travel, including weapons, and leaping around to music had him sweating beneath the warm sun. When the music slowed into a more genteel dance, he tried to beg off, but his pretty partner wouldn't let him. She kept a tight grip on him, forcing him into a sweet but somewhat intimate dance.

"I've not even asked your name, my lord," she said as they looped their arms and turned to the music. "Forgive me for being so rude."

Cassius' pale eyes twinkled. "I've not asked you yours, either," he said. "I am Cassius de Wolfe."

He twirled the girl and when she came around, their eyes met once more. "De Wolfe?" she repeated. "I have heard that name."

"My family is rather large."

"In Yorkshire, mayhap?"

"Northumberland."

She nodded in understanding as he twirled her again. When she came back around, their eyes met again.

"My name is Amata de Branton," she said. "My father's cousin is the Duke of Doncaster, and if my father knew I was being so bold, I would be in for a row. Therefore, if you meet him, do not tell him that I forced you to dance with me."

He grinned. "Who is your father?"

"Hugh de Branton of Silverdale," she said.

"Doncaster's cousin?"

"Aye," she said, looking him over and noticing that he was wearing the crimson standard with three golden lions. "And you serve the royal household."

"Aye," he said, not going into detail. "I am here to see the duke before I continue on home. I have not been home in three years."

"I see," she said. "Do you serve in London, then?"

She wasn't going to let him off so easily. She was curious, this one. Cassius nodded. "I do," he said. "But I do not wish to speak of my service at the moment. It is the first time I have had time away in three years, so all I wish to think of is frivolity and food and more dancing."

That seemed to satisfy her, or at least she respected his wishes. For the moment, anyway. They danced the rest of the dance speaking on trivial things, like her younger sister who was bound for the convent. Amata didn't approve of her sister taking her vows and was very clear on that, evidently thinking that it was because her sister was too round or too plain or too something. Listening to her talk, Cassius could see how shallow the woman was, which made her far less pretty in his eyes.

In fact, he was growing rather bored with her pettiness, so he began to look around for Rhori and Bose, already thinking of an excuse to leave Amata. Before he could make his move, however, fools with their foolish caps and red tunics invaded the dance, pinching the women and making them scream. They were causing quite an uproar and Cassius could see them approaching.

In fact, they were looking at him.

Not that it was difficult to see him. Not only was he excruciatingly handsome, but he was also at least a head taller than any man there. Height ran in his family, as his father was an extremely tall man, so Cassius had inherited those long bones. As the fools drew near, they suddenly let up a cry and completely disrupted the dance.

The music stopped.

"We have found them!" one man with missing teeth cried, pointing to Cassius. "We have found the King and Queen of

Misrule!"

The crowd gave up a cheer, wanting to know who it was, and Cassius found himself swept away by the Lords of Misrule and their happy, drunken minions. He was armed and usually didn't take being pushed around very well, but he realized this was a festive occasion and those doing the pushing weren't doing it aggressively. So what if he was being grabbed by some very happy men and a few women? Someone even pinched his arse but when he turned to see who had done such a thing, all he could see were happy *male* faces. They were all grinning at him.

He wasn't going to ask who pinched him.

Cheeky bastards...

"The king and queen, the king and queen!" the group shouted, funneling them over to the northern end of the town square where a platform had been raised. There were people upon it, and a table laden with food, but Cassius didn't think anything of it until the fool that had him by the arm came to a halt.

"Your grace!" the fool shouted. "We have our king and queen. Will you not crown them, your grace?"

That's when Cassius realized he may have allowed himself to be put into an embarrassing situation. As soon as the fool addressed someone as "your grace", he immediately turned to the platform. That kind of address went beyond any baron, viscount, or even earl. It went higher still. He'd seen the Duke of Doncaster several times in London, so he knew the man on sight. Much to his chagrin, the elderly man sitting at the table on the platform was, indeed, the Duke of Doncaster.

Old Cuffy in the flesh.

Cassius pulled himself away from the fools, and from Amata, and made his way to the stairs leading up to the platform. When he and the duke made eye contact, he came to a halt and bowed respectfully.

"Your grace," he said. "I did not know you were at this festival, else I would have sought you as soon as I arrived. You will accept my deepest apologies for not greeting you sooner."

The duke looked at him curiously. "I know you, I think," he said, noting the royal standard. But more than that, he was noting the enormous knight with the pale blue eyes who was vaguely familiar. "In London, was it?"

Cassius nodded. "Aye, your grace," he said. "I am the king's Lord Protector, Cassius de Wolfe. I accompanied the king on his visit to Edenthorpe two years ago."

"I recall."

"I have come this time with Edward's compliments and a message."

Vincent Rossington de Ryes, Duke of Doncaster, lit up at the mention of Edward. Perhaps there was some recognition there for Cassius, too, but he seemed to be delighted to hear Edward's name mentioned. An elderly man in his seventh decade, Old Cuffy was a favorite because of his generosity and wisdom. He was well loved by his vassals and well liked in military circles. He didn't go to battle like some of the upper crust did, but he could always be counted on for men or material. Edward had a particular fondness for his friend, Old Cuffy.

And his money.

"I am honored," Doncaster said, rising to his feet. "Will you sit with me, Sir Cassius? I should like to hear Edward's message."

Cassius took a few steps towards the table, looking around

at all of the people, not only on the platform, but in general. The area was swarming with them.

"If you please, your grace," Cassius said. "I would prefer to deliver the king's message in a more... private setting. It is for your ears only, after all. Will you indulge me?"

Doncaster was already moving away from the table, nodding his head. "Of course," he said. "How silly of me. Shall you accompany me to my castle?"

Cassius nodded. "It would be an honor, your grace," he said. "Let me collect my men and we will meet you at the castle gate."

As people on the platform began to scatter, helping the old duke down the stairs and clearing off the food, Cassius took the other set of stairs and bolted through the crowd, hunting for Rhori and Bose. He finally found them in the distance, over by the ale table, and he quickly headed in that direction.

Until someone grabbed him by the arm.

"Where are you going?" It was Amata and she did not look pleased. "You cannot leave now. We are to be crowned the king and queen of the festival!"

Cassius paused, though he was greatly impatient. "You shall have to find another king," he said. "I have business with Doncaster."

He patted her hand and headed off, but she followed, practically running beside him because his strides were so long. "You are going to the Edenthorpe?"

"I am."

He couldn't see her petulant frown, and even if he could, he wouldn't have cared. "But when will you return?" she asked.

"I will not, my lady, though I thank you for the dance and the polite conversation."

Amata wasn't about to let him get away so easily. "You will not find anything of value at Edenthorpe," she said. "There will be no one to entertain you and you will not have any fun. You *must* return with me."

"I am sorry, but I cannot."

Amata picked up her pace and ended up running in front of him, blocking his path. When he looked at her, his impatience now evident, she slid her soft hands onto his arm.

"You *will* be back," she said confidently. "The only thing you are going to find at Doncaster is an old duke and his ugly granddaughter, and you must stay away from her. So – you *shall* return here, to me, and we shall dance all night."

Cassius eyed her curiously. "Why must I stay away from the granddaughter?"

Amata lifted her eyebrows as if he had asked a stupid question. "Because she bears the marks of a witch, of course," she said. "You have not heard that of her?"

"I have not. What marks?"

Amata leaned into him as if gifting him with information of great importance. "On her face," she said in a low voice. "She is covered with them. Dacia of Doncaster is her name and she is my cousin, but I pity the lass. To look upon her is to become cursed. You do not want to be cursed, do you?"

Cassius' eyes narrowed. "You have looked upon her," he said. "Have you become cursed?"

Amata shook her head. "I am her cousin and she loves me," she declared. "She would not curse me."

"Then you should be careful what you say about her. Your accusations are serious."

Amata shrugged him off. "Everyone knows it," she insisted. "Oh, I know how good she is and truth be told, she is very sweet. She tends the poor and ill who cannot afford a physic, and she feeds those who cannot feed themselves, but it is purely in penitence because of the marks she bears."

"Marks on the flesh do not make her a witch."

Amata wasn't pleased that he wasn't listening to her. She wagged a finger at him. "Do not say that you were not warned," she said. "Whatever your business is with the duke, you should not stay at Edenthorpe. You must come to my father's home for lodgings. He will be more than happy to have you and I would be honored to entertain you."

At that point, it was all he could do not to roll his eyes at her. "Thank you for the offer, but I will remain at Edenthorpe," he said, moving around her and continuing towards Bose and Rhori. "Good day to you, Lady Amata."

"But –"

"Du Bois!" Cassius bellowed, drowning her out. "De Shera! We ride to Edenthorpe!"

He had all but forgotten about Amata. He didn't even notice when she stopped running after him. He was focused on his knights and as Amata stood there and watched, Cassius and his men ran off towards the livery where they'd left their horses and the dog. The duke was expecting them and they wouldn't keep the man waiting.

But Amata didn't see it that way. She saw a deliciously handsome knight getting away from her, but he wasn't going to get far.

She wasn't going to let him get away.

Her father was somewhere in the crowd and she headed off to find him. She would tell him of the gorgeous de Wolfe knight and make sure her father sent word to Doncaster, inviting the man to their home to sup. As a cousin of Doncaster, it would be rude to refuse. One way or another, she wanted de Wolfe to come to Silverdale.

To her.

Amata was convinced she had just met her future husband.

CHAPTER TWO

"WHAT DO YOU think of this shade, my lady?"

The question had come from an older woman, her neck and head tightly wimpled in white, wearing the brown broadcloth garments of a servant as she held up a piece of wet fabric that she had been stirring in a stone cauldron. The woman she was addressing had just come down the stone steps that led into this den of activity. As weak sunlight streamed in through a series of small, barred windows, the woman on the steps peered closely at the fabric without touching it.

"A lovely shade of yellow," she said. "Well done, Edie."

The older woman carefully put the cloth back in the stone vat and continued to stir carefully. "Onion skins and as much saffron as we could spare, mixed with the alum," she said. "It makes a beautiful color."

She wasn't looking at the young woman, now bending over the vat to inspect the color of the water. If she happened to look up, she would see what she had always seen – a petite lass with a womanly shape, big breasts, and eyes of the purest and palest blue. They were almost unnatural in their magnificent beauty. But she would also see a face full of tiny spots. Some called them witch's marks, some called them sun spots, and some even called them freckles.

Whatever they were, they were that by which Dacia of Doncaster was defined.

It was a pity, too. Dacia, under any other circumstances, would have been one of the most sought-after women in all of England because she was the sole heiress to a vast and rich dukedom. Unfortunately, the fates had not been kind to her, and just after her first birthday, a sea of freckles began to appear on the bridge of her nose and cheeks.

That had only been the beginning.

Her nursemaid had kept her covered up and out of the sun but, still, the freckles kept coming. By the time she was five years old, they covered her nose, her cheeks, and down her neck. Since Dacia's parents had died when she had been very young, the only person to tend to her had been her nursemaid, who had been convinced that the devil was trying to mark her charge.

As a child, she'd had a few friends and had been allowed to interact somewhat normally with allies and children her own age. But as she grew, the freckles darkened and the comments began to come. When the rumors and whispers started, and the children grew cruel, the withdrawal from normal life came.

Dacia of Doncaster retreated from the social circles.

As a result of this stringent and paranoid upbringing, Dacia had never been sent away to foster. She had been kept at Edenthorpe Castle, considered a safe haven, because of her zealously religious nursemaid. Even on her deathbed, the old woman was still convinced that the devil had been trying to mark her beloved Dacia and made her promise to always keep her face covered.

All Dacia had ever known was to hide those marks from the world.

Oddly enough, however, she grew into a thoughtful, intelligent, and well-educated young woman who was determined to do good in the world. She had a genuine desire to help the less fortunate, possibly because she knew what it was like to be an outcast. There was no lingering hint of the strangeness her nursemaid had imprinted upon her other than the fact that she rarely left Edenthorpe and when she did, she was covered from head to toe in veils to disguise the heavy dusting of freckles.

Marks of the devil, the old woman had called them.

Unfortunately for Dacia, she had to live with that stigma.

Even so, she didn't let it weigh upon her as heavily as it could have. She had gotten used to hiding her face from the world, which now was uncovered in a rare moment. The woman stirring the dye happened to look up, right into Dacia's face as the woman bent over the vat. She thought that, perhaps, the freckles had faded with age. They didn't seem as dark as they used to be and, at a distance, one couldn't really tell she had them. But at close range, they were clear.

A pity, too. Dacia had an exquisite face of lush lips, well-shaped nose, and those magnificent blue eyes, but the scattering of freckles marred that picture.

The woman stirring the dye tried not to feel pity for the lonely young heiress. When her days should be filled with parties and her nights with handsome suitors, she'd never attended a party in her life, nor had she ever known a suitor.

No one should have to be so lonely.

"This will make for a beautiful garment, my lady," the old woman said. "It was kind of you to have it made for Lady Amata's day of birth. It will go well with her pale hair."

Dacia Mathilde Violette de Ferrar de Ryes grinned as she watched the woman stir the material. "She is my cousin as well as my friend," she said simply. "Oh, I know you do not like her, Edie, but I do look forward to her visits."

Old Edie lifted an eyebrow as she continued stirring. "She comes here to gawk at your grandfather's knights, pick over your jewelry, and steal your clothing," she said with disapproval. "You should not be so generous with her. She takes but she never gives."

"She gives me her companionship when she visits. That is worth a great deal to me."

Edie shut her mouth after that. She was just thinking on how lonely her mistress was except for occasional visits by her greedy and silly cousin, Amata de Branton, who came to visit regularly even though she was petty, gossipy, and bordered on thieving. She also had a tendency to mimic what the nurse had told Dacia, criticizing her face, insisting that her cousin remained covered at all times. It was Edie's opinion that it was out of jealousy and not concern, as Dacia chose to believe.

Edie had never liked Amata.

For good reason.

"She'll be very grateful for your gift, my lady," Edie said evenly. "You are a kind and generous soul, lamb."

Dacia looked up from the vat, smiling at the old servant. "As are you," she said. "Edie, I know you mean well about Amata... and do not think I am so blind to what she really is... but she is my cousin and I do crave her companionship. It is better than the alternative."

Edie simply nodded. It was that lonely girl speaking again and she had nothing to say to the contrary. "What of her sister?" she said. "Why not have Sabine visit? She used to come quite a bit."

Dacia shrugged. "Sabine is bound for the cloister," she said. "Amata says she spends all of her time praying. She has no time to visit me any longer."

Pity, Edie thought. Younger sister Sabine had been the kind one. Still, she wouldn't dwell on it. "And when shall we expect Lady Amata's next visit?" she said. "It has been a while since the last one."

Dacia returned her focus to the dye vat. "Soon, I hope," she said. "Her father was ill, but he is better now, so she should return soon. I hope so. I have missed her."

Edie glanced up at her. "Mayhap you should ask your grandfather to make it so that Lady Amata stays on longer this time," she said. "She could become your companion, your lady-in-waiting. You are to be a duchess someday and all duchesses need ladies."

Dacia shrugged. "Possibly," she said. "But becoming a duchess is a long time off yet."

"Not as long as you think," Edie reminded her quietly. "Your grandfather is old, my lady. You must prepare for the event of his passing. You must be prepared to take your rightful place."

Dacia knew that. It wasn't as if she hadn't thought on it before, but she didn't like to think of the day her grandfather would pass away. He was really all she had as far as immediate family went. Even Amata was really a distant cousin. But Edie was right. When her grandfather was gone, she would become the duchess of a great empire. Having her cousin for a lady-in-waiting wasn't a bad idea.

And she would have a permanent friend.

"Mayhap," she said. "I will think on it."

"If not a lady-in-waiting, why not a maid?"

Dacia waved her off. "Amata? A maid?" She shook her head. "She would sooner throw herself from the battlements than become a maid. Besides… I have more maids than I need, to be perfectly truthful. They do everything but eat and breathe for me. Sometimes I wish…"

She trailed off and Edie looked at her. "*What*, lamb?"

Dacia stood up from the vat. "Sometimes I wish they would all go away and leave me alone," she said. "It's strange, Edie… I feel so alone sometimes, but I am never really alone. I am always surrounded by people. God's Bones, when I hear myself say that, I sound like a madwoman."

Edie grinned. "You sound like someone who has great responsibilities and many people to help you with them," she said. "That is why you have so many women, my lady. They are all there to serve you."

Dacia nodded her head, but it was clear that Edie didn't understand what she was saying. As much as the old woman loved her, it wouldn't be the first time.

She was a bird in a gilded cage and no one seemed to understand that.

"That is true," she said, but she didn't want to continue along a subject that was both frustrating and sometimes painful. With a sigh, she turned for the door. "Grandfather should be returning soon from the festival. I hope he has brought me something from it."

"You should have gone with him," Edie said. "There is dancing and food and merriment. It would have been fun."

Dacia was climbing back up the stone steps that led out into the bailey. "Not me," she said. "You know I do not attend those festivals. They are not for me."

Edie looked up from her dye vat, a hint of pity in her ex-pression. "But... what happened was so long ago. Surely you could try again. You might enjoy yourself."

Dacia was at the top of the stairs, pausing to look down at her most faithful servant. "Nay," she said softly, firmly. "I am not meant for those gatherings, nor merriment, nor gaiety. Men want to see who they are dancing with or talking to, and you know that I cannot... well, it is not for me. I learned my lesson the first time I went and a young man yanked off my veil. It will not happen again."

Sadly, Edie remembered the incident. A very young Dacia, who had just made that awkward transition from childhood to womanhood, wanted very much to attend the very festival that was going on in the village that day – the Lords of Misrule. She had worn her customary veil, but a naughty fool had pulled it from her face and she'd run home, embarrassed, vowing never to attend another festival again.

Edie wasn't entirely sure that her revealed face had caused a ruckus, because the duke told a slightly different story about the incident, but Dacia was convinced that every person in the village looked upon her and was horrified, so she kept away from anything that had to do with festivals or feasts or celebrations. She went to mass regularly with the duke, but that was the only thing she ever did that involved groups of people.

Dacia of Doncaster had relegated herself to a solitary exist-ence.

But... Edie didn't argue with her or try to change her mind. It would do no good. As Dacia left the tower, Edie simply smiled and waved her on. It was never productive to convince her that perhaps the marks on her face weren't as bad as her old nurse had convinced her of.

The old nurse had left an imprint that could not be erased, leaving a ruined young woman in her wake.

IT WAS A surprisingly mild spring day as far as spring days went.

Sometimes this far north, even the springtime could be cold and wet. It was rare when there was a bright and crisp day that had a hint of warmth to it, as today did. As Dacia stepped out into the bailey, a veritable hive of activity at this time of day, she shielded her eyes from the sun and looked up into the blue, blue sky.

It was difficult not to look into the beautiful day and not feel some depression.

Remorse.

Edie had brought up the festival and Dacia had brushed it off, as she always did. But the truth was that it meant more to her than that. She suspected that Edie knew that, but something in Dacia couldn't let the woman know that it hurt more than she let on. Dacia wasn't one to complain, nor had she ever been. She was stoic and accepted things as they were.

But still...

As a child, she would go with her grandfather and enjoy the silliness and the entertainment of a festival that had been going on for decades. Even back then, she would cover her face at the insistence of her nurse. She remembered sitting on her grandfather's knee and eating off of his trencher as minstrels sang and dancers danced. It had been something that she and her grandfather had shared together, and those opportunities were few and far between. The older she became, the more distant and absentminded her grandfather became, and it was increasingly difficult to hold a conversation with him.

He usually seemed to be busy with his own interests.

But not always. After the evening meal, sometimes, they would play games together, like Queek or Draughts. Her grandfather had taught her to play both of those games as a child and it was something they enjoyed together. Lately, however, she was beating him quite regularly and his male pride was having difficulty accepting that. Therefore, they didn't play either as often as they used to.

Dacia couldn't help but notice the older she became, the more her grandfather seemed to withdraw. In fact, she almost went into town with him this morning to attend the festival simply so she could spend time with him, but her experiences of the past would not let her go. Vincent de Ryes went alone, the benevolent Duke of Doncaster, so beloved by his vassals.

And beloved by his only granddaughter.

In fact, Dacia was eager for him to return so he could tell her all about the festival. She had busied herself around the castle all day long, passing the time until he would return. The older he became, the less his stamina, so she expected him home shortly because she knew he was about at his limit given how long he'd already been gone.

Glancing up to the sky again, she shielded her eyes from the sun, realizing that it was rather warm and bright for her not to be wearing a veil against the sunlight. Her old nurse had been fanatical about covering her face because the sunlight seemed to create more freckles on her face as well as darkening the ones that were already there, so it had become habit to cover up in the sun.

Unfortunately, she'd left her veils in her chamber because

she wasn't really in the habit of wearing them when she was within the walls of Edenthorpe. Everyone knew her and she didn't feel particularly self-conscious around the people she'd grown up with, but she usually stayed away from the gatehouse where visitors arrived or farmers came through on their way to the kitchen yard.

The bailey of Edenthorpe was so vast that she could easily move about freely near the keep and near the kitchens without having to worry about seeing strangers who would notice a girl with a heavy dusting are freckles over her nose and cheeks. Although she did manage the kitchens and the keep quite efficiently, she let the cook do the buying from the farmers who came to peddle their wares. She didn't involve herself in that mundane contact, and the truth was that she kept out of sight as much as possible.

It was simply a habit.

But sometimes, her curiosity and need for freedom got the better of her.

Like today. It was beautiful, and she knew that most everyone would be in Doncaster at the festival. No chance of being seen unexpectedly. There were times when she wandered away from Edenthorpe, down to the River Don that ran alongside. It wasn't a fast-flowing river – mostly, it was a shade of greenish-blue, meandering through heavily forested trees with riverbanks of thick, wet grass. In the summertime, flowers would sprout all around and Dacia spent a good deal of time collecting those blooms for perfumes and salves.

On this day, as she waited for her grandfather to return from Doncaster, something about that slow-moving river was calling to her.

She didn't think it would hurt to answer.

Just for a few minutes.

The postern gate was open as it usually was during the daytime, but it was almost as heavily guarded as the gatehouse. That had only been normal as of late – her grandfather had been having trouble with a neighbor, a minor baron named Catesby Hagg of Hagg Crag, who was convinced Doncaster had claimed land that belonged to him. The land in dispute had a mine on it that quarried fine, white rocks in much demand for building in the area. There was money to be made and no one had cared a lick about that strip of land until her grandfather's men had discovered the rock and had begun to mine it.

Suddenly, Hagg came forward and the dispute had been going on for about three years. Mostly, he raided the mine, or at least tried to, but Doncaster had more men and more power, and Hagg's offensives were always turned away. He hadn't come after the castle yet, but the army remained vigilant.

One could never tell when dealing with Catesby Hagg.

Still, Dacia felt no sense of danger as she headed for the postern gate. Her maids, the women who tended to her every need, would go with her if she asked them to but, at the moment, they were in the keep where they always were, dusting and cleaning and sewing and generally keeping busy, and Dacia was glad. She'd much rather take Amata with her, but she wasn't at Edenthorpe, so she was content to go alone.

It was better than going with those women who seemed to view her as Doncaster's heiress rather than just a woman, an ordinary woman, of flesh and blood.

It was a strange dynamic, indeed.

"Going somewhere?"

Dacia heard the voice as she neared the gate. Startled, she turned to see her grandfather's captain approach.

She grinned sheepishly.

"To the river," she said. "I did not see you around, Darian. Why did you not go with Grandfather into town?"

Sir Darian de Lohr made a face that suggested he found the very idea distasteful. A big man with blond hair and sky-blue eyes, he was unwaveringly handsome, dedicated to duty, and a son of the House of de Lohr. There were few finer families in England and Darian had all the makings of a legend, like many of his ancestors.

There had been whispers for years that he would make an excellent Duke of Doncaster with an advantageous marriage to the heiress, but there was one problem with that idea – he'd been at Edenthorpe for eleven years and Dacia had known him since her childhood. She had essentially grown up with him and he was the closest thing she had to a brother.

Unfortunately for Darian, she didn't view him as husband material.

And he knew it.

"Your grandfather took enough heavily armed men with him to start a small war should he have a mind to," he said in answer to her question. "Besides, someone has to remain here, in command."

Her eyes twinkled at him. "It couldn't be because you might see Amata in the village, could it?"

He turned his nose up at her. "I do not know what you mean."

She laughed softly. "Not much, you don't," she said. "The last time she visited, she told me that she is madly in love with you."

"That was only for a brief moment and quite some time ago," he pointed out. "She is madly in love with every man she meets."

Dacia shrugged. "That is possibly true," she said. "Still, her father is rich. Marry the daughter and you inherit the father's money."

"It would *not* be worth it."

Dacia snorted. "Poor Darian," she said. Then, she threw a thumb in the direction of the postern gate. "Care to go with me to the river?"

He shook his head. "I do not," he said. "But take someone with you."

"I do not want to."

"You have an entire horde of women to choose from."

"Not them. I would rather go alone."

He frowned. "Then stay where I can see you, for Christ's sake."

"I will."

"And do not go in the water," he said, wagging a finger at her. "If something happens, you're too far away. I may not be able to get to you in time."

She grinned, flashing him a lovely smile. "You worry like an old woman."

"It takes one to know one, old girl."

Dacia stiffened at the rather sore subject where her age was concerned. "I have only seen twenty-three years."

The wagging finger pointed at her. "You will see twenty and four years next month," he said. "You forget that I know everything about you. Old age is swiftly approaching, lass."

Dacia had enough. She knew why he was saying such things. He'd never come right out and asked for her hand, but he liked to throw subtle digs her way.

Old age is swiftly approaching, lass.

Meaning the chance for suitors would soon be gone, leaving Darian as the victor by default.

But not today. Sticking her tongue out at him, she turned away and headed to the postern gate, listening to him issue orders to the guards that were standing around. As she passed through, two of them followed her, though not closely enough to be a bother. Just enough to watch the area as she wandered around, enjoying the spring weather and pushing aside the knight who wanted both her and her dukedom.

She'd push it all aside until her grandfather returned.

Unfortunately for Dacia, that was sooner than she had expected.

She had been down by the river's edge, noting the reeds that were starting to grow in and thinking on the baskets and hats her maids could weave from them, when she heard the sentry cry go up. When she looked up to see what the commotion was, she realized she had wandered further away from the castle than she had intended. In fact, there was now a road between her and the castle if she wanted to make it home quickly. Otherwise, she would have to follow the river back the way she had come so she could slip in through the postern gate and that would take time.

Then, she began to see the standards of Doncaster. Bright blue with a golden stag upon it, affectionately named Cuffy. No one knew how it got started, but the stag had been called Cuffy for many years. In fact, that was what the villagers of Doncaster called the duke – Old Cuffy. Not to his face, of course, but he was referred to as "Old Cuffy" by almost everyone.

Cuffy was making his march towards the great gatehouse of Edenthorpe and Dacia could see her grandfather's carriage. He didn't ride a horse these days, too old and too fragile, so he rode in a fortified carriage everywhere he went that was far more comfortable than the bony back of a horse.

Gathering her skirts, she was preparing to walk up to the road to meet the carriage when a dog of enormous proportions suddenly shot out of the tall grass, chasing a squawking duck and heading right for her. He was big, gray, and hairy, and all Dacia could see was a mouth with fangs coming in her direction.

Terrified, she turned tail and began to run.

The dog was right on her heels. She thought he may have even bitten her skirt because she swore she felt tugging. She began to swat at the dog, demanding he go away, but the dog wasn't listening. The river was straight ahead and as she tried to make a sharp turn, away from the river and away from the dog, the beast jumped on her from behind and ended up pushing her right into the water.

Splash!

Dacia went in, but she didn't go down all the way. She fell to her knees in the shallow, rocky shore, keeping her head out of the water, as the dog leapt all around her. Now, the dog was barking happily and the birds that had been gathered on the riverbank, including more ducks, were scattering.

With water in her face, and on her knees, she blinked water droplets out of her eyes as the dog chased the birds around. It was clear that he wasn't interested in her, only the birds. When he ran close to her, he licked her face as she picked up two handfuls of mud and threw it at the animal. It drove the dog away, but not far. Not far *enough*, at any rate.

Damnable dog!

With a heavy sigh at the ridiculous and naughty dog, Dacia struggled to stand up when she was suddenly grasped from behind.

"Here, my lady. Allow me to help you."

Panic set in.

"SUP WITH OLD Cuffy tonight, shall we?" Bose said with satisfaction. "I hear he sets an astonishing table."

"Mayhap," Cassius grunted. "But we're not staying beyond tonight, Bose. It's still going to take us at least six more days to reach Castle Questing and I do not want to delay. I want to get home and spend some time there before I have to turn around and head back to London. Edward will not let me cavort in the north forever."

"Then let us eat, sleep, and be on our way."

As long as de Shera understood this night was simply a duty visit, and a quick one at that, Cassius was satisfied. He nodded at the man as if to emphasize his point before returning his focus to the road. They were riding behind the duke's brightly painted carriage, resplendent with blue and gold colors, all reflecting gaily in the bright sun. Edenthorpe Castle was up ahead and Cassius shielded his eyes, getting a good look at the legendary seat of Doncaster.

"I'd forgotten how enormous this place is," he said, catching sight of the blue and gold standards on the battlements, snapping in the breeze. "When we were here two years ago, I spent the entire night roaming the great hall. I do not think I even ate."

To his left, Rhori snorted. "I spent most of the night on the wall," Rhori said. "I really only saw the outside of the place.

Never the warm and comfortable inside where you always linger."

Cassius fought off a grin. "Did you ever stop to think that Edward is trying to hide you from the good people of England?" he said. "With a face such as yours, he does not want to frighten the women."

Rhori grinned, but he was slightly behind Cassius so the man couldn't see him. "There is something on my body that frightens the women, but it is not my face."

"Now you are starting to sound like de Shera."

"You are not the only man around here with astonishing physical traits, Cass."

"Aye, I am."

That brought snorts from Bose, who shook his head at the ribbing. But this was usual with them. It was how they expressed their love for one another.

"Speaking of women," Bose said, looking at Cass. "I saw you dancing with that blonde lass back in Doncaster. Did you get her name?"

Cassius nodded. "Amata," he said. "She said her father is a local baron."

"She was pretty."

Cassius cast him a long look. "And she knows it," he said. "She was most unhappy when I decided to leave with Doncaster. She told me that I should not stay here because of the man's granddaughter. Correct me if I'm wrong, but I do not believe we saw a granddaughter the last time we were here. I do not even recall being introduced to such a woman."

Bose shook his head. "Nor I," he said. "Doncaster is a widower, as I recall, and his only son died long ago."

"And left him with a granddaughter, evidently," Cassius

said. "At least, that was what Amata said. She also said something strange – she said the granddaughter bears witch's
marks."

Bose frowned. "What are witch's marks?"

"Spots, evidently," Cassius said. "Skin blemishes, mayhap. I
am not sure, to be truthful. She accused the granddaughter of
being a witch and I told her to mind her tongue. The conversation collapsed from there."

Bose cocked his head thoughtfully, looking up to the Doncaster standards in the distance. "Curious," he said, scratching
at his neck. "But I've seen women with spots before. We all
have. On their face or neck, it is not uncommon."

"Freckles," Rhori said. "Sun spots, or whatever one wishes
to call them. Horses are freckled sometimes, as is fruit, food,
and a number of other things. But I know there are superstitious fools that believe they only appear on witches or the
possessed."

Bose looked over at him. "You do not believe that?"

"I do not," Rhori said flatly. "I believe what I can see. If a
woman is evil, then it is in her soul, not because she is possessed
by a demon. Demons are a creation of men."

"You are a pragmatic man, my friend," Cassius said. "My
younger sister, Thora, has a big freckle by the corner of her
mouth. She is a beautiful girl and men swarm her. I've not
heard anyone call her a witch because of it."

"Would you not kill them if they did?" Rhori asked.

Cassius cracked a smile. "I am an excellent brother," he
said. "Between my eldest brother and my two younger brothers,
no one who insults my sisters stands a chance of survival."

Rhori and Bose snorted. "Are they all as big as you are?"
Rhori asked. "I've never met your family, Cass."

"I have," Bose said knowingly. "And, aye, they are all as big as he is. Bigger, even. You think Cass is tall? His father and elder brother are giants. The two younger brothers are also quite tall. Whatever is in the water in the north makes men larger than life. They grow like trees."

Cassius shook his head. "In our case, it is the Northman influence," he said. "I have Scots and English blood on my father's side, and Scots and Northman blood on my mother's. Do you remember that I told you about my grandfather, once? He is the King of the Northmen. They call him Magnus the Law-Mender."

"So you are a god," Bose said, a hint of jest in his tone. "We are mere mortals and you are the grandson of not only a king, but also the grandson of the greatest knight the borders have ever seen in William de Wolfe."

Cassius cast him a long look. "Never forget it."

That brought soft laughter from Rhori and Bose. As they drew nearer to the castle, now looming up before them with great, white-stoned walls mined from local stone that was prevalent to the area, the dog that had been plodding patiently alongside Cassius' horse suddenly took off, chasing something in the grass. They turned to see a duck rising up out of the overgrowth along the side of the road.

"Christ," Cassius muttered. "There he goes, that foolish dog. *Argos!*"

He bellowed at the dog, followed by a piercing whistle, but the big dog was down in the thick grass, heading towards the river. He watched as the dog dashed further and further away.

"He'll come back," Bose said. "He always does."

Cassius was indecisive. "True," he said. "But he is getting older and he tends to get lost in new places, the idiot. If he gets too far away, he might lose his way."

Bose reined his horse towards the side of the road. "Then I shall fetch him."

"Nay," Cassius said. "You stay with the duke. I'll find him. He doesn't particularly like you, anyway. He might never come back if you try to catch him."

"That dog loves me."

"That dog growls at you every time you get near him."

As Bose cocked an eyebrow at the old dog who only seemed to like Cassius and no one else, Cassius directed his horse over to the side of the road, sliding down the slight embankment as he headed towards the river. He could hear barking and whistled for the dog again, but Argos was being stubborn. He was having too much fun chasing ducks.

Until Cassius heard a feminine shriek.

Digging his spurs into his horse's flanks, he thundered towards the river.

CHAPTER THREE

W HEN CASSIUS ARRIVED at the river's side, he spied a disaster.

A woman was in the river on her knees while Argos cavorted around her, chasing ducks and other waterfowl. He was having a grand time. As Cassius watched in horror, the dog ran up to the lady, licked her face, and then shook himself so that the water on his fur sprayed out all over her.

The lady yelped.

Cassius was in the water in an instant.

"Here, my lady. Allow me to help you."

When he touched her, the woman shrieked again, yanking her arm away from him and stumbling forward, splashing down into the water again. Cassius wasn't sure what to do, so he stood there, watching her struggle to her feet, pulling the ends of her wet apron around her face before she ever turned to look at him. In fact, she was covering most of her face, leading Cassius to believe that Argos must have hurt her somehow.

He was mortified.

"My lady, are you injured?" he asked, concerned. "My deepest apologies. The dog is usually harmless, I swear. If you are injured, I shall seek a physic immediately."

The lady finally turned to him, staggering, with one hand holding the apron on her face and the other one gathering her soaking skirts. The only thing he could really see were her eyes and her forehead, and a head of dark, luscious hair that was braided into one long braid that trailed to her buttocks.

But those eyes... somewhere between pale blue and pale green, as if they had a fire all their own.

He'd never seen a color like that in his life.

"Is this your dog?" she demanded through the cloth on her face.

He nodded with great remorse. "Aye," he said. "I am exceedingly sorry, my lady. If you are injured, please let me help you."

She was agitated. That much was clear. "He is a very naughty dog."

"I know, my lady. He is usually much better behaved."

"He *jumped* on me."

"I am very sorry, my lady."

"He... he got me all *wet!*"

Cassius sighed sharply and whistled, one of those piercing bursts, and the dog immediately came to his side. He looked at the dog sternly.

"Do you see what you did?" he scolded the mutt. "You pushed this lady into the river and hurt her, and now I am at her mercy because of you. If she wishes to beat me in retaliation, then I must let her. If she wishes to kick me, then I will have to stand for it. If she wants to light my hair on fire and call it justice, then I will have no say in the matter. Well? Do you see what you have done, you ridiculous creature?"

The dog wagged his wet tail and Cassius frowned deeply.

But he was also trying to catch a glimpse of the lady from the corners of his eyes.

She was still standing there.

Cassius wanted to see how she was reacting, hoping that she was softening with his humor and that the dog escapade was a forgivable offense. He finally dared to look at her and he swore he saw her eyes crinkling, as if she were smiling, but the moment their eyes met, she hastily turned for the riverbank.

"I will not beat you nor light your hair on fire," she said, sloshing through the water. "But Argos had better learn to behave himself. The next woman he jumps on might not be so forgiving."

Cassius was following her, sort of. He was walking parallel to her, holding out his hands as if to keep her from teetering because she was having difficulty with her wet, heavy skirts.

"I will have a stern talk with him," he promised. "Are you certain that I cannot assist you?"

She came to the bank. She had to step up about a foot, and the slope was slippery and wet. She tried once and failed, looking to Cassius reluctantly.

"Mayhap you can help me onto the bank," she said.

He leapt up onto the bank with the agility of a cat, reaching out to carefully pull her up. She was soaking wet and heavy, but he managed to get her onto the shore. She still had the apron up around her face and he peered at her.

"Are you *sure* he did not hurt you?" he asked.

Her pale, bright gaze lingered on him for a moment. "I am sure," she said. She looked at him perhaps a little longer than she should have before tearing her gaze away. "I am well enough. Thank you for your assistance."

She started to walk away, picking her way through the grass

as she headed downriver. Cassius, mesmerized by those brilliant eyes, watched her go.

"May I know the name of the woman my dog sinned against so grievously?" he asked.

She paused, turning to him. "You should tell me *your* name so I know who to avoid in the future."

"Sir Cassius de Wolfe, my lady," he said without hesitation. "I have the great honor of holding the position of Lord Protector to our king. I have come to Doncaster to relay a message to the duke from Edward."

Those great eyes flickered, surprised by what he'd told her. "Then you are an accomplished knight," she said. "I suppose I should be honored that your dog assaulted me."

"It was not an honor, I assure you," he said regretfully. Then, he paused. "Are you really going to avoid me now?"

His explanation of who he was and why he was there gave her pause. Now that she knew, her gaze seemed to go from indignant to curious, although it was truly difficult to tell because her face was so covered up. But something in her eyes suggested that she was no longer angry.

Perhaps interested, even.

After a moment, she sighed.

"Probably not," she said.

He grinned that smile that could melt even the hardest heart. "I would very much like to know your name."

His smile had the desired effect. He could tell just by looking at her. But she steeled herself against the charm offensive, at least as much as she was able, and lowered her gaze.

"Dacia," she said, turning away. "Good day to you, Sir Cassius."

He didn't try to follow her. In fact, he didn't say another

word. He simply watched her walk away, down the riverbank, until she nearly faded from view. Then, he saw her take a turn and head up the slope towards Edenthorpe. As he watched, she headed straight to the castle.

That told him what he wanted to know.

He was going to be on the lookout for those bright, pale eyes.

IT WAS WELL into the evening at Edenthorpe Castle and the great hall was ablaze with light and conversation. It was a big hall with big beams supporting the roof and two enormous hearths, one at each end of the hall.

The hall was built with the same white stone that the castle was built with, but the hearths were made of marble that had been imported all the way from a quarry north of Rome. Italian craftsmen had come along with the marble and had pieced it together expertly, creating an intricate and fascinating work of art. Those hearths weren't the only things that suggested the overall wealth of Doncaster.

The hall was full of such suggestions.

Everywhere one looked, there was something lavish and expensive – tapestries, furs and rugs on the floor instead of rushes, and even the tables themselves were massive, well-built pieces of furniture. Doncaster had a shipbuilder in Liverpool build the tables and he liked to joke that they could withstand a gale-force tempest.

Certainly, they could withstand a gang of drunken soldiers.

And then there was the food. Mounds of it. More food than

Cassius had ever seen in one place, and that was saying a lot. He came from a family of men, hungry men who liked to eat, and the king would have lavish feasts regularly that were nothing compared to what he was looking at now – savory baked egg dishes with prunes and wine and meat, subtleties that were in the shapes of castles and serpents, puddings, breads, giant boiled knuckles of beef, and so much more.

Old Cuffy did, indeed, produce an epicurean delight.

Cassius was given a seat next to the duke while Bose and Rhori were seated across from him. The table was so wide that they may as well have been across the hall, for they could barely hear the conversation between Cassius and the duke and wouldn't have been able to hear it at all had it not been for the fact that the duke was hard of hearing and Cassius had to practically shout in a room that was not conducive to audible nuances. In truth, it was a giant echo chamber, and that made the buzz of conversation somewhat overwhelming.

"The last time you were here, I dare say that you did not partake of the feast," Doncaster was saying over the terrible acoustics. "As I recall, you prowled around the hall like a cat, watching for any threats against our illustrious king."

Cassius nodded. "That is my position, your grace," he said. "Wherever the king goes, I am usually relegated to roaming whatever chamber he is in, ensuring his safety. Once it is secure, I will stand behind him. I am sure that did not escape your notice, either."

The old duke shook his head, his white hair thin but fluffy. It looked like a dandelion head. "Probably not," he said, taking a drink of his wine. "I do not miss much, but these days, I find myself giving over to a lack of caring sometimes."

"Your grace?"

He was asking for clarification and Doncaster shrugged. "What I mean to say is that I am old," he said, his blue eyes twinkling. "Nothing much frightens me any longer. I do not pay close attention to people like I used to. That kind of vigilance is for the young. Truth be told, I am resigned to what comes."

"What comes, your grace?"

"Death."

"Are you ill, your grace? The king will wish to know."

But Doncaster waved him off. "Not ill," he said. "Simply… old. Everyone I love has moved on to the next adventure. I have always believed death is the next adventure, you know. I had a priest tell me once that he believes death is merely a transition to another type of existence. That is not what the church tells us, mind you, but this priest was a radical. He believed there was a great life after this one and everyone we ever loved was waiting for us there."

Cassius found himself in an unexpectedly philosophical conversation. "Of course they are, your grace," he said. "It is my belief that heaven *is* that next adventure."

"Who do you look forward to seeing in your next adventure, Sir Cassius?"

That wasn't a difficult question. "My grandfather, William de Wolfe," he said. "We lost him a few years ago and I miss him every day."

"Ah, yes," Doncaster said. "The great Wolfe of the Border. I was a very young man when he was rising to power in the north. We would hear great stories of feats."

"They were all true."

Doncaster grinned. "I have no doubt," he said. Then, he sighed. "As for me, I look forward to seeing my father and grandfather, too. And my wife and son. But I cannot go just yet."

"You have unfinished business, your grace?"

The old man nodded. "My granddaughter," he said. "She must marry before I go and that will be a difficult task."

Now, they were on to the subject of the mysterious granddaughter and Cassius collected his wine up, drinking of the fine and sweet wine from Bordeaux. "Forgive me, your grace, but I did not even know you had a granddaughter," he said. "I have attended the king in many feasts and festivals and never once have I seen Doncaster's heir. It is a great legacy she bears."

Doncaster sat back in his chair, putting a leg up on the feasting table and kicking aside one of the many dishes on the tabletop. But he didn't seem to care as the dish fell off and the dogs under the table scrambled to eat up the mess.

"She does," he said, sounding weary and resigned. "It all rests upon her. In truth, I pity her. She has over two hundred years of a legacy weighing down on her. No brothers or siblings to help share the burden. 'Tis only her."

Cassius sensed great regret in his tone. Not remorse for what he'd burdened his granddaughter with, but perhaps it was more of the simple fact that she had been born female. A male heir would have brought pride from the old man. But a female heir… it wasn't pride Cassius heard.

It was disappointment.

"I am sure she is a strong and educated woman, your grace," Cassius said. Frankly, he was unsure what to say at all given the old man's obvious mood. "Why is it we have not seen her at the many festivals and gatherings of the nobility?"

The duke looked at him. He'd had a goodly amount of wine and very little food, so he was feeling his drink. He sat forward in his chair, looking Cassius in the eyes.

"Because she refuses to attend," he said flatly. "She is not a social woman, and given the position Doncaster holds in England, that is an unfortunate stance, so I must find her a husband who can take the reins of power. A man who is cunning, political, powerful, and of the finest noble bloodlines. But given her propensity to keep herself away from the world, that opportunity has not presented itself yet."

"But she is still young, is she not?" Cassius said. "There is time."

The old man shook his head, sighing heavily. "You do not understand," he muttered. "She is… well, there is no use in speaking of it. It has occurred to me that God must want my family legacy to die away."

"I do not understand, your grace."

Perhaps he didn't, but the duke wasn't willing to clarify. He changed the subject.

"How many brothers do you have, Cassius?" he asked.

"I have three, your grace," he said. "Markus, who is married, and then Magnus and Titus, who are younger than I."

"And your father? How many brothers did he have?"

"Five, your grace."

"I see," the duke said, looking disgruntled. "That is ten male offspring of de Wolfe, your father and you included. And that is not including the male offspring of your uncles."

"There are many more, your grace."

The duke sighed heavily. "And I only have her," he said. "It is a sad thing to see a great legacy narrowed down to one woman."

Cassius wasn't entirely sure what more to say on the subject. He could see that the duke was disappointed with his one and only heir, and a female to boot. It was puzzling, but the truth was that it really wasn't any of his affair. Trying to remain in a positive mood, he glanced around the hall.

"Where is your granddaughter, your grace?" he asked. "Will she not attend her guests?"

The old duke shook his head. "She does not attend feasts when there are guests present, usually," he said. "She prefers to ensure the meal is perfect from her post in the kitchens."

That sounded strange to Cassius. No hostess at a feast for guests? "She must be very dedicated," he said. "I should at least like to thank her for her kind attention to detail before we depart. May I know her name, your grace?"

The duke took a long drink of wine before answering. "Dacia," he said. "Dacia Mathilde Violette de Ferrar de Ryes, but she is known to all simply as Dacia of Doncaster."

Dacia!

The realization hit him. It was the woman from the river, the one that Argos so thoughtfully shoved into the water. The woman that Cassius was positive the dog had injured because she kept her face covered up. He was certain the dog had hurt the woman's face somehow. Perhaps damaging her mouth or nose.

But then, Amata's words came flooding back to him. She had said Dacia's name and...

Witch's marks!

It occurred to Cassius that the woman must have been covering up what some were calling her witch's marks, something she hadn't wanted a stranger to see. All Cassius knew was that she had the most beautiful eyes he'd ever seen and he couldn't imagine her face was any less glorious.

Marks or no marks.

"Then I hope I am able to make her acquaintance before we

depart on the morrow," he said, not letting on that he'd already met the woman at the river. Given that the duke didn't seem to have a high opinion of his granddaughter, perhaps he wouldn't like to know she was wandering outside of the walls. "She has provided us with a goodly feast and should be commended."

The duke simply nodded, downing more of his wine. "You said you came bearing a message from the king," he said, changing the subject completely. "What does Edward have to say to me?"

With talk of Dacia of Doncaster finished, Cassius went with the new focus. It was why he had come, after all. "He sends you his compliments, of course," he said. "He has instructed me to reiterate his fondness of you and hopes that he can see you personally very soon, but business has kept him in London."

Doncaster looked at him. "What does he want?"

"Your grace?"

The old man waved him off. "I have known Edward long enough to know that he wants something from me," he said. "He strokes me like a kitten, hoping I'll purr loudly enough to cough up money and men for his wars in Scotland and Wales. Well? What is it? How much does he want this time?"

Cassius stared at him a moment before breaking down into a grin. "You have not even let me say all of it."

"There's more?"

"More stroking, flattery, and sickening sweetness."

The duke started to laugh. "Must I sit for all of it, de Wolfe?"

"I must do my job, your grace. I will be ashamed to tell the king that I was unable to spew every last bit of his adulation to you."

Grinning, the duke sat forward to pour himself more wine.

"I will tell him that you did," he said. "Just tell me what he wants."

Cassius paused a moment before leaning towards the duke and lowering his voice. "What I am to tell you is in the strictest confidence, your grace," he said quietly. "May I rely upon your discretion?"

The duke may have been tipsy, but he was still sharp. He nodded. "Of course, de Wolfe," he said. "What is it?"

"Edward is taking a delegation to France," Cassius said. "He intends to create a treaty with the French, thereby breaking the alliance they have with the Scots. Then, he intends to move into Scotland and finally bring the country into submission. If they lose the support of the French, that will seriously cripple them."

Doncaster raised his eyebrows. "The French, is it?" he said, surprised. "They may lose the support, but that will not break them. The Scots are stronger than that."

"Robert Bruce has pledged to side with Edward."

That brought a strong reaction from Doncaster. "The Bruce himself?"

"Indeed, your grace."

Doncaster stared at him a moment before shaking his head. "It seems impossible that the wars with Scotland will finally be over and England will be the victor," he said. "But if Robert Bruce has pledged to side with England, that means something."

"It does, your grace."

"It means that Edward will put The Bruce on the throne and his enemies will be forced to contend with a Scottish ruler backed by England."

Cassius simply nodded. The old duke was sharp and understood the implications of the situation. He'd spent seven decades being entrenched in England and her politics, so he was well aware of the magnitude of what Cassius was suggesting.

It was considerable.

"I see," he said after a moment, looking far more sober than he had only seconds earlier. "And he feels his overture to the French will succeed?"

"He has every confidence, your grace."

"With enough money and gifts."

"Exactly, your grace."

Doncaster was satisfied that he had the truth of it. He was willing to go along with Edward's request with the hope that it would end his expensive wars once and for all, wars that rich barons like Doncaster were paying for.

"Very well," he said. "Then of course I shall pledge money and men for Edward to accomplish this. What does he need?"

"Money, your grace. He is taking an army with him to France."

"Then I shall pledge one hundred pounds in gold and five hundred men."

Cassius smiled. "He will be quite pleased, your grace," he said. "That is very generous."

Doncaster returned to his drink. "It is," he said. "But he had better end these wars once and for all this time. I do not intend to give him another cent for his foolish wars against people who we should let alone. As long as the Scots stay in Scotland, let them be, I say."

Cassius snorted. "The problem is that they do not stay there, your grace," he said. "My mother and grandmother are Scottish. I have aunts who are Scottish. Being that my grandfather's properties protect most of the Scots borders and my father is the Earl of Berwick, we have seen our share of Scots.

We know how they think. Too many feudal clans make it difficult to unite Scotland, but Edward believes it is possible. Still... the Scots can be an unruly and unhappy bunch. I speak from experience."

Doncaster nodded reluctantly. "True enough," he said. "I suppose it is just one of those things we must accept. In any case, I will send the men and the money with you when you leave. When do you intend to go?"

But Cassius shook his head. "I depart tomorrow, but I am not returning to London," he said. "I have not been home in three years and the king has graciously granted me the time to return home for a short while. I would suggest you send your men and money to London directly."

The duke pondered that. "I shall," he said. "I will send them before the week is out. And with that, I shall conclude my business with the king. I do not stay up late these days, you know. No offense, de Wolfe, but my bed is a greater companion than you could ever be. But I insist that you and your men enjoy the food and drink. Do not let me stop you from that. Have you been given your rooms yet?"

Cassius nodded. "Your majordomo took care of that when we arrived, your grace."

Doncaster grunted. "Good man," he muttered. "Fulco will tend to your needs, should you have any. I shall see you on the morrow before you depart."

He was speaking of the small, pale man who ran his castle business most efficiently, a young man who was the son of one of his senior soldiers. Fulco Worthing was a servant worth his weight in gold. Doncaster rose wearily to his feet, weaving slightly with alcohol and fatigue, as Cassius stood up beside him.

"Good sleep to you, your grace," he said, helping the old man move away from the table so he wouldn't stumble. "We shall bid you a farewell on the morrow."

Doncaster simply waved at him as he shuffled away from the table, heading off to seek his bed. Cassius watched him go before making his way around the table to Rhori and Bose, who were well into their food and drink. Argos, who had been laying at his feet under the table, moved with him. As Cassius perched on the edge of the table, Rhori glanced up from his trencher.

"Well?" he said. "Did he pledge money?"

Cassius nodded, slapping the big dog affectionately on the back. "One hundred pounds gold and five hundred men."

Both Rhori and Bose looked at him in surprise. "That is more than Edward was hoping for," Rhori said. "Well done, Cass. The old man fell for the de Wolfe charm."

Cassius didn't have much to say to that. It had simply been a task to perform and nothing more. But he looked around the great hall, vast and smoky, crowded with men, and scratched his head.

"I find something curious about Doncaster," he said. "For all of the man's wealth and social position, I find it odd that he doesn't have a group of courtiers following him around. Odder still that he is not married. He spoke of that elusive granddaughter and seemed either embarrassed of her or disappointed. I could not tell which. You would think he would marry again simply for the opportunity to have another son. For such a great man, he seems very... alone."

The knights weren't hard pressed to agree. They were sitting at a massive table on a raised dais that was virtually empty except for them. Down below, on the floor of the hall, it was crowded with soldiers enjoying their meal.

But the duke's table was empty.

The table of a house about to die out.

"Mayhap he simply prefers it that way," Rhori said. "We have visited here before and it has been that way."

"It has," Cassius agreed. "But Edward brought more courtiers and advisors with him to fill many such tables, so I suppose I never really noticed before. But now, it's just the three of us, a lone duke, and his elusive granddaughter."

"And a massive empire of Doncaster," Rhori finished for him.

"Exactly."

Cassius thought about it a moment longer before shrugging his broad shoulders. "I suppose it seems strange because I have so many members in my family that I can hardly keep track of them all," he said. "Families that aren't by the dozen are something of an odd concept to me."

"The de Wolfes multiply like rabbits," Bose said, mouth full. "That's all you know."

Cassius looked at him, snorting. "I think we know a little more than that," he said. But it began to occur to him that with Doncaster now retired, he was free to roam. Perhaps even free to roam into the kitchens to see if he could catch a glimpse of those bright blue eyes, because he'd put the pieces of the puzzle together and suspected that's where she might be. With that in mind, he slid from the tabletop. "I'm going to see if I can find our hostess and thank her for her hospitality."

"What hostess?" Bose asked.

Cassius was already up, heading towards the servants' alcove. "The granddaughter," he said. "Doncaster said she's usually in the kitchens."

Bose and Rhori waved him on, returning to what was left of

their meal. With the dog in tow, Cassius crossed the great hall, his destination in sight.

And a strong curiosity that was leading him there.

CHAPTER FOUR

Silverdale Manor
12 miles from Edenthorpe Castle

"BUT, PAPA... YOU *must* invite him. Did you not hear what I said?"

The old man bent over a cluttered table in an equally cluttered solar simply nodded his head. "I heard you."

"He's a de Wolfe!"

"A de Wolfe, indeed."

Amata sighed sharply because her father didn't seem to have the same sense of urgency that she did.

"If you truly wish for me to marry well, now is your chance," she said. "Send word to Edenthorpe and invite him to come to Silverdale. Papa, are you *listening* to me?"

Hugh de Branton was writing something, very carefully, on a piece of prepared parchment that was held down on the edges by rocks to keep it flat. A learned man and minor warlord who was a distant cousin to the Duke of Doncaster, he wasn't nearly as ambitious as his daughter. She was determined to be someone, to marry well, and he was content with what he had.

Yet, in her quest to marry higher than her station, her ruthlessness knew no bounds. Neither did her envy, and her slant against her cousin, Dacia, was nothing new.

Hugh suspected that's really all it was.

"I am listening to you," he said patiently, dipping his quill into the inkwell by his right hand. "You want me to invite a de Wolfe son to Silverdale to sup."

"I do!"

He paused and looked at her. "Did you not stop to consider that he is at Edenthorpe for a reason?" he said. "He must be there on business. We have no right to lure him away from his business with dear Cousin Vincent."

That wasn't what Amata wanted to hear. Frowning, she plopped down on a stool next to her father's table.

"Papa, if you do not take the chance, I shall never have what I want," she said. "Of course he came to Doncaster on business. But when the business is over, he can come here if you invite him. He will not come without an invitation."

Hugh's gaze lingered on his oldest daughter's anxious face. "This could not have anything to do with stealing him away from Dacia, could it?"

Her frown deepened but she wouldn't look at him. "I do not know what you mean."

Hugh snorted softly and went back to his document. "Of course you don't," he said. "Little Dacia, your cousin whom you pretend to like but secretly envy to the point of hatred. A lass who will inherit everything you want."

"That is not true!"

Hugh dipped his quill in the inkwell again. "You have tormented that girl long enough, Amata," he said. "You visit her, take her clothing, her jewelry, and she never stops you because, unlike you, she has a kind and generous heart. You speak badly about her to anyone who will listen and, still, she does nothing. Jealousy is an ugly thing, Daughter. It makes you ugly yourself."

Amata's features tightened. "That is a terrible thing to say to me."

"Then do not make me have to repeat it," he said calmly. "I will not send an invitation to the de Wolfe knight. His business is not with us."

Amata came off the stool in a huff, furious at her father. "Then I shall be an old maid and torment *you* all the rest of your days!"

"You have already done that," he said. "So much like your mother, you are. Cruel and vain, although I have tried to raise you otherwise. I have tried to show you that a kind heart is what all men would like in a wife, but I suppose your mother's influence was too great. Therefore, I am still not sending an invitation to the de Wolfe knight. Why would I want to saddle his good name with your petty and envious soul?"

With a scream of frustration, Amata stormed out of the chamber, tears of rage in her eyes. The man wouldn't do as she asked. He rarely did. She didn't even know why she had asked him, only that she had been hoping against hope that, for once, he would do what she wanted.

This could not have anything to do with gaining the upper hand on Dacia?

She wasn't going to admit it even though it was the truth. Dacia *did* have everything Amata ever wanted – money, prestige, titles. Everything. It was true that she pretended to love her cousin. It was true that she visited Edenthorpe with some regularity just to bask in the richness of the duke's residence.

Amata slept in Dacia's lavish bed, dressed in her lavish

gowns, and helped herself to her perfume and baubles and bangles. When they were young, Dacia even had her own miniature castle built near the stables where the girls would pretend that they were princesses. Everything Amata had always wanted.

All of it belonging to a woman made ugly by the marks all over her face.

Amata had tried to warn de Wolfe about Dacia.

He hadn't listened.

In fact, no one listened to her. Neither her father *nor* the de Wolfe knight. But Amata had her own network of friends, young women from lesser houses around Doncaster, and even some village maidens, women who were the daughters of the merchants or other prestigious positions within the village. Amata was the ringleader to this group of young women who would follow rather than lead.

And they listened to her.

Dacia used to be part of that group when she was quite young, but once Amata's jealousy got the better of her and she began to whisper about Dacia behind her back, that paranoid nurse took her into the walls of Edenthorpe and never let her join the group again. Amata and her gossiping friends had defeated the sweet young girl with the freckles all over her face. Though for some reason, Dacia never seemed to blame Amata for that particular incident.

As her father said, she tormented Dacia... and still, Dacia embraced her because she didn't have any other friends. Now with the addition of a handsome young knight, the torment would continue in earnest.

If de Wolfe wouldn't come to her, she would go to de Wolfe.

CHAPTER FIVE

Edenthorpe Castle

"T HEY MEN ARE hungry tonight," the old cook said, wiping sweat from her brow with the back of her hand. "They've already gone through the meat we had. I've sent men to the stores to bring out the salted pork."

It was a busy night in the steamy kitchens of Edenthorpe Castle. The bread ovens were running full-bore and two enormous hearths were cooking all manner of food for the hungry Doncaster men. Servants rushed to and fro, bringing food to the masses, or stirring pots, or helping the cook as she served up the dishes.

And Dacia was in the middle of it. She was keeping track of everything that had been cooked and served, and she was the one who had instructed the cook to procure more meat for the men, who were gobbling up the boiled beef that had been prepared. With so many men to feed, Dacia was always the one to direct the meals and the portions, keeping everything tallied in a neat book she kept in her grandfather's solar.

Doncaster was run quite efficiently. In fact, and the duke

had nothing to do with it. He'd long since relinquished those duties to his majordomo, Fulco, and his granddaughter. If it seemed like real work, then he didn't want much to do with it. He was a very intelligent man, however, and could do complicated sums in his head when it came to his money or expenses. That was never the issue. But he didn't want to work at it or keep daily track of his empire, so he left that to Fulco and Dacia.

Fulco was essentially in charge of everything other than the keep and the kitchens. Anything that had to do with the male sex, like visitors or kings or soldiers or housing visiting knights was his domain. But anything to do with the keep and kitchens purely belonged to Dacia. Although she had never been sent away to foster, she had been well taught by a fastidious Italian priest hired by her grandfather, from whom she received an unconventionally classic education.

Her education had included everything that well-bred young women usually learned, including languages, mathematics, writing, music, and scripture because her grandfather was well-read and insisted that she be also. But the priest went a step further, educating her on the classics of literature from Greece and ancient Rome, things usually reserved for scholarly men. That meant that Dacia was far more educated than most young women who had spent years fostering in the finest households. She was quite smart with household budgets and a master at organization, which was why she was invaluable in the kitchens when her grandfather was feeding his army of fifteen hundred men.

Like tonight.

Food was being prepared, and eaten, at an alarming rate.

"Make sure they know to bring the fatted pork and not the ham," Dacia said, wiping the sweat from the steamy kitchens off her brow. "We are saving that ham. Let them eat the meat the spoils more quickly."

The cook nodded, her red jowls quivering. "I've got enough beans and peas to make a good stew with it," she said. "I'll get it started tonight and make enough to carry us through tomor-row."

"Excellent," Dacia said. "But you'd better keep the bread ovens going. If we can fill them up on the bread and ale, we will not need to feed them so much additional meat tonight."

"Aye, m'lady," the cook said, clearing off a big portion of the kitchen table because the men were starting to bring the sides of fatted pork in. "You needn't worry. I know what to do."

And she did. Dacia stood back as a slab of the meat was slapped onto the old wooden table and the cook went to work on it. Everything was running efficiently, as always, and she backed away from the activity, stealing a hunk of currant bread and chewing on it as she went to the door that overlooked the kitchen yard.

It was her moment to relax, at least briefly.

The cool air on her face felt wonderful. It had been a busy evening and the men seemed hungrier than usual. Mouth full of the sweet-tasting bread, Dacia looked up to the night sky, seeing a blanket of stars across the heavens and a nearly full moon low in the sky. It was a beautiful night, capping off an interesting day.

Cassius de Wolfe.

She'd been thinking of him ever since she'd met him.

It had been a mortifying moment when he'd come across her in the river because being on her hands and knees, with a dog running circles around her, hadn't been exactly the best position for an introduction. They had visitors at Edenthorpe all the time, but it was rare when Dacia had contact with them. She remained in the background, making sure the guests had plenty of delicious food and ensuring their chambers were comfortable and warm. It was rare when she was expected to interact with them, even though she was an excellent conversationalist, witty and intelligent.

But she let her grandfather take charge instead.

It was better than entertaining guests while clad in her veils, self-conscious and unsure.

Therefore, meeting an unexpected knight like she did today was somewhat rattling. She wasn't used to meeting new people. She hadn't been expecting to see anyone so close to Edenthorpe's walls, so it was a reminder to her to always be prepared. Fortunately, she had been able to cover her face a little with her wet apron, so she hadn't been completely exposed, but she knew she had looked like a fool doing it. She should have run for the castle the moment she saw the stranger, but something made her stay.

Mesmerizing blue eyes had been looking at her.

Oh, but he was a beauteous lad. She couldn't have run from that face even if she'd wanted to. With blue eyes and black, curly hair, she had never seen such a handsome man. His features were perfect and even, his nose straight, his jaw square. And he was taller than any man she'd ever seen. The more she stared at him, the more entranced she had become, and her reaction had frightened her. She'd tried to get away from him, but he ended up helping her. His grip had been like iron.

That iron grip had made her feel weak in the knees.

Cassius de Wolfe.

She would remember that moment for the rest of her life.

Dacia continued to stare up into the sky, eating more of her bread and thinking on a blue-eyed knight that had the power to make her feel weak just by looking at her. She thought on his smile, something that had caused a strange buzzing in her head, as if she were about to faint. Even the memory of it made her grin, just a little, a moment to tuck away and revive from time to time when she wanted to think on the most handsome man in all of England who happened to cross her path.

A sweet memory, indeed.

As she stood there and chewed, the last of her bread in her lowered hand, something began tugging at the crust. Frowning, she looked down to see Argos, that naughty dog, pulling the last of the bread from her hand and chomping it down. Her eyes widened when she realized that de Wolfe's dog had found her yet again. When the dog swallowed the bread in two bites, it wagged its tail furiously and bumped into her, licking her hand.

She recoiled.

"*You* again?" she said, outraged. "How did you get into the kitchens?"

"He came with me."

Dacia heard the voice from behind and, instinctively, she lifted her apron, covering her nose, mouth, and cheeks before she even turned around.

Cassius de Wolfe was standing behind her.

Those blue eyes were glimmering at her and Dacia began to feel weak-kneed again. She stepped back, startled by his appearance.

"Why..." she stammered. "Why are you here? Is something the matter? Do you require...?"

He cut her off, though it was gently done. "I require nothing, my lady, I assure you," he said. "Dacia of Doncaster, I presume?"

She hesitated before nodding. "You know?"

He nodded. "Your grandfather told me," he said, a smile playing on his lips. "He told me that his highly efficient and brilliant granddaughter managed his kitchens and I wanted to thank you for an astonishingly good meal. You are to be commended."

Dacia was still feeling lightheaded, now made worse with his flattery. The man made her feel all shades of giddy. She ended up backing out of the kitchens, out into the moonlit yard, simply to put distance between her and Cassius because she didn't know what else to do.

He followed.

"It was all in the course of my duties, my lord," she said, holding up that apron in front of her face and again feeling like a fool because of it. "You honor me with your gratitude."

His smile was growing. "Not at all, my lady," he said. "I am just sorry we were not graced with your presence, but it seems as if you have been very busy in the kitchens."

By this time, Dacia had come to a halt, gazing up at the man who was so tall that she had to crane her head back to look up at him. If she kept backing away, she'd end up backed against the wall of the kitchen yard, so she bravely took a stand.

"That is usual at the evening meal, my lord," she said. "There are over a thousand men to feed and it must be done in an organized fashion, so that is my task."

Cassius nodded. "Your grandfather explained that you were very diligent in your duties," he said. Then, he paused, clearly studying her beneath the moonlight. "Why did you not tell me you were Dacia of Doncaster earlier today?"

She shrugged, lowering her gaze. "It does not matter who I am," she said. "Moreover, it is not polite for a lady to introduce herself to a man. We should have been introduced by others. It is the proper thing to do."

"You are correct," he said. "I apologize if I seem forward. But I have a reason for seeking you out other than thanking you."

"What reason?"

"To ensure that the woman that my dog tried to drown is suffering no ill effects."

She bit her lip to keep from grinning openly. "I am suffering no ill effects."

"Do you swear this?"

"I do."

Now he was flashing his teeth at her, that magnificent smile that dramatically changed his whole face. "I am pleased," he said. "Argo really isn't a naughty dog. He simply becomes excited. He is, in truth, very friendly."

As if on cue, Argo ran up to Cassius, banging into his legs, wagging his tail furiously. Cassius reached down to pet the dog when he noticed something. Curious, he bent over.

"What in the world does he have in his mouth?" he wondered aloud. He reached into the dog's mouth, pulling forth something that was warm. And alive. "Christ... it's a puppy. Where in the hell did he get a puppy?"

Forgetting her giddiness and fear, Dacia was at his side, inspecting the tiny, mewling creature that was newly born.

She recognized it.

"In the stable," she said, pointing to a small stable at the edge of the kitchen yard, butting up against the larger stable meant for the horses. "The cook's dogs had puppies a couple of days ago. Is it injured?"

Cassius held the little creature up, trying to get a better look at it in the moonlight. "I do not think so," he said. "Argos does not normally kill little creatures, but he has been known to bring them to me. Rabbits or anything else he can catch. He likes to bring me gifts. But never a puppy."

"Come," Dacia said quickly, taking him by the elbow and pulling him towards the stable. "We must return the puppy to its mother. It is quite possible she will reject him if your dog's scent is on him."

Cassius knew that. He knew something about animals. But at the moment, he was quite interested in the fact that she had him by the arm, escorting him towards the small stable where two goats lay in the straw. He followed her into a second stall were a big, gentle mother dog was nursing her litter of pups.

Cassius carefully handed Dacia the puppy and she put it down with the mother, who began licking it furiously. Argo, standing next to Cassius, was wagging his tail happily, as if confident he'd done the right and true thing by bringing his master a puppy. Cassius frowned at his dog, who licked his hand.

"Strange that the mother dog did not fight him when he tried to take a puppy," he said. "Truly, Argo is a big, stupid beast who would never hurt anyone or anything. He's very gentle that way."

"Except when he is shoving women into the river," Dacia said.

Cassius pretended to concede the point. "Aye, except that," he agreed. "But I am coming to think that was a good thing."

She looked at him as she stood up. "Why would you say that?"

He smiled. "Because I got to meet Dacia of Doncaster as a result," he said. "Had Argo not been such a wild bull, I would never have had the opportunity to meet you."

Beneath the apron, Dacia was smiling at his flattery. The entire time, she'd kept the apron up over her face with one hand, never once failing to keep it in place. She'd gotten used to doing that over the years.

But she was coming to wish that Cassius could see her smile.

"It is kind of you to say so," she said. "But you have not caught me at my best. First in the river, now in the kitchens. You must think I'm quite common."

Cassius shook his head. "Not at all," he said. "In fact, I respect the fact that you are unafraid of work, or even fall into a river without becoming a hysterical mess. I've never found much use for pampered, fragile women."

She looked at him in astonishment. "Oh," she said, off guard by the continuous stream of compliments. "Do... do you know a lot of pampered, fragile women, then?"

He grunted, scratching his head. "I have spent the past three years in London, my lady," he said. "I have met my share."

They headed out of the stable, back out into the moonlight, but Dacia was interested in his statement. "I have never been to London," she said. "It seems to me that it is the center of the entire world."

Cassius shrugged. "It is a busy city," he said. "Great castles, great buildings, great cathedrals, great houses."

"Have you been in any of them?"

"All of them."

"I meant the great houses."

He nodded. "Several times," he said. "Where the king goes, I go, and he is invited to many a feast."

That seemed to have her curiosity. For the first time, she

seemed to be warming to both the conversation and his presence. "And these feasts," she said. "Are they different from the ones here at Edenthorpe?"

"What do you mean?"

She shook her head. "I am not certain," she said. "I... I never fostered, you see, and my travel experience is very limited. I have heard that the feasts in the great houses can be quite elaborate and beautiful, with a thousand tapers and dishes shaped like castles. I even heard that sometimes they bury jewels in bread loaves for the guests to find."

He peered down at her curiously. "You never fostered?"

"Nay."

"Why not?"

That brought the conversation to an immediate halt. Dacia looked as if she were going to respond but, suddenly, she lowered her head and ran on ahead of him towards the kitchens.

"I am sorry, my lord," she said. "We should not be wasting time with idle conversation. I have... duties to attend to and I am sure your time is better spent elsewhere. Good eve to you."

But Cassius wouldn't let her get away. "Wait," he said, taking long strides after her. "It was quite forward of me to ask such a question. Forgive me. It is truly none of my affair. I would be happy to tell you about some of the more fanciful feasts I have attended if you would care to hear about them. I have attended some truly festive ones."

She still wouldn't look at him, but at least she had come to a tense halt. It appeared as if she weren't quite sure what to do – keep running or stop and speak to him.

She was coming to like speaking to him.

"I... I would like to, but I really do have duties to attend to," she said. "Mayhap another time, if you are still so inclined."

He shook his head. "Alas, I wish I could, but we are depart-ing tomorrow morning," he said. "I have no way of knowing when I shall return to Edenthorpe."

She looked at him, then. "You are going away so soon?"

"I have only come to deliver a message to your grandfather from the king."

She nodded in understanding. Then she glanced over her shoulder, back to the open kitchen door, before hesitantly returning her attention to him.

"I suppose I could spare a few more moments," she said. "I would like to hear of the feasts you have attended. Briefly, of course."

"Of course," he said quickly, pleased that she was willing to continue the conversation after his misstep. Those bright eyes had him hypnotized. "You are correct about lords baking jewels into bread for their guests to find. I attended a feast once where there was an entire treasure hunt, all of it buried in food."

"Is this so?" she said, immediately interested. "Where was this feast?"

There was a bench over near the buttery, used by servants when they churned butter. It was simple but suited his purposes. He began to casually move in that direction.

"It was at a great manse along the Thames called Hollyhock House," he said. "It is a property belonging to the Earls of Surrey. The king was in attendance, of course, and I was simply there as his protection, but it seemed to be great fun. Everyone was searching for golden coins and they had baked them into bread, buried them in egg dishes, put them in fruit – every-where. People were breaking teeth on a regular basis biting into dishes in their search for coins."

Beneath her apron, Dacia chuckled. "Sounds charming," she said with some sarcasm. "How can it be so much fun when people were breaking teeth?"

He shrugged. "It was the spirit of the event, I suppose," he said, sauntering close to the bench and noticing that Dacia, as hoped, was following him. "It was hilarious to watch drunkards make fools of themselves in their quest for gold."

"Sounds terrible."

He shook his head. "Sometimes, one must surrender one's dignity in order to have a bit of fun," he said. "I attended another feast where riddles were written on little pieces of vellum that were shoved into women's garments. Sometimes down the neck, sometimes in the sleeve, and men went from one woman to the next, guessing who the next woman would be and what her clues were. That one grew rather wild because the treasure they sought was a bag of coins and jewels that were tied to a woman's leg."

Dacia's eyes were wide. "Tied to her *leg*?"

He gestured as if pulling up skirts. "Aye," he said as if it were terribly scandalous. "Right above her knee."

Dacia gasped at the shocking nature but, in the very same breath, she started to giggle. "How naughty!"

"Indeed."

He had reached the bench. Dacia had followed him, closely enough that he indicated for her to sit on the bench, hoping she would take his direction. Truth be told, she wasn't holding the apron up to her face as tightly as she had been, and he could see the edges of it drooping. She was losing herself in their conversation, hardly paying attention to the apron across her face.

In the bright moonlight, Cassius really couldn't see anything terrible underneath that apron. Certainly nothing she should be hiding. In fact, the very fact that she was warming to him emboldened him a little. He had to admit that he was greatly curious about the features beneath the apron.

"Sit, please," he said. "I shall tell you of more naughty and scandalous feasts I have attended. There was one that had an entire parade of white ponies, each one of them with a different dish upon its back. The servants led the ponies among the diners and they selected their food right off the backs of the animals."

Dacia sat down without any hesitation, entranced with the tale. "And the ponies behaved themselves?"

He nodded. But then, he shrugged. "Well, for the most part," he said. "I remember one tried to bite Baron Lulworth when he shoved it by the head because it came too close. The little beast was not to blame for that."

Dacia frowned. "It is a man of sin who would be so cruel to a little animal," she said. "But what an enchanting feast that would have been. I should like to be served by ponies."

He grinned. "All of the ladies at the feast thought so, too," he said. "Mayhap you could try it here, sometime. Gather twenty ponies and have them carry around dishes on their backs. It would be a way to impress any future guests."

Cassius could tell by the way her eyes were crinkling that she was smiling. "Mayhap," she said. "But I would give you all of the credit for the idea."

"It is not my idea. You are, therefore, welcome to use it freely."

She looked at him, her eyes glimmering with warmth. "If I can find some well-behaved ponies, I might."

He shook his head. "I have not met many of those, to be

sure," he said. "I've met warhorses with better dispositions."

"That is true," she said, looking over into the darkened stable area. "We have two ponies here now who are nasty gluttons. One is named Day and one is named Night, and they would rather eat than anything else. If you try to make them do something, they will kick. Night will even lay down and refuse to get up."

Cassius laughed softly. "Sounds like some men I know of."

"Sounds like my grandfather when he has had too much to drink."

They shared a moment of laughter, something that had Cassius increasingly boldened. She had a good sense of humor and he liked that. After a few moments, he sobered.

"May I ask you a question, my lady?" he said.

Dacia shrugged. "That depends on what it is."

"It has to do with my dog."

"Then you may ask."

"Did he hurt your face today and you simply do not want me to see what he did?"

Her expression went from warm to cold, all in a split second. He was positive that she was going to get up and run away, and was quite surprised when she didn't. Something was forcing her to remain even though her entire body was tense, preparing to take flight.

But she didn't.

She did, however, lower her gaze, keeping that apron up, turning her head away from him so he couldn't look at her.

The defenses were up again.

"Nay," she said after a moment. "My face is not injured."

"That is good," he said, trying to look her in the eyes. "Then I can only assume you are covering such magnificent beauty that for me to gaze upon it would immediately make me your devoted slave for life. Is that it?"

He heard her sigh faintly. "Sir Cassius," she said. "I like speaking to you very much, but I do not wish to speak about... *this.*"

"About my becoming your devoted slave?"

He could see, even from a side view, that she had rolled her eyes. "Nay," she said. "About... the apron. I... I am very modest with men I do not know, and this is part of that modesty. Suffice it to say that it is simply my way. It always has been."

The mood could have taken quite a serious turn there, but Cassius didn't let it. He wanted her to know that he wasn't particularly concerned with whatever lay beneath that apron.

"Then you do not want to make me your devoted slave for life?"

She was embarrassed, uncomfortable, but his charm had her chuckling in spite of herself. "That seems to be all you care about."

"It would change my entire life."

He could hear her chuckle. "I am afraid that it simply would not work out," she said. "The king might become angry if I stole you away from him."

"Mayhap," he said, thinking that if she was willing to joke about it, then mayhap she understood that he wasn't being critical of whatever was beneath the apron. "But you are much prettier than he is. He would understand."

She looked at him, then. "I am not sure how you can say that when all you can see are my eyes."

"They are the most magnificent eyes I have ever seen."

Her gaze lingered on him a moment and he swore he could see the flicker of longing in them. Perhaps she wanted to believe him.

Perhaps she was afraid to.

Somehow, that made sense to him. He was coming to think that if the only reaction or reference she'd ever had to her beauty were the nasty comments of petty women like Amata de Branton, then surely she wasn't used to someone telling her that anything about her face was magnificent.

But it was.

In truth, he felt rather sorry for her.

"Lady Dacia?"

They both heard the voice, standing up from the bench in time to see Darian coming through the kitchen door. He was looking over the yard but quickly noticed Dacia and Cassius over by the buttery. He headed in her direction, hardly giving Cassius a second look.

"My lady, forgive me," he said. "Old Timeo is at the gatehouse asking for you. It seems that his wife has grown worse and now their daughter is ill as well. He has asked for your help."

Dacia was on the move. "I thought the woman was doing much better."

"Evidently not."

"I need my medicament bag."

"I've already sent a servant for that and a cloak."

Dacia wasn't thinking about anything but what lay ahead at that point. The conversation with Cassius was forgotten. Darian was behind her and Cassius was further back, bringing up the rear, but Dacia forgot herself completely and dropped the apron the moment she came through the kitchen door. She was so used to moving freely around Darian that it didn't even occur to her not to keep the apron over her face.

She was completely focused on the task ahead.

"Make sure Edie knows that I am going," she said, turning briefly to Darian. "She will have to ensure the comfort of our guests while I am gone."

"Aye, my lady," Darian said. "And I will ride with you, but I do not want to take any of the other knights. Given the issues we've had lately with Hagg, I am uncomfortable giving you more than one knight for an escort. This could be a ruse, you know."

Dacia came to a halt and turned to Darian in the shadowed light of the kitchen. "Old Timeo a ruse?" she said, aghast. "That old man is as loyal to Doncaster as much as you or I are. He would never let Catesby Hagg use him so."

"Unless he threatened the man's family."

She threw up her hands. "Then if you believe that, why let me go at all?" she demanded unhappily. "He could be waiting for me at Timeo's home."

Darian eyed her. "That is possible," he said. Then, he turned to Cassius, who was still standing back by the kitchen door. "My lord, may I ask you to ride with me to escort the lady? We can leave your knights here at Doncaster in case this is a ruse."

Cassius came closer, interested in what Darian de Lohr was saying, but more interested in the fact that Dacia had dropped the apron from her face. In all of the fuss with the subject of Old Timeo and his ill family, she seemed to have forgotten the defenses she'd so carefully held up. Her face was now exposed to the dim light of the kitchen.

And what a face it was.

Magnificent didn't quite cover it.

She had freckles, that was true. A fairly heavy dusting covered her nose, her cheeks, and she even had a few down around

her mouth. They weren't even very dark in coloring and
nothing, in his opinion, that needed to be covered up. No
amount of freckles could take away from her sweetly oval face, a
nose that was a little wide, and lips that could only be described
as lush and bow-shaped. With her dark, arched brows, brilliant
eyes and dark hair, he was smitten by what he saw. Perhaps she
wasn't the pale, fragile beauty that was the romantic ideal to
some men, but if one took time to really look beneath the
freckles, she was something astonishing.

For a moment, he was actually speechless, but for necessi-
ty's sake, he quickly recovered.

"What ruse do you speak of?" he asked, focusing on Darian.
"Is Doncaster having trouble the king is unaware of?"

Darian sighed heavily. "Some," he said, unaware that Cassius was studying Dacia closely. "He hasn't wanted Edward to
know. He believes it will resolve itself."

"*What* will resolve itself?"

Darian's gaze lingered on the king's Lord Protector. The
House of de Lohr and the House of de Wolfe were family
because Cassius' cousin, William de Wolfe, had married
Darian's cousin, Lily. Although he didn't know Cassius well, he
had met him a few times in the course of his duties with
Doncaster and knew that Cassius was one of the most elite
knights in England.

Given that they were family, even if they didn't personally
know one another well, it was implied that there was already
trust between them. When Cassius had appeared earlier that
day, Darian was more than happy to welcome the man to
Edenthorpe and, now, he was more than willing to let him in on
Doncaster's troubles.

Had he known what Cassius was thinking about Dacia,

however, he might have changed that opinion.

"We have a neighbor named Catesby Hagg who is laying claim to lands that belong to Doncaster," Darian said. "It is a long story, so suffice it to say that Hagg has been bold enough to launch a few raids on the disputed land."

"But nothing on Edenthorpe?"

"Nay, nothing on the castle," Darian said. "But we must be vigilant."

Cassius' gaze drifted to Dacia, standing partially in the shadows of the kitchen. He couldn't believe she hadn't realized that she'd dropped her apron, waiting for the moment when she would remember and suddenly cover herself up again.

"And this old man who has summoned help?" he said. "Is he to be trusted?"

Dacia nodded. "Very much so," she said. "His wife has not enjoyed good health over the past couple of years and I have helped her."

"You are a healer, my lady?"

Dacia shrugged. "I have some knowledge, aye," she said. "It is part of my responsibilities as the Lady of Edenthorpe. I tend the sick and the poor to the best of my abilities."

That was very true in many houses all over England. The lady of the castle was always expected to tend to the sick and the weak.

That was good enough for Cassius.

"Then I will go with you," he said to Darian. "Let me find du Bois and de Shera and tell them where I am going. Who are you leaving in command?"

Darian gestured towards the gatehouse. "I have four knights under my command," he said. "Lesser knights, young and hungry, but experienced. I will leave one of them in command,

Sir Clifton St. Marr."

"You trust him?"

"Implicitly."

"How old?"

Darian lifted his shoulders. "Young," he said. "He has only been a knight for a few years, but his judgment is impeccable."

Cassius digested that. "Then let me leave du Bois in command," he said. "He has been a knight for twenty years and can command a battle better than almost any man alive. He would submit to St. Marr if I told him to, but let us not strip the man of the respect he has earned, shall we?"

Darian was agreeable. "Absolutely," he said. "I will tell my men that the king's knight is in command while I am gone. They will be most agreeable to taking orders from a man who is in royal service."

"Better than that, he is one of Edward's Praetorian guards," Cassius said. "That's what they call the king's personal guard, you know. Praetorians."

"Prestigious, indeed."

With that, they headed out, following Dacia as she scurried away to collect her things. Cassius went about his business, finding Rhori and Bose still in the great hall and explaining to them what their duties would be until he returned from his escort duty. When Bose offered to go in his stead, Cassius brushed him off. Perhaps *too* quickly. He didn't want anyone else taking the escort duty.

If Dacia was going out, he was going with her.

He wanted another look at that sweetly freckled face.

CHAPTER SIX

T HE NIGHT SEEMED still and calm enough, but thirty soldiers were spread around Old Timeo's small farm as Dacia worked inside with a sick old woman and her equally ill daughter. Their mood was tense, as if the night were too still for their liking.

Something was in the air.

An icy breeze was coming off the meadows, chilling everything in its path as the moon rose higher in the sky and bathed the landscape in silver. The cottage was small, but warm light burned in the windows as Cassius and Darian stood outside the doorway, watching the darkened land for any signs that this might have been the ruse Darian had been wary of.

But everything seemed still.

The cottage was in view of Edenthorpe Castle, the massive-walled bastion to the south, the white stones gleaming silvery beneath the moonglow. It sat on an elevated position, with forests to the east and west of it, but from the cottage, there was a clear field of vision across a wide-open meadow. With torches burning on the walls against the dark night, it made for an awesome sight.

Cassius was in full battle gear, lingering on the edge of the line of men around the cottage. Every now and then, the cold breeze would bring a scent of the pine trees that grew heavily in these parts. A nightbird would call, the screech filling the air, but that was nearly the only sound.

Cassius was starting to think that Darian had been wrong about Hagg.

He walked along the road, passing the line of Doncaster soldiers, as Argos plodded alongside him. The dog went everywhere he went, even to battle. In fact, the dog was a seasoned veteran as well as any old soldier. He may have been silly and clumsy, but he was smart when it came to sensing trouble. He'd also been known to sniff out an attack or ambush before it happened, and Cassius trusted the dog's instincts. But even Argos was calm on this night.

Darian was standing at the mouth of the path that led to the front door of the cottage. He, too, was looking south at the great fortress of Edenthorpe in the distance, but he turned his attention to Cassius as the man came near.

"It is a cold night," Cassius commented. "Men tend to stay close to their hearth and bed on nights like this."

Darian's blue eyes glimmered. "What you mean to say is that I was mad to think this was a ruse."

Cassius fought off a grin. "You were simply being prudent," he said. Then, he gestured to the cottage. "Does this kind of thing happen often?"

Darian turned to look at the small, neat home. "You mean illness at this house?"

"I mean Lady Dacia being called forth to tend the sick."

Darian nodded. "As she said, it is expected of her," he said. "She was being humble when she said she only knew a little about healing. The truth is that she knows a great deal. She had a teacher for years, a former priest from Rome, who taught her many things, a knowledge of healing potions included. She knows more than most physics."

Cassius looked at him. "Impressive," he said. "Then she is a lady of skill."

Darian snorted softly. "Skill is where she begins," he said. "Where she ends, it is not yet known."

"What do you mean?"

"I mean that she speaks several languages," Darian said, leaning against the stone wall that surrounded the cottage. "She can do mathematics better than I can. She sews, manages the household efficiently, paints beautifully, and can debate the bible and philosophy with the greatest scholars in England. Intelligent doesn't even begin to describe her."

Cassius stared at him. "And she is not yet married?" he asked, incredulous. "Why in the hell not? With talents like those, and the Doncaster dukedom, she should be the most sought-after bride in the country."

Darian shrugged. "You would think so," he said. "But… well, there are a few dynamics in play that prevent it."

"Like what?"

Darian turned his attention back to the fortress in the distance, crossing his big arms thoughtfully. "When she was a young girl, she had a nurse who was convinced she was being marked by the devil because of the freckles across her face," he said. "I know it sounds silly but, in these parts, the fear of Satan is a real thing. The freckles became more plentiful as Lady Dacia grew up and the nurse was convinced that she was just this side of being possessed. When that gets into a young girl's mind, it is difficult to get it out."

Cassius frowned. "Does *she* think she's possessed?"

Darian shook his head. "Nay," he said. "She never speaks of it. But she keeps herself covered. She has no real friends except for a petty cousin because when she was young, the girls from the village would whisper behind her back about the freckles on her face. Witch's marks, they would call them. Truthfully, I think her cousin started those rumors, but it does not matter now. Thanks to that radical nurse and her cruel friends, she has learned to cover herself up, convinced she is just as ugly as they have said."

Cassius grunted, shaking his head in disgust. "And she refuses suitors because of that?"

"Refuses them, rejects them, all of that," Darian said. "It wasn't as if she really had any, but anyone who has come to her grandfather with marital interest is sent away. The duke will not entertain any suitors for her."

Cassius eyed him. "Don't tell me that he thinks she is ugly," he said. "She's his heiress, for Christ's sake. You would think he would simply select the best husband for her and force her to wed."

Darian couldn't disagree. "You would think so, except he doesn't," he said. "She refuses and he listens to her. He will not force her."

"Does he not care?"

"I am not entirely certain," Darian said pensively. "He loves her, but it is almost as if he has lost his will to do anything about her. The older he becomes, the most distant he becomes. I have not yet figured out why."

"Resentment, mayhap?"

"It could be."

Cassius scratched his neck, thinking on the lovely Dacia.

While the situation shouldn't concern him in the least, he found that it did. She was beautiful and witty. At least, he thought so. Hearing how educated and bright she was from Darian, he wasn't surprised. It made her much more alluring to him. She seemed to be quite the perfect lady except for the fact that in her childhood, someone had planted the seed that she was unattractive because of her freckles.

It had stayed with her.

After a moment, he shook his head at the sadness of the situation.

"When I was coming to Edenthorpe earlier today, we were caught up in the Lords of Misrule festival," he said. "When I mentioned I was going to Edenthorpe, a young woman I met there told me about Lady Dacia's witch's marks."

Darian looked at him. "What was the young woman's name?"

"Amata de Branton."

Darian snorted, shaking his head in disgust. "That is her cousin," he said. "That little chit does all she can to tear Dacia down. It's truly despicable. But on the other hand, Dacia's marks are common knowledge in the village, so she is not repeating anything that isn't already known. Whenever Dacia goes into town, which is rare, she always covers herself so as not to frighten or offend anyone with her face."

Cassius frowned. "I saw her face," he said. "She is a beautiful woman. Surely you think so."

Darian nodded. "I do," he said. "Truth be told, I have entertained thoughts of marrying her myself."

"Why don't you?"

Darian shrugged, looking at his feet. "I am not entirely sure the duke would approve," he said. "And Dacia... truthfully, she has never shown the slightest interest in me. Whatever feelings I have for her are entirely one-sided. I know that feelings do not matter in a marriage, but it would be nice to have a wife who actually wanted to be married to me."

Cassius looked at him as if he'd lost his mind. "You are a de Lohr," he said. "You are a cousin to the Earl of Hereford and Worcester. That makes you quite appropriate."

"Not for a duke's granddaughter," Darian said, smiling without humor. "She should marry a royal relation or an earl at the very least. Not a mere knight. But... I shall not give up. Dacia is already twenty years and three, so I am biding my time. When she grows a year or two older, her grandfather may be ready to accept any offer."

"And then you shall strike."

"Exactly."

Cassius simply nodded, understanding the man's plan and completely understanding his admitted attraction to Lady Dacia. Cassius was having some of his own attraction to the woman going on, but he suspected that Darian was subtly laying his claim so Cassius knew the situation.

Not that Cassius had any designs on her.

... did he?

"Then I wish you luck," he said, clearing his throat and fighting off a stronger sense of disappointment when it came to Lady Dacia. Disappointment that Darian had perhaps a stronger claim, and intentions, than he did. "I think you would make an excellent Duke of Doncaster."

Darian grinned nervously. "It is a heady thought, indeed," he said. But then, he sobered. "May I tell you something?"

"Of course."

"I would take Dacia even without the dukedom."

Cassius was quite positive that the statement was, indeed, staking a claim. "Then I will again wish you luck," he said. "From what you told me, you may need it. But never forget you are a de Lohr. Doncaster can do no better than that."

Darian's smile turned genuine. "You honor me," he said. "I am glad we have had this chance to speak, my lord. It has been a great honor."

"You will call me Cassius," Cassius said, cocking an eyebrow. "You will not address me formally. We are family, after all. My cousin, Will, married your cousin several years ago. That marriage linked the de Wolfe and de Lohr families forever."

Darian nodded in agreement. "It did, indeed," he said. "In fact, I…"

He was cut off when one of his men shouted, pointing, and everyone turned towards the great bastion of Edenthorpe. Beneath the silver moonglow, they could see something moving in the distance, near the castle walls. There were gangs of men on horseback, bearing torches, as they watched, a barrage of flaming arrows launched at the men upon the walls. It took everyone a moment to realize what they were watching.

A raid.

"I thought you said Hagg had never attacked the castle," Cassius said, incredulous. "*What* in the hell is that?"

Darian was momentarily flabbergasted. "Damn," he finally hissed. "He never has attacked the castle."

Cassius could see that the activity was growing. "That, my friend, has changed," he said, giving Darian a shove. "If not him, then someone is, and at night, no less. Get your men back there. I will go inside and sit with the lady."

Darian looked at him. "I cannot leave her unprotected,

Cassius," he said. "I must…"

"You cannot take her through those lines and you know it. She must remain here."

"But if they move in this direction…"

Cassius cut him off, though not unkindly. "If they see thirty Doncaster soldiers around this cottage, they are going to suspect that they are protecting something," he pointed out quickly. "You must get these men away from here so as not to attract attention. Get them away from here and I will protect the lady with my life. I swear they'll not get her as long as there is breath left in my body, Darian. But you have a castle under siege."

Darian was torn, but only for a split second. He knew that what Cassius said was true. Soldiers around the cottage would only attract attention, so it would be best to move them. After a moment of indecision, he nodded.

"Very well," he said. "Get inside and stay with her."

"I will."

"Do not leave her for any reason."

"I will not, I promise."

Darian emitted a sharp whistle between his teeth and his men began to run for their horses. He, too, started to move, but not before he looked pointedly at Cassius.

"I will return," he said.

Cassius was heading for the cottage door, whistling for Argos as he went. "I know," he said. "Be cautious. There are only thirty of you and more than a few hundred of the enemy."

Darian waved him off, now rushing for his steed. Cassius bolted for the cottage door, yanking it open, and dashed inside with the dog on his heels. As he threw the bolt on the door, he happened to catch a glimpse of Dacia's startled gaze.

"Shutter the windows," he commanded softly. "Close them all up. Quickly, now."

The occupants of the cottage were an older woman, a middle-aged woman, two young children, an old man, and Dacia. The old man began to move without question, but Dacia stood up from where she was bent over the older woman.

"What is it?" she asked, concerned. "What has happened?"

Cassius went to help the old man place the shutters in front of the window closest to the door. "It seems there is a raiding party at Edenthorpe," he said. "Darian has taken your escort because we are afraid it would attract their attention. Therefore, we are going to fortify this cottage and settle down until the raid is finished.

Her eyes widened. "Hagg?"

"Possibly."

Dacia didn't say anything. Cassius was moving to the next window when he happened to look at her. She was still standing there and he knew it was because she was concerned, perhaps even indecisive about what she should do. Her home was under attack, as outlandish as that sounded, and she was understandably shaken.

Confused.

He spoke softly.

"Everything will be all right, my lady. Return to your work."

Dacia looked over at him and her gaze lingered for a moment. She was wearing a series of gossamer veils across her face and on her head, essentially only revealing some of her hair and both eyes. Everything else was covered. It was the apron all over again except with finer material.

But there was no mistaking those magnificent eyes, now filled with concern.

"Do you really think so?" she asked quietly.

"I do."

"You do not think it is too serious?"

"Probably not, but it is best to be prudent. Do not fear."

She continued staring at him before finally nodding her head and turning away. But her movements were slow and uncertain, apprehensive with the turn the night had taken. Cassius watched her return to work, trying to ease the fever of an old woman who didn't look as if she would survive the night. He went about helping the old man secure all of the shutters in the two-room cottage, returning to the larger common room and taking position next to the door where he could peer through the shutters at the castle in the distance.

It was going to be a long night.

"WELL?" DACIA WHISPERED. "Is the fight still going on?"

Cassius had been watching the battle for quite some time. The bright moon had sunk low in the sky, indicative of the late hour, but he could still see some movement near the castle. Whoever had attacked Edenthorpe had not quite given up yet.

"A little," he said, turning to look at her. "I can still see activity at the gatehouse, but it seems to have dissipated elsewhere. Where does this Catesby Hagg live?"

"South and west," she said. "A half-day's ride from Edenthorpe."

Cassius nodded before turning to watch the activity. "The moon will set soon," he said. "Their light will be gone, so I suspect they are heading home after a fruitless attempt to assault Edenthorpe."

He heard Dacia sigh. "Do you really think so?"

"I do. It is all but over."

She paused a moment, grateful that the attack on her home hadn't been worse. "In all my years living at Edenthorpe, I can only remember two assaults," she said, breathing heavily with relief. "I do not even remember why or who, but I know they did not last long. They were both so long ago. Edenthorpe has always been peaceful."

Cassius cocked an eyebrow. "Because only a fool would attack such a place," he said. "With those tall walls and those berms around it, I would say that it is impenetrable. It is demoralizing to attack a castle, knowing you have no chance."

He spoke like a man who knew his way around a fight. "Have you seen many battles?" she asked. "Mayhap that is a foolish question, given your profession."

"It is not foolish," Cassius said. "There are knights who see little battle and knights that see constant conflict. In answer to your question, I have seen many. Too many to count."

"All of them in England?"

"Some in England, some in Scotland, some in Wales, and a couple in France."

"Your family is a warring family, isn't it?"

He shrugged. "We are knights and we have property to protect," he said. "If someone wishes to take our property, we will fight. If the king needs our support, we lend it. There are other reasons to fight, of course, but good reasons. We do not go to war simply for war's sake."

"I did not mean it the way it sounded," she said. "I simply meant you have a great deal of experience in warfare."

"Definitely."

"And you have seen much of it with Edward?"

"The king has many enemies."

Dacia could hear something in his voice, something deadly. There was a stool next to the door and, wearily, she planted herself upon it, thinking of the events of the night, of Edenthorpe, and of Cassius.

It had been a most eventful evening.

"They have seen my strength for themselves, have watched me rise from the darkness of war, dripping with my enemies' blood," she murmured.

Cassius looked at her, his expression flickering with curiosity and recognition. "From *Beowulf*," he said softly. "How would you know that?"

Dacia glanced him, feeling perhaps a little embarrassed. "Forgive me," she said. "I did not mean to sound like a doomsayer. It is simply that what you said... the king having many enemies and you fighting his wars... made me think of that passage."

He came away from the window. "You did not answer my question," he said, though not unkindly. "How do you know *Beowulf*?"

"Because I have had an education in classic literature," she said. "An old priest who taught me everything he could, everything I would learn. I not only know *Beowulf*, I have debated it."

"With whom?"

"With the priest and with my grandfather," she said. "I will debate it with anyone."

A flicker of a smile pulled at Cassius' lips. "Even me?"

He saw her eyes crinkle up as she smiled beneath the veil. "You *are* Beowulf," she said. "You are a great warrior from the

House of de Wolfe. *Wulf* is even in your name."

He chuckled. "But I do not defeat the Grendel nor dragons," he said. "That old poem is a tribute to godless people in a godless time. But I will tell you that mayhap more of those bloodlines are in me than you realize. My mother's father, my grandfather, is a Norse king."

Her eyes lit up; he could see it. "*Konungr*," she said softly, using the Norse word for king. "I would believe that completely."

"You know the Norse language?"

She shrugged. "As I said, the old priest schooled me on many things."

Cassius nodded faintly, digesting the fact that this was truly a remarkable woman. He didn't want to give away what Darian had already told him because he didn't think she would take too kindly knowing the man had been talking about her. Cassius thought that whatever she wanted him to know should come from her, and he realized that he wanted her to tell him.

He wanted to know more.

"Did he teach you how to tend the ill?" he asked, with the intention of leading into more personal subjects. "You seem to know what you are doing."

Dacia glanced over at the old woman and her daughter, sleeping quietly in the corner with their family around them.

"I know enough," she said. "The woman has a recurring fever that does not seem to completely go away. Now her daughter is showing symptoms, too. I have given them both a potion of willow bark, which will ease the fever, but I suspect it is coming from a worm or an insect of some kind."

"A disease?"

"Possibly," she said. "I do not believe it to be contagious, but it may even be in the food they eat. I do not know."

Cassius was studying her as she was watching her patients. By the time she turned around, she caught him looking at her and she cocked her head curiously.

"What is it?" she asked.

Embarrassed that he'd been caught staring at her, he thought he might as well be straightforward with her. He hoped they had reached some level of comfort between them, but he wasn't entirely sure that level of comfort would be all that tolerant of what he was about to say.

He was about to find out.

Lifting a hand, he gestured at his own face.

"I was just noticing your modesty panels," he said. "You said that you always wear them?"

Something in her eyes flickered anxiously and she lowered her gaze. "I told you that I was modest with men I do not know," she said. "Or when I am outside of Edenthorpe for all to see. As I explained, it is my way."

Given everything Cassius had been told about her, he knew that was the truth. Before he made his next move, he took into account where they were – located in a tiny cottage where they were both essentially captive until the trouble at Edenthorpe was finished. If he spoke to her know about her reasons for keeping her face covered, she couldn't run from him.

She would have to hear him out.

Cassius honestly didn't know why he should even bother discussing something that wasn't his business, but there was something inherently tragic about a beautiful young woman who thought she was ugly because of the cruelties of others. From what he had seen, Dacia was more than accomplished in many areas. She was bright and well-educated.

And... she was beautiful.

Perhaps if he told her his opinion, it might make a difference to her.

Or not.

But something was compelling him to speak.

"I understand," he said. "But I would like to speak plainly. May I?"

She eyed him warily. "That depends," she said. "If you are offensive, I shall tell you so."

He nodded. "And I hope you would," he said. "But it is not my intention to offend you. I would never knowingly offend you, Lady Dacia. I swear this to you."

She continued to eye him. "Well, then?"

Cassius had her attention. Knowing that, he thought hard about what he was going to say. He wasn't sure he'd ever have another opportunity to speak his mind, so he knew he had to be careful.

"We have only just met this day, my lady," he said quietly. "But I wanted you to know what it honor it has been to come to know you. It is rare to find such a witty, educated young woman. You are a fine tribute to the House of de Ryes."

He saw her eyes widen, just a little, as if surprised he should say such a thing. "You have my thanks," she said. "It has been an honor to meet you, as well. In spite of our introduction."

She looked straight to Argos, who was sleeping on his back next to the hearth. The big dog was all stretched out, soaking in the heat. Everyone else in the cottage was huddled up for warmth, but not Argos. He was living the good life, warming his belly. Cassius looked at his big, silly dog and grinned.

"I will always thank him for introducing us," he said, returning his attention to her. His smile faded. "I want to say something more, if I may."

"Proceed."

He did. "Earlier this evening, when Darian came into the kitchen yard to tell you of the vassals in need, I do not know if you realized it, but you removed the apron from your face as you went into the kitchens," he said. "I saw your face without its covering and I realized that what I had said to you earlier was true. Mayhap you cover your face for modesty, and that is a well and good thing, for never in my life have I seen such beauty. That kind of beauty is not meant for the masses, my lady. It is meant only for the few and the fortunate who are privileged to glimpse upon it. Thank you for giving me such a vision. I shall never forget it."

He held his breath, waiting to see which direction she would go. Would she run away in outrage? Or would she realize he meant every word?

Instead, she did the unexpected.

"It's not true," she breathed. "You do not have to feed me false flattery, my lord, for I know what you say is not true."

The fear radiating from her was palpable and she began to tremble. Cassius could see it. "I do not lie, my lady," he said steadily. "What I saw tonight was a woman of astonishing beauty. Has no one ever told you so?"

She stared at him, blinking rapidly, and her trembling grew worse. "Of course not," she finally hissed. "For it is not... I am not... it is *not* true."

"Then you are accusing me of lying?"

He had her cornered and she stood up quickly from the stool to put some distance between them. She couldn't run, however, as he knew, so she was forced to face this conversation, as unpleasant as it was for her.

But the fear bristling in the air around her was static, like lightning.

It was everywhere.

"Sir Cassius, I know you mean well," she said. Even her voice was trembling. "You are trying to be polite to the duke's granddaughter, but I am not a fool so I would appreciate it if you would simply stop telling me things because you think I wish to hear them. I don't, you know. I do not need to hear any of it."

Cassius sighed faintly. She was standing up, looking away from him and wringing her hands. He came away from the window and moved towards her, coming up behind her.

It was time for total truth.

He had a feeling this might be his only opportunity.

"My lady," he said softly. "'Tis not idle compliments, I assure you."

"Please… no more."

He didn't listen to her and for good reason. If he didn't get it all out now, he probably never would.

He had a point to make.

"May I tell you a story?" he asked, hoping he wasn't about to watch her crawl through a window to get away from him. "When I first came to Edenthorpe, I was told of a young lass with a nurse who was convinced that the spots on the lass' face were the work of the devil. Now, I do not subscribe to the devil, or demons, or witches or curses. I was told that the reason you wear veils over your face is because your nurse covered you as a child and you continue doing it as an adult to hide the freckles that your nurse called witch's marks. When I first met you, you held the apron over your face and I asked if it was because my dog had injured you. Do you recall? You assured me that was not the case, but I will admit that I found out why you covered yourself. And not God or king could force something out of my mouth that wasn't the absolute truth, so when I say that I saw your face and thought it beautiful, that was nothing less than complete honesty. I am a knight of the highest order. I do not deal in half-truths, lies and flattery simply for flattery's sake. I swear this upon my oath."

With that, he turned around and headed back to his post next to the window. He resumed his task of peering through the shutters at Edenthorpe in the distance, but his senses were attuned to Dacia.

He was wondering if he had made an impact.

For the longest time, he heard nothing. No movement of any kind. Then, she slowly moved to the other side of the hearth, nearer to the sleeping family, and sat down next to the fire. He could hear the chair creak when she sat.

She remained there for the rest of the night.

And so did he.

CHAPTER SEVEN

"**Y**OU LOOK NO worse for the wear," Cassius said as he exited the cottage, bent over so he wouldn't strike his head on the doorway. "I take it the enemy has fled?"

It was dawn on the morning after the night battle at Edenthorpe and Cassius opened the door to a parade of knights. Rhori and Bose were there along with Darian and one of his junior knights, along with about one hundred heavily armed Doncaster men.

"Of course they have fled," Rhori said imperiously. "With the threat of a du Bois in command, they turned tail and ran like the cowards they are. Some of them are probably in Scotland by now."

Cassius grinned. "Good lad," he said. "We could see the battle from here. No slight against your ability, Rhori, but it never looked like they had a genuine chance of breaching the castle."

"They did not," Darian said, dismounting his horse and pushing past Rhori. "They harried the gatehouse mostly, but the walls are too tall. Where is Lady Dacia?"

Cassius threw a thumb over his shoulder. "In the cottage,"

he said. As Darian went to check on Dacia, Cassius went over to Rhori. "I am sorry this wasn't a true test of your command ability. I shall try to throw a more worthy enemy your way the next time."

By now, Bose had dismounted his steed and had joined them. Rhori slithered off his horse, holding on to the jumpy animal as he faced Cassius.

"This enemy may be quite worthy," Rhori said, lowering his voice. "We noticed something strange."

Cassius' eyebrows lifted. "What?"

"The yellow shield with the black lion," Bose muttered. "Three-point shield on some of the tunics, though they tried to cover it up. Still, we were able to see them. A lion with bloody paws, Cass."

Cassius stared at him a moment before cocking his head in confusion. "Yellow shield with the bloody black lion?" he repeated. "*Here?*"

"Here."

"That's Marcil Clabecq."

"It is."

Now, Cassius' eyes widened. "He and his men were with Edward at Falkirk," he said. "Are you telling me that professional Flemish mercenaries were part of that attack last night?"

Both Bose and Rhori nodded. "This may be more than simple harassment by an unhappy neighbor," Rhori said, keeping his voice low. "Clabecq goes where the money is, so Baron Hagg must be paying him a fortune."

Cassius shook his head in disbelief. "I had no idea the man had that kind of money," he said. Then he paused as if a thought had just occurred to him. "Or mayhap he does not. Mayhap Clabecq was promised part of the spoils. That would be quite an incentive."

Rhori nodded. "Quite," he agreed. "The party last night rode all around the castle, stopping at the barbican, at the postern gate, and at the gatehouse, but they never really did much of anything other than ride in circles, launch a few arrows, and look around. *Look around*, Cass."

Cassius knew exactly what he was driving at. "Studying her weaknesses," he said. Everything they were saying made sense. "So Hagg has hired himself Flemish mercenaries and they are studying Edenthorpe for her weaknesses."

"That would be my guess," Rhori said. "And if they take Edenthorpe, the spoils would be immense."

That was a very true statement. Suddenly, a little raid wasn't so little any longer. "Did you tell de Lohr your suspicions?" Cassius asked.

Rhori shook his head. "Nay," he said. "The man has seen one siege since he took command of Edenthorpe. Only one. While he wasn't terribly rattled, he was somewhat overly concerned given how few antagonists there really were. He spent most of his time reporting to Doncaster, who was sending the majordomo for information every few minutes. We wanted to give you our observations before speaking to Darian or to Doncaster. Something like this cannot be treated lightly."

Cassius shook his head. "Not at all," he said. "With Clabecq involved, the stakes have grown considerably. In fact, Clabecq was with Edward when he took Caerlaverock Castle in Scotland a couple of years ago. We were all there. We saw how Edward used them like a hammer to break down Caerlaverock."

Bose and Rhori nodded gravely. "Did you have much contact with Marcil Clabecq, Cass?" Rhori asked.

Cassius shook his head. "Not directly," he said. "Like you

two, I was with Edward the entire time trying to make sure the man didn't get himself killed. My focus was on Edward, not his allies or the Flemish scum he'd hired. They raided Caerlaverock heavily once it was breached and I heard that they also raided the Scottish countryside before they took a cog out of Edinburgh for home."

Rhori shook his head at the despicable nature of the mercenaries. "'Tis a good thing they did not go south into de Wolfe territory," he said. "I have a feeling that your father and uncles would have made short work of that group."

Cassius grinned. "They would have chewed up those Flemish bastards and spit them out," he said. But his grin quickly faded. "And now they're here, sizing up Edenthorpe."

"Old Cuffy needs to be told, Cass," Bose said. "He carries a big, lazy army and they could be in for a good deal of trouble."

Cassius knew that. "The problem is that they've never had trouble here," he said what they all knew. "Darian is a fine knight, but it's very possible he's become complacent. The Doncaster army has contributed to some of Edward's campaigns, but that was a while ago. If Flemish mercenaries really are here and Edenthorpe is their target, then they must be prepared."

Bose opened his mouth to reply, but Dacia and Darian chose that moment to quit the cottage. Darian was carrying Dacia's big leather satchel containing all of her herbs and potions, and she was giving the man orders as she walked.

"… and then I want to see Emmeric to see what he has for a parasite," she was saying. "I'm convinced that Old Timeo's wife has a worm of some kind. Mayhap the physic has something to kill it. I would like to go into the village today."

She walked right by Cassius without acknowledging the

man. Not that he had expected her to, for ever since their conversation last night, there hadn't been another word spoken between them.

But Cassius wasn't going to let it bother him.

In fact, he was perturbed at himself for giving a damn in the first place. He'd had the rest of the night to stew about the situation and by morning, he was fairly cooked with regret. He'd met a young woman whom he felt sorry for and had tried to help. Or was it more than that? Truthfully, he wasn't sure and perhaps that perturbed him the most – because he didn't know *why* he really did it when it was none of his business. He thought maybe his ego had gotten the better of him and he thought he could make a difference to a rather isolated young woman when, in fact, she clearly didn't want any help. She didn't want or need his opinion.

It would be the last time he tried to do something kind for someone.

He was done.

As Dacia made her way out to the palfrey that had been brought around from the stable yard of the cottage, Argos suddenly bolted out of the cottage, past Cassius, and headed straight for Dacia. She was almost to her palfrey when Argos butted up against her legs, wagging his tail so hard that he kept smacking her with his tail. She came to a halt as if uncertain what to do with the dog when Cassius emitted a whistle so piercing that the horses jumped.

"Argos!" he boomed. "To me!"

The dog may have been big and silly, but he wasn't stupid. He knew when his master was calling him. With a final lick to Dacia's hand, he loped over to Cassius, who turned for the stable yard where his warhorse had been housed last night.

He didn't give Dacia another look.

"We return to Edenthorpe, tell Doncaster what we suspect, and leave it at that," he said to Rhori and Bose, pushing the woman from his mind. "And then we get out of here. We are not staying any longer than necessary. Mount up. I shall meet you in a moment."

As Rhori and Bose headed off to gather their horses, Cassius made his way into the stable yard where the warhorse he called Old Man await him. A husky Belgian charger, the animal was as red as a stormy sunrise and built for battle. His saddle was in the small barn, in a pile of hay, and he quickly put the tack on his horse as Argos wandered around nearby. He knew the dog was looking for a meal, which was something he could find for him at Edenthorpe. But once the dog was fed and Doncaster knew that there were Flemish mercenaries involved in Hagg's presence last night, they were departing Edenthorpe.

Hopefully forever.

The ride back to the castle was uneventful. The gatehouse opened wide for the returning knights and sealed up quickly once they passed through. Cassius took Old Man and Argos into the stables where he made sure both animals were well-fed and the horse bedded down, at least temporarily. He left Argos with the horse, knowing the dog wouldn't wander far away from the steed he was familiar with, as he joined up with Rhori and Bose once more. Darian, who had just stabled his blond beast, emerged from the opposite end of the livery and headed in their direction.

"Well?" Rhori said, eyeing the approach of Darian. "Do we tell him now and let him tell Doncaster?"

"That might be best, Cass," Bose put in. "If we remain to tell Doncaster as you suggested, there is no telling when we will be able to leave."

It would have been easy for Cassius to agree to that with his need to get out of Edenthorpe. That feeling grew worse when he saw Dacia emerge from the stable, carrying her leather satchel, heading for the keep. She was covered in her customary veils, glancing in his direction before quickly looking away when he happened to look over at her.

That was enough to disgust Cassius completely.

"Tell Darian now," he muttered. "Let him tell Old Cuffy. This is their problem, not ours. The longer we remain here, the more chance there is of us getting sucked into something that does not concern us."

Rhori and Bose nodded in agreement. As Darian came near, it was Rhori who finally spoke out.

"De Lohr," he said. "My colleagues and I have been discussing the attack last night. I believe this is something you should hear."

Darian looked between the three knights with interest. "Oh?" he said. "What about it?"

Cassius looked at Rhori, silently urging the man to continue. Rhori and Bose had seen everything firsthand last night and Cassius hadn't. Therefore, the information was best coming from them.

"De Shera and I noticed something that we wanted to discuss with Cassius before we brought it to your attention," he said. "I'm curious… you said you've had dealings with Catesby Hagg in the past?"

Darian nodded. "Aye," he said. "Over in the disputed lands. Raids on the mining operation, mostly. Why?"

"And they've never attacked Edenthorpe before?"

"Never."

"Did you ride out to defend the disputed land against their raids?"

"I did," Darian said. "I led a contingent of men three times. Why are you asking these questions?"

Rhori folded his big arms over his chest. "The men that were here last night," he said. "Granted, it was somewhat dark, but the moon was still bright, bright enough to see them with a goodly amount of clarity. Did you notice anything different or strange about them?"

Darian's brow furrowed. "I do not believe so," he said. "Why do you ask?"

"Nothing different?"

"Nothing at all." Darian paused, looking at the knights. "If there is something you wish to say, I wish you would say it."

It was Bose who spoke. "Last night, Rhori and I were northwest tower," he said. "The earthworks are fairly high there and we were watching the raiders ride up over the crests, coming close to the castle walls. We noticed that some of them were wearing tunics of yellow with a black lion upon them. They were trying to cover them up, but when they rode towards us, the cloak one man was wearing flipped up so we could easily see the standard. Is the black lion the banner of Catesby Hagg?"

Darian looked puzzled. "Nay," he said. "He flies a red boar. I did not see any tunics with a black lion."

"You were so busy with Doncaster and his majordomo, I am not surprised," Bose said. "But we saw it. We've seen it before."

"You have? Where?"

At this point, Rhori and Bose looked at Cassius. "It is the standard of Marcil Clabecq, a Flemish mercenary whom Edward has used in the past to bolster his ranks," Cassius said seriously. "Clabecq is a killer, Darian. His men are highly trained and he goes where the money is. It is my thought, and the thought of Rhori and Bose, that Hagg has hired Clabecq to lay siege to Edenthorpe. Last night wasn't an attack as much as it was surveillance. They are looking for the weaknesses of the castle so that the next time they come, they'll bring a larger number of men and they'll attack the weaknesses of the fortress. Last night was nothing compared to what is to come."

Darian was trying not to openly react to the news, but it was difficult. "Are you certain?" he asked. "Catesby Hagg is not a wealthy man, at least not wealthy enough to hire mercenaries of that caliber."

Now came the second part of the bad news. "It is possible Hagg has promised Clabecq a percentage of the spoils," Cassius said. "Edenthorpe would be an enormous spoil. They would strip it."

Now, Darian's jaw was hanging open in surprise. "But Edenthorpe cannot be breached," he said. "The fortress is invincible. There is no possible way they can take her."

Cassius could hear the shock, the denial, in the man's voice. "Clabecq was with Edward two years ago when he took Caerlaverock Castle," he said. "The mercenaries were instrumental in helping Edward breach that castle, which is surrounded by a moat as big as a lake and walls that are nearly as high as Edenthorpe's. Do not make the mistake of thinking they cannot get in here. If they want to, they will find a way. You must warn Doncaster and all appropriate steps must be taken to prevent this from happening."

Darian closed his mouth, looking at Cassius in astonishment. "Do you truly think this will come to pass?"

"It is very possible, Darian. You must warn Doncaster and

make the necessary preparations."

Darian sighed heavily, running his fingers through his cropped, blond hair. After a few moments of deliberation, he nodded his head.

"Very well," he said. "Will you please come with me? Doncaster will want to hear this from you."

Cassius shook his head. "Nay," he said. "We have relayed our concerns and observations to you, so do what you will with the information. I am expected in the north and will not be delayed."

Instead of agreeing, Darian reached out and put a hand on Cassius' arm. "Please, Cassius," he said, a hint of desperation in his tone. "I will not keep you overly long, but please come with me and speak to Doncaster about this. He respects and trusts you. He will have questions I possibly cannot answer. I would consider it a personal favor."

When he put it that way, Cassius couldn't very well disagree. After a moment, he nodded shortly, but it was under protest. Rhori and Bose could both see it. Still, he did as he was asked, accompanying Darian into the keep of Edenthorpe with Rhori and Bose bringing up the rear.

Something told both men that Cassius would not be leaving for the north as soon as he had hoped.

Call it a hunch.

HE'D GONE INSIDE the keep.

Dacia had been watching Cassius since their return to Edenthorpe from her chamber high atop the keep. Of course, she had been watching him the entire ride back to the castle. And, of course, when they were sequestered together in the cottage.

There had been nothing else on her mind but him.

Oh, she'd pretended to ignore him and, in truth, she *did* ignore him after he'd told her she was beautiful. But she wasn't ignoring him to punish him – she'd been ignoring him because she didn't know how else to react, torn between denial and hope. She'd spent so many years being convinced she was a hideous creature with spots all over her face that to hear the most handsome man she'd ever seen say that he thought she was beautiful had been enough to stun her into silence.

She just couldn't believe he meant it.

Once Dacia saw Cassius go into the keep with Darian and the other two knights, she came away from the window of her extravagant bower. It took up nearly the entire third floor of the octagon-shaped keep, separated into three chambers. One chamber was for her bed while another was for her possessions like clothing, trunks, and a dressing table. Still another was where her army of maids would sit and work. It was a magical suite of rooms filled with everything a young woman could possibly hope to have. She wanted for absolutely nothing.

With Cassius out of her sight, Dacia wandered into the smaller chamber that contained her dressing table. Her maids were in their little chamber, mending the dress she'd worn yesterday when that silly dog had pushed her in the river, and that included Edie. She could hear the woman bossing the others around.

There were six maids in all, Edie plus two older women who had served her mother long ago, and then three of whom had come into service over the past few years. All of them had a function, from cleaning her bed to emptying her chamber pot to sweeping floors and lighting fires.

It was that veritable army of maids that Dacia was so unfond of, except for Edie, but they had sense enough to leave her alone when the mood dictated it.

Like now.

She was in a mood.

Next to the dressing table was a small cabinet that contained all manner of potions, creams, cosmetics, and herbs meant for the care and hygiene of a well-bred young woman. Given that Dacia was quite familiar with herbs and potions, she probably had more than most, including a potion given to her by Emmeric, the local physic, guaranteed to reduce the marks on her face.

But she had never tried it.

Her old nurse had told her once that the marks on her face were her penitence. For what, she didn't know, because they had started developing at such a young age that she surely hadn't had time to sin too terribly. Still, the nervous woman was convinced dark forces were at work through her young charge, something that made for a contentious relationship between the nurse and the priest who taught all manner of lessons.

Growing up with that pair had been an interesting time.

Even now, Dacia smiled when she thought of the old priest teaching her about herbs and flowers, and potions that could possibly help clear her skin, and the nurse screaming about it. Even now, as Dacia looked at all of the medicaments she had collected over the years, there were at least three things in her possession that were said to ease skin blemishes.

Truthfully, she didn't see the use of even trying them.

Until now.

Cassius had called her beautiful.

As she gazed at herself in the mirror, she began to pull off the veils, one at a time. They were carefully and artfully arranged, and they ended up in a pile on her dressing table as she stared at her reflection in the polished silver mirror.

Big, blue eyes gazed back at her from under dark brows. Her freckles went across her nose, on her upper cheeks, and faded away once they came to her mouth and chin, although she did have a big one next to the corner of her mouth.

Leaning forward, she touched the freckles, thinking they weren't as dark as they used to be when she was younger, but to her, they were still quite obvious. And ugly. Everyone said so. Only a woman with pure and clear skin was considered beautiful.

Maybe Cassius had bad eyesight.

Even so... his words had meant something.

Dacia had never been called beautiful in her life. She was so very puzzled why Cassius would say such a thing to her. It had been unsolicited. He'd just come out with it. But he'd heard about the nurse, about her freckles, so he knew something of her embarrassing history.

But mayhap... *mayhap*... she could try something to ease those marks. With her nurse gone, there was no one to tell her that they were penitence. There was no one to make her feel ugly and harassed by demonic forces. It had been a habit to cover up her face, to hide behind those veils, but the truth was that she hated it even if she was resigned to it.

But maybe she didn't need to be.

Cassius was the first man she had ever met who took the time to give her a little unexpected hope.

With that thought, she went to the cabinet that held all of

the treatises and books that the old priest had given her before he'd returned to his monastery in Lincoln. She was a collector of these things, but kept them tucked away. It was considered unseemly for a woman to collect books, and with her freckles already creating an undesirable issue, she felt compelled to hide one more unbecoming trait away from the world.

Reverently, she pulled them forth.

From the pages of these leather-bound, hand-painted books came recipes for so many things, but she was looking for something in particular – recipes to banish unsightly skin blemishes. Onion and garlic were recommended, mixed with vinegar, as were various herbs and roots. She'd seen these recipes before in the quest for mixing certain potions to help with the sick that she'd been called upon to tend, but she hadn't paid any attention to them until now.

Even as she looked through the books, she felt guilty. Guilt that her old nurse had instilled within her, that old woman who had believed in omens and demons and insisted that fae roamed the land. Ironically, the woman's name had been Mother Mary, the name of Christ's mother, the most holy woman in Christendom. But Mother Mary believed in the worst far more than she had faith in the good.

Thumbing through her books, she found six recipes that had to do with correcting blemished skin, but they were all for unsightly eruptions, which Dacia never had. She was looking for something specifically to remove or ease freckles. Towards the end of a book translated from an old Arabic treatise, she began to find what she was looking for. From Adnan, apothecary to Sultan Bakir ibn Faizon, she found several recipes.

Wheat flour, dragonwort, and vinegar, boiled together, and then smeared upon the skin shall remove blemishes and spots.

Or…

Buttermilk mixed with flour, applied as a paste, shall fade freckles.

Or…

Cut a lemon in half and rub the halves upon the skin to elim-inate skin spots.

Dacia read all of the recipes she could find, but those three seemed to be the least radical. She drew the line at smearing the blood of her enemies on her freckles. She knew she could find the ingredients and was willing to give them a try. To the devil with her nurse's superstitions and the guilt she had thrown over her charge like a weighted blanket. Dacia was going to shrug off that blanket, push past the superstition, and step out into the light.

All because Cassius de Wolfe had called her beautiful.

It was amazing what just a few words could accomplish.

Dacia knew where some dragonwort grew, down by the river's edge, so she quickly changed out of the clothing she had worn all night and into something more functional. As two of the maids helped her, she donned a simple garment made from very fine lamb's wool. It was the color of cornflower, almost the exact color of her eyes, gathered under the breasts and flowing freely below. It even had two big pockets sewn into it that Dacia's maids had stitched honeybees on. With her hair in a braid and no veils on her face because she would slip in and out through the postern gate, Dacia left her maids behind and headed out to find the dragonwort.

It was, literally, the beginning of a new day.

"AND YOU ARE certain of this, Cassius?" Doncaster said seriously. "A Flemish mercenary?"

In Doncaster's solar that smelled of leather and smoke from a chimney that liked to back up into the chamber, Cassius faced an old man who suddenly looked older just in the course of the short conversation. Once he'd been told that what he thought was a manageable adversary had evidently hired professional and deadly soldiers in the land dispute, the lines on his face became ten years deeper.

"Am I certain that the bloody lion is Marcil's banner?" Cassius said. "Aye, I am certain. But I was not here during the attack last night, so I did not see the tunics that du Bois and de Shera saw. However, they would not lie and they are not fools. I would trust them both with my life a thousand times over. If they said they saw Clabecq's bloody lion, then they did."

Doncaster looked as if he'd just been hit in the gut. He suddenly slumped, staring off into the chamber as he pondered what he'd been told. A mood seem to settle, something uncertain and edgy, and Cassius glanced at Darian, who lifted his eyebrows as if to confirm what they all knew.

They had a problem.

"I must speak to Hagg," Doncaster finally said. "In the past, we were never enemies, but we were never allies, either. I must speak to the man and discover if this is the truth. This entire situation has gone far enough."

It was clear by the expression on Darian's face that he didn't think that was a good idea. "Your grace," he said, frowning. "If the man is hiring mercenaries, then it is past the negotiation stage. He means to destroy us."

Doncaster shook his head. "There is always room for talking, Darian," he said patiently. He looked up at the four big seasoned knights standing around him. "I am a man of peace. I have always been a man of peace. I keep a big army because I have much to protect, but to go to war? That is another matter altogether. If I can make peace with my neighbor through talking, then I shall do so."

Darian looked at the man as if he had lost his mind. "He wants the disputed land," he said. "At least, he did. Now he seems to want everything you have, too. How do you think he will agree to make peace, your grace?"

Doncaster eyed his knight, perhaps a bit unhappily. "Mayhap I shall agree to share the disputed land with him," he said. "He cannot have it all, but I will share it."

"But he may want more, your grace. What more are you willing to concede?"

Doncaster cocked his head thoughtfully. "I do not know," he said. "I know that he has a son. If the lad is not married, mayhap a marriage will seal the peace. I have Dacia to bargain with, you know."

"Nay!"

Both Darian and Cassius shouted the word at the same time before looking at each other in surprise. In fact, everyone was looking at them in surprise. Chagrinned, Cassius held up a hand.

"Your grace, a marriage to the son of the man who has been harassing you would only be condemning your granddaughter to a life of misery," he said evenly. "I have seen marriages like that and it is the women who suffer. I am sure you do not wish your granddaughter to suffer. Moreover, if you marry her to Hagg's son, he shall become the Duke of Doncaster. Is that who you want to entrust your legacy to?"

Doncaster seemed to ponder that suggestion as if he hadn't considered it at all. Then he shook his head. "I suppose not," he said. "But I will speak with Catesby nonetheless."

Cassius, like Darian, didn't think that was a good idea. He sought to drive that point home where Darian hadn't.

"Your grace, he has already made his intentions known," he said. "The Flemish mercenaries are here and even if you try to negotiate with Hagg, those mercenaries are going to want some kind of payment. Hagg may agree to peace, but the mercenaries will not and they will more than likely go on a rampage on your lands for what they will consider just compensation. This is not a situation where you can simply will peace to happen."

"Then what do you suggest, Cassius?"

Cassius cleared his throat softly. "I realize you will not like my suggestion, but for your own sake, you must consider it, your grace," he said. "You must reinforce your ranks and you must hit Hagg before his mercenaries have a chance to move on Edenthorpe. Destroying them is the only option at this point. If you do not, they will destroy you."

Doncaster sat back in his chair, staring up at the ceiling as he mulled over the advice. He was an old man and, like most old men, all he wanted was peace. He wanted to sit in front of the fire and read his books, and not have to worry about his safety or the safety of his fortress. This conflict with Hagg had been both unexpected and unwelcome, and the fact that it was escalating did not please him.

Now, Edward's Lord Protector was suggesting more military action.

That wasn't what he wanted to hear.

"I do not know if I want to strike first," he finally said. "That makes me look like the aggressor. That is not how I want to live out the remainder of my life, as an aggressor attacking neighbors."

Darian sighed sharply, struggling to keep from rolling his eyes. "But *he* attacked us first, your grace," he said. "If you do not take Cassius' advice, then we will suffer the consequences. This situation will not simply go away. Something must be done."

Doncaster looked up at the host of faces around him. Three men that the king trusted implicitly and one that he trusted implicitly. All seasoned knights, highly trained warriors. They wanted him to fight. He didn't want to fight. But he also didn't want to lose his legacy to an envious neighbor and Flemish mercenaries.

Unfortunately, Vincent had never been a warrior. His father had been one, and his father before him, but Vincent had been the scholar. He was at home with his books, not on a battlefield.

He was going to have to trust others for better advice than he could give himself.

After a moment, he simply shook his head.

"Very well," he said, looking to Cassius. "I know that you were only meant to deliver Edward's message to me and I have given my pledge of money and men to him, but now I need something from Edward."

Cassius nodded smartly. "Anything, your grace."

"I need you."

Cassius blinked as if he didn't understand the statement. "I... I am not sure what you mean, your grace," he said. "I am sworn to Edward, so if you..."

Doncaster cut him off, though not harshly. He simply waved a hand. "Not permanently," he said. "But at the moment, I need your might and the might of the knights you brought with you. I also need reinforcement from crown troops. There are some at Pontefract Castle and some at Tickhill Castle. Send for them and then you will remain to command them. In fact, you will command my army. Darian is a good knight, but he doesn't have your battle experience. If we are to go to war, I want a de Wolfe in command."

Cassius didn't dare look at Darian. "Your grace, if I…"

"Do this and Edward can have anything he wants for his wars in Scotland."

That stopped Cassius in his tracks. He stared at Doncaster a moment before sighing heavily. Truthfully, he didn't have a choice. He knew Edward would want him to help his old ally if the man was requesting assistance, so declining wasn't an option. In fact, if it got back to Edward that he was resistant, Edward would not be pleased. Not in the least.

If Cassius wanted to keep his position, he was going to have to do as Doncaster asked.

Damn…

"Very well, your grace," he said, but it was clear that he wasn't happy about it. "I will send to Pontefract and Tickhill. They are the closest. I will ask for half their numbers to reinforce your ranks."

"Good," Doncaster said, visibly relieved. "Bring all of those men here and when Hagg sees how big my army has become, he will think twice about turning the mercenaries loose. Mayhap a mere show of force will be enough to scare him off."

"Except that the show of force cannot remain forever, your grace," Cassius said quietly. "If I summon that many men, I must have free rein to do what I feel is necessary to protect the peace of Doncaster. Will I have this freedom, your grace?"

Doncaster hesitated a moment before nodding his head. "You will."

There wasn't much more to say after that. They all knew the stakes, and now Cassius had committed to remaining with Doncaster for the duration of the conflict.

So much for returning home.

With a nod to Doncaster and a long look to Darian, who was looking back at him with clear disappointment, Cassius quit the solar with Rhori and Bose on his heels. He managed to get out of the keep before he exploded.

"Damnation!" he boomed. "This was *not* part of my plan. I did not come here only to involve myself in another man's war. But if I do not agree to his request, Edward will hear about it and there will be hell to pay. I cannot refuse the man and he knows it."

Rhori sighed heavily. "I am sorry, Cass," he said. "I know how badly you want to see your grandmother. She's just going to have to wait a little longer."

Cassius threw his arms up in the air in frustration. "The woman is in her ninth decade," he fumed. "She does not have all the time in the world. I swear upon my oath, if my grandmother passes away while I am wasting my time with Doncaster's foolishness, then Doncaster need not fear Marcil Clabecq. He will have to fear *me* because I will burn this bloody place to the ground."

He was stomping around angrily, expending his rage. Rhori and Bose let him. Cassius had spent the past three years without a rest of any kind and now he'd been forced into another man's war just when rest was within his reach. He had every right to be angry.

It was Bose who finally stopped him from stomping around, putting his hands on Cassius' shoulders to stop his pacing.

"Then let us make short work of this," he said. "Think, Cass – send word to Pontefract and Tickhill Castles, just as you told Old Cuffy. Get those men here and then we'll merge them with the Doncaster army and obliterate Catesby Hagg. Doncaster said he would give you full control, so the sooner you destroy Hagg, the sooner you can leave."

Cassius was still twitching. "Stupid, ridiculous old men," he muttered. "And what about him putting me in command right in front of Darian? How do you think that made de Lohr feel? If I were him, I'd be bloody furious."

"Then you find Darian and apologize to him," Bose said steadily. "Tell him you did not mean to usurp his command, that you happily defer to him in all things. And then just do what you want, anyway. But make him feel as if he had part in the decision making. I've seen you do this, Cass. You're a master."

Cassius sighed sharply, struggling to push down his temper. He focused on Bose's words. The man was making sense. Taking a deep breath, he smiled weakly.

"That was the Scots side of me raging like a madman, you know," he said. "I get that from my mother and grandmother."

Bose grinned. "What about the Viking side?"

Cassius shrugged. "That side wants to raid the countryside, burn villages, and steal women," he said. "I keep that side well restrained."

Bose laughed softly. "I hope not *too* restrained," he said. "You must let it out for the battle against Marcil if we are to win this quickly. We need your mighty sword, Cass."

Cassius' smile faded. "It will be unleashed, I assure you," he said. Then he took a deep breath to steady himself and looked off towards the stables. "I suppose I should find my dog and make sure he is fed before I take a few hours' sleep. I did not sleep all night."

Relieved that he was calming down, Bose waved him on. "Go," he said. "Find that stupid dog. Du Bois and I will be in the hall, finding something to eat. It was a long night for us, too. Do you want me to send word to Tickhill and Pontefract?"

Cassius nodded. "If you would, please," he said. "Do it before the day is out. I'd like to get this over with as soon as we can."

"I'll make sure the messengers go out within the hour."

Cassius merely lifted a hand before heading off towards the stables. With missives being sent, he was focused on other things. He wanted to check on his horse to make sure the animal was well-fed and bedded down, and he knew the dog would be somewhere around the horse.

But he was wrong.

A hunt for Argos went on for fifteen minutes until he finally found a stable servant and asked if the man had seen a big gray dog about. The man had, pointing to the postern gate. It seemed that Lady Dacia and the dog had gone back to the river.

With a frown, Cassius followed.

CHAPTER EIGHT

T HAT SILLY DOG was following her again.

Dacia had been nearly to the postern gate when the dog came out of nowhere, wagging its tail and licking her hand. At first, she was greatly annoyed, but that annoyance fled because the dog, for all of his ridiculousness, really was a sweet animal. Happy, too, especially when he was pushing young women into the river. Dacia did like dogs, but she wasn't entirely sure what to make of Argos.

He belonged to Cassius, after all.

Still, the dog seemed to like her quite a bit.

He followed her as she passed through the postern gate, which was guarded after last night's raid. She was in full view of the soldiers who were at the gate as she and the dog headed down to the river's edge.

It was a bright spring morning, not too cold, and the grass was wet with dew. She was looking for the tall, slender bushes that grew wild in a land where so many other flowers and grasses grew wild. Around the River Don, there seemed to be an inordinate amount of heavy foliage of all kinds, and she began to hunt for the dragonwort, pulling apart bushes, looking around the base of the earthworks that formed some of the defenses of Edenthorpe.

The dog wandered around behind her, sniffing around, running over to the river and peering into it. There were a great deal of water fowl in and around the river and as Dacia finally found what she thought was a small dragonwort bush, Argos managed to catch some kind of small water bird with a great deal of noise and splashing.

When she looked over at him, he had killed it and was already starting to eat it, feathers and all. But it didn't take him long and as she pulled out a small knife to cut through the long, slender branches that contained the dragonwort, he wandered over to where she was and plopped down beside her. She glanced over at the animal in time to see him burp up some black feathers.

"God's Bones," she said distastefully, turning back to her task. "You are a brutal and disgusting creature. Do you know that?"

"So I have been told."

Startled, she turned to see boots next to her, shielding her eyes from the sun and looking up enough to see that Cassius was standing next to her. Quickly, she looked back at her task, a reflex action so he couldn't see her uncovered face.

It was purely habit.

"I did not mean you," she said, her heart racing furiously. "I meant your dog. He just ate a bird."

"That is because he is hungry," he said. "I went to the stable to find him so I could feed him and was told he had gone with you."

Dacia shook her head. "He did not *go* with me," she said. "I came out here and he simply followed. I have no control over him."

Cassius put his hands on his hips, looking down at his dog. "Clearly, you do and you do not even realize it," he said. "He seems to like you a great deal."

Dacia continued to cut and tug, turning her head slightly and still seeing his boots standing there. As she tried to ignore her wildly thumping heart, she reflected on the evening before and the very reason why she was out here.

Cassius *was* the reason.

Considering they hadn't spoken since he'd delivered the fateful compliment that had sent her spiraling into confusion, she was quite aware that she was glad to see him but also terrified at the same time. Considering the way she'd reacted last night, she was certain he thought her ungrateful and rude. She didn't think she'd be seeing him so soon, so she hadn't had the opportunity to work up her courage to seek him out and apologize for her behavior, but she knew they might not have another perfect opportunity like this one. They were alone and he would soon be leaving.

There might not be another chance.

"I have forgiven him for pushing me into the river," she said after a moment. "Mayhap he senses that."

Argos burped again and stretched out on the grass. Cassius shook his head at his lazy, rude dog.

"Mayhap he does," he said. "Even so, I will relieve you of his burden. He needs a proper meal and some sleep, as do I."

He whistled for the dog, who simply raised his head, looked at him, and laid back down again. Cassius frowned as Dacia looked over at the mutt, fighting off a grin.

"He does not obey very well, does he?" she said.

Cassius grunted. "Usually, he does," he said. "Again, I can

only imagine that he has taken a great liking to you and I apologize if he is being an annoyance. I will lock him in my chamber from now on."

She turned her head slightly again, still keeping her face turned away. "I am sure that is not necessary," she said. "He is not being an annoyance."

Cassius wasn't going to argue with her. "Suit yourself," he said. "When you tire of him, put him in the stables near my charger. He'll remain there until I come for him."

He turned to leave and Dacia summoned her courage. She could see this moment slipping away and she didn't want it to.

She had something to say.

"Wait," she said quickly, hearing his footsteps come to a halt. "I... I would like a moment of your time, if you would be so kind."

She could hear him draw in a long breath, perhaps fortifying himself for another unpleasant conversation like the one last night.

"I am at your service, my lady," he said neutrally.

Dacia was still cutting on the dragonwort even though she had enough. She simply didn't want to look up at him.

At least, not yet.

Speaking her mind was harder than she thought.

"I... I wanted to apologize for my manners last night," she finally said, putting bunches of the dragonwort in a pile next to her. "You were kind and I reacted poorly. I should not have insinuated you were telling me untruths when you... when you spoke of..."

She still couldn't bring herself to say it. Cassius folded his big arms over his chest.

"When I told you that I thought you were beautiful?"

She nodded quickly. Sighing heavily, she put down the knife and rocked back on her heels.

"It is simply that no one has ever told me that," she said quietly. "You must understand, Sir Cassius... the marks on my face developed at a young age. My nurse, Mother Mary, was convinced that a demon was trying to possess me, so I've simply learned to cover them. All I've ever done is cover them. I am afraid to let anyone see them because they are so ugly. That is why when you... said that to me, I have never heard it before and I reacted poorly. I have often dreamed of being like other women, of having fair skin that is considered beautiful, but I am afraid it is only a dream. At least, it was until you told me that you thought I was beautiful. Now I am afraid to believe it, but I thank you just the same for your kindness in saying so."

She couldn't see Cassius' face as he looked at the back of her head, a faint smile on his lips and his eyes glimmering with warmth.

"Will you do something for me, my lady?" he asked softly.

She nodded. "If I can."

"I want you to stand up."

Dacia was puzzled, but she did as he asked, hesitantly. She was still facing away from him as she heard him come up behind her. Her heart, which had momentarily calmed, was now thumping so loudly that she could hear it in her ears. His presence behind her made her feel so giddy that her head was starting to swim.

"Now," he murmured. "Turn around and look at me."

She started to move but quickly came to a halt. Her entire body began to tremble. "I... I cannot. I am not covered."

"I know. Turn around and look at me."

She wanted to. God knew, she did. But she was terrified.

The tears began to pool.

"I… I cannot."

Cassius could tell that she was close to weeping. "Please, Dacia," he whispered. "Turn around and look at me."

She stood there for a moment. But very slowly, she began to move. With the pace of a snail, she managed to turn around, all the way around, with her head lowered and tears dripping off her chin. She couldn't stop them. Cassius found himself looking at the top of her head, the tip of her nose, and little more.

Reaching out, he tipped her head up until she was looking him fully in the face.

Those magnificent blue eyes, filled with tears, gazed back at him with panic. He could see how frightened she was, her naked face for all to see. But he smiled at her to let her know that there was nothing to be frightened of as he reached up, pushing a stray lock of dark hair from her face and wiping the tears that had streaked down her face. It was a sweet and gentle action.

Very closely, he looked at her.

"I see nothing imperfect," he murmured. "I see a beautiful young woman with the most beautiful eyes I have ever seen. I see smooth, soft skin. I see lovely lips."

Her lower lip began to tremble and her eyes spilled over again. "But… but the spots…"

His smile grew. "Let me explain something to you," he said. "In nature, many creatures have spots. Dogs, cats, birds, even horses. Now, a horse of one color is an unexciting thing. Boring. It's the horses with spots and blazes that are truly interesting and beautiful. And flowers; when you see a flower with many colors, does that not make it the most interesting and beautiful of all of God's creations? Of course it does. We see plain creatures and flowers every day. They are nothing special. But when we see creatures with spots and streaks, or flowers with multiple colors, it makes me think that God was in fine form when he created them. They are his most beautiful of all creatures because he was showing his talent when he made them. Just like he was showing his talent when he made you, Lady Dacia. You are one of his magnificent creatures."

By the time he was finished, her tears were gone and she was looking at him in awe. Her hand came up to touch her face, where she knew the freckles were, stunned by his words.

"No one has ever said that to me," she muttered. "I've only had others tell me I was a witch, and girls I thought were my friend tell me that I was ugly."

"Don't you know why?" he asked with feigned incredulity. "Because they are jealous, my lady. Don't ever believe them. I have known my share of women to know exactly how they are when faced with a creature that outshines them. Jealousy overtakes them. That is the only reason they said such things to you."

Shocked, she pondered that for a moment because the concept had genuinely never occurred to her. "Do you really think so?"

"I really think so." Eyes glimmering, he shook his head faintly. "Do not ever cover yourself up again when you see me, please? I consider it a privilege to see you as God meant you to be seen – one of his best creations."

There were those words again, giving her hope. This man she'd only known a couple of days had given her more hope than men she'd known a lifetime, her grandfather included. That hope reminded her of why she was out by the river in the first place. Weakly, she gestured to the pile of dragonwort she had collected.

"I came out here to collect an herb that was part of a recipe I found," she said. "I have some old Arabic treatises and one says to use dragonwort to… well, it helps with the skin."

"Helps it do what?"

Now, she was embarrassed with her admission. "Helps to fade skin spots."

"I see," he nodded, looking over to the pile of herbs next to his sleeping dog. "Have you tried it before?"

"Never. I never saw any reason to before."

He looked at her, a glimmer of mirth in his eye. "But you have a reason now?"

Her cheeks turned bright red and she lowered her head. "I thought… it could not hurt."

His lips tugged with a smile. "Who is this reason, Lady Dacia?" he asked, teasing her gently. "Is it anyone I know? You must tell me so that I can fight him for your affection."

She grinned. He saw it. But she put her hand to her flaming cheek and turned away, back to her herbs.

"It does not matter," she said.

Cassius was smiling broadly. "It matters a great deal," he said. "I will challenge him. Give me his name immediately."

"He will not fight you."

"Why not?"

"He is too lazy."

Cassius started to laugh. "A lazy lover? What a horrible man."

Hearing him laugh made her giggle. "I did not say it was a man," she said. "If you must know, it is Argos. He likes me so much so I thought I should make myself more presentable with recipes to fade these spots."

130

Cassius continued to smile as he looked at his dog, now on his back in the sun. "Argos likes you just as you are," he said. "He does not need for you to fade anything on his account. But if you feel as if you want to, then do as you please. He wants you to be happy."

Dacia bent over, collecting the herbs and putting them in her pockets. "It might make me feel as if I could go without my veils and not be stared at."

"If you are being stared at, it is because you are beautiful. Not because you have freckles."

She turned to look at him, smiling at the compliment for the very first time, and Cassius could see that she had big dimples in each cheek. It was absolutely charming. More and more, he found himself enamored with her.

Attracted to her.

Suddenly, he was very glad he was staying on.

"I will thank you for saying so this time and not call you a liar," she said. "I may even come to believe you someday."

"I hope you do," he said. "And I am glad we are on speaking terms again because it seems that I am going to be staying on a little while, at the request of your grandfather. I should like our continued association to be pleasant."

Her smile faded as she looked at him curiously. "Oh?" she said. "Why should he ask you to stay?"

Cassius didn't want to tell her all of it. He didn't want to frighten her. "Because of the attack last night," he said. "He seems to think I can help with your neighbor problem, so I have agreed to remain until it is solved."

"That could take more than a week or two."

That didn't displease Cassius in the least to hear that. With a cock of his head, he simply shrugged his shoulders in a coy gesture that was both sincere and flirtatious.

He was quite adept at such things.

"Only if I'm lucky, my lady," he said softly. "Only if I'm very lucky."

The way he said it made Dacia blush furiously once more. She was about to reply when they both heard the cry from the sentries go up. Thinking that it was, perhaps, another raiding party sighted, Cassius grabbed Dacia by the hand and raced with her back to the postern gate where the gate guards were preparing to lock it. They just made it through, with Argos right behind them, before the men slammed the two iron gates shut and bolted them.

They soon discovered that what the sentries sighted wasn't a raiding party.

It was much, much worse.

Amata had arrived.

CHAPTER NINE

Hagg Crag

"I WANT EDENTHORPE."

Catesby looked at Marcil in shock. "What's this?" he asked, aghast. "You *want* Edenthorpe?"

Marcil nodded. He was dirty and exhausted from being up all night and in no mood to negotiate with Catesby. He was resolute in what he wanted, so this was going to be an interesting exchange. There would be no negotiation.

He seriously wondered if Catesby was going to survive it.

"I do," he said, moving to Catesby's table where a pitcher of stale wine sat. He didn't even hunt for a cup; he simply downed it straight from the neck before licking his lips. "I have spent all night looking at that beastly fortress and with eighty-one men, it will be quite difficult to secure it. Therefore, if I am going to capture this castle, then I want the castle itself."

Catesby faced off against Marcil in his low-ceilinged solar, having failed to notice that a few of Marcil's men had trickled in through the door. He was only focused on the greedy mercenary and the man's ridiculous declaration.

"The castle is *mine*," he said sternly. "That is why I brought you here, Clabecq. You will help me gain that castle once and for all and then I shall share the spoils with you. That was the deal."

Marcil eyed him. "That deal has changed," he said. "You failed to tell me how big and how impenetrable it was. You lied to me, Catesby. Therefore, the terms have changed. You can keep most of the spoils and the disputed strip of land that started this mess, but I will keep the fortress. My men and I can stop wandering about and settle in one place. Edenthorpe suits me perfectly."

Catesby was too angry to realize that he should probably disengage with the conversation and regroup when he wasn't so livid. Instead, he marched on Marcil, coming close enough to the man to snarl.

"I never lied to you," he hissed. "How dare you call me a liar. I paid you good money to come to England and assess the situation. That was your job. I told you Edenthorpe was an enormous castle. That information was never withheld from you. Clearly, you are simply not up to the task. I would have hired someone else if I'd know you were such a coward."

Those were the magic words as far as Marcil was concerned. He turned on Catesby, his eyes narrowing dangerously.

"You will never speak that term in my presence again," he growled. "Do you understand me? You want me to do a job with only eighty-one men of my own and three hundred of your men and I am telling you that it is going to cost you dearly. I want Edenthorpe when all is said and done. It will become mine."

Catesby took a step back, shaking his head. "Never," he gasped. "You will do the job for the price agreed upon or you will leave."

Marcil took a deep breath, perhaps one of annoyance, and set the wine pitcher back to the table. "And that is your final word?"

Catesby was back by the table he used to write on, perhaps just now noticing that his solar had about five heavily armed mercenaries in it. The situation was spiraling out of control very quickly and he was trying not to look nervous, but it was difficult.

He suspected that he and the mercenaries had come to an impasse.

"It is my final word," Catesby said bravely. "I will not be tricked or coerced by you, Clabecq. We made a bargain and now you are trying to change it. There will be a great deal of wealth to go around once Edenthorpe is captured, but you cannot have the fortress. That becomes mine. I have staked my claim."

Marcil looked at him a moment, appraising him, before turning casually to his men.

"Kill him."

His men gladly moved in, weapons drawn. Catesby, seeing that he was about to be cut into pieces, drew the sword that he kept on the wall near the hearth and began swinging it like a madman. Soon, the small solar was filled with sounds of metal upon metal.

Servants hearing the fight ran for Catesby's men, who were in the bailey. Unfortunately, Clabecq's men were at the entry to the manse and managed to stop all but one of the frightened servants. The man that got through sounded the alarm. Soon, the entire bailey and manse of Hagg Crag was alive with the sounds of battle, blood, and chaos.

Three hundred adequately trained troops were an even match against eighty-one highly trained mercenaries. Hagg Crag deteriorated very quickly into a roiling mass of death and violence. By sheer number, Hagg's men should have overwhelmed the Flemish mercenaries. But as the battle wore on and more Hagg men dropped, the more evident it became that the mercenaries were gaining the upper hand.

Holding true to their nasty reputation, they tore through the Hagg army.

Even so, the Hagg men put up a good fight. There were pockets of fighting all over the bailey that eventually ended with death, surrender, or escape. When some of the Hagg men saw which way the winds were blowing, they escaped through the gatehouse and out into the countryside. For those who remained behind, they were poorly matched against the mercenaries, who eventually triumphed.

Inside the manse, Catesby put up a good fight but, in the end, he was no match for four highly trained mercenaries. They not only killed him, but they quartered him and tossed the body parts out of the window. Catesby's son, who hadn't even been involved in the situation, was the victim of bloodthirsty mercenaries who did to him what they did to his father.

Edward Hagg ended up in pieces thrown from a window.

The battle, from start to finish, only lasted for a couple of hours. When everyone related to Catesby was either dead or had run off, Marcil and his men began to ransack the manse for anything of value. They started in Catesby's solar, tearing apart walls, tearing through chests and any solid vessels they could find in their hunt for valuables.

They'd killed the master.

Now, they were going to kill the manse.

With no one to stop them, they were ruthless in their hunt. Nothing escaped their notice or destruction. When they had sufficiently torn apart the solar, they made sure to light it on fire and shut the door. Since the manse was made mostly of stone, it would take some time for the fire to burn through the wooden floors and furnishings, giving them time to search the rest of the place.

As the fire smoldered in the solar, they ran through the rest of the rooms, looking for anything of value. Catesby only had one son, as his wife had died many years before, and they tore apart his son's chamber on their continued hunt for anything valuable. They even ransacked the dead wife's chamber, stealing her jewelry and fine things that had been stored away after her death.

They left that chamber on fire, too.

Every room in the manse was searched for anything of value that they could carry with them. There were pieces of good furniture, but they were left behind because it wasn't practical to haul them around.

The rape and ransack of Hagg Crag went on for most of the day. They also ransacked the kitchens for anything they could carry, knowing that it might be awhile before they had the opportunity to replenish whatever foodstuffs they could carry with them. They did not intend to stay at Hagg Crag because now that they were in England, they knew the Yorkshire countryside was rich and they intended to take what they could before they headed home.

The men from the Hagg army that weren't killed and did not run away were given the opportunity to join the mercenaries, but no one did. There were about eighty men left, the same number of mercenaries, but no one would join them. Marcil was hoping they would so he'd have a better chance at laying siege to Edenthorpe, but it was a fool's dream. He knew that. He couldn't take the castle with only eighty-one men, so once all of the horses were confiscated and any other livestock was turned loose in the kitchen yard, Marcil's men rounded up the remnants of the Hagg army and corralled them in the stable. Shutting the door behind them and bolting it, they set the stable on fire.

Marcil and his men welcomed the dusk to the soothing sounds of men being burned alive. They had taken everything they could from Hagg Crag and were now burning any witnesses to what they had done.

No survivors, no trace.

But Marcil had planned it this way.

With Hagg Crag burning and in ruins, Marcil turned his attention to the nearby village of Doncaster. It was nearing evening, which meant people would be in their homes for the night and would be caught off guard by a gang of mercenaries who planned to raid the town before they fled off into the night. Of course, Edenthorpe would send out troops to fight off the marauders, but Marcil and his men could do a great deal of damage before that event occurred. They'd managed to glean a good deal of valuables from Hagg Crag, but it wasn't enough. It wasn't enough to make up for the fact that the mighty bastion of Edenthorpe would be lost.

Marcil intended to take what he wanted from the village.

It was small compensation, of course, but it would have to do.

As the sun set behind the smoke rising from the burning manse and stable, Marcil and his men gathered their booty, mounted their horses, and rode off in the direction of Doncaster.

CHAPTER TEN

Edenthorpe Castle

"Ceecee, it is wonderful to see you again," Amata said, hugging her cousin in a flagrantly insincere gesture. "Papa is finally feeling much better, so I thought I would come and visit you. It has been such a long time since we were last together."

Dacia, as always, was thrilled to see her cousin. She didn't care if the woman was being insincere or not. She was just glad to have the company, as always.

"I am so glad you have come," Dacia said happily. "It has been a very long time, indeed. I am having something special prepared for your day of birth next week. We must make this visit a celebration!"

She had Amata by the hand, pulling the woman towards the keep as Amata's escort unloaded her capcases and disbanded the horses and wagon. Several Doncaster men were lending a hand.

But Amata seemed to be looking everywhere but at her cousin, who she had allegedly come to visit. As Dacia pulled her across the bailey, her head was on a swivel.

"And we shall," Amata said, spying an unfamiliar knight over by an outbuilding that housed male visitors. "We shall make it a great celebration. But let us talk of that later. Tell me of your activities since I last saw you, CeeCee. Have you had any unexpected visitors? Have you been well?"

Dacia nodded. "Very well," she said. "Grandfather has been well, too. You did not contract what your father had, did you?"

Amata shook her head. "Nay," she said. "Whatever Papa had is something recurring. He just seems to come down with a cough he cannot shake, and then it goes away. But he is quite well now."

Dacia smiled. "That is good," she said. "But you must send for me the next time he becomes ill. I may have something to help him. Mayhap I can even cure him."

Amata squeezed her hand but she still wasn't looking at her. "Dear CeeCee," she said, using a nickname Dacia had since childhood. "You are always so good and kind. So willing to help."

"It is no trouble."

"Then you've not had any exciting visitors since the last time I was here?"

It was a reminder of an earlier question that Dacia had failed to answer, but where Amata was concerned, that wasn't unusual. Amata always wanted to know everything that had gone on in her absence, demanding every little last detail. She was nosy that way.

"Nay," Dacia said, but quickly recanted. "Wait, that is not true. We had three of Edward's knights visit us yesterday and last night, Edenthorpe was attacked."

Amata looked at her sharply. "Attacked?" she repeated

fearfully. "By whom?"

Dacia pulled her along. "By Lord Hagg," she said quietly. "That's what I was told. You know he wants that land to the south that Grandfather is mining. Last night, he decided to harass us."

Amata didn't look any too soothed. "That is terrible," she said. "Was there any damage?"

Dacia shook her head. "None," she said. "Fortunately, the king's knights were still here and they helped protect the castle."

"Are the king's knights still here this morning?"

"Aye," Dacia said. "I was told that Grandfather asked them to remain a little while. He wants their help with Lord Hagg."

Amata's head resumed its eager swiveling. "Where are they?"

Dacia shrugged as they passed the great hall, with the keep directly ahead. "I am not sure," she said. "But you will meet them at some point. I know how eager you are to meet fine, young knights."

Amata gasped. "CeeCee!" she scolded softly. "You make it sound as if I lust for them constantly."

"Don't you?"

Dacia turned to look at her, seeing an unhappy expression on her cousin's face. But Amata couldn't keep it up for very long. She cracked a smile and looked away.

"Well… not constantly," she said, giggling. "But it would be nice to meet a knight to marry and take me away from this place. I do so long to see the big cities and meet interesting people. I…"

She suddenly came to a halt, her gaze on the great hall. Dacia was forced to stop as well, turning in time to see Cassius emerging from the hall entry. He had Argos with him, catching sight of the young women immediately. It was difficult not to see them because they were right in his path. Amata lifted a hand and waved it furiously.

"Greetings, Sir Cassius!" she called. "It is agreeable to see you again!"

Dacia looked at her cousin in surprise. "You know him?"

Amata couldn't take her eyes from him. "He came through town during the Lords of Misrule feast," she said excitedly. "Yesterday, in fact. He's so handsome, CeeCee. The most handsome man I have ever seen. Don't you think so?"

Bewildered, Dacia looked at Cassius as he came upon the pair, his expression bordering on unfriendly as he looked at Amata. Still, he politely bowed.

"Lady Amata," he said with a hint of disapproval in his tone. "What brings you to Edenthorpe?"

Amata was beside herself with glee. "*You*, silly," she said. "You would not come to me, so I have come to you. Are you surprised?"

Cassius just looked at her. "It would have been best had you sent word ahead to ask for permission to visit," he said, avoiding her question. "We had some trouble here last night and it may not be safe for you to travel."

Amata sensed a rebuke, but it didn't spoil her enthusiasm. "If you had trouble last night, then surely you and your powerful knights chased them away," she said, letting go of Dacia and looping her hands through Cassius' elbow in a possessive gesture. "I am positive Lord Hagg took one look at you and fled. How could he not?"

She was clinging to him, something he was clearly displeased with. "There is a little more to it than that," he said. "If you will excuse me, I must be along my way."

He started to move away from her, but she held fast. "Please do not go," she said. "I have come all the way to Edenthorpe to see you. Will you not sit with me and talk a while? I never did thank you for the dances yesterday. You are a wonderful dancer, by the way. I have never seen finer. You made me feel lighter than air when you lifted me in your powerful arms."

Cassius had about all he could take of her sappy adoration, but before he could shoo her away, Dacia spoke up.

"You… you two danced yesterday?" she said, looking between Amata and Cassius. "Where?"

"At the Lords of Misrule feast," Amata said. "I told you that was where I met him. Sir Cassius and I were crowned the king and queen of the feast. Well, *almost*. But he had to leave because he had business to attend to with Cousin Vincent. Still, it was great fun while it lasted."

Now, Dacia's focus was on her cousin. For a moment, she just looked at her, processing the foolish words that were coming from her mouth and coming to understand that Amata's visit here was no casual happenstance.

She had a motive.

Perhaps it was jealousy or perhaps it was disappointment, but Dacia did something at that moment that she wouldn't normally do.

She confronted Amata.

"Then you came today because you knew he was here," she finally said. "It was not to visit me at all. It was to see Sir Cassius."

Amata looked at her as if suddenly realizing she'd given away her entire reason for coming. "I… I knew he would be here, that is true," she said quickly. "But I very much wanted to see you, CeeCee. Seeing Sir Cassius is just a happy coincidence."

It was a lie.

Dacia knew it was a lie and she felt like a fool. A silly, duped fool. Everything Edie had ever said about Amata came tumbling down on her. Although in the back of her mind she'd always known that her cousin only used her, she had always been willing to overlook it. But no longer. That selfishness had never been more apparent than it was now.

And Cassius… the only man who had ever shown Dacia any attention had evidently done the same with Amata. There had been nothing special in the compliments he'd paid her because he'd done it before – with a young woman who didn't have the handicap of freckles all over her face, and perhaps a thousand others, too.

It wasn't just her.

God… she felt like an idiot.

"Then please visit with him since you came to see him," she said, lowering her gaze and backing away. "I will not interfere."

At that point, she was already turning around, heading for the keep, but Cassius called out to her.

"Lady Dacia," he said. "Wait, please."

Dacia kept going. Cassius called to her again and she started to run, all the way up the stairs and disappearing into Edenthorpe's keep.

Cassius watched her go with a heavy heart.

"I wonder what's the matter with her?" Amata asked as if she didn't really care. "It is of little matter, I suppose. I shall find out later. Will you come into the hall with me, Sir Cassius?"

Cassius turned to look at her. Then, he pulled his arm away from her grabbing hands, stilling them rather firmly when she tried to grab him again.

"Nay," he said steadily. "I shall not go into the hall with you.

You came to see your cousin, so go see her."

Amata's face fell. "But... but we had such a nice time yesterday," she said. "I thought you would be glad to see me."

"I have no time for a visit, my lady."

Amata was starting to look hurt. "What have I done to make you cross with me, Sir Cassius? Please tell me so that I might make amends."

He looked at her, seeing the petty, vain, and spoiled girl he'd suspected from the start. She had been pretty to him, once, when he'd first met her. But her manner and her personality had cancelled out any beauty he thought she might have had. The disappointment on Dacia's face when she had realized why her cousin had really come had sealed that opinion.

Cassius didn't do very well with petty, vain women.

He'd seen too many of them in his lifetime.

"We had three dances yesterday and that was all," he said evenly. "I've danced with a hundred pretty girls and they are all the same to me, including you, so think not that there was anything special with a few leaps and twirls. You were a few pleasant moments to pass the day with and nothing more. So if you've come to Edenthorpe because you thought I wanted to see you again, I am afraid you are gravely mistaken. Anything you thought I might want is a creation of your own mind. If you've really come just to see me, then you may as well return home. I am not interested."

Amata was red in the face when he finished, deeply ashamed. "That is a terrible thing to say to me," she said. "How dare you!"

Cassius cocked an eyebrow. "Feeling humiliated, are you?"

Amata was near tears. "If that is what you intended, then you succeeded."

He pointed to the keep. "Now you know how your cousin feels," he said. "Clearly, you made her think that you had come to visit her when it was me you really wanted to see."

Amata opened her mouth to retort but nothing came forth. She huffed and stomped her foot, grunting unhappily.

"You'll not school me on manners, Knight," she said. "Dacia is my cousin. She knows I love her."

He sighed impatiently. "Does she?" he said. "It seems to me that when I told you that I was coming to Edenthorpe, you made a point of warning me against your cousin with her witch's marks. You mentioned that to simply look upon her was to be cursed. Is that what you tell everyone, Lady Amata? That your cousin has witch's marks and she turns men to stone like Medusa?"

Caught in a web of her own design, Amata backed away from him. "She *does* have marks on her face," she said defensively. "You just saw them, for she was uncovered. Everyone knows she has the marks!"

"Everyone knows because you tell them," he said. "I was a virtual stranger and you told me, humiliating your cousin in the presence of a stranger. Why on earth would you do such a thing?"

Amata didn't have an answer. Instead, she began to seethe. "Rude," she hissed. "You are rude and horrible and I hope I never see you again, Cassius de Wolfe!"

Cassius looked at her for a moment before breaking down into a weak grin. "That can be happily arranged," he said. "But remember one thing – you, my lady, are not nearly as pretty as you think you are. Your cousin, Dacia, is more beautiful than you could ever hope to be."

With that, he walked around her, heading towards the keep

because it was clear that he cared more about Dacia's feelings than her own cousin did. He felt badly enough that he wanted to see to her, to make sure she knew he had no designs or intentions towards Amata. Odd that he should want to make that clear to Dacia, but he did. But as he walked, he noticed that Argos was not beside him and turned in time to see the dog lifting his leg on Amata, peeing on the back of her dress.

He didn't even call the dog off.

He just started laughing.

Amata's screams of rage were like music to his ears.

SHE HAD KICKED the maids out.

When Dacia arrived in her chambers, four of the six maids were there, cleaning part of the floor, and she had no patience for their presence at the moment. With a shriek, she threw them all out of the chamber and slammed the door, bolting it.

She needed to be alone.

The tears came. Tears of shame, tears of hurt. Shame because of Amata's motives, hurt because Cassius had evidently spewed words of flattery to Amata, enough so the woman had come all the way to Edenthorpe to see him. Hurt because Cassius had turned those same words of flattering on her, making her feel special.

But she wasn't.

She was angry at herself for ever believing his compliments.

Her pockets were bulging with dragonwort and she pulled it out angrily, tossing it on the table in her smaller dressing chamber. She felt like an idiot for having sought out the weed in the first place, an idiot for letting herself get swept away by Cassius' presence and sweetness. God, the man was sweet, and she'd fallen for it.

She wondered how many other maidens had fallen for it.

A knock on the door distracted her from her thoughts.

"Go away!" she yelled.

Whoever it was hadn't heard her because she was in another chamber, so she stepped out into the big chamber just as the caller knocked again.

"Go *away!*" she boomed. "Get away from that door!"

There was no reply, only more knocking, this time continuous. Enraged, Dacia went to the door, threw the bolt, and yanked the door open.

"Stop knocking, you stupid –"

She had started yelling before she'd ever seen the caller and now she found herself looking into Cassius' somewhat surprised face. His mouth was open in astonishment and, for a moment, neither one of them moved. Finally, he lifted his eyebrows.

"Would you care to finish that sentence?" he said.

Dacia looked at him, dumbfounded and hurt. "What?" she said, then realized what he meant. Quickly, she lowered her head. "Nay, I will not. I thought you were one of my maids. Sometimes they can be rather insistent and annoying, and… oh, it does not matter. What do you require, Sir Cassius?"

Cassius watched her lowered head. "Require?" he repeated. "Nothing. I came to see you."

Given what had just happened, she was understandably on the defensive. "You do not have to keep up the pretext, my lord," she said. "Please have Amata entertain you. She is better at it than I am."

He cleared his throat softly. "I am not sure why you think I have been keeping up a pretext," he said. "I am an honest man, my lady. Pretexts are excuses and I do not make excuses. I came to see you because I wanted to assure you that whatever your cousin said out in the bailey was completely one-sided."

Dacia lifted her head slightly to look at him. "She said she met you in town."

He nodded. "She did," he said. "We were passing through, as she said, on our way to see your grandfather. We stopped because we were tired and hungry, and there was enough free food to feed an army, so we stopped to refresh ourselves before continuing on. Lady Amata grabbed me and pulled me into a group of dancing people, so that is how I ended up dancing with her. I did not ask her, I assure you."

Dacia lowered her head again. "She is a good dancer," she said. "Pretty, too. I do not blame you for dancing with her."

Cassius could see how hurt she was. It was in everything about her. It began to occur to him that only someone with an emotional investment in the situation could feel hurt, and it further occurred to him that he was rather pleased about it. It made no difference to him that Amata was sweet on him, but Dacia?

That was a completely different story.

Truth be told, he might have been just the slightest bit sweet on her, too.

"I danced with her because I did not want to be rude," he said. "And also because it has been a very long time since a pretty girl asked me to dance, but I discovered something about Amata."

She was back to peering at him again. "What is that?"

"She is annoying."

Dacia's eyes widened briefly and she began fighting off a smile. "Mayhap a little."

Cassius grunted. "From what I've seen, it is more than just a little," he said, pleased that he'd at least lightened her mood somewhat. "The fact that she used you as an excuse to come to Edenthorpe because she wanted to see me is an appalling lack of tact and I told her so. I also told her something else."

"What is that?"

"That no matter how pretty she thinks she is, you are more beautiful than she could ever hope to be."

Dacia's head came up and she looked at him full-on, her eyes wide with astonishment. "You told her *that*?"

"I did."

She blinked. "But *why*?"

"Because it is the truth."

Dacia stared at him a moment before finally shaking her head. "I… I do not even know what to say."

He clasped his hands behind his back, bracing his legs apart as he looked at her. "You need not say anything," he said. "I came up here to tell you not to let your cousin hurt your feelings. I do not have the slightest interest in her and she is quite upset about it. She seems to think that I would die for a taste of her lips."

Dacia shrugged. "Some men would."

Cassius shook his head. "Not me," he said. "In fact, I have come here to ask something of you."

"What is it?"

His eyes took on that warm glimmer again, something that seemed to happen every time he looked at her.

"I know you like to tend the kitchens and not attend the evening meal," he said. "But I was hoping, just for this evening, that you might rethink that usual practice and sup with me. I would very much like you to."

Dacia's cheeks began to turn that familiar shade of pink. "Me?"

"You."

Dacia lowered her gaze, as if thinking very hard on his invitation. She'd just convinced herself that every bit of flattery out of his mouth was insincere, but here he was, being kind to her again. He'd thought enough of her to explain her cousin's comments and his side of things.

Perhaps a man like that deserved better than what she thought of him.

He seemed to be making the extra effort.

"I suppose I could," she said. "If you'd really like for me to."

"I would. Very much."

"Then I shall attend."

"Will you do something more for me?"

"What is it?"

"Do not wear your veils."

She looked at him as if he were suggesting something scandalous, but the lure of his sweet invitation took precedence.

"Are you sure you will not mind?"

He smiled, flashing that smile that had caused many a maiden to swoon. "My lady, I prefer it," he said. "I've noticed you have dimples that would cause most men to fall at your feet."

The blush was back, ragingly so. She wasn't very adept at flirtation, or kind words, so she said the first thing that came to mind.

"But not you?" she teased.

In one swift and fluid movement, Cassius took a knee in

front of her, reaching out to take one of her hands. Dacia was so startled that she took an instinctive step back, but he held her fast. He was so tall that on one knee, he was nearly eye-level with her. Leaning over, he gently kissed her hand.

"Does that answer your question, Dacia?"

The way he said it made her heart beat painfully against her ribs. She couldn't seem to catch her breath. Before she could answer, however, they both heard a gasp coming from the stairwell, turning to see Amata standing on the top step.

The woman's eyes were bulging.

"What is the meaning of this?" she demanded.

Dacia looked at her cousin curiously, having no idea what she was talking about. "The meaning of what?" she asked as Cassius stood up. "What are you talking about?"

Unfortunately, Amata was a woman scorned, a petty and volatile creature, indeed. She looked accusingly between Cassius and her cousin.

"Is this what has happened since I last saw you, Dacia?" she said. "You now permit men to display unrestrained gestures of affection? Now I understand why Sir Cassius rebuffed me. It was because of *you*!"

Dacia was starting to catch on. Truth be told, she was flattered that her cousin thought she was finally doing something scandalous but, in the same breath, she was quickly furious about what the woman was suggesting.

Furious enough to snap back.

"And what if it is?" she said. "Sir Cassius was doing nothing I haven't seen you permit with twenty different men at twenty different times. In fact, I've known you to permit something worse than a simple kiss to the hand, so if you do not want your father to hear about it, I suggest you shut your lips this instant."

As Cassius stood back and folded his arms across his chest, an approving smile playing on his lips, Amata features flushed with fury and embarrassment.

"I am your cousin," she hissed. "You cannot say such things to me in front of a stranger. You promised to keep them in confidence!"

Dacia took a few steps in Amata's direction. "And you used me as an excuse every time you stole away to meet yet one more man in your vast collection of suitors," she said. "You would tell your father that you were coming to visit me, but you'd go into Doncaster and spend time with any man who caught your fancy. Did you think I did not know this? I have known it for years. And then when you do come to visit me, it is to steal kisses from Darian's knights or steal pieces of my jewelry, and the fool that I am, I simply looked the other way. I was so happy to have you visit me that I overlooked your lies and your thievery. Therefore, your accusations against me are sadly misplaced, Amata. You saw nothing untoward and you know it. You're simply angry that it wasn't your hand Sir Cassius was kissing."

Amata's jaw dropped in abject humiliation. "This is how you repay the only person who will talk to you?" she screeched. "No one will talk to you or be your friend because of your ugly spots and this is how you repay me? You ungrateful wench!"

She was hitting Dacia where it hurt. In times past when they fought and Amata brought up Dacia's freckles, Dacia would usually surrender the argument. She'd taken a beating for so many years about her freckles that, like a whipped dog, she knew when to tuck her tail between her legs and hang her head. That was what she usually did.

But no more.

Thanks to Cassius, Amata didn't have that power over her anymore.

"I would rather be an ungrateful wench than a whore," Dacia said in a low voice. "You heard me, Amata – *whore*. I know you for what you are. I know you gave your innocence to one of my grandfather's soldiers a few years ago and there have been men between your legs ever since. Everybody knew it; I knew it. But I overlooked it. I will overlook you no longer. Go find another place to sleep tonight. And then tomorrow, you can return to Silverdale. I do not want to see you again, ever."

Amata was so angry that she was trembling. "I knew it was a mistake to try and help you," she said. "This is the thanks you give me for my friendship, you ugly, silly chit. I will leave tomorrow and I will never come back. You have made a big mistake this day. *Very* big."

Dacia simply shook her head. "I have *fixed* a very big mistake today," she said. "Poor Sabine to have a horrible sister like you. A whore that will bring down the whole family. No wonder she chose to commit herself to a convent – she could not live with the shame of a trollop for a sister."

Amata's face contorted with rage and her mouth worked as if she wanted to say something more, but she wisely kept silent. She'd just been humiliated in front of Cassius, horrified that her darkest secrets had a witness.

But this wasn't going to be the end of it.

She was going to make sure of it.

Gathering her skirts, she headed back down the stairs. Dacia stood there a moment, listening to her footfalls fade away, before returning her attention to Cassius. She smiled weakly, chagrinned that he had witnessed that exchange, but not sorry.

She was definitely not sorry.

"She is correct, you know," she said quietly. "She is the only friend I have."

Cassius shook his head. "She is *not* correct."

"What do you mean?"

He smiled. "You have me."

Dacia laughed softly. "You are not exactly a ladylike companion," she said. "I cannot speak to you of silly or frivolous things that would only interest a woman."

"You have not yet tried."

She cocked her head. "Is that so?" she said. "Then at the feast tonight, I shall make sure to talk about the most frivolous of frivolity and see how long you can stand it."

His grin broadened. "I look forward to it, my lady."

Dacia's smile faded. "Would it be too forward for me to ask you to address me as Dacia?"

He shook his head. "Nay," he said. "In fact, I was hoping that you would give me permission, although I have used your name informally once or twice."

"I hardly noticed," Dacia said, feeling lighter of heart than she had in her entire life. Something wonderful was happening to her that she could hardly begin to describe. "I would be honored if you called me Dacia."

"And I would be honored if you called me Cassius. Or Cass. I'll answer to anything you call me, Dacia."

It was enough to return the blush to her cheeks. "Thank you," she said. "Then I shall see you tonight?"

"Of course you will."

Dacia smiled bashfully, heading back into her chamber as Cassius stood there and watched her go. He'd never noticed how gracefully she moved. In fact, there was nothing about her that wasn't graceful, beautiful, and bright.

More and more, he was coming to see that.

And strength… he'd never seen such a strong woman. It had taken great strength to stand up to her abusive cousin. That impressed him perhaps more than anything else – shy, suppressed Dacia of Doncaster had great inner strength.

But it never occurred to him that he'd helped bring it out.

The evening's feast couldn't come soon enough as far as he was concerned.

CHAPTER ELEVEN

"I WAS TOLD that Amata arrived today," Doncaster said. "Where is she? She usually eats with Dacia, but I at least expect her to greet me when she arrives. I've not yet seen her."

The evening's meal was well under way, the hall crowded with eating, drinking soldiers and massive fires in both hearths that were spitting smoke and sparks into the room. At the dais, the duke was seated with Cassius, Rhori, and Bose along with Darian and one of his junior knights, a young man from a fine family named Sir Everard Allington.

The duke was addressing Fulco, his majordomo, who was hovering nervously at the man's right elbow. A pale man with stringy brown hair, he always seemed to have the look of a frightened rabbit.

He very much wanted to please his lord.

"Lady Amata has retreated to the chamber we usually reserve for her father and refuses to come out, your grace," he said. "She says that she is ill."

The duke looked at him curiously. "Ill?" he said. "Is Dacia tending to her?"

"Not that I am aware of, your grace."

"Why not?"

"Because Lady Dacia is in her chamber and says she will come out when she is ready, your grace," he said.

"And they are not together?"

"Nay, your grace."

The duke sighed with exasperation. "What is happening with these women?" he demanded. "Dacia and Amata are usually quite close, especially when Amata visits. What nonsense is going around?"

The majordomo simply shook his head, which didn't satisfy Doncaster. Frustrated, he turned back to his food and drink.

"Women," he muttered to Cassius, seated at his right. "Dacia's grandmother was not like that. She was a calm and sensible woman."

Cassius had watched the exchange about the women carefully, knowing exactly why Amata was pleading illness. Frankly, he was glad because that meant he wouldn't have to deal with her on this night. He was much more concerned with Dacia making an appearance.

He found that he was eagerly awaiting it.

"Sometimes they are unpredictable creatures, your grace," he said. "I have two sisters, a mother, a grandmother, and a host of female relatives. I've seen just how unpredictable they can be."

The duke snorted in agreement but, in truth, he couldn't give the subject of women much more attention than he already had.

He moved on.

"Have you sent word for reinforcements as we discussed earlier?" he asked Cassius.

"De Shera did," Cassius said, rolling with the change of

focus. "The missives went out earlier today and with the castles being so close, I should expect an answer in a day or two. We'll assemble enough men to wipe through Hagg easily."

Doncaster was holding his cup, staring into the ruby-red liquid. "I still wish I could have spoken to Catesby," he said. "All of this seems so… unnecessary."

Cassius wasn't sure what to say to that. The duke wanted a peaceful resolution but Hagg had already dictated the terms and they most certainly weren't peaceful. He was about to take another drink of his wine when he caught sight of someone entering through the servants' alcove.

Dacia had finally arrived.

His heart skipped a beat.

She was wearing a gray gown with silver silk panels that reflected light as she walked. The front of the gown was laced up with silver ribbons and there was elaborate silver thread embroidery around the neckline. The sleeves were long and belled, with white fur trim, and as she drew closer, Cassius could see just how beautiful she looked.

And no veils.

He was on his feet.

"Lady Dacia," he said. "Please come and sit. It is good of you to join us."

Rhori and Bose, in their customary places across the table from Cassius and the duke, glanced up at the lady without much interest until they saw how beautiful she was. Then, she had their attention. But Cassius had beat them to the punch. He was already holding out a chair for her, which she took graciously.

"I hope I am not disturbing your conversation," Dacia said, looking over to her grandfather. "I hope I am welcome,

Grandfather. Sir Cassius asked me to join the feast and I could not refuse."

Doncaster was looking at her strangely. "You are always welcome, child," he said. "But why are you not covered up?"

He was gesturing at her face, asking a rather blunt question for all to hear. Cassius could see the mottle coming to Dacia's cheeks and he hastened to answer.

"Because I asked her not to," he said. "It is rude to hide from guests as she does. Men like to see who we are speaking to."

Doncaster looked at Cassius with surprise. "You asked her not to wear her veils?" he said, sounding confused. "She knows that if she attends a meal here, with guests, that she is to cover herself."

"Why?"

The duke pointed at her. "Look at her face," he said. "Men will see that she bears the marks."

Poor Dacia looked at her lap. Already, the situation was taking a downturn. She had come into the hall, radiant and lovely, and now her own grandfather had embarrassed her. Cassius could feel his temper rise, which wasn't a good thing. As he'd mentioned to Bose and Rhori, he had the Scots temper. Usually, it took a great deal to rile him but, in this instance, the reaction was instant.

"She has freckles on her face that are unique and charming, your grace," he said, trying to restrain himself from sounding angry. "You have a beautiful, cultured granddaughter that you keep hidden away as if she were a shameful secret. The marks on her face are of God's creation, not the devil's, and no man has a right to cover up God's careful work. Whoever told you that Lady Dacia should be covered up was grossly mistaken."

The duke looked at him as if he'd lost his mind. "You are not offended by her?"

Cassius cocked an eyebrow. "Not in the least," he said. "She is quite beautiful."

That brought a squint from the duke, as if greatly puzzled by Cassius' statement. "But she is marked," he said. "You *like* this?"

"I like it very much."

Baffled, and for lack of an argument, Doncaster simply returned to his wine. He didn't know what to say to Cassius' rather strong opinion.

And neither did Darian.

Sitting next to Rhori across the table, Darian had heard the entire exchange. He was shocked to see Dacia show up for the meal and even more shocked to hear Cassius speak strongly in her defense. Then, he watched the way Cassius looked at her. He watched how attentive the man was to her.

The embers of jealousy stirred.

"It is good to see you at the table, Lady Dacia," he said steadily. "I hope you do not feel coerced by our guest. If you were not comfortable, you did not need to come."

Dacia looked over at Darian, already knowing why he was saying such things. There had never been any competition for her hand and now that Cassius had shown up, and had shown interest in her, suddenly there was very viable competition. In fact, it was competition that could easily oust Darian from the consideration and she could tell that he was well aware of the fact.

Although Dacia liked Darian a great deal, he was like a brother to her and nothing more. He knew it, which made this situation delicate because Dacia genuinely never expected to face anything like this.

Someone else who might be interested in her.

She didn't want to hurt Darian.

"I do not feel coerced, I assure you," she said evenly. "It was nice to be invited to sup. I'm usually so busy making sure everyone else has been well fed that, sometimes, I forget to eat myself."

Remembering how Darian staked his claim when they were at Old Timeo's cottage, Cassius wasn't oblivious to the mood radiating from the man. He was essentially jumping his claim, although not in an official capacity. He'd not made any formal offers, but his behavior definitely suggested interest. He didn't want to upset Darian, but he was also quite conscious of what he was feeling when he looked at Dacia.

As if nothing could spoil his evening.

"Would you like to sit with us, Darian?" he asked generously. "We would be happy for your company over here. It is a big table."

Darian's gaze moved from Cassius to Dacia and back again. "Mayhap later," he said. "But thank you. That was kind."

Over on Cassius' left, Doncaster suddenly snorted. "You have competition, Darian," he said. "Your lack of action may cost you but, of course, Cassius has not expressed any real interest in her. But he probably will not – with as handsome as he is, I'm sure he has armies of women following him around. I am sure you will be thankful when he leaves, eh?"

The old man had obviously had too much to drink and it was showing. Darian didn't say a word. He simply returned to his food, while Cassius looked at Dacia to see how she was reacting to all of this. She was still looking at her lap and Cassius reached over to the pitcher on the table, pouring her some wine himself.

"I do *not* have armies of women following me around," he said quietly. "Well, not big armies, anyway. I suppose that all depends on your point of view. Are hundreds of women considered armies?"

He was teasing her and he could see her profile as she smiled. "Probably," she said. "It would seem that my grandfather speaks the truth. *In vino veritas.*"

He lifted his cup. "*Et vinum non opus ad pulchritudinem tuam.*"

Dacia's head snapped up, looking at him with wide eyes. *I do not need wine to see your beauty.*

Her mouth popped open.

"Your Latin is flawless," she said.

He shrugged. "Like you, I have been well-educated," he said. "Besides, my mother was a postulate before she married my father, so if I do not know Latin, she would probably beat me."

Dacia's smile grew. "Where do your parents live?"

"Berwick Castle," he said. "My father is the Earl of Berwick."

She looked surprised. "I did not realize that," she said. "But I suppose I should have, given your elite status. The de Wolfe family is well-titled, are they not?"

He nodded, pouring himself more wine because the conversation was starting to flow effortlessly and he wanted to keep it going. "My grandfather, William de Wolfe, was the Earl of Warenton," he said. "My uncle, Scott, now holds that title, while his youngest brother holds the title of Earl of Northumbria by marriage. Uncle Thomas married well, needless to say, but my father was granted the title by Edward years ago. My eldest brother, Markus, holds the title of Viscount Ravensdowne and the property of Cheswick Castle. There are a dozen other titles floating around to various uncles and sons, inherited or earned, and as for me, I had to earn mine. When I accepted the position of Lord Protector, I was given Penton Castle and the title Lord Westdale. Penton Castle guards a major road from Scotland that leads into Carlisle. It is a very big place, built upon the ruins of a Roman fort, and it has seen more than its share of action from the Scots."

Dacia was listening closely. "And that is where you shall retire when your role of Lord Protector is finished?"

He smiled faintly. "That is my intention," he said. "My entire family rules the Scots border. Penton will anchor a nearly unbreakable line of de Wolfe castles from one end of the border to the other. Even now, I have four hundred men who man it for me plus a cousin, Adonis de Norville, and another very old friend of the family, Gethin Ellsrod. His father, Deinwald, served my grandfather many years ago, and now Gethin serves me."

"Then your property is well staffed."

"It must be, given its strategic location," he said. "If I do not man it, the Scots certainly will."

"I see," she nodded in understanding. "They are aggressive, then?"

"You could say that."

She smiled at what was probably a silly question on her behalf. "Being so far from the border, we do not have any engagement with the Scots in Doncaster."

"Just greedy neighbors."

She laughed softly, taking a gulp of her wine, probably more than she should have, but social situations were very rare for her. She was nervous and trying very hard not to be.

"There is truth in that," she said. "But hopefully, you can help make a swift end to the harassment. Given your experience with the Scots, subduing an Englishman must be a far simpler thing."

He chuckled as he poured her more wine. "They can be more difficult because they are more cunning than the Scots," he said. "But let us not speak on such depressing things. Let us return to your vast education. My excuse in knowing Latin was that my mother was once intended for the veil, so she insisted. What is your excuse?"

"My tutor was a priest."

He laughed softly. "Ah, yes," he said. "You told me that. Therefore, your excuse is better than mine. Do you consider yourself fluent in Latin?"

"More than most."

"Are you up to a challenge?"

She eyed him, seeing from the gleam in his eyes that he was being quite impish. "That depends," she said. "What is the challenge?"

He sat back in his chair. "We shall play a game with du Bois and de Shera," he said, looking over at the knights. "Did you hear me? A challenge is about to be proposed."

Rhori and Bose looked up from their food. Bose groaned. "God, now what?" he said. "Can I not even eat a meal in peace before you are leveling threats and challenges at me?"

Cassius snapped his fingers at him, abruptly. "Still your tongue," he said. "We are going to play a game. Since you and du Bois were educated just as I was in Latin, among other things, we shall see just how much we remember of our Latin lessons. I will say something in Latin and whoever cannot properly translate it must drink as much wine as those who issued the challenge will dictate. Whoever is the most drunk at the end of the game shall bear the title of Stupidest Man in the World."

Bose pointed to Dacia. "What if she is the drunkest?"

Cassius looked at Dacia, who was grinning at him. "Something tells me she will not be," he said. "Now, I shall begin. Tell me what this means – *Sapere Aude*."

Dacia started to laugh while Bose just looked confused. Rhori rolled his eyes. Cassius looked at Dacia. "Do you know what it means?"

She nodded. "Aye."

"Whisper it in my ear."

Leaning over, Dacia put her lips against his ear, a gesture that sent bolts of excitement racing through his big body.

"Dare to know," she murmured.

Cassius had to take a deep breath. He'd never had such a reaction to a woman in his entire life. Fighting off the urge to pull her into his arms, he looked over at Bose and Rhori.

"What about you two?" he asked. "Do you know?"

Bose cocked his head thoughtfully. "Something about knowing?" he said. "Seeking knowledge?"

Cassius looked at Rhori. "You?"

Rhori yawned. "Dare to know."

Poor Bose was forced to drink most of his cup of wine by cruel friends after that. Unfortunately, it wasn't much better for him the second, third, and fourth time around and in a short amount of time, he was quite drunk. Angry, he stood up and went to the other side of the table to sit with Darian and his knight, men who weren't ridiculing him and punishing him with wine consumption.

As Bose wandered away, the game continued.

"It occurs to me that you have not been given any Latin phrases yourself," Dacia said. "You've been the one dealing them out. It's my turn now."

A smile played on Cassius' lips. "Go right ahead, my lady," he said. "Do your worst."

She was smiling as well, gazing into the eyes of a man who grew more handsome with each passing moment. Certainly, he was gorgeous in appearance, but it was his manners, his kindness, that were endearing him to her even deeper than he already was. That, coupled with his sense of humor, made him positively glorious.

"Very well," she said, eyeing both him and Rhori. "*Audentes fortuna iuvat.*"

Cassius' smile grew, a sure sign he knew the answer, as Rhori drank his wine, seemingly bored. Dacia focused on Cassius.

"Well?" she said. "What is it?"

He crooked his finger, beckoning her close. When she leaned into him, he put his lips against her ear.

"Fortune favors the bold," he murmured. "May I be bold, my lady?"

She pulled back, her cheeks flushing pink, a smirk on her face that carved big dimples through her cheek. She managed to give him such a coy look that he started laughing. For a woman who hadn't any experience in the subtle dance of flirtation between men and women, she was doing an admirable job. Across the table, Rhori slammed back what was left in his wine cup and stood up.

"You two finish this game," he said. "I have a feeling you do not need an audience."

With that, he headed over to Bose and Darian, both of them arguing about something Cassius couldn't quite hear. Dacia watched the man go.

"Did I offend him somehow?" she asked.

Cassius shook his head. "Of course not," he said. "He senses that he is not wanted."

"But I never said that."

He looked at her, an impish look in his eyes. "You did not have to," he said. "But I was screaming it from every bone in my body. Thank God he finally got the message."

Dacia was feeling as giddy as she had ever felt in her life. In fact, it was overwhelming her. So much of her was feeling unrestrained and free, something she'd never felt. But there was a part of her that was feeling some doubt in letting the situation go too far. Cassius de Wolfe was not a permanent resident of Edenthorpe, nor would he ever be. She didn't want to fall for the man only to have him leave.

But it was certainly difficult not to fall for him.

"You are quite charming when you want to be, Cassius," she said, an appraising twinkle in her eyes. "I suspect you have had much practice at it."

He sat back in his chair, wine cup in hand. "*Ut ameris, amabilis esto.*"

Dacia chuckled softly. "If you want to be loved, be lovable."

He lifted his cup to congratulate her. "Indeed," he said. "I am coming to think there is nothing you do not know."

She shrugged. "I am sure there is a great deal I do not know," she said. "For example… I do not know the motives of handsome knights who come to Edenthorpe and ply me with flattery. Can you tell me if I should be suspicious?"

The smile never left his lips. "I would not blame you if you were," he said. "But I have a family reputation to uphold and that does not include taking advantage of women with rash compliments and empty promises. Were I to do that, my grandmother would find me wherever I happened to be and take a switch to me. She is particularly fond of willow branches and I do not wish to incur her wrath. But more than that, I do not wish to shame myself."

It was a good answer. "Your honor means a great deal to you, then."

"It means everything."

There was a lull in the conversation, but it wasn't unpleasant. Dacia began to realize that they hadn't even touched the food that had been brought, so engrossed they were in the games they'd played. Reaching out, she picked a piece of boiled beef from her trencher and put it in her mouth.

"If you are the king's Lord Protector, then you must have great honor, indeed," she said. "I did not mean to question it. But... but I will admit that I have never had anyone be quite so friendly to me before."

"That is probably because you have never given them a chance, hiding yourself away as you do," he said. "You should not do that, Dacia. You are witty and charming. Truly, you are an ideal companion. I could talk to you all night."

She smiled, bashfully. "You must sleep."

"I can sleep when I'm dead." When she giggled and put more meat in her mouth, he leaned forward, his eyes riveted to her. "May I ask a personal question?"

"You may," she said. "But I reserve the right to decide whether or not to answer it."

"Fair enough," he said. "How old are you?"

She faltered, just a little. "I have seen twenty years and

three."

He leaned just a little closer. "I'm told you reject all suitors who come your way."

Her smile faded. "Who has told you that?"

He shook his head. "It does not matter," he said. "But you know in a castle this size, people talk. They *all* talk. I am coming to think that it is a good thing you have rejected suitors who have come for you because you are far superior to any of them. No man is worthy of you."

She smiled, rather sadly. "Then I shall be a very lonely woman."

He shook his head. "I think not," he said. "There will be a man who will come along, worthy of you. But you cannot chase him away."

"How will I know this shining example of manhood, then?"

He sat back, his eyes glittering at her. "You will know him," he said. "He could be right in front of your face right now for all you know."

"You are in front of my face."

"I *am* the shining example of manhood."

"That is established."

"See? You knew that before I even told you."

He was talking in riddles, perhaps declaring his interest, perhaps not. It was difficult to tell. Dacia kept putting pieces of beef in her mouth, wondering where the conversation was going.

"Tell me something, Cassius," she said. "Where are you going when you leave us? You told me that you had only stopped to relay a message to my grandfather, so you must have another destination once you leave Edenthorpe?"

He nodded. "That grandmother I spoke of," he said. "She is

the matriarch of our family. All eighty-five of us. She had nine living children and more than seventy grandchildren, with some of the most powerful knights in all of England. But she is our guiding star and I very much want to see her. I've not seen her in three years."

Dacia smiled. "That is very sweet," she said. "Where does she live?"

"Castle Questing, in Northumberland," he said. "That is why I am hoping to finish this business for your grandfather sooner rather than later. Edward is expecting me back in London next month and I do not want to return before I've seen her."

Her smile faded. "Did you tell my grandfather that?"

"Nay," Cassius said, shaking his head. "It is not necessary. This should only take a few days and then I shall be on my way."

Dacia didn't press him. She knew he had given his word to her grandfather that he would stay and help and after their conversation about honor, she knew he wasn't going to break his word. So she smiled weakly.

"However long you remain, just know that you are most welcome," she said. "I am grateful that you are here to help my grandfather and Darian. But I do hope you will visit us again whenever you have the opportunity. You have made a friend of me, Cassius, and I do not have many. In fact, after the incident with Amata today, I really do not have any."

His smile faded as he watched the flickers of regret across her face. "You stood up to her today," he said. "I was proud to witness that. I have a feeling Amata has been beating you down and taking advantage of you for a very long time, so I am proud that you finally took a stand against her."

She tried to force a smile, but it was unconvincing. "Sometimes you overlook the obvious when you are desperate for companionship," she said. "I have spent more than my share of lonely hours. I do not see that improving any time soon, but I am not complaining. It is simply the way things are. But... but I do thank you for what you have done for me."

He was leaning into his hand, chin in his palm, as his eyes glimmered. "What have I done for you, CeeCee?"

She heard her childhood nickname from his lips and she smiled broadly, touched that he should use that intimate term.

"You have given me a view of myself that I have never seen before," she said. "All I have ever heard is how unsightly my face is. That has been my whole life. But you... you see something different. You see what no one else sees and I shall always be grateful. You have given me... hope, Cassius. I shall never forget you for it."

She felt embarrassed even as she said it, so she stopped talking and picked up her cup, drinking deeply of her wine. Cassius watched her, a smile tugging on his lips.

"You're sweet," he murmured. "I think I like you, Dacia of Doncaster."

She just looked at him and giggled, unsure what more to say because she was quite certain she'd said enough.

"And I like you," she said. "I am glad we are friends."

"So am I. In fact, I am glad that I will be remaining here for a few more days. Mayhap we can become better friends."

Dacia didn't say anything more because she didn't want to sound too happy that he was remaining. She wasn't adept in the ways of men and women, and there was a fine line between gentle flirtation and reading too much into the situation. She'd seen that from Amata and she didn't want to do the same thing.

But if Cassius had been this charming with her cousin, she didn't blame her for thinking there was something more to it.

But something told her Cassius hadn't been like this with Amata.

Call it a hunch.

Before she could reply, however, there was a commotion at the hall entry. One of Darian's junior knights had just come through the door, pushing through the crowd as he approached the dais. He had a harried look about him, young and excitable as he was, and some of the soldiers in the hall were standing up, curious as to why he seemed so agitated.

Darian stood up as well when he saw him.

The knight headed right to him.

"My lord," he said. "There is trouble in Doncaster."

Darian frowned. "What trouble?"

The knight gestured in the direction of the gatehouse. "We have many panicked villagers pouring through the gates," he said. "Someone is looting and burning the town. We have been asked to help."

"Looting and burning?" Darian asked, incredulous. "*Who?*"

"It does not matter who," Cassius answered for the knight. He and Rhori and Bose were already on their feet, already on the move. "Rouse your garrison, de Lohr. You have a village to defend."

Rhori and Bose began shouting to the men, ordering them to arms, and Darian's junior knights began to take up the cry. Darian, caught off guard by the announcement of raiders and Cassius' subsequent action, caught up to Cassius and grabbed him by the arm.

"This is my command, Cassius," he said. "I will give the orders."

Cassius could see that the pleasant relationship between them threatened to deteriorate into a competition. It was something he'd feared when Doncaster has asked him to stay but, at this moment, he could see that very thing reflected in Darian's eyes. The man was a good knight, but he'd rarely dealt with trouble at Edenthorpe.

He wasn't moving fast enough.

"Then give them," Cassius said, not backing down. "While you are asking questions, men are burning down your village. If I were a gambling man, I would say it was probably the same men who attacked Edenthorpe last night, so it is quite possible that this is a ruse. Keep that in mind when giving orders and do not empty your garrison of men or you might find someone else in possession when you return. Take half with you and put the other half on the walls or you might be very sorry."

He didn't even wait for an answer. He pushed past Darian, heading out to the knights' quarters to don his armor. Doncaster wanted his help even if Darian didn't.

Doncaster was going to get what he asked for.

CHAPTER TWELVE

I T WAS CHAOS.

By the time Doncaster's men arrived, the southern section of the village of Doncaster was burning. Cassius, leading a large contingent of men, charged first into the town, a street that happened to have metal merchants and smithies. The raiders had hit this side of the village first, decimating businesses, but the owners had appeared with swords and clubs and had chased many of them off, so the mercenaries had circled around to the market street.

That's where Cassius found most of the fighting. The tunics of Clabecq were recognizable in the flames and moonlight, as they were not trying to hide them any longer. He unsheathed his de Wolfe-standard sword and plunged into the fight.

And a nasty fight it was.

Cassius was enormous and made quite a target, but he was also something to run from. Half of the mercenaries were moving away from him while the other half were moving towards him. Rhori joined him and, together, along with several hundred Doncaster men, engaged in a terrible battle that saw men falling, men running, and a few dying.

And Cassius was right in the middle of it.

The mercenaries were few, and highly skilled, but they were also highly clever. Knowing they couldn't match Doncaster's numbers, they scattered, which caused small groups of Doncaster men to go in chase. They were separating the army in a tactical move, piece by piece, that Cassius saw early on. He began ordering the Doncaster men to remain grouped and to not run after the individual mercenaries.

But those individual mercenaries were creating an issue.

They were the ones who were setting the fires and generally causing havoc, trying to force the army to splinter. Darian had his hands full because he was over by the church dedicated to St. George, trying to keep a gang of mercenaries from raiding the church. That put him in a stationary position, meaning he couldn't move away and manage the battle.

Cassius, once again, took charge.

He broke up his troops into four big groups and assigned each group a section of the town. The men formed lines and began to move through the streets, fighting with the mercenaries, but sweeping them towards the town gates to essentially sweep them out of the town. It worked well enough for the metal worker avenue and for the avenue of the bakers, but the avenue of the merchants was a more difficult fight.

That's where things got down and dirty.

There were three gates leading into Doncaster's village and Cassius made sure those gates were covered with a heavy presence of Doncaster soldiers as the fighting on the avenue of merchants turned into hand-to-hand combat. The mercenaries were resorting to dirty tricks to battle the Doncaster men, including climbing on roofs and either dropping heavy things on the Doncaster men, like pots or rocks, or by jumping on top of them.

Cassius saw more than one soldier go down by someone jumping off the roof on top of them. He even saw one of Darian's junior knights get toppled off his horse that way. Bose was able to help the young knight, who was badly injured, but he took a blade to the arm for his efforts. Still able to fight, Bose had dispatched his enemy in a spectacularly gruesome way before making sure the young knight was taken away from the fight.

And the battle raged on. The Doncaster men had the mercenaries overwhelmed, but they didn't go down easily. Cassius had also given the order for the men to take away whatever booty the mercenaries happened to be carrying, so it soon became a fight for the mercenaries to purely keep what they'd already taken.

That's when the punches began to fly in earnest.

There was so much blood being splattered around that it was difficult to tell where it was coming from and who, exactly, was injured. Bose had beaten down a man who was carrying hams as well as finery he'd taken from a merchant stall, pounding him unconscious until he could finally take the items away from him. All of the ill-gotten gains were being hauled back to the church for protection so the merchants and villagers could reclaim their items when the fight was over.

"Cass," Rhori called above the sounds of battle. "The south side of the village is burning heavily. We should put men to help fight the fire. The villagers are afraid to come out of their homes and if we don't do something, the town will be gone by morning."

Cassius could see the heavy smoke rising to the south and he knew Rhori wasn't wrong. With the brittle material the cottages were built with, they could go up very easily in a blaze.

"Select a contingent of men to fight the fire," he directed. "Some to protect the villagers and some to help fight. Where's de Lohr?"

"Still at the church as far as I know," Rhori said. "Do you want me to fetch him?"

Cassius shook his head. "Nay," he said, lashing out a big boot and kicking a mercenary in the face when he came too close. "Leave him where he is most needed. In fact, I think…"

He was cut off when the sounds of bolts being launched filled the air. Two arrows sailed past his head, striking both a mercenary and a Doncaster soldier. But before Cassius could get out of the way and under cover, two big bolts sailed into him, one hitting him in the shoulder and the other somewhere down on his torso.

The force of the strikes were hard enough to nearly topple him from his horse, but he held fast. He didn't want to end up on the ground where he would surely be set upon. As he struggled to stay upright, Rhori was beside him, shoving him up onto his saddle.

"Christ, Cass," he muttered. "We need to get you back to the castle. Can you ride?"

In extreme pain, Cassius grunted. "Bloody bastards," he muttered as another series of bolts sailed through the air, missing him and barely missing Rhori. "Get the hell out of here. Tell the men to retreat to the church. Go!"

"But –"

"*Go!*" Cassius boomed. "I will make it back to the castle on my own, but you are now in charge. Find out who's shooting off those arrows and cut their bloody heads off!"

Rhori wanted to go with him; he truly did, but a direct order from Cassius wasn't meant to be disobeyed. With two ugly projectiles sticking out of him, Cassius took off down an avenue, heading towards the gate that led back to the castle, while Rhori bellowed at the men to retreat back to the church. It was really all they could do as more bolts began to fly and Doncaster men began to go down. Somewhere in the mayhem, Rhori sent two men after Cassius to ensure he made it back to the castle. The last thing they needed was for Cassius to pass out and end up in a ditch somewhere.

Or worse.

Retreat to the church they did, with tales of Cassius de Wolfe being struck by arrows and still managing to fight his way out. Brave and strong, Cassius wasn't going to let a group of barbaric mercenaries end him.

He was a de Wolfe, after all.

A minor skirmish with mercenaries turned into an all-night murder spree for the Doncaster men, Rhori and Bose. Now, they had a personal score to settle.

Marcil and his mercenaries did not survive the night.

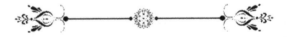

THERE WERE ALREADY men trickling into the great hall.

Dacia was ready for them. She knew that, with any battle, there needed to be a place to tend the wounded and that logical place was the great hall. In the skirmishes she could remember from the past, she seemed to recall the servants setting up an infirmary in the great hall with the help of Mother Mary. Dacia had been quite young at the time and didn't remember much of it, but she knew enough to know that men would be returning from battle soon, some of them injured, and she had to have a place to put them.

Already, men were trickling in, mostly with bloody head and upper body wounds, and she put those with more severe wounds closer to the hearth and tended them first. Edie was with her, as was Fulco and her maids, and between the eight of them, the men were well covered.

Argos the dog was also in the hall, mostly following Dacia around, and she was learning to ignore him. It seemed that he simply wanted to follow her about so she let him, and the casualties were light, so he wasn't in the way. But Dacia was coming to believe that the fight hadn't been too terrible because of the limited wounded. In fact, it was so light that her grandfather went to bed. He didn't see any need to stay up and help, not even to manage his castle's own defenses.

That left everyone else at Doncaster overseeing the safety of the fortress and with Dacia in charge of the wounded, everything was organized brilliantly. Men were receiving the best of care. When one of Darian's knights was brought in with a myriad of wounds, he was put in a more secluded area of the hall so he could have some privacy.

Dacia was tending to the knight when she caught sight of someone entering the hall through the servants' alcove. She thought it was another servant until she glanced up again and caught sight of Amata.

Immediately, she returned her attention to the knight, who had several puncture wounds and what she suspected to be a broken jaw. She'd brought her medicament bag with her, which included a sewing kit, and she finished sewing up the last puncture wound on the knight's hip with very fine silk thread. The knight was young, and trying hard to be brave, and she had one of the servants bring the man some beef broth. With his jaw, he didn't have to chew it, so she was just packing her things up when Amata approached.

"What happened?" she said, looking around the hall with shock. "Why are these men wounded?"

Dacia wasn't ready to play nice yet. She continued putting her things away. "There was a raid in the village," she said. "The men rode out to chase them away. Some were wounded as a result."

Amata was still wide-eyed. "The chamber I am in faces the rear of the castle," she said. "I did not know this was going on until I heard some of the servants speaking of it. Can I help?"

Truth be told, it would be nice for her help, but Dacia wasn't sure just how much help Amata was capable of. She didn't like blood or dirt, and she had never seen her cousin work very hard at anything other than attracting men, so she thought carefully on her answer.

"If you can go to each man and see if he would like something warm to drink or some broth, that would be helpful," she said. "They should not eat anything solid, like meat, so only liquid for now. You can help the men who cannot eat very well. Can you do this?"

Amata nodded. "I can," she said. Then, she started looking around again. "Where is Cousin Vincent?"

"He has gone to bed."

Amata looked at her curiously. "He did not stay to help his own men?"

Dacia shrugged. "You know that he does not like war," she said. "He has never been comfortable with it. He provides the money and the titles and lets other men do the fighting."

Amata simply nodded, looking around at the men nearest

her. "Where should I begin?"

"Anywhere. Just pick any man and start with him."

Dacia started to move away, but Amata stopped her. "CeeCee," she said. "I… I am sorry I became angry with you. I really did come to Edenthorpe to see you."

Dacia paused, looking at her cousin. The hurt and humiliation from Amata's treatment still hadn't vanished. "You came to see Cassius," she said. "Amata, I know you. I know how you think. Lying to me is only going to make this worse, so do not think I will fall for your false apologies any longer. The only way we will find forgiveness is if you are completely honest with me."

Amata frowned as if she were going to become angry again. "I'd hoped to see him," she said. "I will not deny that. But I wanted to see you, too. I did not come here only hoping to see Sir Cassius, but now I see that my efforts were in vain. His focus is on you."

Dacia was careful in her answer. "His focus is *not* on me," she said. "He has simply been kind to me, much as he was kind to you at the Lords of Misrule feast, but the difference is that I did not follow him to someone else's castle. If he had wanted you to come to him, he would have sent for you."

Amata was beginning to lose her temper. She had come into the hall perfectly calm and willing to forget about their earlier argument, mostly because she knew Dacia had been right. But her willingness to be humble only went so far.

"How would you even know what a man wants?" she demanded. "You have never known a man in your life."

"And you have known too many."

Amata didn't have the restraint she'd had earlier when Cassius had been witnessing everything. She and Dacia had experienced plenty of arguments in their lifetime together and Amata had always emerged the victor. Lifting her hand, she slapped Dacia across the face, not hard enough to really hurt, but the message was obvious. She didn't want Dacia to gain the upper hand. She wanted her to shut her mouth and be submissive like she usually was.

But Dacia wasn't having any of it. Feeling the throb of Amata's slap on her cheek, she set her bag down, turned fully to Amata, and slapped her so hard that the woman toppled over onto a chair behind her. Amata ended up sitting in the chair, her hand to her stinging cheek and looking at Dacia as if the woman had just done something horribly wrong.

Dacia's eyes narrowed.

"Hit me again and I shall give it back to you stronger than you can imagine," she said. "I am tired of being your pawn, your obedient dog, and anything else that strikes your fancy. You are a petty, vain, and terrible girl, Amata. I told you I did not want to see you anymore. I meant it."

Amata rubbed her cheek, her eyes spitting daggers at her cousin. "You are wicked," she hissed. "Everything Mother Mary said about you was right – you *are* a demon. The devil has taken you over!"

"Then if that is the case, you had better not push me too far or I will wave my hand and incinerate you," she said. "If I were you, I would be very afraid of someone possessed by a demon. It will not end in your favor if you provoke me again."

Amata stood up from the chair, one fist balled and the other hand on her stinging cheek. "I am going to tell Cousin Vincent what you have said!"

Dacia took a deep breath. "If you do, I will tell your father every secret you have ever kept from him," she said. "I will also make sure he knows that you steal from him. Do not cross me, Amata. You will not like the results."

Amata was furious that she couldn't gain the upper hand. She started to say something more, but a woman was suddenly between them. Edie had made an appearance, having seen the exchange and heard some of the argument.

Her focus was on Amata.

"Lady Amata," she said evenly. "Might I escort you back to your chamber? This is no place for you."

Amata scowled at the maid. "I shall go where I please," she said. "Go away and leave me alone."

Edie shook her head. "Alas, I cannot, my lady," she said. "Lady Dacia has a job to do around her and if you are not going to help her, then you must leave. 'Tis shameful for two well-bred young women to be slapping each other for all to see."

Amata was outnumbered and grossly upset about it. She stomped her foot angrily and started to berate Edie, but more men coming in through the hall entry caught Dacia's attention.

She didn't have time for Amata's temper tantrums.

Completely forgetting about her cousin, she headed towards the entry to see what the casualties were. She was met by a wide-eyed, bloodied, and exhausted soldier.

"My lady," he said, trying to catch his breath. "De Wolfe has been wounded. We've brought him back, but he shouldn't... he can't..."

The man was cut off when Cassius suddenly appeared in the doorway with two big arrows sticking out of him. He was dressed in full battle gear, including his helm, and there was a great deal of blood all down the left side of his body. One arrow was in the left shoulder and the other was somewhere down by the curve of his torso, in his gut. He was holding on to that arrow to stabilize it, but the expression on his ashen face was nothing less than calm, steady strength.

It was all Dacia could do not to cry out at the horrific sight.

"Cassius," she said as evenly as she could. "Please... let me take you someplace to lie down. You must lie down so I can look at your wounds."

He just stood there, but he was weaving unsteadily. "I never saw them coming," he said. "I heard them before I saw them and, suddenly, they hit me."

"I can see that."

"They came out of nowhere."

Dacia sensed that he might not have been as in control as he wanted her to think. As he wanted everyone to think. Cassius was all about honor and the de Wolfe name, so it was possible he didn't want to show weakness in front of the men. In front of anyone, really. He had a reputation as Lord Protector to uphold, but Dacia could see that he was hanging on by a thread.

Perhaps the hall wasn't the best place for him.

"It will be all right, Cassius," she said, moving to him and putting her hands on his arm. "Come into the keep with me. You can rest there while I remove these. Will you come?"

He was looking at her. In fact, his pale eyes never left her. "How are the men?"

"No one will die," she said. "Most of the wounds are minor. But you... you must come with me. Please, Cassius."

"They came out of nowhere."

He was repeating himself, indicative of the fact that he probably didn't have much longer on his feet. She could feel him trembling violently as she gripped his arm. She looked at the soldier who had announced his arrival.

"Help me," she said quietly, then looked over her shoulder.

"Edie! I need you!"

Edie rushed over, getting in behind Cassius because he was now having difficulty walking as Dacia turned him for the keep. Argos, seeing his injured master, came bounding over and Dacia had to push him away. With the soldier on one side and Dacia on the other, Cassius began to walk haltingly towards the keep. More soldiers, men who had seen him ride in with arrows sticking out of him, had followed him to the hall, astounded that the enormous knight was still on his feet.

But, then again, he was a de Wolfe.

De Wolfe strength, as evidenced before them, was legendary.

Dacia saw the men gathering, looking at Cassius in shock, and she didn't want them gawking. She focused on two older soldiers who had served her grandfather for many years.

"You two," she said. "Help me get him into the keep. Edie, get my medicament bag. Then I want you to send someone into the village to find Emmeric the physic. With the village in flames, I do not even know if he is still there, but send men to find him. I will need help with Cassius, so hurry. Hurry, Edie!"

As the two older soldiers got in behind Cassius to help him cross the bailey, Edie fled back into the great hall to gather Dacia's medicament bag. The other maids were still there, wide-eyed at what they had just seen, and Edie encouraged them to continue tending the men. She instructed the other servants to do the same, and put Fulco in charge, but as she came to the bag, she noticed that Amata was still standing where they had left her.

Head down, she quietly collected the bag, but Amata stopped her.

"I shall take it," she said, reaching out to demand the bag. "I will help Dacia with Sir Cassius. You will stay here."

Edie knew about the earlier fight with Dacia and Amata because she had been in the chamber across the landing when she'd heard it. She had heard everything. She had never been so proud of her mistress than she was when she heard her tell Amata everything that had ever needed to be said to the spoiled young woman.

Therefore, she knew that Amata's demand for the bag and the insistence to help Dacia were not altruistic. Amata had a motive in mind, as she always did, so Edie politely shook her head.

"Nay, my lady," she said. "She asked for me. I shall take it to her."

Amata reached out and grabbed it, but Edie held firm. "Let it go," she insisted. "I will take it to her."

"Nay, my lady. Please release it."

Amata yanked on it, but Edie wouldn't let go. "I said give it to me," Amata said angrily. "You are a stupid servant. You cannot be any help to her, so let it go."

Edie's dislike of Amata had reached its limit. She wasn't going to let Amata help Dacia, and in a sense, she was protecting Dacia against a woman she'd long tried to protect her from. She'd seen years of abuse and selfishness from Amata towards Dacia. It had been heartbreaking to watch.

Now, she wasn't going to take anything more.

Amata never saw the hand that shot out and slapped her across the face. Suddenly, she was falling onto her backside as Edie slipped from the hall, out into the night, where Dacia and the escort of soldiers were just reaching the steps leading up into the keep.

As Amata screamed, Edie just kept on walking.

CHAPTER THIRTEEN

"ONE MORE STEP, Cassius," Dacia said gently. "We're almost there."

Cassius could hardly lift his leg. He'd been functioning on a battle high ever since those arrows carved into his body, but now, that high was wearing off. His entire left side was soaked in blood and he was starting to feel faint.

But he couldn't let his guard down.

He had to make it into the keep under his own power.

Once inside the keep, there was a constable chamber inside the door to the left. It wasn't a big chamber, but it had a good-sized bed in it and a hearth and, at the moment, that was all that was needed. There hadn't been a constable in the chamber in years, so it sat cold and unused except by visitors on occasion.

Dacia took him inside the chamber.

"Sit, Cassius, please," she said softly as she and several soldiers lowered him onto the bed. Once he was down, she looked to the men around her. "Bring light in here, as much as you can, and get a fire going in the hearth. I need hot water and as much wine as you can find, so get that for me right away. Hurry, now. There is no time to waste."

Two of the men fled, but the older two didn't move. They were looking at her with some uncertainty.

"My lady?" one man finally ventured. "Have you...?"

She looked at him sharply. "Why are you still here? I gave you orders."

The men nodded patiently. "I know, my lady," the first man said. "And we shall follow them. But after we've helped you remove those bolts. Have you ever removed them from a man's body before?"

Dacia looked at Cassius, who was gazing at her with complete and total trust. There wasn't anything in his expression other than the full knowledge that she would heal him. There wasn't a doubt in his mind. But Dacia had to be truthful in her answer.

"Nay," she said reluctantly. "I... I suppose you were right to remain because I am sure I will need your assistance. Help me lay him on the bed and remove what clothing we can. I must see the wounds."

Between Dacia and the two old soldiers, they manage to lay Cassius flat on the bed and straighten him out as much as they were able. He was so tall that his booted feet hung over the end of the bed at least a foot.

"Hurry," Dacia commanded softly. "Help me get this clothing off."

They tried. They removed his belt and scabbard, carefully setting aside his sword and purse, and other things that were contained on his belt. With that off, Dacia was forced to cut through the royal tunic. Cassius had finally closed his eyes. He was deathly pale as Dacia and the others rushed to help him, but when it came to his mail coat, they could go no further. It was sticky with coagulated blood and the bolts were pinning it to Cassius' body.

"I cannot cut through this mail coat," she said. "We have no choice but to remove the arrows before we go any further."

Edie had entered the chamber by that point, setting the medicament bag next to the bed. There were boiled linen bandages in the bag, but they were forced to wait until men started returning with the hot water and wine that Dacia had sent them for. She couldn't start anything without the things she needed. As soon as she had the water, the wine, and the bandages, she nodded to the soldiers hovering around the bed.

"Am I to understand that you have done this before?" she asked quietly.

The older solders nodded. "Aye, my lady," the first man said.

Dacia bent over the gut wound, trying to get a close look at it, but it was difficult with the mail and tunics he had on. Gently, she prodded around, determining where, exactly, it had penetrated.

"If this arrow had been just an inch or so to his left, it would have missed him completely," she said. "I do not know if it has hit anything vital but I assume that if he was going to bleed to death, he would have already done so. But we must remove them both, so I shall let you take charge. Tell me what you wish for me to do."

The two soldiers spread out around the bed.

"Removing these requires some strength, my lady," the first man said. "I'll yank this one out and Bardo will remove the one in the shoulder at the same time. 'Twill be better for him that way if we can do it all at once. You will hold him still, if you can."

Dacia nodded, struggling not to feel sickened by the whole

thing. She was trying very hard to be clinical about it, to not feel any emotion, but the shock of seeing Cassius impaled had faded, being replaced with a strong sense of horror.

God, help me to help him!

She had to stick to what she'd been taught, to everything the priest had taught her. But it was difficult when her patient was Cassius.

All she wanted to do was weep.

But she fought it.

"Let me douse the wounds with wine first before you pull," she said, forcing herself to focus. "The wine helps kill any poison."

Edie handed her a wine jug but before she poured it, she bent over Cassius as he lay there with his eyes closed. She put a warm, gentle hand on his forehead.

"Cassius?" she said softly. "Can you hear me?"

It took him a moment to answer. "I do."

She stroked his sweaty forehead, smoothing back his dark, dirty hair. "We are going to remove the bolts," she said. "Please try not to move. We shall be as swift as we can."

His eyes lolled open, focusing on her. "As you say, Angel," he murmured, his tongue thick. "I am in good hands."

Dacia smiled faintly at the man as his eyes shut once more, exhausted from blood loss. She stroked his head one last time before moving to the bolt in his shoulder. Quickly, she doused the wound and the one in his torso with the wine. Alcohol on an open wound was excruciating, but Cassius didn't flinch.

"Go," she commanded huskily. "Pull them out."

They did. Both bolts came out fairly easily, one after the other. As the soldiers took them away, Dacia and Edie went to work.

Quickly, they placed the boiled linen over both wounds, which were now starting to bleed again. Edie held tightly to the one on his shoulder while Dacia held tightly to the one on his torso. They pressed them down, stemming the flow of blood because Cassius had already lost a goodly amount. Dacia had her eyes on his face as she held the linen down and she only saw him twitch once. Considering the pain he must have been in, it was remarkable that he'd not uttered a sound.

As the bleeding lessened, Dacia was finally able to get a look at the wound. As far as she could tell, it was really only as deep as the head on the bolt, which was maybe three inches at most. But the head of the arrow had pushed all kinds of debris into the wound – fabric, pieces of mail, and other things. Dacia knew she had to get those out. When the soldiers returned, she had them strip Cassius to the waist so she could have a clear field to work in. As the men hauled out Cassius' clothing and armor, including his boots and sword, Dacia had Edie shut the door so they would have some quiet and privacy.

The worst part about wounds like the ones Cassius had suffered was the debris the arrows had pushed into the body. That was where the poison and fever could kill a man and Dacia was only too aware of that. Some of the Arabic treatises that she had in her collection of books had recipes on how to combat those poisons, including one that called for salts from the human organ – the liver.

The physic in Doncaster, Emmeric, had concocted the potion several times, having purchased bile salts from a man in York who harvested such things from the dead. It was probably immoral, but Emmeric still bought the salts because mixing them with wine, garlic, and onion often produced a cure unmatched in fighting fevers and bodily poisons. She knew that he would bring his potions when he came, provided the man could be found. Meanwhile, she would have to do what she could do for Cassius and, at the moment, that meant picking the debris out of the wounds – one piece at a time.

With the man stripped down, the fire in the hearth blazing, and Edie hovering to be of assistance, Dacia went to work on the gut wound with a pair of tweezers. She tried not to look at his naked flesh, how absolutely perfect he was, muscular and powerful and formed like a marble statue.

Interestingly, he had a big *stigmat*a on his left shoulder, a wolf's head set within a five point shield in black ink, an unusual marking on a knight but clearly one with significance to him. But she didn't do anything more than simply glance at it. She kept her focus on the wound and bit by bit, she plucked the debris out of it, which must have been agonizing for Cassius, but he simply lay there.

Not a sound came out of his mouth.

Dacia got a good look at the wound between washing it with wine and picking out the debris, and it didn't seem to her that it had hit anything vital. It had passed through skin and fat and muscle, embedding itself about three inches into the side of his torso. It was a miracle it hadn't done more damage.

Even so, it still took Dacia a couple of hours to remove every particle she could find and when she was certain there was no more, she stitched him up with her careful, tight stitches and applied a wine-soaked chamomile poultice to keep any swelling at bay. As Edie bandaged up the wound with more clean linen, she moved to the shoulder wound.

This wound wasn't as clean and it had already begun to coagulate, so she had to pick out the newly formed clots to get into it and remove the same debris that she had found in the other wound – pieces of cloth, mail, and leather, all of it shoved down into a wound that went into his armpit. This one seemed to be deeper and she thought it might have nicked a bone, but it was difficult to know. It had torn up the muscle of his shoulder and once she picked out the rubbish, she washed it with more wine before applying another chamomile poultice and stitching it closed. Packing boiled linen on top of it, she bound up the shoulder tightly.

At that point, it was well after midnight, but she didn't feel any fatigue, only great concern for Cassius, who had fallen into a deep, exhausted sleep. Edie cleaned up the bloody bandages and rags, tossing out bowls of bloodied water, moving quietly about her duties. Dacia remained seated next to Cassius, putting her hand on his forehead every so often to gauge his temperature, and generally watching how he was handling everything. She was so wrapped up in watching him that it took her a moment to realize there were two big, gray paws sticking out from underneath the bed.

A smile came to her lips as she realized Argos had somehow gotten into the chamber and she hadn't even noticed. Bending over, she caught sight of big doggy eyes looking at her from underneath the bed. Reaching into the darkness, she petted the dog on the head, comforting the animal. He may have been a silly fool of a dog, but he was sweet and loyal.

She was coming to like him, just a little.

Sitting back in her chair, Dacia took a moment to breathe. She also took a moment to thank God that Cassius hadn't been more badly injured. All things considered, it wasn't as bad as it could have been, but time would tell whether or not any poison took hold. That was the big fear with battle wounds. If they survived the actual wound, all of that could be ruined in an instant if a fever came upon them as a result of the injury.

He wasn't out of the woods by any means.

Dacia looked over at Cassius, sleeping heavily, and put a gentle hand on his forehead. His dark hair was dirty, oily, but it didn't matter to her. She stroked it softly, feeling a great deal of affection for the man lying before her. He was magnificent to look at. And he was witty, charming, brave, and strong. There was nothing about him that wasn't perfect in her opinion. There wasn't anything about him that wasn't to love.

Love...

Dacia realized that she was falling in love with him. She wasn't shocked by the awareness, mostly because it seemed completely natural. She never thought she'd find someone she could love, so the moment was both unexpected and a little intimidating. She reminded herself that Cassius wasn't meant to remain at Edenthorpe, that he would soon be moving on once he healed, and she didn't want to love a man who would soon leave her.

But it was too late.

Thoughts about Cassius leaving Edenthorpe reminded her that he had not come to Edenthorpe to stay, but to relay a message. That had been his only in purpose in coming, but that brief visit had turned into something far more than anyone had anticipated. He had ended up fighting a battle and now he was lying here, wounded because of it. Wounded because of his knightly sense of honor and duty. He had spoken of his desire to see his grandmother, and now those plans were in jeopardy because of her grandfather's selfishness in asking Cassius to stay.

Somehow, it didn't seem fair.

Dacia loved her grandfather, but even she could see how

selfish this had been on his part. He had never considered what Cassius had wanted or why he had ever really come to Edenthorpe in the first place. Cassius had made it clear he had not come to stay, but her grandfather had clearly ignored that.

Now, Cassius was paying the price.

As Dacia sat there and watched him breathe, slowly and heavily, it occurred to her that his family might like to know that he had been wounded. He had mentioned Castle Questing as well as Berwick Castle, so she decided to send them word about his injury.

She thought, perhaps, that they might want to know.

As she sat there and thought on Cassius' family, Argos suddenly let out a growl. Curious, she looked at the dog just as someone knocked on the door, softly. Rising to her feet, she went to the door and quietly opened it.

Rhori and Bose stood outside, covered in grime and sweat and blood. Their expressions were grim as they looked at Dacia.

"My lady," Rhori greeted, his voice hoarse from screaming battle commands. "How is Cassius?"

Dacia opened the door so they could come in, but she had her finger to her lips in a gesture of quiet.

"He had lost a great deal of blood by the time he got here," she said softly. "We removed the arrows and I cleaned and stitched the wounds. It does not look as if anything vital was hit, miraculously, but the wounds were dirty. There was a good deal of debris in them. I removed everything I could see, so I hope it was enough."

Rhori bent over Cassius, taking a good look at him. "He is sleeping heavily," he said. "Did you give him something?"

Dacia shook her head. "Nay," she said. "Exhaustion and blood loss will do that. But I will give him something for the pain when he awakens."

Rhori simply nodded, a lingering glance to his friend before turning away. "You have my thanks for tending him, my lady," he said. "Cassius is... important to me. He is important to many people."

Dacia could see how grieved he was. It was actually quite sweet that the man should be so loyal and concerned but, then again, Cassius seemed to bring that out in people. He'd certainly brought it out in her.

"I will do everything in my power, I assure you," she said. "I will not leave him, not even for a moment. But I was thinking that we should send word to his family. They will want to know about this and if the worst happens and a poison takes hold... his father will want to know, don't you think?"

Rhori nodded. "I will send word to him immediately," he said. "And to Castle Questing. You have never seen a family so devoted to one another, my lady. If one suffers, they all suffer. They will want to know."

"And the king," Bose said quietly. "We must send word to him also. He must know that Cassius was wounded defending the Duke of Doncaster. It will elevate Cassius in the king's eyes tremendously for his heroic deeds."

Dacia thought of her grandfather, who was even now asleep in his bed. He couldn't have been bothered with remaining vigilant all night while other men were fighting his battle. While he slept, a fine and strong knight had been wounded defending Doncaster's village. Thinking on that very thing made her quite furious.

Furious enough to act.

"May I ask you to remain with Cassius for just a moment?" she asked the knights. "Just a quick moment is all I ask. I shall return as fast as I can."

As they both nodded, she fled the chamber, racing up to the floor above where her grandfather's chamber was. His chamber was literally above Cassius' bed, taking up the entire floor, and she charged into his chamber without knocking.

The chamber smelled like a man who never bathed, that heady aroma that filled the nostrils and clung like dirt. There was a fire burning low in the cluttered hearth and a bank of candles somewhere near the bed to give the duke some light, for he was up several times a night, peeing in a chamber pot that was never full. He had an old man's bladder, as he often said.

Dacia marched right up to the bed.

"Grandfather," she said, reaching out to gently shake the man. "Grandfather, awaken."

Doncaster stirred a little, groaning, before trying to go back to sleep. Dacia shook him again.

"Grandfather," she said, more loudly this time. "You must awaken. Something has happened."

He lay there a moment as if trying to ignore her, but one eye popped open. "What has happened?" he demanded, muffled because half of his face was in the pillow. "Dacia, what do you want?"

Dacia gave him a good shake, so much so that he batted a hand at her, trying to push her away.

"Grandfather, I know you are not a warring man," she said. "But men have gone to war for you this night while you have slept safe and warm in your bed. You must awaken. Cassius de Wolfe has been wounded."

That brought a reaction. The duke rolled onto his back before struggling to sit up. "De Wolfe?" he said. "Where is he? What happened?"

Dacia stepped back from the bed as he swung his legs over the side. "He is in the constable's room," she said. "I have just spent hours picking debris out of two arrow wounds. He sleeps now, but you must send word to the king that this has happened. It is your duty to tell him that his Lord Protector went to war for you and has been injured. Do you know he was heading home to see his elderly grandmother when all of this happened? And you demanded he stay here and help you with Catesby Hagg. As a man of honor, he did, and now see what it has cost him. He may never get to see his grandmother now and it is your fault."

Dacia wasn't in the habit of talking to her grandfather so angrily, but she was genuinely upset about the situation. To Doncaster's credit, he took it seriously. He rubbed his eyes.

"Is it that bad?" he asked. "Have you sent for Emmeric?"

Dacia nodded. "I have," she said. "But half the village was burned this night and he may have fled. I do not know where the man is. You cannot sleep while men are injured and your village is in chaos. You must show the men that you are strong and in control, and that you care about them, so get up and do your duty. Send word to the king about Cassius and I will do all I can to ensure the man survives this."

Doncaster was nodding before she even finished. He stood up, a bit unsteadily, and headed over to the wardrobe where his clothing was kept. "Where is Fulco?" he asked.

Dacia was pleased that the man was at least up and moving. "In the hall the last I saw of him," she said. "There are many wounded. They will need your encouragement, Grandfather. They have all risked their lives for you this night."

Doncaster found his breeches, turning to Dacia before pulling them on. "They have," he said. "But they have sworn their fealty to me. That is why I provide them with food and clothing and a place to stay. I am not an unkind lord, Dacia."

"I know," she said, softening her manner a little. "But Cassius… he is not your knight, yet he was injured fighting for you. I feel sorry for him, Grandfather, and also angry. Angry that you kept him here rather than let him go along his journey."

Doncaster's gaze lingered on her for a moment. "You like Cassius, don't you?"

There was no use denying what was probably very apparent. "He has been very kind to me," she said quietly, turning for the door. "I intend to repay that kindness by nursing him back to health."

She was nearly to the door when her grandfather spoke out to her. "I like him, too, CeeCee," he said quietly. "He is a fine knight from a most powerful family. He would make an excellent duke."

Dacia didn't say anything, but she did turn to look at him as she lifted the doorlatch. There was no mistaking the smile on her lips as she left the chamber.

She rather thought so, too.

CHAPTER FOURTEEN

T HE NEXT DAY dawned a bright and beautiful morning. The sky was cloudless and the temperatures warming, as the hint of spring that had been in the air was now transforming into a kiss of summer. It seemed that on a day like this that nothing could touch the languid atmosphere of the land, as if nothing had been amiss the night before, but that was certainly not the truth. All one had to do was look to the great hall and see all of the wounded soldiers who had done battle against the mercenaries the night before.

Amata had decided to leave this morning and return home, considering she wasn't needed and she no longer wanted to remain. After the scuffle with Edie, she had retreated to her borrowed chamber. She had no intention of helping out with the wounded, especially when it was made clear that she wasn't wanted, so she went to bed and pulled the covers over her head.

Her selfish heart rendered her incapable of doing anything more.

Now, on this fine morning, she intended to go home and never return. She had sent a servant for the soldiers she had brought with her from Silverdale, and the men had assembled her escort as the sun began to rise. Amata sent another servant to bring her some food so she could eat before she headed home and rather than eat it in her borrowed chamber, she decided to stand in the bailey impatiently as her escort assembled.

She figured that if her soldiers saw her waiting, they might move faster, so it was her intention to rush them along as much as she could. But as she stood in the dewy morning and chewed on the bread that she had been given, she could see the Doncaster soldiers moving about the bailey, men who had fought last night in the village skirmish. In fact, there was a heavy smell of smoke in the air and she heard some of the soldiers say that the fire in the village was still smoldering.

She also heard them say that several of the mercenaries had been killed and those who had remained had realized that the tides were turning against them and fled into the darkness. Nosy as she was, she wandered about in the bailey a little, chewing on her bread and listening to the men speak on the battle of the night before. What she mostly heard was the men who had been there speaking to the men who had not been there, men who had been left behind in case the raid in the village had been a ruse.

There was much to tell on this fine morning.

As Amata finished her bread and pretended not to pay attention to what the soldiers were saying, she heard a great deal. She had heard that the church had remained untouched, as had the northern part of the village. She heard the men speak about the burned out southern section of the village and how the avenue of the smithies had been partially destroyed.

It seemed as if the village of Doncaster had taken a serious beating at the hands of the mercenaries, but the body count of dead mercenaries numbered into the forties and those bodies had been dragged over to the church until something could be done with them. For now, however, the village was quiet and she heard someone mention that they were trying to resume a sense of normalcy on this very morning.

All of the talk about the village made Amata very curious to see it.

In fact, Amata had friends in the village, the same girls who scorned and ostracized Dacia. Amata was understandably concerned for her friends and decided to pass through the town before heading home to see how bad the damage really was. One of her oldest friends was the daughter of the richest merchant in town, a young woman by the name of Eloise Saffron. She hadn't seen Eloise in quite some time, so she thought today might be a good time to see how her friend was faring after the terrifying night.

It was also quite possible that she was looking for a friendly face, considering she found none of that here at Edenthorpe.

Her escort, spurred on by the sight of their lady pacing around, was ready by the time she finished her bread. She was ready to depart without a word of farewell to anyone and, soon enough, her escort was riding through the gates. Usually, her escort turned south before they reached the gates into Doncaster village but, this time, her escort continued on and entered the berg.

Immediately, Amata could see the damage from the raiders because the avenue of the smithies was directly in front of her, and she could see the damaged and half-burned stalls. The smell of smoke was heavier here and, to the south, she could see plumes of dark smoke still rising, evidence of the fire started last night that continued to burn.

In truth, it was a little eerie to see the village so beaten down. But she could also see that the soldiers had been correct – it looked to her as if the villagers were trying to resume some sense of normalcy and over on the street of the merchants, she could see a few people going about their business.

Eloise's father had the biggest merchant stall on that avenue and Amata directed her escort to the Saffron stall. She craned her neck to see if it was open and as they drew closer, she could see that the shutters were indeed open for business. Her escort came to a halt just as Eloise herself exited the stall, shaking out a piece of fabric that seemed to be inordinately dusty or dirty.

"Eloise!" Amata called, waving her hand at the women. "Greetings, Eloise!"

Eloise Saffron looked over to the woman calling her name, smiling when she recognized Amata.

"Amata!" she cried happily, running over as Amata climbed from her carriage. "What in the world are you doing here?"

Amata hugged her friend, grateful to be in the presence of someone who wasn't going to slap her. "I was at Edenthorpe last night and heard about the attack," she said. "I came to see if you and your family had weathered the storm."

Eloise's smile faded. "It was terrible," she said. "So much fighting and pillaging. My father's stall didn't suffer too much because he employs his own soldiers, so they were able to fight off those trying to do damage. But so many others were not so fortunate."

Amata could believe that, given the damage around her. "And our friends?" she asked. "Beatrix and Ursula and Claudia?"

Eloise pointed down the avenue. "Beatrix and Ursula's father suffered a great deal of damage," she said. "You can see that his stall has been torn to shreds."

"And Claudia?"

Eloise shrugged. "I do not know," she said. "I have not seen her, though I hear the metal workers' stalls were all badly damaged. Her father is a goldsmith, so I imagine he was one of the hardest hit. I heard my father say that the attackers last night were stealing the most expensive things they could find."

Amata shook her head, clucking sadly. "What a terrible thing," she said. "You must have been horribly frightened."

Eloise nodded. "I was," she said. "Thank God it is over. And you? You were at Edenthorpe last night?"

Amata averted her gaze. "I helped tend the wounded," she said modestly. "You know that they depend on me for such things. I was overseeing the servants as they tended the wounded, but the more badly injured men were referred to me for my care. I did what I could."

Eloise smiled. "Brave Amata," she said. "You are always so willing to help and do good."

Amata lowered her head, appropriately humble. "I do as God asks of me," she said. "Except... oh, Eloise, it was simply awful!"

Eloise nodded. "I am certain that it was," she said. "We are very grateful to the Doncaster army for riding to our aid. I saw knights, too. The fighting was very bad."

In that moment, Amata saw her salvation. The salvation to ease her humiliated soul. She'd been doing this kind of thing for years, spreading lies while making herself look like an angel, which was why no young woman in the village would speak to Dacia. They almost exclusively knew of Dacia through Amata's lips. But at this moment, Amata saw a perfect opportunity to punish her cousin for being bold enough to stand up to her. For stealing the man she wanted.

Aye, she saw the perfect opportunity.

This was where Dacia was going to pay.

"It was very bad," she agreed. "But some of the knights were from King Edward's stable. They were not Doncaster men. And that was why I had to leave Edenthorpe – I am banished, Eloise. Banished by my own cousin."

Eloise's brow furrowed. "By Dacia?" she said, incredulous. "What has that terrible girl done to you now?"

It was the sympathetic ear Amata had hoped for. "One of those knights you saw fighting last night," she said, lowering her voice to a whisper. "This great knight is one of Edward's knights and he had eyes only for me, but my wicked cousin seduced him."

Eloise's eyes widened. "Seduced him?" she gasped. "You mean...?"

Amata nodded firmly. "They kissed right in front of me," she said. "Or, I should say, Dacia kissed him. And you know Dacia – she spends all of her time seducing her grandfather's soldiers. She has had more men between her legs that I care to count, all the while telling her grandfather that *I* am the wicked one. But this knight belonged to me and she knew it, yet she stole him from me anyway. Last night, I saw them retreat into the keep – together!"

Eloise's mouth opened in astonishment. "Did they –?"

"Of course they did," Amata said. "He bedded her and that is what she wanted. She did it to steal him away from me. So this morning, I fled. I will never go back to that terrible place where my terrible cousin does such immoral things."

Eloise patted Amata's shoulder in sympathy. "Poor Amata," she said. "Your cousin is despicable in her behavior. If I ever see her again, I shall tell her so!"

It was the pity Amata had needed. She pretended to be quite heartbroken. "The knight and I were talking of marriage, but not any longer," she said. "I would not be surprised if Dacia married the man. Little does he know what an awful person she is. Why... why, her own maid has told me such tales of her. Such tales! She told me that Dacia gave birth to a baby last year and buried it in the garden. A poor bastard baby!"

"Oh!" Eloise gasped, hand to her mouth. "Do the priests at St. George's know this?"

Amata shook her head. "If they do, they will not speak of it," she said. "The duke is a powerful man. He probably paid them to pray for Dacia's black soul. So you mustn't say a word, Eloise. Promise me."

Eloise shook her head. "I will not, I promise," she said, but it was a lie and they both knew it. "Poor Amata. Why not come inside and have some warmed wine? It has been a long time since we last saw one another and we can have a nice, long visit."

Amata gladly followed Eloise inside, where the rear portion of the stall was the family home. Eloise's mother and grandmother were there, welcoming Amata graciously, and the four of them sat down to warmed wine and bread with cheese. It was a lovely visit, but one in which Eloise forgot her promise and told her mother and grandmother about Dacia's terrible behavior while Amata played the wounded cousin throughout the entire thing.

But inside, she was smiling.

It wasn't long before that bit of gossip went flying around Doncaster, from ear to ear, finally reaching the priests at St. George's. It was a morbidly glorious bit of rumor mongering, with Dacia of Doncaster at the center of it thanks to her liar of a cousin.

Dacia may have had the last slap, but Amata would have the last laugh.

CHAPTER FIFTEEN

Three long days...

T HAT WAS HOW long Cassius had slept. Dacia knew it was only sleep because he would wake if she roused him, but he had slept like the dead for two long days. She woke him periodically to force him to drink a small cup of boiled, salted water because she knew that the human body was comprised of fluids and if he didn't have enough, his body would take longer to heal. She was also giving him a poppy potion for the pain, which contributed to his heavy sleep.

The poultices and the bandages on the wounds were changed regularly. There was a dousing with wine and a poultice of chamomile, repeated several times during the night and day. The wounds seemed to be doing well enough, which was good news, and Cassius had not developed a fever.

Dacia said prayers hourly for that very critical blessing.

No fever, no poison, and Cassius had a good chance of recovering completely.

Rhori and Bose were regular visitors to the sick room, as well. It was Rhori who would sit with Cassius while Dacia slept for a few hours, but the truth was that she was seriously sleep deprived because she didn't want to leave him. Sometimes, it took both Edie and Rhori to convince her that it would be okay for her to leave him for a short while. She would go to her chamber, fall asleep for a couple of hours, and then rush back to Cassius.

It had become a regular cycle.

On the morning of the third day, Dacia was sitting at Cassius' bedside, reading a book from the faraway, mysterious kingdom of Harsha. The book was written in their mysterious language but, at some point over the centuries, someone had translated it into French, which Dacia could understand. It wasn't a book of treatises or recipes, but more of a religious book, something that she was certain the priests of St. George's would not approve of. As the fire in the hearth snapped softly, she continued to read, noting that the sky outside was becoming lighter as a new day dawned.

Edie slipped into the chamber, bringing food and tending to the hearth. She put a big pot of porridge over the flame, bringing honey and butter, bread and warmed wine for Dacia to eat when she grew hungry. The problem was that Dacia wasn't eating much at all and often let Argos have her food. The previous night, Rhori and Bose had brought their meals into the chamber to eat with her, gently forcing her to eat with them so they would not be ashamed to eat in front of her. They coerced her to eat a full meal that way and Dacia was touched that they would be so concerned for her. Until she'd met Cassius, she'd never had anyone show such concern in her entire life.

Now, his knights were doing it, too.

When Edie brought the food this morning, Argos came out from his position under the bed and immediately turned eager

WOLFESWORD

eyes to the food being set out. Exasperated, Edie lured the dog out of the chamber with buttered bread, promising to take him to the kitchen and feed him a decent meal. That left Dacia as the only partaker of the food left behind but, true to form, she didn't touch it.

She was more interested in her book, and in Cassius, unable to relax enough even to eat.

The morning progressed. Dacia could hear men out in the bailey, going about their duties, and the occasional neigh of a horse. There were birds all around the keep because they had made their nests high in the eaves. She could hear them tweeting, feeding their newly hatched babies because spring was here. In fact, everything seemed to indicate a fine spring day. She would have thought so, too, had Cassius not been laying in a bed, recovering from battle wounds.

The morning continued towards noon. Dacia was still reading her book, now listening to Cassius as the man began to snore. He was breathing heavily now and she put her book aside, standing up to go to the bed and put her hand on his forehead, something she did twenty times a day. Only this time, it was different.

He was hot.

Her heart sank.

Quickly, she went to her medicament bag, pouring a little white willow powder into some wine. White willow was known to fight fevers. After three days, Emmeric the physic had not yet been located, so Dacia was having to rely entirely on her knowledge and what ingredients she had with her. Though she was confident in her knowledge, she was hoping they would be able to find the physic at some point, especially if Cassius was going to run a fever. She didn't want to do this all on her own if his condition grew more serious.

Mixing the powder with her finger, she went to Cassius, gently rousing the man.

"Cassius?" she said softly. "Cassius, please awaken."

He snored a few moments longer before abruptly falling silent. Dacia shook him again.

"Please, Cassius," she said. "Wake up and look at me."

He remained still, his eyes closed. But then, his head turned in her direction. "I will gladly look at you, my angel," he mumbled, though his eyes were still closed. "What is amiss?"

Dacia sat on the bed next to him, putting her arm behind his neck. "I need you to sit up a little and drink this."

His eyes lolled open but he was having a difficult time staying awake. Still, he did as she asked, weakly lifting his head as she helped him and draining the wine cup. Carefully, Dacia lay him back down.

"Good," she said. "I am sorry to have awoken you. Go back to sleep."

She tried to move away but his hand shot up, grasping her wrist. "Nay," he muttered. "Do not move away. Stay here with me."

She set the cup aside but remained on the bed. His hand moved to hers and he grasped it, bringing it to his lips and kissing it sweetly. "Sweet Dacia," he slurred, his eyes finally closing. "What would I do without you?"

Dacia smiled in spite of herself. "You would be in the hands of someone not as competent as I am," she said. "Consider yourself fortunate."

He grinned, dimples carving through his unshaved cheeks. "I consider myself the most fortunate man in England," he said. "How am I faring?"

Her smile faded, just a little. "As well as can be expected," she said, not mentioning the hint of a fever. "The arrows didn't strike anything vital and I was able to clean out the wounds and stitch them up. Barring anything terrible, you should recover."

He kissed her hand again. "Sweet girl," he said, laying his cheek against her palm. "You have my unending gratitude."

He was rather adorable in his sleepy, slurring state. Dacia could have quickly become accustomed to his touch as he held his face against her hand. There was something so comforting and intimate about it, something she'd never experienced before. She'd never been close enough to a man not her father or grandfather to be hugged or touched in any way, and she knew that she liked it. Very much.

His touch was magic.

"And you have my undying gratitude for riding off to save the village from the raiders," she said. "You did not have to go. You could have very well remained in the hall and let the Doncaster men go forth, but you did not. You risked yourself for us. The least I can do is tend to your wounds."

His eyes rolled open again and he looked up at her, the pale eyes studying her. "Be under no false impression," he said. "I risked my life for you and no one else. Those bastards weren't going to come anywhere near my sweet angel."

Dacia flushed furiously. "I think I must have given you too much of my potion," she said. "You are being silly now."

He shook his head, slightly. "Not at all," he said. "I am quite within my right mind. Dacia, will you do something for me?"

"Anything."

"Kiss me."

Her eyes widened. "*K-Kiss* you?" she stammered. "Now?"

"Now." When she hesitated, off guard by his bold request,

he sighed heavily. "I am dying right before your eyes and you will deny me a simple kiss? How can you be so cruel? I would have done better had I asked my dog to kiss me."

He said it so dramatically that she knew he was jesting, but she still wasn't over his request. It was titillating, wildly exciting, and wildly intimidating all at the same time. Fighting off a smile, she started to look around.

"That can be arranged," she said. "Argos has been under your bed nearly the entire time. I will happily put him next to you so he can kiss you to your heart's content."

"It's not the same."

Their eyes met and Dacia knew she was going to honor his request no matter how much she was pretending to debate it. He smiled at her, lifting a weak finger to teasingly poke her nose. That freckled nose she'd always been so ashamed of, but something he found beautiful. The next thing she realized, she was kissing his bearded cheek.

But that wasn't enough for Cassius.

He turned his head, his lips latching on to hers, and that weak hand holding her head had surprising strength. His hand was so big that it encompassed more than half her head, holding her fast to him. It was a sweet, delicious, and alluring kiss, and just when he shifted himself so he could embrace her with his good arm, he torqued his torso and the wound in his gut pained him greatly. He grunted and the momentum of their kiss was shattered.

"Did you hurt yourself?" Dacia asked, leaping off the bed to get a look at the bandages around his midsection. "This is my fault. I should have let the dog kiss you."

Cassius had been wincing from the pain, but he suddenly started laughing. Dacia was trying not to laugh as she checked the bandages, making sure he hadn't torn anything. She was bent over, peering at the edges of the bandage, when there was a soft knock on the door and Rhori entered.

"Cass," he said with surprise. "You're awake!"

Cassius nodded faintly, his good arm up over his eyes and somewhat thankful for his knight's sense of timing. Any earlier, and there would have been some explaining to do.

"Aye," he said. "For a short time, anyway."

Rhori came over to stand next to the bed. "How are you feeling?"

Cassius grunted. "Well enough until I moved too much and strained my wound," he said. "Lady Dacia is making sure I did not ruin her good work."

Rhori stood back as Dacia evidently felt the need to rebandage the wound on the torso. He watched her for a moment as she moved around.

"Her work is excellent," he said, returning his attention to Cassius. "She has hardly left your side the entire time. We have tried to force her to sleep, but she has been reluctant to leave you at all. I have never seen such a devoted nurse."

Cassius' eyes opened and he looked at Dacia, bent over his belly. He could tell that she had heard Rhori's words because her cheeks were flushing red. Before he could reply, Dacia spoke up.

"It is because it is my grandfather's fault that Cassius was wounded at all," she said. "Had my grandfather not been so demanding to insist that the king's knights fight Doncaster's war, none of this would have happened. I have much to atone for."

Rhori seemed pleased with her answer, but Cassius wasn't. There was something cold and unemotional about a woman tending a wounded man purely out of guilt. In fact, he didn't even reply to it. His attention moved to Rhori.

"What happened after I left?" he asked.

Rhori cocked his head thoughtfully. "We killed many of them," he said. "Call it what you will, but your injury spurred the men into a sort of revenge. Clabecq's mercenary force is in ruins. I would say no more than thirty or forty escaped with their lives."

"What about the wounded?"

"We left no wounded."

Cassius was rather pleased to hear that. "Good," he said. "And Marcil himself?"

"Dead," Rhori said. "I saw the body myself, dragged into the field next to the church."

"Did the church hold?"

"Aye. De Lohr did an excellent job of it."

Cassius sighed, relieved. "That is good to hear," he said. "So the mercenaries ended up buried at the very church they tried to raid, did they?"

Rhori nodded. "In a sense," he said. "Doncaster went to the church himself to speak to the priests about the burial, in fact, but the priests do not wish to bury them in the churchyard, so they are burying them in the field next to it."

"I see," Cassius said, rubbing his eyes wearily. "What about Hagg? Has there been any word from him?"

Rhori shook his head. "Nay," he said. "De Lohr sent a scouting party to Hagg's property yesterday and they returned to tell us that everything was burned to the ground. There is nothing, and no one, left."

Cassius' eyebrows lifted curiously. "So the mercenaries burned Hagg to the ground and then went to work on the village," he said. "Interesting. I wonder why? Mayhap Hagg refused to pay them and they went on a rampage."

"That is as good an explanation as any," Rhori said. "Doncaster wants to ride out there later today to look it over and de Lohr is planning to take him."

Cassius took on a pensive expression. "He seems to be taking an active role in all of this. Strange for a man who seemed so reluctant for any kind of military activity."

Rhori shrugged. "He has expressed his gratitude to Bose and me," he said. "He is thankful for our assistance. In fact, he sent a missive to Edward about your injury and to thank the man for your sacrifice. I sent a missive to your family so they know what happened and why your visit will be delayed."

Cassius grunted. "That is good," he said. "Because I plan to send a missive to Edward asking to extend my time away because of this. My plans have not exactly been adhered to, but I do not intend to abandon them entirely. I was supposed to be nearing Castle Questing by now."

"You will at some point," Rhori said. "I do not expect to see you down for much longer. But until such time as you are on your feet, do you have any instructions for me?"

Cassius thought for a moment before shaking his head. "Nay," he said. "Nothing at this time. But assure everyone that I am on my way to recovery."

Rhori nodded, quitting the chamber and shutting the door quietly. When he was gone, Cassius looked down at Dacia, still fussing with his bandages.

Thoughts shifted from his family and the king to Dacia. *I have never seen a more devoted nurse.* It did Cassius' heart good to hear that. Certainly, he'd had many women show attention and devotion to him, and it had fed his pride. Cassius de Wolfe drew women like bees to honey, and he'd been arrogant because of that fact. But Dacia's devotion fed something else inside of him, something he'd kept buried. A true and genuine heart he'd spent his lifetime protecting from his big ego and overzealous females.

This was different.

"Did I ruin your careful work?" he asked softly.

His voice was soft and warm, something Dacia wasn't immune to. "Nay," she said. "The stitches are still intact. I am simply fixing the bindings."

He watched her focus on his wrappings, the way her dark lashes fanned out over her cheek when she blinked. At one point, she bit her lip in concentration and her dimples carved deep ruts into her cheeks. For a woman with many alluring qualities about her, he thought those dimples were just about the most alluring thing he'd ever seen.

"Is it true, then?" he asked.

She was still fussing. "Is what true?"

"That you are only tending me out of guilt?"

She stopped fussing and her head came up. "Who told you that?"

His pale eyes were glittering at her. "You did," he said. "You said you have much to atone for because your grandfather was the reason I was injured."

She blinked in surprise as he repeated her own words back to her. "I do not feel any guilt," she said. "I simply meant that I feel as if I need to make things right with you. My grandfather had no business asking you and your men to fight his war for him. He was wrong and I told him so."

The corners of his mouth tugged with a smile. "Ever my champion, are you?"

She stood up, looking at him full-on. "Cassius, you have been kinder to me than anyone has ever been in my life," she said. "I will champion you until the day I die. There is nothing I would not do for you."

His smile broke free, spreading across his face. He held out his right hand to her and she stared at him a moment as if not understanding his meaning. But after a moment, it occurred to her what he wanted, and she put her hand in his. He pulled her closer, lifting her hand to his lips again and kissing her fingers softly.

"You are the best friend I have ever had," he murmured.

She smiled. "And you are the best friend *I* have ever had," she said. "If it is within my power, I will always ensure you have the best of everything. When you came back to Edenthorpe wounded, Amata wanted to assist me but Edie would not let her. Amata is not very good with the ill or wounded. She would have caused... problems."

"Who is Edie?"

"My maid," she said. "The only maid that really matters to me. She is very protective of me and she has always disliked Amata intensely."

He chuckled. "I like her already," he said. "I shall have to thank her for not letting Amata into this chamber. Where is she, anyway?"

Dacia shrugged. "I was told she left the morning after the battle," she said. "She has gone home and I hope she stays there. I am not sure if I can explain this to you, but I will try. Until you came to Edenthorpe, I clung to Amata as the only friend I had. Edie had often tried to tell me what a petty soul Amata was, but I ignored it. I'm sure you heard that on the evening she arrived, when we were arguing outside of my chamber. It was Amata who would tell me that the girls in the village were gossiping about me, saying terrible things about me, but Edie always told me that Amata was the one saying those things. I didn't really believe her until you came to Edenthorpe."

He squeezed her hand. "How did I change your mind?"

She looked down at his enormous hand as he held hers. "Because you told me something she never did," she said quietly. "You told me I was beautiful. No one has ever told me that in my entire life. Oh, Amata is not entirely to blame. My nurse, Mother Mary, shoulders most of that responsibility, but Amata was not much better. And then you came. You were a stranger, yet you told me something I didn't realize I needed to hear. You made me think that everything I'd ever been told about my appearance was wrong."

He tugged on her gently, pulling her closer. "It *was* wrong," he said. "If your cousin told you that you were ugly, then she was lying. Ask Rhori or Bose. Ask any man who has not lived and served at Doncaster and has been poisoned by these lies. They will tell you that you are quite beautiful, but you've been surrounded by idiots who look at your freckles and think the devil is trying to mark you. Those are ridiculous, lying fools. And I think your cousin told you all of those things because she was jealous of you. She didn't want the competition."

Dacia smiled timidly. "That is why you are my dear friend," she said. "You make me believe that mayhap I am not as bad as everyone says I am."

Cassius rolled his eyes before tugging on her a final time so she was sitting on the bed next to him. She was sitting on his wounded side and when she accidentally bumped into his left arm, jostling the shoulder, she quickly put her hands on him in an apologetic gesture. But to Cassius, her touch was worth a thousand such jostles. He held her hand against his chest, tightly.

"Dacia, I want you to listen to me and listen carefully," he said. "What I am about to say may mean something to you, or it may not. Only you can be the judge. But I think it is important."

He sounded serious and she nodded. "Of course, Cassius," she said. "What is it?"

He gazed up into her magnificent eyes. "Would you say that I am a comely man?"

She nodded without hesitation. "The most handsome man I have ever seen," she said. "In fact, my maids have been buzzing about it. Evidently, every woman at Edenthorpe thinks the same thing."

He gave her a look that suggested he was quite pleased and also not surprised, which caused her to chuckle. But he reached up, capturing her chin between his thumb and forefinger, forcing her to look at him.

"This is going to sound quite arrogant of me, but it is the truth," he said. "They are not alone. When I said I had armies of women following me around, it was the truth. The king has long suspected that he will not die in battle, but trampled by a stampede of women in their haste to get to me. It is, therefore, fair to say that I have seen many, many beautiful women."

Her smile faded. "And you've not yet found a wife in that horde?"

He shook his head, releasing her chin but reclaiming her hand. "Nay," he said. "Not to say that there haven't been a few viable candidates but, in the end, it would be unfair to take a wife because of my position with the king. I would be with him more than I would ever be with my wife and that is not fair to her."

Her smile vanished completely at that point. "That is understandable," she said. "No one would blame you."

His big fingers began to caress her soft flesh. "You are the only female who sees it that way," he said. "I have been sent gifts, expensive gifts, and plied with money and wine from rich women who thought I would drop everything to lay down by their side."

"But you did not?"

"I did not."

She cocked her head in a gesture of understanding. "I do not blame you," she said. "You have a great position that is very important to you. You should not give it up for a woman."

He cleared his throat softly. "That is where you would be wrong," he said. "There *is* a woman I am considering giving it up for."

She looked at him and he could see the light go out of her eyes. All of the warmth she had in her face was gone, replaced by something cold and sorrowful as much as she tried to hide it.

"I... I am happy for you, then," she said, averting her gaze and pretending to focus on his shoulder wound. "I shall do my best to heal you so that you may return to her. Would you like me to send her a missive telling her of your injury? Mayhap she would like to come to Edenthorpe and tend you herself."

He was back to rolling his eyes. "Christ," he muttered. "You do not understand, do you?"

"Understand what?"

He fixed on her. "Dacia, what I was trying to tell you, though not so eloquently, was that I have seen many women in my life," he said. "Too many women to count, so I know a beautiful woman when I see one. I also know a good heart when I see one, but it is rare to find both a beautiful woman and a good heart together. I'd have better luck looking for a unicorn. But I have found one such woman, the rarest find of all. I have found you."

She was still puzzled; he could see it. "But what about the woman you are considering giving everything up for? Surely she is beautiful with a good heart."

He groaned, putting a hand up to cup her face. "Are you truly so dense?" he said. "You *are* the woman I am considering giving everything up for, silly wench."

Dacia stared at him. For a long, uncertain moment, she simply looked at him. Then, she bolted off the bed, bewildered and overwhelmed, and ended up sitting in a chair over against the wall. About as far away from him as she could get. She sat there, staring at him as he gazed back steadily.

"Can you hear me from over there?" he asked, touched and amused by her response.

She nodded stiffly. He chuckled.

"Are you *happy* sitting over there?" he asked wryly.

Again, she nodded. He tried to shift his body so he could get a better look at her.

"Dacia, this is not helping my pride," he said. "I have just bared my soul to you. The least you could do is say something. Tell me you feel the same way. Or tell me to go outside and throw myself into the river. Say what you will, but say *something.*"

Truth be told, Dacia was stunned. She didn't know what to say. She stared at the man, gorgeous and glistening, bandages over his damaged body, and she could only think of one thing.

It was on her tongue before she could stop it.

"I love you," she said, barely audible. Then, she slapped her hands over her mouth. "God's Bones, I cannot believe I said that."

He laughed, low in his throat. "Did you *mean* it, lass?"

She hesitated before nodding, so firmly that her hair came out of its braid. It was waving all around her face. "I do," she whispered. "I do mean it, but I should not have said it like that. No one has ever said such things to me, Cassius, so I have never had any practice on how to respond. I may have impeccable manners, but sometimes my social graces are raw and honest. I should have at least told you how I felt before telling you that I loved you. But… it simply came out. It is the truth."

He crooked his finger at her, beckoning her to come near. She shook her head, staying planted in the chair. Cassius started to laugh, a joyful and giddy sound.

"So you do not intend to come near me, ever again?"

"Nay."

He laughed harder, then suddenly put a hand over the wound in his torso as if the movement hurt. "Damnation," he said. "I think I felt something snap."

Dacia was off her chair, running over to the bed to check the bandages. But the moment she drew near, a massive hand shot out and grabbed her. Before she realized it, she was on the bed, laying half on him. She was laying over the bandaged left arm and shoulder, but Cassius was so strong that he didn't need two arms to hold her with.

Just one.

She was trapped.

"When one is trying to catch the elusive Dacia, one must use the right bait," he murmured, his face very close to hers. "The right bait is evidently a Cassius."

Dacia tried to pull away, briefly, but she quickly gave up. "You are a trickster, Cassius de Wolfe," she said, feigned disapproval in her tone. "I shall remember this."

He pulled her closer, his lips seeking hers. "I hope you do," he purred. "Tell me again that you love me."

She could feel his hot breath on her face and it made her feel weak all over. "Why?"

"Because I want to know that I mean something to you."

"You mean everything to me."

His mouth slanted over hers hungrily. After the first small kiss before Rhori had arrived, Dacia was more than willing to explore a deeper and more passionate kiss as her emotions swept her away. She welcomed it, in fact, knowing that Cassius was feeling something more for her than simple friendship.

You are the woman I am considering giving everything up for.

It was too good to believe.

But surely... it was impossible. They had only known each other a matter of days. But, oh, what days they were! Dacia had never known such monumental days and even though they'd only known each other a short period of time, she felt as if she'd known him forever. As his hand wound itself in her hair and his lips suckled hers, she felt as if she'd always known him. As if she had always been meant to be here, in his arms. By his side.

Loving him.

But things were getting heated. He had positioned her so that she was across his body and he was cradling her against him. She was somewhat trapped by his right arm as his mouth did wicked things to her neck, suckling on a little earlobe and making her gasp. The moment she opened her mouth, he was on her again, his tongue licking at her, demanding entry. The thrill of his tongue licking at her, of his lips suckling on her tongue when she finally opened her mouth, was nearly too much for her to bear.

She was starting to feel faint.

"Cassius," she whispered in between his heated kisses. "You must let me up. Someone might come in and see us."

He slowed his pace, eventually pulling back to look at her with smoldering eyes. "You are correct, of course," he said, carefully pushing her up so she could find her feet on the floor. "Forgive me, angel. I could not help myself."

She wiped his saliva off her mouth, grinning sheepishly. "I seem to have suffered a lack of control myself," she said. "But... but it was worth it."

He smiled broadly, reaching out to touch her cheek. "It was," he agreed softly. "Will you let me court you, then?"

She couldn't keep the smile off her face. "Was your kiss part of your scheme to coerce me into agreeing?"

"Of course."

She burst out laughing. "Well, at least you are honest about it," she said. As she looked at him, her smile faded. "Truly, Cassius, that is all I shall ever ask of you. Honesty."

"And that is what you shall have," he murmured. "That... and my heart."

He said it so sweetly that, this time, she reached out to grasp his hand. "And you shall have mine," she murmured. "And if you wake up tomorrow and still wish to court me, I will not resist."

"I must wait until tomorrow?"

She nodded. "Sleep on it," she said. "Make sure it is what you wish to do, for once you have me, you shall have all of me. I shall never love another, Cass. If I give you my heart, it belongs to you forever. It will not be mine to give again."

He squeezed her hand, kissing it before releasing it. "Thank you, my lady," he said quietly. "Then let me sleep now. The sooner I sleep, the sooner I shall awaken and speak with your grandfather."

"As you wish," she said. "Would you like something to eat before you do? You've not eaten in two days."

He shook his head. "Not now," he said wearily. "When I awaken, mayhap."

Dacia touched his cheek softly before helping him get comfortable in the bed once more. She put her hand on his forehead, realizing that he still felt hot to the touch. But she didn't say anything to him, not wanting to plant that seed that might worry him. He wanted to sleep and she would let him, but she was most certainly not going to sleep.

She had to remain vigilant.

All she could do now was pray.

"My lady, you really should sleep," Rhori said quietly. "You have been at this for three days now. If you become ill, you'll not do him any good."

Dacia could hear the knight's concern, but she couldn't give in to it. Not tonight.

Cassius' fever had worsened.

Throughout the day, he'd grown hotter and she gave him willow potion regularly. But by nightfall, he was shivering with chill while perspiration beaded on his forehead. He slept heavily but awoke on occasion so she could ply him with more willow potion. She had all but given up on Emmeric, knowing she was Cassius' only hope. She stuck to the belief that she could heal him.

She wasn't going to give up.

"I will not become ill," she said, putting a cool cloth on Cassius' forehead. "I am weary, but not terribly so. I am well enough, so please do not worry for me."

Rhori wasn't so sure. He looked over at Bose, who simply shook his head sadly. The maid that was known to help Dacia, a woman she'd called Edie, was busy brewing something over the fire while more maids brought the buckets of fresh, cold water. Dacia was working as hard as they'd ever seen anyone work.

Still, the knights felt as if they were entering into a death watch. They'd both seen this kind of thing before, puncture wounds that festered until the man eventually passed away from a fever that shut down all bodily functions. But there were also times when there would be a small fever for a day or two and then the man would recover completely. At the moment, it was difficult to know which way Cassius was going to go, but Dacia was doing everything she could to help him.

Rhori made his way over to Bose.

"Thank God we sent that missive to his family," he muttered to the man. "I'm wondering if we should not send them another one and tell them to come immediately."

Bose's dark gaze was on Cassius. "Nay," he said quietly. "By the time they receive it, he will already be gone, if it is God's will that he passes. If the fever grows worse, it will take him quickly. He is already weak."

Rhori, too, looked at Cassius, laying pasty upon the bed, shivering beneath the heavy blankets that Dacia had put on him.

"I've seen worse," he said after a moment. "He is weak for Cassius, but given that he is the strongest man I know, he's not too terribly weak. If the lady has anything to say about it, he will pull through."

They both looked at Dacia, sitting at Cassius' bedside, bathing his torso and arms with cool water to help the fever. Bose scratched his head wearily.

"She will wear herself out if she continues," he said. "But she will not leave him and I suspect there is a reason behind that."

Rhori glanced at him, knowing exactly what he meant. "You saw that, too, did you?" he asked. "The night of the feast?"

Bose nodded. "I have never seen Cassius look at a woman like that, and God knows, he has looked at plenty of women."

Rhori's focus returned to Dacia. "She's a beauty," he said. "I do not blame him. But I also received the impression that de Lohr was... fond of her, shall we say."

Bose simply lifted his eyebrows. "No man can compete with Cassius de Wolfe," he said. "If de Lohr was fond of her, then he has waited too long to declare his interest. I suspect she is already spoken for."

Their conversation was cleaved when someone knocked on the door. Bose opened it to reveal Darian standing in the doorway. The knight greeted Bose and Rhori with a nod.

"The duke is on his way to see Cassius," he said. "How is he?"

All three knights looked over to the body on the bed as Bose answered. "He is feverish," he said. "Lady Dacia is doing all she can for him. Have you managed to locate that physic you were looking for?"

Darian's gaze was on Dacia, not Cassius. "Aye," he said quietly. "We found his burned body in some of the rubble on the south side of the village about an hour ago. As near as we can determine, he was tending to a patient when the roof burned over his head and caved in. I've got my men bringing in what they could collect of his medicament bag. Mayhap Lady Dacia can use some of it."

That changed the situation somewhat. They all knew that Dacia had been hoping for the physic to join her. Bose turned to say something to Darian, but he caught sight of the duke on the landing outside and he pulled on Darian to move the man out of the way.

"Your grace," Bose greeted.

Doncaster moved into the doorway, his gaze immediately finding Cassius lying supine on the bed in the corner with Dacia bent over him, swabbing him with cool water.

"I came to see how Cassius is faring," he said. "Is he better?"

Rhori answered. "He is the same, your grace," he said. "He is still with fever."

That wasn't what Doncaster wanted to hear. He pushed into the chamber, heading over to the bed to gaze grimly upon Cassius. Dacia caught sight of him, looking at him but giving the man no hint of warmth.

"I am doing all I can," she said before he even asked. "If he does not start to improve soon, I will have to reopen his wounds to see if there was something I missed when I cleaned them out."

The duke nodded, looking at Cassius with a pained expression on his face. "I am so very sorry for this," he said. "Edward will never forgive me if something happens to de Wolfe because of me. 'Tis a terrible thing, indeed."

Dacia paused in her swabbing. "I would not worry about the king," she said. "*I* will not forgive you if something happens to him, Grandfather. It was your selfishness that brought Cassius to this point. All he wanted to do was return home to see his grandmother, but you commanded him to assist you and you knew he could not refuse. It was cruel and terrible of you to do that."

The duke opened his mouth to defend himself, but a faint voice came from the bed. "Dacia," Cassius whispered. "It was not his fault. You will not blame him. Tell the man you are sorry for your short temper."

They both looked at him with some surprise. Dacia leaned over him, wiping a cool cloth on his cheeks.

"You are awake, listening to a private conversation?" she teased him gently. "What a terrible thing for you to do. You should have plugged your ears."

He peeped an eye open, looking at her. "Bold words, my girl," he said. "Apologize to your grandfather and then you will go away and let me speak with him alone."

She frowned. "I will not leave you."

"You will if I tell you to or I shall rise up out of this bed and spank you soundly. Is this in any way unclear?"

She wasn't offended in the least. In fact, she sensed some mirth, but she also sensed seriousness. Heavily, she sighed.

"It is clear," she said unhappily. "I will go away, but only for a few moments. I shall be right outside the door."

"Stay there until I send for you. And take that motley group with you."

She sighed again, sharply, and cast him a long look, but she did as she was told. After kissing her grandfather on the cheek to apologize, she moved away from the bed, shooing the knights out of the chamber because Cassius had told her to. When she was gone and the door quietly shut, Cassius opened both eyes to look at the duke.

"Cassius," Doncaster said before the man could speak. "You

must know how terrible I feel about this. It never occurred to me that something like this would happen, of course. I would never deny you the opportunity to see your family. I hope you know that."

Cassius nodded weakly. "I know, your grace," he said. "I was honored to be of service. But now I must ask you an important question."

"What is it?"

"I would like your permission to court Dacia with the intention of a marriage."

Doncaster's eyebrows lifted at the swift and shocking change of subject. "You would?"

Cassius could see the old man's astonishment, sensing that he had spoken the words that Doncaster had never expected to hear where it pertained to Dacia. Realizing that, he felt some anger. As much as his fever-ridden body would allow, he could feel his anger rise at the attitude of a foolish old man when it came to his granddaughter.

"And why not?" he said. "She is a beautiful, talented woman that any man would be proud of. I have heard that she was raised by a woman who covered her up because she believed her freckles to be the work of the devil. But as I told you before, I think Dacia is God's most magnificent creation. I further realize that she is your heiress and she brings with her the great legacy of the House of de Ryes. Know that this situation has no bearing on my request."

"It doesn't?"

"I would take her without the title or the name."

Doncaster looked at him, awed by his position. "If that is true, then you must truly be serious about her."

"I am, your grace," Cassius said. "I will go one step further in my declaration. Though it is not usual for a man to change his name when he marries, when it is the case of a woman of higher social standing, men have been known to take their wife's family name. I will not give up the name of de Wolfe, for it is a storied and proud heritage, but I will add de Ryes to my name if it pleases you, so that our children will bear the name. Your family is an old and distinguished one."

Doncaster stared at him, his features softening and his eyes growing moist with emotion. "Would you truly, Cassius?" he said. "I had a son, you know. Dacia's father, Dacian. Dacia was named for him. But she was his only child, as his wife died when Dacia was quite young, and then he died of an ailment when she was about seven years of age. She is all I have left. What you have said… it gives me more joy and hope than you could possibly imagine. Would you truly add my name to the great de Wolfe name?"

Cassius could see how touched the man was. "Of course," he said. "That way, our children will be born of the House of de Wolfe-de Ryes, but known as Doncaster formally, as Dacia is. Would this be acceptable?"

Doncaster was already nodding his head, reaching out to take Cassius' hand. "You have made an old man very happy," he said sincerely. "If you wish to court Dacia, then you have my blessing. You will make a fine duke, Cassius. Greater than I could have ever hoped for."

Cassius smiled faintly, giving Doncaster's hand a squeeze before letting him go. "Thank you," he said. "Now, you may let your granddaughter back into this chamber before she beats the door down."

With a grin, Doncaster moved for the door, lifting the latch and being faced with four serious faces – Dacia, Darian, Rhori, and Bose. He crooked a finger at Dacia, but kept the knights from following. He had something to tell her and given Darian was part of that group, he didn't want the man to hear the news just yet. There was the little matter of Darian having his heart set on Dacia.

Doncaster wasn't immune to that.

Therefore, he would let Cassius inform Dacia that she was now spoken for and he would personally handle Darian. He loved the man like a son, so he knew how delicate the situation was. He wanted to be kind. He genuinely tried to be.

As expected, Dacia was thrilled at the news.

Also as expected, Darian was not.

By morning, Cassius' fever had broken.

CHAPTER SIXTEEN

The village of Doncaster
One week later

"I SUSPECT SHE is never going to speak to me again."

Cassius, astride Old Man, spoke loudly to Rhori and Bose. Riding ahead of a column of about fifty Doncaster men, he was leading the escort into town with Dacia on a small gray palfrey several feet behind him and Argos plodding along beside her. His own dog wasn't even walking beside him, but *her*. He kept glancing back, casually, to make sure she heard him, but she ignored him soundly.

That only made him grin.

"She is angry that I am back to my usual duties," he said. "She was so angry with my plans to come into the village this morning that she locked the chamber door on me. I could not get out until Rhori came to my aid. And, by the way, that makes her angry with you, too, so watch yourself today."

Rhori and Bose were snorting at the antics that had been part of this venture into town since the escort was formed this morning. Cassius was recovering swiftly from his wounds, gaining strength every day thanks to Dacia's diligent and excellent care, but she hadn't been able to keep him in bed as long as she had wanted to.

Hence, the trip into town.

As far as Cassius was concerned, he was feeling completely normal. His wounds were healing nicely even though they were still bandaged for the most part, but Dacia was concerned that he was doing too much, too soon. She nearly had a temper tantrum when she saw him yesterday, bare-chested in the morning sun, as he worked a little with his sword in the bailey.

With the wound in his shoulder, he was feeling some weakness as a result and, as he had explained to her, he wanted to be aware of what limitations the wound had temporarily imposed. It made perfect sense to him, as a warrior, but little sense to her, as a healer. He needed to recover before he could work the shoulder, in her opinion. She tried to take his weapon away and he wouldn't give it to her, so she went away angry.

She was still angry.

And he was still laughing.

In fact, he was as joyful as either Rhori or Bose had ever seen him. He was betrothed to the heiress to the Doncaster dukedom, a massive triumph for a lowly knight, but Cassius was a de Wolfe and they were some of the most sought-after grooms in England. It was only right that one marry the Doncaster heiress and everyone agreed on that account.

Everyone but Darian, that is.

It had been a very fine line to walk for everyone all week, trying to be sensitive to Darian's feelings while celebrating Cassius' betrothal. Dacia had tried to speak with Darian about it, but he had avoided her. She finally gave up trying, hurt that he didn't seem to want to talk to her at all because he had been a dependable friend for years when she'd had few people to talk to. His coldness stung, but there was nothing she could do to ease it. She had never intended to marry him even if he thought there might be hope. Any perceived future marriage had been concocted only by him.

But he had been professional nonetheless, at least to Cassius and his knights, so his behavior with them had been admirable given the circumstances. Cassius hadn't brought up anything about the betrothal to him and their discussions had been purely professional. But Rhori had mentioned that Darian had become ragingly drunk the night he found out about the betrothal and had to be carried to his bed.

Still, everyone was trying to stay above it and not let the situation deteriorate in any way.

But it was a difficult fight.

The trip into Doncaster today was a good example. Usually, Darian would accompany Dacia whenever she left the castle. But this time, he had remained behind while Cassius and his men took the lead. Considering Cassius was now her betrothed, that was appropriate. But there was still something sad about leaving Darian behind.

Yet, it couldn't be helped. Both Cassius and Dacia knew that.

They put it behind them to enjoy the day, or at least, Cassius had. Dacia was still angry at him for the fact he was even up and moving, so he'd spent the short jaunt into town mostly taunting her. He also did it for another reason – to take her mind off the fact that she wasn't covered in her veils.

He had insisted.

It had taken a good deal of coaxing to convince her not to cover herself up. Cassius thought she was a radiant creature and he didn't want that radiance covered up, but Dacia was very nervous about it. She wore her hair in a braid, with a lovely bejeweled cap and a white gossamer veil that was attached to it. The veil went around the neck, covering the neck and chest, before being pinned up on the other side of the cap. Therefore, she was covered up a little in an elegant and fashionable sort of way, but her face was still exposed.

Cassius thought she looked magnificent.

She thought she looked naked.

As the escort approached the St. Sepulcher gate, the one that faced northwest, Cassius slowed his horse down so the escort passed him. He was waiting for Dacia, wanting to be next to her when they rode into town so she would not feel alone and nervous in her uncovered state. As her horse came near, he smiled at her.

"Well?" he said. "Are you speaking to me yet?"

As she came upon him, she gave him a reproachful look. "I've not decided," she said. "You are a cheeky, naughty lad, Cassius."

"I know, my lady."

"And quite difficult."

"I know, my lady."

"And ungrateful."

"For what?"

"For all of the hard work I have put in to you," she scolded. "Look at you, riding around as if nothing has happened. You are not even keeping your left arm immobile while your shoulder heals. A week ago, you were feverish and in bed, and I was genuinely fearful that I would lose you."

He reined his horse next to hers, reaching out to take her hand and lift it for a contrite kiss. "I know," he said softly. "But your miraculous talent healed me. There was never any real danger for me as long as you were there."

It was difficult to be stern with him when he was being so sweet. "You will be careful, won't you?" she asked. "You will not exert yourself today."

He shook his head. "Nay, my lady," he said. "I promise I will not."

"How are you feeling?"

He winked at her. "Rather well, lass," he said. "Why do you ask? Do you have something in mind for later when we are alone?"

She yanked her hand away, shaking her head at him. "You are impossible," she said, fighting off a grin. "Cheeky *and* impossible."

He laughed low in his throat. "Admit it. That is how you like me."

Her grin broke through. "How can I not?" she said. "I fear that, very quickly, you have learned how to get around me. One flash of that smile and I am like butter, melted and pliable to your wishes."

He continued laughing at her. "Just wait until you realize the power you have over me," he said. "That will be the day your life changes forever."

Her smile faded as she looked at him. "My life is already changed forever," she murmured. "You have changed it, Cass, and I shall always be grateful."

He looked at her, winking again. "That statement goes both ways, angel."

She smiled, watching him for a moment, perhaps looking for any sign of fatigue from her powerful, invincible knight. She still could hardly believe he was hers. But she saw nothing in his manner that suggested lethargy. He looked as if he had never been wounded. She lifted her hand, shielding her eyes from the sun as she continued to watch him.

"You are sweet to want to take me into the village to purchase a few things for me," she said. "Truly, you do not have to. I have more possessions than I need."

"But *I* did not buy them for you," he said. "Never argue with a man who wants to buy you something. It will not go well in your favor."

She chuckled, softly. "I was not arguing," she said. "I was simply saying that I have a great deal already."

"Do you have a ring that expresses my devotion to you?"

"Nay."

"Where can we find one?"

The mere suggestion made her heart flutter as she thought on this question. "There are a few merchants that sell jewelry," she said. "But our best chance of finding something like that will be on the street of the smithies. There are silversmiths and goldsmiths there, too."

"Then that is where we shall go," he said. "And then we shall find a merchant who can supply some pretty things for your trousseau."

She was starting to flush again, thinking on their wedding, and wedding night, and all the nights afterwards.

"If you insist," she said. "And have you finally decided when this event shall take place?"

He nodded. "We shall leave here in a few days, when I am feeling strong enough to travel great distances, and go north to Berwick Castle," he said. "I want to be married in my father's home, with my family about me. It is important to me. I hope that is agreeable with you."

She smiled at him, at the sentimentality when it came to his beloved family. "Of course it is," she said. "And your grandmother will be there, too."

"She will have a place of honor to witness the marriage."

"What of your mother's father? The Norse king?"

Cassius shrugged. "He is very old these days and does not travel like he used to, but I will send him word. Be prepared for his response."

"What response will he give?"

Cassius snorted. "He claims the right to name every firstborn male child in our family," he said. "He named my oldest brother and my oldest brother's firstborn son. But he also named me and my two younger brothers, so he will undoubtedly lay his claim to name our firstborn son."

Dacia was laughing because he was. "God's Bones," she said. "The Norse have some very strange names. I do not wish for my son to bear a name that no one can pronounce."

Cassius continued to chuckle, this time because she was absolutely right. "Then we shall give him a suitable Christian name as a second name and call him by that," he said. "But we cannot deny Magnus the Law-Mender. That was a rule established in our family long ago so you may as well know now."

The gate to Doncaster loomed overhead. Dacia looked up at it, seeing the familiar walls and the familiar massive wooden gates, and was reminded of how her future had changed. She was Doncaster, and always would be, but she would have a husband who served at the king's side. When he became the duke, things would change drastically for him. She knew he realized that, but the practice of it would be something altogether different.

It made for an uncertain paradox.

"Cass," she said slowly. "I was wondering... once we are married, what then? Do you plan to return to Edward? You once said you never took a wife because of your position with him, but marrying me changes that a little. I am Doncaster and when my grandfather passes away, you will inherit the title. That means that there are... expectations. What will you do?"

He was looking up at the gate, too. "It is true that things will change when your grandfather passes," he said. "But let us hope that will not be for a long while yet and we shall deal with one problem at a time. I'm not yet sure what I shall do for the immediate future, but I do know that wherever I go, you will be with me. I will never be without you, angel."

It was a good enough answer for her and she didn't press him. The party bearing the Doncaster standard moved into the village now, distracting her. It still smelled of smoke almost two weeks after the mercenary raid. It was the first time Dacia had been to town since the incident and she could see the scorched and burned buildings, the open village center that had piles of charred wood on it and other debris.

Immediately, she could see that there had been a good deal of trouble.

The church of St. George's was to her left, on the north side of the village, and it was unscathed. The churchyard was next to it and the empty field to the north of it, the one where the mercenaries had been buried.

In spite of the damage and rebuilding, people in town were going about their usual business. When the Doncaster party rode into town, they became the center of attention. People were pointing, whispering. Some were even running to other streets to announce the presence of Doncaster.

It didn't bother Dacia, as she had seen this kind of behavior every time she came to town with her grandfather. But this time, she felt more apprehension than usual. Her face was exposed, which was cause enough to be anxious. She'd never gone out in public like this and it was an effort not to lower her head so her face wouldn't be obviously seen.

Cassius glanced at her, watching to see how she was responding to everything. He saw her drop her chin once or twice, looking at her saddle, her hands, her lap, but she always lifted it again. He knew this was something new to her, something she would have to become accustomed to, but she was trying very hard no matter how much discomfort she felt.

"Dacia," he murmured. "You are the most beautiful woman in this village, if not all of England. Let these people see you for what you really are. They've never seen a face like yours in their entire lives."

She looked at him, smiling gratefully and he winked at her encouragingly. Then, he pointed up ahead.

"Is this the street of the smithies ahead of us?" he asked. "My visits to town have been limited to a feast and a raid, so I do not know the layout."

Dacia nodded. "Aye," she said. "There are several up ahead, but it looks as if they suffered a good deal of damage."

That was quite true. This was the street that had been the worst hit. Stalls that hadn't been burned completely were in shambles, and there wasn't one stall that was untouched. Still, men were working in them. Smithies were shoeing horses, or fashioning things on their anvils, and the heat from their forges could be felt as soon as they entered the street proper.

There were a great many people about, conducting business or rebuilding what had been damaged. People paused to stare, although no one greeted Dacia. All they seemed to do was stare at her. More and more, she was becoming self-conscious, struggling not to let the attention bother her.

But it was difficult.

They came to a stall that Dacia knew was a goldsmith because the man was the father of a girl that she had been friends with, long ago. Cassius ordered the escort to a halt and dismounted his horse, handing the reins over to Rhori before going to Dacia and lifting her from her palfrey. He smiled at her when their eyes met.

"Come," he said softly.

Tucking her hand into the crook of his elbow, he forced the clingy dog to remain behind as he took her to the stall that wasn't as badly damaged as some of them had been. Goldsmiths usually employed their own security, and this stall was no different. They were stopped at the door by three heavily armed men who allowed Cassius to pass when he surrendered his sword to Bose and swore to enter unarmed.

Once inside the stall, they were met by the goldsmith, a little man in flowing robes with rings on every finger. The man's focus was on Cassius, a positively enormous knight filling up his stall.

"My lord," he said. "I am Lockwood. How may I be of service to you this day?"

Cassius looked down at the man, who was shorter than Dacia. "My lady and I wish to look at rings," he said. "The very finest you have. Do you have some to show us?"

The man nodded eagerly until his gaze fell on Dacia. He stared at her for a moment before his eyes widened, as if realizing who she was. His mouth popped open.

"My lady," he said. "You are Doncaster's granddaughter."

Dacia was tense. Cassius could feel it in her hand as it clutched his right elbow. But to her credit, she didn't try to lower her head or avert her gaze. She looked him in the eyes.

"I am," she said. "This is Cassius de Wolfe. We are to be married. Will you show us some modest rings, please?"

"The biggest rings," Cassius said.

She looked at him. "Modest."

"*Big.*"

She sighed sharply and looked to the goldsmith. "Do whatever he wishes," she said. "He will have his way in the end, so do what he wants."

Lockwood looked between the pair in a most hesitant manner before beckoning them to follow. They did, following him into a smaller chamber in his stall where three men were working over various pieces on the tables before them. He indicated two chairs in front of one of the tables.

"Please," he said. "Sit down. This is Flavio and he will show you whatever you wish."

Cassius didn't even think it strange that Lockwood left him with a subordinate, who promptly showed him several big, gold, beautiful rings, all with precious stones in them. But Dacia was a little more uncomfortable. She was wondering why the man had suddenly run off, heading back into the living quarters. She suspected that he was telling his wife and daughter who had come to his shop.

Dacia hadn't seen Claudia Lockwood in years, not since she'd been a girl. She was certain that Claudia would come out to greet her purely to be polite and she braced herself. Not being covered in her veils was soul-rattling to someone who had always gone into public well-camouflaged, but having Cassius by her side fed her courage. His mere presence made her feel strong and brave.

"Well?" Cassius said. "What do you think?"

Dacia had been so focused on the possible appearance of Claudia that she hadn't been paying attention. But Cassius was holding a gorgeous ring in front of her, one made from gold fashioned into glorious, intricate designs. The entire ring was like that, all the way around the band, and at the crest was an enormous diamond.

It was absolutely spectacular.

"Oh… Cassius," she said in awe, plucking it from his fingers to get a good look at it. "It is the most beautiful ring I have ever seen."

He watched her face as she inspected it. "Do you like it, then?"

She nodded eagerly. "I do, but it must be quite expensive," she said, looking at the other rings that were on the table before them, each one sitting upon different colored pieces of silk. "The one with the amethyst is beautiful, too."

She was indicating a much smaller, far less elaborate ring. He ignored her, took the ring from her hand, and slipped it onto her wedding finger. It was a little snug, but it fit well enough.

"Look," he said. "The ring was made for you. It fits."

Dacia looked at the enormous diamond ring on her finger. "But it is so big."

He wouldn't hear her argument. "It is a suitable ring for a future duchess," he said. "And it is exactly what my wife deserves. I will have you in nothing less."

"A diamond will represent your strength and loyalty to your husband, my lady," the clerk said timidly. "It is a ring to be greatly admired."

Dacia wasn't sure she wanted a ring to be admired, but Cassius seemed so certain about it, so she simply nodded. In truth, it was a magnificent ring. He held her hand up, watching the ring catch the light.

"Are you sure?" she said to Cassius. "I am sure we can look at other rings. Smaller. Less expensive. I do not need a massive ring, Cassius."

He looked at the clerk. "We shall take this one," he said, completely ignoring her protests. "But I will look at other rings for her. She has ten fingers, after all. She should have a ring for each one."

Dacia could only giggle at him. He was being thoughtful and excessive, a potentially dangerous combination for a man's purse, but he didn't seem to care in the least. He started pawing through the other rings presented, including the one with the amethyst, which he liked very much. Dacia watched him hold the rings up to the light and inspect them.

"I always thought it was a strange custom for the woman to wear a ring symbolizing her loyalty to one man, but a man does not wear a ring symbolizing his loyalty to one woman," she said. "History abounds with male lovers giving their female lovers a ring, but you do not see men wearing any rings at all."

Cassius was looking at a ring with a brown stone on it. "Would you like for me to wear one?"

"Of course not. I was simply making an observation."

Cassius set the ring down and looked at the clerk. "Do you have any rings for men?"

The clerk looked surprised. "Elaborate and bejeweled, my lord," he said. "They would not be suitable for a fighting man."

"Why not?"

"Because they are enormous, my lord," the clerk insisted.

"Unless you wish to use them as another weapon."

That brought a chuckle from Cassius. "Nay, I do not wish to do that," he said. "But she is right. Women are expected to show their loyalty, but men are not. I should like for you to do something for me."

"Anything you wish, my lord."

Reaching out, he pulled the ring off of Dacia's finger and handed it to the clerk. "You will put my name on this ring, on the inside, so all will know who she belongs to," he said. "My name is Cassius, so make sure it is clear. As for me... measure the same finger on my hand that she is wearing the ring on and make me a gold circlet. Just a simple golden band, smooth and strong. You will inscribe her name on the inside, so all will know to whom I belong. Her name is Dacia."

Dacia smiled at him, at his sweet and utterly romantic gesture as the clerk went to find something to measure his finger with. When he was gone, she spoke quietly.

"Are you certain you want to wear it?" she said. "Men do not wear such things."

"My grandfather did, as I recall," he said. "It suddenly occurred to me that I saw him wear a ring my grandmother had given him, years after they'd been married. She wore a very simple ring that he'd given her and years after the fact, she gave him one also. When my father asked her why, she said because she wanted him to wear her heart as she wore his. I am happy to wear your heart, Dacia."

It was one of the most touching things Dacia had ever heard. "That is such a sweet gesture," she said, leaning against him affectionately. "I have a book from the Far East, something that was left to me by my tutor, and it is all about the love between men and women. There is one passage in it that has always stayed with me."

"What is that?"

She looked at the big diamond ring on the table before picking it up, inspecting it. "The world moves for love," she murmured. "That is what it says – that the world moves for love. It does, doesn't it?"

"My world does," Cassius murmured. "It moves for your love. Tell me again that you love me."

Immediately, her cheeks flushed red and he laughed softly, giving her hot cheek an affectionate stroke. But he did no more than that, not wanting to make a spectacle in public, even though he very much wanted to kiss her.

The clerk returned, distracting them from each other as he measured Cassius' finger with a marked ribbon. Then, Dacia watched in horror as Cassius paid an enormous sum for the diamond ring, but when it came to his ring – the simple gold band – he paid the clerk almost as much.

But he had a purpose in mind.

"How soon can you have these rings finished?" he asked.

The clerk put the money, all of it, into a pouch under his table. "At least two days, my lord," he said. "Three, more than likely."

"Make it in two days, including the name etching, and I shall pay another silver coin," he said. "Can you do it?"

The clerk nodded firmly. "Aye, my lord."

"Good," Cassius said, rising to his feet. "I do not know where your master went, but thank him and tell him that I shall return in two days for both of those rings."

As the clerk nodded, Cassius took Dacia by the elbow and escorted her outside. Rhori and Bose were standing by their mounts, watching some pretty women down the avenue. The women were flirting and the men were watching, like hunters sighting prey. Cassius had to slap Bose on the back to get the man's attention.

"Our business is concluded," he said, taking Dacia to her palfrey. "Now, we must find the best merchant in town and make some additional purchases."

Before Bose could reply, Dacia caught sight of someone that she recognized and she stopped Cassius from lifting her up onto her palfrey.

"Wait," she said. "Look over there. It is Old Timeo and his wife. She looks much better. Let me inquire on her health, and then we may continue."

With Cassius remaining with his knights, Dacia walked across the avenue, lifting her skirts to keep the dust off the hem as Argos, not to be left behind this time, followed alongside her. The old man and his wife were at a smithy stall across the street, evidently having a piece of farming equipment looked at or repaired. They didn't see Dacia until she was standing next to them.

"Good day to you," Dacia said pleasantly, looking at the man's wife. "You appear much better today, Leoba. How is your daughter faring?"

The old man and his wife looked at Dacia, startled by her appearance. But very quickly, it seemed to be more than that. They obviously moved away, putting distance between them.

He began backing off.

"All is well, my lady," Old Timeo said as his wife got in behind him, putting her husband between her and Dacia. "Everyone is well."

Dacia wasn't blind. She could see that they were shrinking away from her and it occurred to her that there could only be one reason – it was because she wasn't covered with her veils like she usually was.

Old Timeo was afraid of her marks.

Her heart sank.

"I... I am glad to know that," she said, lowering her chin, going into self-protection mode to hide her face. "Should you need any further help, please send for me. I suspect that the problem may be... a worm."

They didn't even hear her last two words. They were too busy scurrying away from her as fast as they could go. Feeling deeply ashamed and embarrassed, Dacia went back to her escort and mounted her palfrey before Cassius could help her.

He had been standing with Rhori and Bose in quiet conversation, surprised when she returned so quickly. She jumped on her horse before he could lend a hand and when he reached her, he could see that she was close to tears.

She was looking at her lap again.

"Angel?" he said quietly. "What is the matter?"

She shook her head. "Can we please return home?" she whispered tightly. "I... I do not wish to go to the merchant's stall today."

His brow furrowed. "Why not?"

"I just don't," she said. "Not today. Please, Cassius... I want to go home."

He didn't move. He leaned forward, onto the saddle, trying to look her in the eyes. But she wouldn't lift her head to look at him.

"Dacia," he murmured. "Tell me what happened. Why are you troubled?"

The tears began to come, then. "Old Timeo and his wife ran from me because I am not covered," she said. "It was a mistake for me not to wear my veils, Cassius. Please... I want to go home before I face any further humiliation."

His heart sank, just a little. He looked down the street to see the old man and his wife, nearly to the village walls by now on their way out of town. Reaching up, he clasped her hands in his big, gloved mitt.

"Did they say anything to you?" he asked gently. "Did they tell you that you should be covered?"

She was starting to weep, struggling desperately not to embarrass herself. "Nay," she said. "But the way they looked at me... and then they ran... they did not need to say anything. Their actions were enough."

Cassius was proud of her for coming into town without her usual covering. She showed great courage when he forced her out of her comfort zone. But he could see that he had pushed her too far. He couldn't control the actions of a few village idiots and he didn't want to subject her to anything more she might consider embarrassment, so he squeezed her hands and let them go.

"Very well," he said. "If you want to return home, then we shall. Mayhap you will feel like going to the merchant when we return to collect our rings."

She simply nodded, wiping at the corner of her eye, and he felt like a monster for forcing her into town without the comfort she was used to. It was a learning process for them both, but he knew she would do whatever he asked her to do, whether or not she was comfortable with it, simply to please him. And, being a man who was used to having his way in all things, he didn't even realize it until they had moments like this.

Now, he felt terrible.

Turning for his horse, he lifted a hand to Rhori and Bose.

"We are returning to the castle," he said. "I... I suppose I am feeling a bit weary. I think I have had enough excitement for today."

No one questioned him. They assumed the lady's upset was because of Cassius' condition, so Rhori and Bose began moving the escort out, heading back the way they had come.

Dacia kept her head down. It seemed that people were still looking at her, pointing and whispering, and now she knew that it was because she wasn't covered up. She couldn't even bring herself to look at anyone, more ashamed than she had ever been in her life. Mayhap she could go out in public, in any other city, without covering on her face, but here in Doncaster... there was history here, with people knowing about the duke's marked granddaughter.

She was glad to be going home.

The escort moved towards the gate, passing from the avenue of the smithies and coming upon the church. Dacia wasn't paying any attention to her surroundings, too afraid that someone might see her freckles and run away from her, so she kept her head down, following the knights with the soldiers riding around her. She was counting the seconds until they were able to get free of the town.

But that countdown stopped when someone was blocking their path.

"Halt!" someone shouted. "Dacia of Doncaster, you will show yourself!"

Dacia's head shot up. She had to look around Cassius' enormous form, since he was directly in front of her, but she could see one of the priests from St. George's blocking the escort. Curious, she reined her palfrey forward.

"I am Dacia," she said. "I have seen you before. You are new to St. George's."

The priest was tall, with silver hair, dressed in immaculate brown woolen robes. He pointed to the ground.

"They told me you had come to town," he said. "Get off your horse, Woman. Come here and face me."

"You will address her as Lady Dacia, Priest," Cassius growled. "Use that tone with her again and you'll not like my reaction. She remains on her horse until I say otherwise. What do you want?"

The priest lifted his chin at Cassius, looking him over. "Who are you?"

"Sir Cassius de Wolfe," Cassius answered without hesitation. "My master is King Edward himself, as I hold the position of Lord Protector to the king. Now, who are you and why are you making demands of the lady?"

He said it in the most unfriendly way possible, conveying to the priest the pain and anguish the man would suffer if he continued along his present path where Dacia was concerned. Even Argos, who had been so contentedly traveling beside Dacia, trotted forward and growled at the priest. But the priest wasn't looking at the dog; he was looking at Cassius.

"Then it is you," he said. "*You* are the one. You will come here and face me, also."

Cassius was becoming exasperated. He had no idea what the man was talking about. "Get out of my way," he said. "If you do not move, I will trample you, so it would be best to do as I say."

He started to move forward, as did the rest of the column, but that seemed to throw the priest over the edge. He backed up, but he didn't get out of the way.

"You cannot run and you cannot hide, Dacia of Doncaster," he boomed. "I know your dark soul and if you do not repent immediately, hell awaits you!"

Cassius looked at Bose, who was off his horse in a flash, grabbing the priest by the neck and tossing the man aside. But at this point, there were other priests who had heard the yelling and had come to see what the fuss was about. As Bose manhandled a priest who was surprisingly strong and resistant, Dacia saw a priest that she recognized.

Father Lazarus had been with St. George's as long as Dacia had been alive and he knew her grandfather well. It was Father Lazarus who put up his hands, trying desperately to prevent Bose from breaking the neck of the silver-haired priest. Confused and concerned by what was going on, Dacia reined her palfrey to a halt.

"Wait, Cass," she said. "Something is not right. Wait a moment, please."

She was off her horse before he could stop her, making her way over to Father Lazarus as Bose and the silver-haired priest began throwing punches. Concerned that Dacia might get caught up in something unpleasant, Cassius bailed off his horse and followed her, avoiding Bose as the priest kicked the man hard enough to send him onto one knee. A full-scale brawl was erupting between de Shera and the priest as Dacia and Cassius made their way over to the priest that Dacia recognized.

"Father Lazarus?" she said, apprehension in her voice. "What is happening? Who is that priest and why should he speak to me so?"

Father Lazarus was an old man who had seen a good deal in life. He knew all about Dacia and her grandfather, and he shared a good relationship with them. He never believed in Dacia's witch's marks even if some people had, but he was a man without a big voice. He was a rather timid soul, quiet and unassuming, and was therefore at the bottom of the hierarchy of priests at St. George's. But he pulled Dacia away from the fight going on, pulling her away from the ears of the others.

"We had heard you'd come to town, my lady," he said. "I was hoping to see you before Father Alfrick did."

"Father Alfrick?" Dacia repeated, bewildered. "Do you mean the man who shouted at us?"

Father Lazarus nodded. "Aye," he said. "Lady Dacia... I am not sure how to say this, but people in the town have been spreading rumors and I am sure they are lies, but the people of this town are unfortunate sinners. They like to listen to idle tongues who have nothing better to do but vilify the innocent."

Dacia still didn't understand and neither did Cassius. "What idle tongues, Father?" he asked. "Who are people speaking of?"

Father Lazarus had to jump aside when Bose and his priest rolled past him, fists swinging. But his focus remained on Dacia.

"They are speaking of you, my lady," he said as quietly as he could. "They are saying that you stole your cousin's intended by fornicating with him. It is also being said that you bore a bastard infant last year and buried his little body in the garden."

Dacia's eyes opened wide and she clapped a hand over her mouth in horror. "My God," she hissed. "The villagers are saying such things about *me*?"

As Father Lazarus nodded, Cassius grabbed the man by the arm, his big fingers biting in. "Who is saying these things, Father?" he demanded. "You will tell me immediately who is spreading this slander."

Father Lazarus looked at him without fear, an enormous knight with piercingly pale eyes. "I heard you give your name to

Father Alfrick," he said. "You are part of these slanderous lies, I am afraid. I have heard the name of de Wolfe spoken."

Dacia was beside herself with shock and dismay. "Not him," she said. "He has nothing to do with anything. But I do not understand... the only time I have come to town is to attend mass and then I return home again. I have not seen or spoken to anyone at all."

Father Lazarus wasn't without sympathy. "Even so, that is what is being said," he said. "I am afraid that by the time it reaches us, everyone in town knows about it."

Dacia just stared at him, unsure how to react to what she was being told, but something in what he said was sticking with her.

A clue as to where this all came from.

"You said that they are saying I stole my cousin's intended?" she asked.

Father Lazarus' gaze moved to Cassius. "Aye, my lady," he said. "As I said, the name de Wolfe has been spoken."

The color left Dacia's face. She looked at Cassius, who was gazing back at her with anger that was smoldering in his expression. She could tell just by looking at him that he was close to exploding. But she also knew, in her heart of hearts, where this had come from.

Who it had come from.

You have stolen your cousin's intended by fornicating with him.

Dacia had never been more disgusted or angry in her entire life.

"No wonder Old Timeo and his wife ran from me," she said, her voice starting to tremble. "They must have heard this, something that could only have come from Amata. She is the only one who would say such things, especially about you, Cass. She's the only one who knows about you, so it has to be her. Isn't it, Father Lazarus?"

She was looking at the priest by now, but he didn't want to give away too much. There was a certain confidentiality he was expected to keep, even with his gossiping flock but, in this case, he was reconsidering that stance. He knew Amata de Branton, too, and a more spiteful creature did not exist.

Especially when it came to her cousin.

Aye... he knew the history.

"She was in town when the rumors started," he said after a moment. "I do not know if they came from her because she did not speak of it to me directly, but I heard that she is the one you stole from."

Dacia closed her eyes to the reality of the situation, sickened by it, before looking to Cassius. "Now I know why she left Edenthorpe so swiftly," she said. "She came to town and told her friends all of her lies, which they, in turn, spread around the entire village. Cassius, I am so sorry for this. I knew Amata was angry and I surely did not care, but I did not think she would go this far."

Cassius wasn't sure what to do at that point. He was beyond furious, but they were dealing with a malicious young woman. Not a man he could fight or kill, but a spurned, spoiled young woman who was trying to ruin them both in the eyes of the villagers of Doncaster. He'd seen his share of petty women in his life, and there seemed to be an abundance of them in London, but he'd never heard of anything like this. He tipped his helm back, trying to restrain the powerful sense of revenge he was feeling.

"You needn't apologize for her," he said. "She has made her

choice. I shall have to make mine."

Dacia wasn't sure she liked that. "What do you mean?" she said. "You cannot harm her, Cass. I know she is a mean-spirited and vindictive, but you cannot harm her."

He looked at her sharply, offended by the mere suggestion that he might go to such lengths. But he had to remind himself that they hadn't known each other that long. All she knew was that he was the king's Lord Protector, a seasoned knight with a brutal reputation. With a heavy sigh, he shook his head.

"I have never lifted a hand or a sword to a woman and I never will," he said. "But Amata and her lies cannot go without punishment."

Father Lazarus intervened; he had to. The knight's sense of justice was building this into something that would not go in their favor. "My lord, if you punish her, it will appear as if you are trying to silence her."

Cassius looked at the man as if he were an idiot. "I *am*."

The priest shook his head. "Nay, that is not what I mean," he said. "I mean that it makes you look cruel and barbaric, as if you are preventing her from telling the truth about you. Does that make sense?"

It did, but Cassius was still exasperated. "But it is *not* the truth," he said. "She is spouting lies because I rejected her and for no other reason than that. She had an interest in me, but I had no interest in her, and now she is punishing us for it. My attention has been, and always will be, on Dacia, who has done no wrong. She is completely innocent in all of this."

Father Lazarus nodded. "I assumed as much," he said. "Dacia and her grandfather are kind and good. Everyone knows that but, unfortunately, they are swayed by rumors and gossip. Most weak-souled people are."

Dacia was looking at Cassius, wondering what the man was going to do. She could see how angry he was and she was deeply touched by his willingness to punish Amata.

But she couldn't let him do it.

"Father Lazarus is correct," she said softly. "Though I adore you for wanting to protect me and my reputation, if you confront Amata, it will only make things worse. She will tell everyone you tried to intimidate and threaten her, or worse. She has the ear of the people in this village and always has."

Cassius looked at her, his expression between rage and knowing she was right. "Dacia…"

She cut him off, gently. "It is true," she said. "I've known it all along, for when I was younger, I was friends with many of the girls in the village. One day, they all decided to shun me. I no longer had any friends. Amata told me that it was because they were afraid of the marks on my face, but I know it was because Amata turned them against me. Edie told me that, but she really didn't need to. I knew. So this is just one more web of lies in a forest of lies that Amata has told against me."

Cassius could see that beaten young woman again and he didn't like it. He hated it. It made him want to sell Amata to the pirates and burn her house down. But he knew, deep down, that she was right. So was the priest.

He couldn't do a thing about it or his actions would prove Amata's lies.

"Then tell your grandfather what she has done," he said, sounding as if he were pleading with her. "Surely he can repair the damage."

"And have him fight my battles for me?" Dacia said. Then, she shook her head. "I must learn to fight my own battles, Cass. You have taught me that and it is a lesson I have been learning, quite nicely. I will deal with Amata in my own way."

Cassius didn't know what that meant, but it exasperated him. The whole situation exasperated him. As he shook his head, frustrated, Bose happened to walk past him, a bloodied nose and a cut above his eye. But he was walking tall and proud, as if he hadn't just beat up on a priest, who was sitting on the steps of the church, hand on his head. As Cassius watched him walk back to the horses, Father Lazarus spoke.

"All of the priests know what has been said," he said, mostly to Dacia. "Some believe you have been fornicating with this knight, so marrying the man immediately will ease their outrage, at least for that. But the rumor about the dead baby is another issue altogether."

Dacia stared at the man. "I will not marry him immediately simply to ease their outrage," she said angrily. "I will not be coerced into anything by those faithless fools."

Cassius turned to look at her. "Angel, if it will ease the situation, then…"

She cut him off with surprising strength. "I told you that I will not do it," she said, her rage returning to Father Lazarus. "I refused to be pushed into anything by those men who have nothing better to do than listen to idle gossip."

Father Lazarus could see that she was quite enraged. "My lady, it is the only solution," he said. "Right now, some of priests are considering sanctioning your grandfather as well as you, preventing you both from taking communion or praying within these walls. They are even considering sending word to the bishopric of York to investigate you, and something like that will only lead to heartache and terror. You cannot allow that to happen."

She was nearly irate. "Investigate me for *what*?"

Father Lazarus didn't dare look at the enormous knight. "The situation with the baby," he said. "They want it to be considered a crime. A murder."

Dacia's hand flew to her mouth and a sob escaped. "You cannot be serious."

"I wish I wasn't. With God as my witness, I wish I wasn't."

Tears filled her eyes. "But... but I have never even been with a man in that sense," she said tightly. "There has never *been* a baby. Amata is lying, covering up for the fact that she has bedded more men than she can count on her fingers and toes. She is trying to punish me and punish Cass because we love one another. Amata's lies *are* the crime."

Father Lazarus wasn't unsympathetic. "I know, my child," he said gently. "And there are others here who know, but there are still others who believe the lies. If you marry de Wolfe, then he can take you away from all of this. A marriage will be seen as a husband gaining control of you. Mayhap he can take you from Doncaster and you can start a life where people do not speak against you."

Dacia was devastated. "I am *not* marrying him for that reason," she said. "Why would I punish him so when these terrible things are being said about me? Why would I do that to him?"

Cassius stepped in. He had to because the situation was veering out of control. Dacia was veering out of control. He put himself between Dacia and the priest, his big hands on Dacia's arms.

"Breathe, angel," he said softly. "Calm yourself. We can work through this, but I need your level head."

Unfortunately, Dacia was beyond that. The lies, the far-reaching implications of what had happened were not lost on her. Amata had set out to ruin her.

And she had.

But she couldn't let her ruin Cassius.

"Cassius, I am sorry, but I will not be forced into a marriage under these terms," she said, weeping. "Don't you see? We cannot start our marriage to comply with Amata's lies. She knew this when she spread these rumors. If we marry, then it makes it look like she was right."

"It does not."

"You heard the priest," she said. "They want me to marry you to stop the rumors. If we do that, it is as good as confirming them."

Cassius held on to her, afraid of what would happen if he let her go. "Dacia, listen to me," he said calmly. "We would not be confirming anything, but if it shuts up the gossip mongers, I am willing to do it."

Her tears were flowing all down her face. "You wanted to get married at Berwick Castle, with your family around you," she sobbed. "You said it yourself. That is what you wanted to do and what I wanted to do, but now... Cass, I cannot marry you, not when I am the focus of such terrible things. You are a man with a pristine reputation. You cannot marry a woman with a lesser reputation than you. It would tarnish that which you have worked so hard for."

His brow furrowed. "This is madness, Dacia," he said. "Doncaster is not the world. It is only a small part of England. No one else cares what these people think."

"But I do," she said, wiping the tears as fast as they fell. "It is *my* world. If you marry me, it will be your world, too."

He was trying not to get into an argument with her. "You are overwrought," he said, hoping against hope to stop her momentum. "Let us return to Edenthorpe. Tomorrow, the outlook will be different."

Unfortunately, Dacia wasn't listening to him. She pulled away from him, out of arm's length.

"Nay, Cass," she said. "I cannot do that to you. I cannot let them ruin you like they are trying to ruin me. It is not fair to you. I love you too much to let that happen."

At first, Cassius had been in genuine disbelief about the entire situation. But now, he was feeling real fear. Dacia was afraid he would be hurt by his association to her and it cut him to the bone.

"They cannot hurt me, angel," he said steadily. "We must stand strong together. That is the only way we can triumph in the end."

Dacia was backing away from them. "You are a strong, talented knight," she said, tears and mucus running down her face. "You are *my* knight. You said that Doncaster is a tiny part of this world but, in a sense, I *am* Doncaster. These lands have belonged to my family for hundreds of years. I can never leave it, so I must stay and face this crisis, but I will do it on my own. I do not want you singed by the fire that burns around me. And if the church becomes involved, I cannot let you be touched by that. Please, Cass... above all else, you must stay safe. These horrors are mine and mine alone."

He was starting to feel sick to his stomach. "I will not leave you," he said. "What they say cannot hurt us as long as we remain strong, together."

"Nay, Cass."

"If I go, then Amata wins. Is that what you want?"

She shook her head, her lower lip trembling. "Nay," she murmured. "But I cannot let you be hurt by what she has done.

You have my heart; you always will. I love you as the moon loves the night, as the stars love the darkness. But because I love you, I will not marry you."

With that, she turned and ran back to her palfrey as Cassius followed. She leapt onto her little horse, tears soaking the veil around her neck and chest, and spurred the little beast onward with Argos running after her. She was galloping by the time she hit the gate, heading out on the road that led to the castle.

Cassius boomed at the escort, sending the soldiers after her as he collected Old Man and pursued. Outside of the village walls, they kept an eye on her up ahead, all the way into Edenthorpe's bailey.

Even then, Dacia was too fast for Cassius. She flew off her horse and ran into the keep before he could stop her. He followed as quickly as he could, ending up in front of her barred chamber door with Argos sitting outside of it, waiting patiently to be let in. But no amount of pounding or pleading could coax Dacia into opening that door. Cassius spent two straight days sitting at her door, begging her to let him in.

On the beginning of the third day, he knew that his future was slipping away from him no matter how hard he tried to hold on.

With his back against her chamber door, the tears finally came.

And a fragile heart was shattered.

CHAPTER SEVENTEEN

Silverdale Manor
Two Weeks Later

H E'D JUST RETURNED from mass at St. George's.
Hugh de Branton left his horse in the small stable
yard, tended to by a servant. As he made his way across the
bailey, his gaze moved to the manse that had belonged to his
family for three generations. Big, squat, and covered in vines, it
had always been a house of honor and comfort.

But that's not what it was now.

Now, the chaos within was starting to make sense.

Amata had refused to come to mass for a couple of weeks
now, ever since her visit to Edenthorpe to see her cousin had
been cut short. His daughter, usually so bold and vocal,
wouldn't tell him why. She had sequestered herself, hardly
coming out of her chamber, hardly visiting with her father,
which she usually did gleefully and on a regular basis. As of late,
she seemed subdued, avoiding eye contact, avoiding conversation. It seemed to him that she was trying to stay clear of him
for some reason.

Now, Hugh knew why.

His daughter had been hiding something.

He entered the manse, through the cool and dark entry, heading up the mural stairs to the floor above. This was the level where the bedchambers were, at least most of them, and his daughter occupied a chamber on the northwest corner. He made his way to that room, knocking on the door with more restraint than he felt.

He had his anger in check, but barely.

"Amata?" he called. "Amata, are you there?"

"I am, Papa."

Hugh could hear footsteps coming towards the door and the bolt was thrown. The panel opened and Hugh was faced with his daughter's pretty face. More surprising to him, however, was the fact that there was someone in the chamber with her, a young woman he recognized, whose father was one of the premier goldsmiths in town.

Claudia Lockwood stood up and curtsied when she saw Amata's father.

"My lady," Hugh greeted, but his focus turned to his daughter. "I was unaware that you had a visitor."

Amata smiled timidly. "Just Claudia, Papa. She has come to visit."

Hugh eyed the goldsmith's daughter. "She is welcome, of course," he said, but returned his attention to his daughter. "Amata, I must speak to you. Privately, if I may."

Amata looked a little uncertain, but she agreed, stepping out into the corridor and shutting the door behind her. But it didn't shut all the way. It was open just enough for Amata's visitor to hear everything that was said. Amata hadn't planned it that way, and had she known what her father was about to say, she would have made sure that Claudia was nowhere near that cracked door.

But that oversight was to be her grave mistake.

"Aye, Papa?" Amata said. "What is it?"

Hugh was genuinely trying to hold his temper. "I have just come from mass."

"I know, Papa."

Hugh held up a finger in a knowing gesture. "You have not come with me to mass for several weeks now," he said. "You have been pleading fatigue and illness, but now I see that you have a visitor today."

Amata nodded hesitantly. "Claudia came this morning, after you left," she said. "I am surprised you did not see her on the road."

Hugh just looked at her for a few moments, pondering what he was going to say next. There was so much he needed to say that it was difficult to know where to start.

"I did not," he said. "But it is of little matter. Something interesting happened in town today."

"What do you mean?"

"I mean that I was approached after mass by Father Lazarus," he said. "Evidently, there is a good deal going on with you that I was unaware of, and all of it centering around that de Wolfe knight I would not invite to Silverdale."

Something rippled through her expression. He could see it. He thought it might have been fear or shock, but he couldn't be certain.

"What do you mean, Papa?" she said, sounding innocent. "Do you mean Cassius de Wolfe?"

"I mean Cassius de Wolfe."

Amata shrugged. "I have nothing to do with him."

Hugh shook his head. "That is not true," he said. "From what I've been told, you were betrothed to the man until Dacia stole him away by seducing him."

Amata's breathing began to quicken as she began to lose control of the conversation. "Who told you that?" she demanded. "I haven't even seen the man!"

"That is also not true," Hugh said. "You went to Edenthorpe two weeks ago to visit Dacia, you claimed, but I knew you were going there to see that knight. Did he propose marriage to you, Amata?"

Amata was caught and sinking fast. She averted her gaze, backing away from her father. "He... he was glad to see me, of course, but..."

"Did he propose marriage to you and did not have the decency to ask my permission?"

Amata took another step back but Hugh reached out and grabbed her wrist so she couldn't get away. She flinched. "Papa, you're hurting me!"

Hugh yanked on her, pulling her towards him. "He did not propose marriage to you, did he?"

Amata's eyes were filling with tears as the petulant little girl began to emerge. "You would not invite him here so I could have a chance to entertain him. You would not give me the chance to prove how witty and charming I can be!"

Hugh's rage was starting to build. "Give me the truth or I shall lock you up in the vault and leave you there until you decide to be honest," he seethed. "*Tell me!*"

"Nay!" Amata burst into tears. "He did not propose marriage."

"But you told everyone he did, am I to understand that?" Hugh said. "Worse still, you have told everyone that Dacia seduced the man away from you, is this correct?"

Amata was already sobbing. "He kissed her. I saw it!"

"*Where* did he kiss her, Amata?"

"On… on her hand. But he still kissed her!"

"And you equate that to her seducing him?"

Amata's sobbing was growing louder. "Papa, you're hurting my wrist," she wept. "Please let go."

Hugh was too furious to release her. "I will not let go until you tell me what you have done," he said. "There are rumors all about the village that Dacia stole your betrothed and even worse than that, there are rumors that she bore a child and buried it in the garden. Do you know that the church is considering bringing murder charges against her for that?"

Amata's eyes opened wide. "Murder?" she sputtered. "I… I did not know…"

"Then you told that lie?"

"I… I…"

"*Tell me!*"

Amata howled because he shook her, bruising her flesh. "I did!" she cried. "I did and I am not sorry! She stole Cassius away from me and she knew that I wanted him!"

Hugh was so angry that his entire face was red. "So you spread these lies to turn people against her?"

"To punish her!" Amata screamed, spittle flying from her lips. "I wanted Cassius and she stole him!"

Hugh watched his daughter weep, fluid spilling from every part of her face. He was so angry that he was actually afraid of what he might do to her.

But that wouldn't solve the problem.

He'd just come from a village that was whispering about Dacia and her witch's marks, and how she was truly a witch because she used her powers to seduce Amata's betrothed and sacrificed her own baby to the devil. Hugh knew as soon as Father Lazarus told him that it was untrue and he also knew where the rumors had come from. There had been no doubt. He suspected that Father Lazarus knew it, too.

Amata.

But this was the last time it was going to happen.

He'd had enough of his daughter's lies.

"No more, Amata," he said. Then, he lashed out a foot and kicked open the chamber door, smacking Claudia in the arm because she had been eavesdropping. "You! Go home and tell your parents that everything you told them about Dacia of Doncaster is a lie. Do you hear me? If you do not, you shall never be welcome here again!"

Claudia whimpered and fled. Hugh didn't bother watching her go. He was more interested in his hysterical daughter.

"And you," he said, his voice filled with disgust. "You are coming with me."

He began to drag her towards the stairs. She tried to dig her heels in, but it was to no avail. Hugh was stronger, and bigger, and easily pulled her along.

"Papa, please!" she cried, trying to hold on to the walls as he tugged. "Please do not put me in the vault!"

Hugh had her on the stairs. She didn't want to go down, so she sat, and he ended up pulling her all the way down on her arse.

"I am not taking you to the vault," he said. "I am taking you to St. George's, where you will tell the priests what you have done. You are going to tell everyone in the village that you have lied against Dacia and that she has done nothing of which you have accused her."

When Amata realized that, she began to weep loudly again, trying to kick her father to force him to release her.

"Nay, Papa, please!" she wept. "I cannot shame myself so!"

Hugh had to heave because she was showing surprising strength. "If you feel any shame at all, then you will know how Dacia feels," Hugh said, catching a flailing foot. They had reached the bottom of the steps and instead of dragging her by the arm, he was pulling her by a leg, all the way across the wooden floor. "I have let your wickedness go on for too long, Amata. Your jealousies have ruined you, but you are going to start making amends. I do not know if you can undo the damage you have caused but, by God, you are going to try. And then, I am going to take you to Edenthorpe where you will apologize to your cousin for what you have done."

Amata was screaming, trying to hold on to furniture or walls, anything she could, to prevent her father from dragging her from the manse and taking her into town. But everything was slipping from her grasp.

Everything.

Hugh ended up dragging her across the bailey, all the way into the stables where he forced the stable servant to find a measure of rope. He used it to secure his daughter's hands and feet so she wouldn't run away, and then he put her over his horse and took her into town tied up like a hunting trophy.

Once they reached the village, he took her into St. George's where he forced her to confess her lies to Father Lazarus and Father Alfrick, among others. He forced her to confess every little lie she'd ever told, and the big ones, too. It was the priests who forced her to confess those same lies to the worshippers who came to attend vespers. Amata was a sobbing, exhausted, dirty mess by then, but Hugh showed no mercy and neither did the priests.

She would reap what she sowed.

Father Lazarus, in particular, was especially angry.

God frowned upon the wicked, and Amata's confessions had revealed that she was the most wicked of all. So in penitence, they left her sitting in the sanctuary, all night, so she could confess her sins to those who arrived at dawn for matins. Amata was forced to humiliate herself in front of the entire village, including Old Timeo and his family, and Hugh finally untied his daughter and dragged her exhausted carcass over to Edenthorpe to perform the last of her penitence for this most egregious sin.

There was someone else she needed to apologize to. After all of these years of her lies and malicious behavior, Amata was finally forced to confront what she'd done to a woman who had never hurt anyone in her life. But Hugh seriously wondered if the damage caused by his daughter this time could even be undone.

They were about to find out.

CHAPTER EIGHTEEN

Edenthorpe Castle

"DACIA?"

Darian had been knocking at her door for several minutes before finally being bold enough to open the door and stick his head in. The first person he saw was Edie, sitting near the hearth in the large chamber, sewing on a piece of yellow fabric. He didn't see any of the other maids, who were usually bustling around the chamber.

But these days, nothing was usual.

Dacia herself wasn't usual.

It had been a difficult and uncertain time, ever since the day that Dacia had returned from town with Cassius and locked herself up in her chamber. There had been a good deal of banging as Cassius had pounded at her door on that day, begging her to open it, but Dacia didn't comply. It was the first time in her relationship with Cassius that she didn't do what he wanted her to do.

He wanted her to open the door.

Darian was understandably curious as to what was going

on. He'd asked Bose, who had told him to mind his own business, but Rhori had taken him aside and explained about the rumors and about the priests, everything Cassius had told him about the situation. At least, as much as he could while they had been riding like the wind as they had departed from Doncaster. Rhori didn't know all of it, or why Dacia wouldn't speak with Cassius, but something serious had happened between them.

Something tragic.

At first, Darian had been secretly glad. He had been hoping that Cassius was only a passing fancy and it seemed that he had been correct. He saw renewed hope in his quest for Dacia that had been shattered by Cassius' pursuit. But the more the days passed, and the more Cassius would not leave Dacia's door until she opened it, the more Darian began to feel some guilt for gloating in Cassius' failure. The man was clearly broken up over what had happened, so Darian began snapping at the men who would comment on the situation. It wasn't any of their affair, he would tell them.

And the vigil went on.

The duke, having been told of the situation by Rhori, went to see Cassius as the man camped at Dacia's door. Cassius told him everything, the rumors and the lies, and Doncaster was sick over it. He never involved himself in the trials or tribulations of others and had, thus far, kept himself out of the situation between Amata and Dacia. Somehow, they always seemed to work things out, or so he believed. But the latest rumors from Amata's lips were beyond what he believed the girl capable of.

Now, he was involved.

Mostly, he was involved with Cassius, who was grief-stricken by Dacia's solution to the situation. The duke didn't agree with her and tried to tell her so through the closed chamber door, but she never answered him. She never answered the door, not even when he demanded it. The situation went on for two agonizing days and by the third day, Cassius seemed to resign himself to the inevitable.

But it was with a good deal of anger and resentment.

After almost three days of banging on Dacia's door and demanding that she open it, Cassius finally left for good, going to his borrowed chamber and packing his belongings. His movements were crisp and silent, and Rhori and Bose packed along with him. They had a destination that had been put off long enough and Cassius decided that it was a good day to continue their journey to Castle Questing.

Without another word, he left.

But Rhori had spoken to Darian just before leaving, telling the man that he would keep him appraised of their movements in case Dacia came to her senses. Perhaps there was hope, perhaps there was none at all, but it seemed that Dacia was truly convinced that sending Cassius away and breaking their betrothal was the only way to protect him against the accusations against her. Still, no one really knew what she was thinking because she wouldn't tell anyone.

Now, it had been that way for two long weeks, but a few moments ago all of that had changed. Amata and her father had arrived, bearing news, and the duke had sent Darian up to Dacia's chamber.

But he approached her with the same caution as one would approach a wild lion.

Both Dacia and the lion, in his opinion, were unpredictable creatures.

When he finally opened the door and spied Edie, the old

woman's head came up, looking at him with wide eyes, and silently they communicated with gestures and expressions as to whether or not this was a good time for him to communicate with Dacia.

Edie finally motioned him in.

"'Tis good to see you, Sir Darian," she said, her voice elevated so Dacia could hear her. "It is a fine day today, is it not?"

Darian stepped into the chamber, but he was coiled, ready to run for his life if Dacia came flying at him.

"It is a fine day," he agreed. "I do believe it is going to be a warm and dry summer. The temperatures are rising and we've not seen any rain, so I fear we are looking at a dusty season to come."

Edie set aside the sewing in her hands, a beautiful yellow piece. "I can remember in years past when we've had such dry summers," she said. "But come September, the rains will come heavily."

They were speaking casually, knowing Dacia was somewhere about, wanting her to hear them so she wouldn't be startled by his appearance.

"They will," he agreed. Then, he gestured to the sewing she had set aside. "It looks as if you are making something lovely. Mayhap for the warm weather to come?"

Edie held up the piece. "Aye," she said. "'Twill be a lovely frock for my lady. In fact, I've been going through her clothing and pulling out the heavier garments to pack away until the colder weather returns. I've also been mending the garments she likes to wear when she works in the garden. Why, we shall have the very best herb garden in all of Doncaster this summer. Lady Dacia wants to grow some of the herbs that Emmeric used in his potions."

She was pointing to a table where two bags sat side by side – one was singed and worn, while the other was Dacia's very nice leather satchel.

"And be mindful of those poisons," Darian said. "I told you that when I brought the bag."

"You did, my lord."

"Did you keep them?"

Edie shrugged. "My lady may wish to keep some," she said. "It is not my place to remove them, so I put everything in her bag."

She had a point. Darian snorted. "Poisons," he said with irony. "What on earth did he have poisons for?"

Edie chuckled. "The maids and I were wondering the same thing," she said. "Mayhap to use if his patient did not pay him properly."

Before Darian could reply to what had become meaningless banter, Dacia picked that moment to enter the chamber from the smaller dressing chamber.

Darian stiffened when he saw her, wondering what direction she was going to go. Would she chase him away? Or would she let him remain? As he held his breath, she simply glanced at him, putting a pin in her hair to tuck back the unruly strands.

"Greetings, Darian," she said. "What brings you here?"

She sounded completely normal. Utterly, completely normal and Darian was truthfully the slightest bit wary. He hadn't expected her to be so... *normal.*

Carefully, he proceeded.

"My lady," he greeted evenly. "You are looking well."

That was a lie. As she came out from behind the table that was in the middle of the chamber, the one that held flowers or shoes, or anything else tossed upon it, he could see that her clothing was hanging on her. Not eating and hardly sleeping, she'd dropped a noticeable amount of weight, enough so that it was obvious.

Her clothing was hanging at her. It occurred to him that Edie wasn't making new clothing because she wanted to. It was because she had to. Her mistress was wasting away before her very eyes.

It was a sobering realization.

"Well?" Dacia finished fussing with her hair and faced him. "What do you want?"

That was it as far as greetings went. She may have been normal enough, but she wasn't exactly being amiable.

But Darian had come to change that, he hoped.

He had something to tell Dacia, something he thought her grandfather should tell her, but the duke had given that task to Darian because the man had just sat through several long and excruciating minutes of Hugh de Branton forcing his daughter to confess all of her worldly sins to the duke, including all the recent rumors about Dacia and Cassius, and was emotionally exhausted by the rant. Therefore, he sent Darian to summon his granddaughter because Amata needed to apologize to her, most of all.

Darian hoped that it was enough.

"My lady, I have been sent by your grandfather on an important matter," he said. "May we sit?"

Dacia eyed him, considering his request. "I do not want to sit," she said. "Tell me what you have come to tell me."

Darian sighed faintly, thinking this wasn't going to be a simple thing. But it was necessary.

"Very well," he said. "Have you been watching the bailey today?"

Dacia shook her head. "Nay," she said, her mood immediately darkening. "It does not interest me."

Darian knew why. It was because Cassius was no longer in it. "Then you would not see any new visitors," he said. "I have come to tell you that Amata and her father have arrived."

Dacia looked at him in shock, for just a brief moment, before immediately turning away from him. "I do not wish to speak to either of them, Darian," she said firmly. "Tell them to go away. I have nothing to say."

"Dacia, please," he said, trying to be gentle. "Amata has just spent the past several minutes with the duke, but she wants to speak with you. You have shut out the world for two weeks, but I am here to bring you some hope."

She was marching away from him, but she suddenly turned around and marched towards him. "Hope?" she repeated as if he'd said something outrageous. "Why should you want to bring me hope? When you learned of my betrothal to Cassius, you would not speak to me at all, so why now the sudden need to be kind to me? Save your breath, Darian. I do not want to hear it."

That was a blow to his ego, but he resisted reacting. "I am sorry I did not speak to you when I learned of it," he said. "I suppose… I suppose I needed to reconcile myself to it before I could speak to you. I am sorry if I offended you with my silence."

Dacia had started pacing with pent-up nervous energy that was verging on rage. "You did offend me," she said. "You hurt me, but I left you alone. Now I am asking you to leave me alone. I do not want to talk about anything and I most certainly do not want hear anything Amata wants to say."

Darian wasn't leaving. He watched her pace in circles,

wringing her hands, before deciding to tell her what their business was. He could see that she wasn't going to agree to see them, so perhaps she needed an incentive.

"Hugh de Branton forced Amata to confess her lies about you," he said. "Amata confessed them to the priests of St. George's and she was forced to confess the lies to all of those who came to worship for vespers and matins. She told everyone that she spread those lies about you and Cassius and that they were not true. She wants to apologize to you personally. Now, will you see her?"

As he hoped, that brought a big reaction from Dacia. She stopped pacing, turning to look at him with eyes so wide they threatened to pop from her skull. For a moment, she simply stared at him, trying to process what he had said.

"You must be jesting," she said, sounding weak and hollow.

He shook his head. "I am not," he replied. "Her father has brought her here so that she may apologize to you. Dacia, she told everyone that she had lied. Now the entire village knows that you are innocent. According to her father, the priests know that you are innocent as well. Will you not at least let her apologize personally?"

Dacia stood there, her entire body quivering. Her gaze lingered on Darian for a few moments before looking away, struggling to digest what she had been told.

It was a hard fight.

"Where is she?" she finally asked.

"In your grandfather's solar."

Dacia flew from the chamber, slamming the door behind her and trapping Darian until he could yank it open and pursue her. But by that time, she was already down the stairs. The duke's solar was on the first floor and even as Darian raced down the stairs, he could hear Dacia's voice as she called Amata by name. He was running for the solar when he suddenly heard Amata scream.

By the time he entered the solar, Dacia had thrown herself at Amata and was pounding her with her fists as she lay on the floor. Hugh was trying to pull them apart, but the duke was doing nothing. He was sitting at his enormous table, watching Dacia beat on her cousin as Amata screamed.

Darian flew into action.

Reaching down, he yanked Dacia off of Amata as Hugh pulled his daughter to her feet. Dacia was still struggling against Darian, still trying to beat her cousin to a pulp.

"For everything you have done to me, I hate you until my last breath, Amata de Branton," she shouted. "You have spent years turning everyone against me so that I had no friend but you. You made me dependent upon you, craving your companionship, and manipulating me and lying to me all the while. You have tried to ruin me for the last time, do you hear? I will kill you if I see you again!"

Darian was having a difficult time holding on to her. He pulled her back towards her grandfather's table, his mouth by her ear.

"*Stop*, Dacia," he said. "Calm yourself."

Over on the other side of the room, Amata was weeping loudly. "Forgive me," she wept. "I am sorry I hurt you, CeeCee, truly. Please do not hate me."

Dacia's surge of anger faded and the tears began to come. In Darian's grasp, she began to tremble as a wave of emotion washed over her.

"Why?" she finally hissed. "Why did you do it? What did I ever do to you that you would hurt me so?"

Amata was exhausted and ashamed. She'd spent all night confessing her lies, telling her friends from town that nothing she had ever said about Dacia had been true. Girls that had been her friends for years looked at her with disgust and walked away, and now she was seeing that same disgust in Dacia's eyes, only worse.

There was anguish there.

"I... I do not know," she sobbed. "I suppose it was because you had everything and I had nothing. You are to be a duchess. I will be nothing unless I marry well and I hated you for what life had given you and not me. Never me! I wanted to see you suffer."

Dacia was unmoved. "Then you accomplished your task," she said, her voice quivering. "I suffered. I suffered all of my life, and I suffer worse now because you took away the only man I ever loved. You knew when you told those lies that you would be separating Cassius and me. That was your intention and it worked. He is gone and I am nothing without him. I will hate you with everything for the rest of my life, Amata. Go home and never come back. I do not want to see you ever again."

Amata was a pitiful sight. "Please, CeeCee," she begged. "Please forgive me. Do not turn your back on me. I am so sorry for everything."

But Dacia simply shook her head. "You are only sorry because you were caught in your lies and forced to confess," she said. "If you had not been caught, you would still continue perpetuating these falsehoods against me. Ruining me. Therefore, I do not accept your apology. You have wasted your breath."

It was a harsh response, but there wasn't one person in that chamber who blamed her except for Amata. She frowned.

"Have you no soul?" she demanded. "A good Christian would accept my apology. It would please God."

Dacia smiled without humor. "As you have told everyone for years, I bear the marks of a witch," she said. "Mayhap it is those marks that prevent me from accepting your forced and insincere apology. Now, get out of my sight. You are no longer welcome at Edenthorpe."

Amata looked at her father for support, but he gave her no comfort whatsoever. He simply took her by the arm and pulled her towards the solar door.

"Lady Dacia," he said quietly. "I hope you can find peace someday. Know… know that I am very sorry for my daughter's actions. I am sure it is of no comfort to you, but I am sorry just the same."

Dacia couldn't even reply. She genuinely liked Hugh, or at least she had, but he had bred that horrific beast and she could not spare him the attention. Not now. She simply turned away, pulling herself out of Darian's grip, as Hugh took the sobbing Amata away.

When the door to the solar shut behind them, there was a finality in the gesture.

It was over.

Amata was gone, for good.

When the solar was quiet, Dacia sat down in the nearest chair, exhausted and overwrought. Darian watched her a moment before looking to the duke, who was still sitting there.

"You did not stop her from attacking Amata, your grace," he said with a hint of reproach. "Why not?"

The duke was watching Dacia carefully. "Because it needed to be done and it was best that Dacia do it," he said without remorse. But his next words were directed at Dacia. "What do you intend to do now?"

Dacia was pale and shaking. Slowly, she looked over at him. "What do you mean?"

"Just that," the duke said. "Amata's confession has made you blameless, child. The priests know it, the village knows it. Everyone knows it, but I wish you had let me settle this matter sooner. This dragged out far longer than it should have."

Dacia shook her head. "How, Grandfather?" she said. "There was nothing you could have done. The priests were going to believe what they believed, as were the villagers, and anything you did would have simply made it look as if you were defending your guilty granddaughter. The only resolution to this had to come from Amata and, quite honestly, I am shocked that she confessed. She has never accepted blame for anything."

The duke grunted. "Her father forced her," he said. "Hugh is a good man, Dacia. You must not hate him for his daughter's crimes."

Dacia looked away. "He let her get away with it," she said. "He knew what she was doing and he had for years, yet he did nothing and he said nothing. He is not innocent in my torment, Grandfather, and he knows it. Mayhap I will forgive him someday, but not now."

"You are holding a grudge, child."

"Of course I am!" she practically shouted. "Because of Amata, I have lost something that was more important to me than anything on earth. I've lost my moon and my sun. How can I forgive or forget that?"

The duke sighed faintly. "You should have never sent him away to begin with," he muttered. "Cassius wanted to help you and you would not let him."

Dacia shot out of her chair. "I could not let him be tainted by those lies," she fired back. "I was the target and he would have been damaged simply by his association with me, and I could not stomach that. I loved him enough to let him go."

"You sent away a man who wanted to protect you."

They hadn't really spoken of this subject since it happened, mostly because Dacia refused to. In fact, she still wouldn't be talking about it had Amata's appearance not forced her hand. To think of it tore her guts to shreds. To imagine Cassius' face brought her heartbreak that shattered into a million pieces of pain. She'd never experienced anything like it but she would always believe, until the end of all things, that she had done the right thing for him.

Her grandfather simply didn't understand.

"He could not have protected me," she finally said. "This was something I had to face alone, Grandfather. If you cannot understand that, I cannot explain it to you any better."

"Would you have let *him* face a situation like this alone?"

Her first reaction was to voice her support for Cassius in any given situation, but she shut her mouth. It would open an entirely new world of argument and she didn't have the strength. She didn't want to face the possibility that she might have been wrong.

At the moment, she didn't want to face anything.

She was so very weary.

"We shall never know," she said quietly. "I am going to rest now. It has been a trying day."

The duke and Darian watched her go, hearing her footfalls fade away as she mounted the stairs. The duke sat back in his chair, sighing heavily at the apex of a most eventful day.

"Do you know where Cassius is, Darian?"

Darian looked at him. He could have easily lied to the man,

anything to keep Cassius away from Dacia and preserve what little hope there was still for him to marry her. But after seeing what her heartbreak had reduced her to, he couldn't bring himself to make it worse.

Certainly, Dacia would heal. Broken hearts always did, eventually. But even he had to admit that there had been something very special between Dacia and Cassius. Just because he couldn't have her didn't mean he wished her heartbreak equal to his own. It occurred to him that he had to do to Dacia what she had done to Cassius –

He had to let her go.

He loved her enough to do that.

"Du Bois sent me a missive a few days ago that said they were at a tavern in Pontefract," he said. "They were heading north to Castle Questing, but Cassius apparently hasn't been able to move out of Yorkshire. According to du Bois, they are in a place called the Blood and Barrel."

The duke mulled over the information. He finally shook his head. "I think she is making a terrible mistake," he said. "She is letting Cassius slip through her fingers. I never agreed with her sending him away to begin with, but now… now that Amata has confessed her sins, there is no reason for Cassius not to return."

"Do you want me to send him word?"

Doncaster nodded. "Aye," he said. "But do not tell Dacia. If you do, she'll have time to be furious with us. But if she knows nothing and suddenly opens her door one day to find Cassius standing there, she'll thank us."

Darian nodded. "It may be more complicated than that, but at least she may speak to him. She wouldn't before he left, you know."

"I know."

"I'll send word today."

Darian turned and headed for the door, the duke stopped him.

"Darian," he said. "I realize that this cannot be easy for you, but I will say that you have shown remarkable composure through this situation. You are to be commended."

Darian knew what he meant. Losing the woman that a man had his heart set on was never easy. Weakly, he smiled.

"I simply want her to be happy, your grace," he said. "I have reconciled myself to the fact that it is not with me."

The duke nodded faintly, unwilling to comment more. He had acknowledged that sad dynamic as much as he was going to and he suspected Darian did not wish to discuss it further, either. Therefore, he waved his hand.

"Go, then," he said. "If she will not send for the man, then we will. Mayhap you *will* make her happy, Darian. Just not in the way you had hoped."

Darian smiled weakly and quit the solar to go about his business, leaving the duke sitting at his table, wondering if this entire situation was salvageable.

They were going to find out.

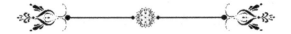

AN APOLOGY.

Dacia still couldn't believe that Amata had come to deliver an apology. Instead of being pleased by it, or happy with it, it just seemed to make things worse.

Her anger had returned.

Perhaps it would have been best had Amata simply faded away, forgotten by a world she tried so hard to control. It seemed to Dacia that her father had involved himself too late in this situation – where had he been during the most formative years when Amata should have been taught right from wrong, love from hate, and how not to build a life on lies? Perhaps she should not have blamed Hugh, but it seemed to her that the man did a terrible job of raising his daughter.

Cousin or no cousin, she had no use for him.

And she did not accept Amata's apology.

The past two weeks had passed in a fog. Every day was the same and every night was endless. Dacia had slept, of course, but fitfully and only periodically, waking into a darkened room with Cassius on her mind. She wondered where he was, and what he was doing, and if he hated her overly for what she had done.

Although Dacia had convinced herself that sending him away had indeed been the best thing for them both, there was also a part of her that wondered even if she had allowed him to remain, if the pressure of being married to a hated woman would have taken its toll on him. If he would have risen every morning and wondered why he had stayed. She wouldn't have been able to live with herself had she seen resentment in his eyes when he looked at her.

It was thoughts like those that convinced her that she had done the best thing for them both.

But, oh, how glorious it had been to have known such love and happiness and acceptance for just a few days. Those few days with Cassius had been the best days of her life and something she would always remember. Perhaps the old saying was right – perhaps it was better to have loved and lost than to never have loved at all, and she was grateful that for a brief and shining moment in time, she had loved and had been loved.

She would have to cling to that memory in the dark years to come.

But the situation had markedly changed. With Amata's confession, she knew that she could send for Cassius and tell him that everything was all right. She could hope for his return. But given the circumstances of their separation, she wasn't entirely sure that he would want to return to her. She had shut herself away and refused to speak with him, and he had spent two solid days outside of her door, begging her to open it.

It had been the most painful time of her life.

There had been moments when Cassius simply talked about anything he could think of, having a one-sided conversation as if there were two people involved. She would hear him speak of his grandparents, his father's parents that he loved so dearly, and he spoke on how they met and married under somewhat clandestine circumstances. He would tell her that most of the men in his family had not had easy paths to marriage. He would tell her that everything would be all right if she would only open the door.

But she had refused.

On the morning of the third day, Cassius had finally given up. Dacia had awoken to silence. She was so used to waking up to the sound of his voice, that the silence had been deafening as well as heartbreaking because she knew he had given up the fight. So much of her wanted to open that door and run after him, but she didn't. She couldn't. She couldn't bring Cassius into the hell that was swirling around her.

He needed a wife who wasn't being accused of unspeakable things.

After that, the depression set in. Hardly eating and hardly sleeping had taken its toll. Dacia's clothing was beginning to hang on her and Edie had been trying to take in some of the things that were obviously bagging. The beautiful yellow fabric that she had dyed for Amata's birthday was being turned into a new surcoat for Dacia. Edie had been a great comfort to her, the only comfort she would allow near her.

Dacia simply couldn't handle anyone else.

Now, with Amata's apology, her emotions were fresh and brittle once again. She had run all the way from her grandfather's solar and now stood in the middle of her larger chamber, reliving the apology over and over again. She was reliving beating up on Amata, thinking that she should have been satisfied from physically expressing her rage but realizing there was no satisfaction at all.

The damage to her life was irreparable.

It was over before it even began.

"My lady?" Edie was standing in the doorway of the smaller chamber. "Are… are you well?"

Dacia looked over at the woman who tried so hard to take good care of her. "I am."

"Did you see Amata?"

"I did."

"And she apologized?"

Dacia nodded. "For everything, she did."

She didn't elaborate and Edie didn't push. She was intuitive that way. She knew that if Dacia wanted her to know something, she would tell her. For now, however, Edie was just glad Amata had made amends, but Dacia didn't seem too relieved or overjoyed.

She simply seemed weary.

"Come and lay down, lamb," she said gently. "I'll mix you a sleeping position and rub your forehead. Would you like that?"

Dacia smiled weakly. "Dear Edie," she said. "You are always trying to tend to me, just like a child."

Edie went over to the big bed and pulled back the coverlet. "That is because sometimes we all need careful tending," she said. "This is your time. Come and lay down, lamb. Let me take care of you."

Dacia didn't fight her on it. She was weary and, truth be told, feeling weak. The day had been too much for her. She needed to rest and organize her thoughts, which were centering more and more on Cassius. Perhaps if she apologized to him, he might forgive her for being cruel and come back to her. If he truly loved her as he said he did, perhaps he'd be willing.

She needed to sleep on it.

"There is some wine over there," she told Edie. "There is a phial in my medicament bag, in the back row, four from the left, that are the sleeping powders that Emmeric gave Grandfather last year. They worked for him. I may as well try them."

Edie looked at the two bags, side by side. "I put the things from his bag into yours," she said, worried. "I thought you wanted his medicines in your bag."

Dacia sat on the bed to remove her slippers. "I did," she said. "Look for the word *somnum* scratched into the glass. That is the sleeping powders."

Edie knew the letters of the alphabet, but she couldn't read very well. Dacia was aware of that and she had tried to educated Edie further, but Edie had been embarrassed about it and she had told Dacia she understood far more than she actually did.

Therefore, reading the etchings on the glass phials was nerve wracking for her because she wanted to find the right powders. She didn't want to admit to Dacia that she couldn't read them properly. The young woman had enough to worry about without an incompetent servant. She came to a phial with "um" at the end of the word and held it up into the light.

"*Somnum?*" she said.

Dacia was already laying down. "Is that what is says?"

"I think so, my lady. I see *um* at the end of it."

"Is it a white powder?"

Edie held it up for her to see, but she was several feet away. "It is, my lady."

Dacia only glanced at it from afar. "Good," she said. "Use one of those little spoons to put a goodly amount in a cup of wine and bring it to me."

"Are you certain?" Edie said reluctantly. "I put Emmeric's potions and powders in here, and some of them were poisons."

But Dacia didn't seem concerned. "If the phial says *somnum*, then it is a sleeping powder," she said. "Put it in the wine, Edie."

Edie did as she was told. She put a heaping spoonful into a cup of wine and stirred it around, dissolving it. Bringing it over to Dacia, she helped the woman sit up so she could drain the entire cup. Edie took the cup away as Dacia lay back down, rolling onto her side.

"Edie," she said. "Will you do something for me?"

"Of course, lamb," she said. "What is your wish?"

Dacia yawned, her eyes already becoming droopy because she was so exhausted. "Would you speak with those you know in Doncaster and see if Amata's apology has had any affect?" she said. "I know you know some of the villagers. Mayhap they can tell you if the situation is truly forgiven."

Edie looked at her sympathetically. "It means a great deal to you, doesn't it?"

Dacia paused before answering. "I told Cassius that I *am* Doncaster," she said quietly. "When Grandfather is gone, I will be all that is left. I love these lands and the people. I want to take care of them and protect them. They must not think ill of me because of Amata's viciousness."

"If they do, then they're fools."

"But will you ask around to make sure Amata's apology was accepted?"

"And if it is?"

Dacia sighed faintly. "If it is…" she began, then stopped herself. But the pause was only momentary. "If it is, then I will send word to Cassius. He said that he was going to Castle Questing in Northumberland, so he must have arrived by now. I will send him a missive and tell him what has happened. At least he will know."

Edie smiled at her. "Will you ask him to return?"

Dacia closed her eyes. "I treated him so terribly," she said. "Mayhap he does not want to return."

"But you can ask him, lamb. Ask him and let him make his choice."

"But what if he refuses?"

"Then at least you will know."

It was a sobering but true statement. "You are correct," she said sadly. "If he does not return, I will have my answer. But if I do not say anything at all, I will never know."

Edie was close enough that she put her hand on Dacia's head. "Sleep, now," she said softly. "Stop worrying about such things for the moment. Make your decision after you've had some rest."

Dacia simply closed her eyes again, drifting off to sleep.

It wasn't until a few hours later when Edie tried to wake her than she realized something was wrong. Dacia wouldn't awaken and her breathing was slow and labored. In a panic, Edie snatched the phial of sleeping powder and rushed to Darian, who was in the middle of writing out the missive to Cassius and couldn't be bothered until Edie mentioned that the phial had to do with Dacia. She needed to know the full name on the glass. Darian held the bottle to the light and read out the name…

Nenum.

Venom.

Edie had accidentally given her lady one of Emmeric's poisons.

CHAPTER NINETEEN

Pontefract
The Blood and Barrel Inn

THE MAN WENT sailing through the open tavern window.

In fact, there were several men sailing around the tavern, through doors, out of windows, or ending up in a heap in the corner. A tempest named Cassius was in full-swing and the fists were flying faster than lightning.

"And that is for your foolish and ineffective lord, who refuses to agree with the king!" he bellowed at the man he'd just thrown out of the window. "Tell him that Cassius de Wolfe has said he is a coward!"

The entire tavern was in disarray and had been for more than a week, ever since Cassius, Rhori, and Bose had shown up and virtually took over the establishment. They had arrived after a few slow and aimless days wandering northward from Doncaster, but once they reached Pontefract, Cassius refused to go any further. He was as far away from Dacia as he wanted to be, so like a tick on a dog, he dug in. Rhori and Bose dug in alongside him. Cassius became drunk the day of their arrival and had not been sober since.

Neither had Bose. An emotional man, he had great sympathy for Cassius. If Cassius drank, he drank. If Cassius fought, he fought. With a man of Cassius' considerable size, those fights could be quick and violent. Cassius had broken nearly every table in the tavern by either throwing men on them or breaking them with his bare hands, using the legs for clubs. Sometimes he used two legs, one in each hand, and Bose went right along with him.

It had made for a ferocious and difficult week.

And then, there was Rhori.

The calmer, less-impulsive knight was drunk for the first two days, too, but being a little more sensible and able to control himself better than Bose, he sobered up quickly. He had been sober ever since and every time Cassius broke a table or a door, Rhori slipped the tavernkeeper a few coins to pay for it.

In fact, it had been Rhori who had kept the tavernkeeper from running to the Pontefract garrison for help by explaining that Cassius had just lost his wife. He didn't elaborate, but he led the man to believe that Cassius was grieving a death. Being sympathetic, and a little frightened, the tavernkeeper simply kept himself and his servants out of Cassius' way. They had tried to go about their business as usual, trying to work around a man who was tearing up their world because his had evidently been destroyed.

And that's where they found themselves today.

Another fight.

Unfortunately, men wearing the black and white standard of William de Ros of Helmsley Castle decided to visit the tavern on that day. De Ros was a crown supporter, but a finicky one. Cassius took exception to the men as soon as they entered and in little time, a room-clearing brawl had started. Even Rhori had to get involved because there were seven de Ros men and only Cassius and Bose. Not that they couldn't take care of seven men on their own, but one of them jumped on Bose's back and tried to strangle him, so Rhori crowned the man with a chair.

The remaining de Ros men tucked their heads down and fled.

"Another victory for the House of de Wolfe!" Cassius crowed, drinking deeply of the cheap ale that had kept him inebriated for days. "I shall best every man in England at this rate and then they shall have to bring in some Scots for me to pummel. It has been a long time since I pummeled a Scot just for the pleasure it brings me."

Rhori pulled him down into a chair. "All hail your mighty fists, Cass," he said, stroking the man's ego. "You are a magnificent beast."

Cassius threw his arm around Rhori's neck and pulled him close, kissing his dark head loudly. "I love you," he said. "You are my brother and I love you. I have real brothers and I love them madly, but you are my friend and my brother. I love you, du Bois. I truly do."

When Cassius wasn't tossing men around, he was being silly and sappy. Rhori was forced to push him away or risk being suffocated by all that love.

"Aye, Cass, we love you, too," he said, motioning to the tavernkeeper for some food. "Come, now. Let us eat something and discuss your future plans. We've been here a week, but your grandmother is waiting. We must go to Castle Questing soon."

Cassius looked at him, the pale eyes flickering with unchecked emotion. "My grandmother," he muttered. "Jordan Mary Joseph Scott de Wolfe. She was named for the River

Jordan, you know. A stronger woman you will never find. I love her dearly."

"I am sure she loves you, too."

"And my father and mother. I love them more than anything."

"Aye, Cass, I know. And they love you."

"But I love my grandmother so very much and I must see her soon. I *must*."

The tavernkeeper arrived. Bread and meat were being set upon the table in copious amounts as Cassius declared his love for everyone in Northern England.

"Then let us go to her," Rhori said, pulling the wine away from Cassius and hoping he didn't notice. "Let us leave this place and not look back. Look at all of this glorious food! Eat and tell us of Berwick Castle, where you were born. I've never been there."

He was trying to distract Cassius and get some food in him, hopefully to help ease his drunken state somewhat and bring him back to his senses. Thankfully, Cassius complied and shoved meat in his mouth, sloppily.

"It is by the sea," he said, chewing. "A massive place by the sea. When my brothers and I were young, we used to run like wild colts on the sand. My father would take us there when we became too much for my mother to handle and he would make us run from him. Whoever got caught was thrown into the icy waves. I was never caught and neither was my oldest brother, Markus, but my two younger brothers, Magnus and Titus, were caught often. My father would throw them in the waves and they would run home to my mother, weeping and shivering. She would yell at my father for it and he would blame it on Markus and me."

He laughed at the memory of his beloved father casting blame for his actions. The tavernkeeper brought around boiled cider, putting it in front of Cassius instead of the ale he'd been drinking. Rhori and the tavernkeeper had been trying to replace the ale for three days, but Cassius always caught on and always went to find his own drink. But again, they would try.

Rhori tried to distract him, keeping up a running stream of conversation. "Your father had many brothers," he said. "He learned to deflect the blame."

Cassius snorted, drinking the cider and realizing it wasn't his ale. He hurled the cup across the room and yelled for his favored drink. "Ale!" he bellowed. "Who keeps putting that putrid juice in front of me? I will kill the next man who forces me to drink that stuff."

Rhori couldn't even look at Bose because he, too, was sotted with drink. In fact, Bose agreed with Cassius, giving the man his cup, and Rhori grunted in exasperation.

"Cass," he said, trying to sound casual. "How do you expect to ride the rest of the way to Castle Questing if you are drunk? It will not work well in your favor."

Cassius was still chewing on his meat. "I will make it," he said. "When I decide we should leave."

"Edward is going to expect you back in London next month. We cannot remain here forever."

Cassius looked at him as if he wanted to say something angry in response, but he couldn't bring himself to do it. He simply drained the cup in his hand.

"I do not want to talk about that right now," he said. "Bose, find me more drink."

Bose was on his feet, staggering away, as Rhori watched Cassius' profile. The man was as drunk and out of control as he'd ever seen him, but it wasn't as if he didn't have his reasons. Frankly, no one blamed him. It had been a tragic happening with Dacia, but they simply never realized Cassius would take it so hard.

Yet, he had.

He was bleeding grief out of every pore in his body.

"Is it helping?" Rhori finally asked softly.

Cassius was staring, half-lidded, out into the room. "Is what helping?"

"The drink. Is it helping you to forget?"

Cassius turned to him, so swiftly that he nearly lost his balance. He had to grip the table. "I told you that I do not want to talk about it," he said. "You'll not bring her up."

"I didn't say a word about her."

"I know what you meant!"

Rhori held up a hand to ease him. "I simply asked if drinking was helping you forget about her," he said. "Is the drinking and fighting helping you heal? Is it doing you any good?"

Cassius' lip flickered in a snarl. "Shut your mouth, du Bois," he said. "You have no idea what you are asking."

Rhori lifted his eyebrows. "Aye, I do," he said. "I've been through this, Cass, only worse. There was no chance of reconciliation when it happened to me. At least you are not mourning her death."

Cassius was geared up to throw a punch at a man he had been professing his love for only moment's early when he suddenly came to a halt. His expression morphed from furious to remorseful in a quick moment.

"God," he groaned, putting a hand on Rhori's arm. "Forgive me. I had forgotten about Lucy. Forgive me for not being more sensitive to that."

Rhori brushed him off. "Four years later, it is not as painful as it used to be," he said. "Though I will admit that I think about her almost every day. Watching you fall in love with Dacia has brought back the memories of when I was courting Lucy. Those were good days. I remember them when I feel particularly sad sometimes. It helps."

Cassius sighed heavily, leaning back in his chair and nearly tipping over because his balance was so bad. "Lucy was such a pretty girl," he said. "Her death was very sad for us all, Rhori."

Rhori nodded faintly, remembering the red-haired, blue-eyed lass he was so deeply in love with. Pretty, vivacious, and naughty at times, she had been the fire to his ice until a sudden and horrific fever had taken her from him. She had been perfectly well and then a week later, he was weeping over her body. They'd never even had the chance to wed. He had to admit that watching Cassius go through the pangs of grief brought back a good deal of grief for him, too.

He understood what it was like.

"I will admit I wonder how things would have been," he said after a moment. "Would we have had a son with her fiery hair and disposition? Or my dark hair and calm manner? I cannot imagine having a son with Lucy's fire. A lad like that would have been the death of me."

Cassius smiled weakly. "He would have been your pride and joy and you know it," he said. "I told Dacia that the first born son must be named by my father's mother."

"Magnus the Law-Mender?"

"Aye," Cassius said. "He has named all of his male grand-children and one great-grandchild. He would have undoubtedly laid claim to any first born son of mine."

"Will you raise Northmen sons, then?"

Cassius laughed softly. "Not me," he said. "They will be English to the bone. But it looks as if I may raise no sons at all. Not if I cannot raise them with Dacia."

Bose came out of the kitchens at that point, carrying a pitcher of ale in one hand and leading a servant girl with the other. They'd all seen this girl around. She was young and pretty, with big breasts and big hips. She swung them for any man who came in through the door and they'd seen her fondle a few men that had taken her into a corner of the tavern. Bose came up to the table and set the pitcher down.

"This is Helen," he said. "She told me that she thinks you're very handsome, Cass."

Cassius looked up with disinterest as the servant girl smiled seductively at him. "M'lord is magnificent," she said. "I'd be happy tae spend some time with ye."

As she said that, she pulled at a string that was keeping her bodice laced up. The string unraveled and the top of her shift fell open, exposing her cleavage. Another casual tug and her right breast nearly fell out. But Cassius simply looked away while Rhori shook his head in disapproval.

"Go away, girl," Rhori told her. "We have no need for you."

The girl's face fell, but Bose grabbed her by the wrist. "Speak for yourself," he said. "If you don't want her, I'll take her. Remember... I'll put anything in my mouth. Just ask the ladies."

Being very drunk, it made him do things he wouldn't normally do. Rhori watched in morbid fascination as Bose sat down with his back to the wall and pulled the girl on top of his lap. She giggled, straddling him, as he reached into the top of her shift and exposed both of her breasts. When he began suckling on them, Rhori had to turn away.

"Christ, Bose," he grunted. "Take her back into a chamber if you're going to do that. We don't need to see it."

Bose did. He stood up, with an erection lifting his breeches like the pole of a tent, and carried the girl back into the chamber he had been sharing with Cassius and Rhori. He threw the door open, startling Argos sleeping on one of the beds, but the door wasn't hung properly so it hit the jamb and bounced back open. They could still see Bose's naked arse as he dropped his breeches and began to ram into the girl, who groaned in delight.

Frustrated, Rhori stood up, went to the chamber door, calling to the dog before he slammed it shut and headed back to the table he shared with Cassius. Argos, smelling food, was happy to go sit next to Cassius and beg for a few bites.

As Cassius fed the dog a few chunks of beef from his plate, Rhori was about to take his seat when the front door to the tavern flew open. He glanced up, purely as a reflex, but when he realized who stood in the doorway, his eyes widened.

"Christ, Cass," he hissed. "*Look.*"

Cassius didn't look up until Rhori elbowed him. Then he looked to the entry with disinterest until he recognized the man who had entered.

Darian de Lohr was coming towards him.

Cassius dropped the beef and bolted to his feet.

"Darian?" he gasped in disbelief. "What are you doing here?"

Darian was in full armor and he had a host of Doncaster soldiers with him. They could see the men filtering into the tavern. He tilted his helm back, peering at Cassius as if he couldn't believe his eyes.

"Cassius," he said, bewildered. "What in the hell is the matter with you?"

Cassius didn't know what to say. He was weaving so unsteadily that he had to sit back down or he would fall down. It was Rhori who answered.

"We have been sequestered in this disgusting hovel for a week," he said quietly so Cassius wouldn't hear. "Ever since I sent you that missive."

"Cassius still refuses to leave?"

Rhori nodded. "The further we move away, the further he is from Lady Dacia. So… we have been watching him feel sorry for himself."

Darian sighed heavily, ripping his helm off and slamming it onto the table. "He must sober up," he said, irritated and brittle. "We have a long ride back to Doncaster."

Cassius heard him. "I am *not* going back to Doncaster," he declared. He may have been terribly drunk, but he wasn't out of his mind. He understood what was being said. "I am never going back to Doncaster, Darian, and you cannot make me. She does not want me back."

Darian cast a pleading look at Rhori. "You must sober him up," he said quietly. "Something has… happened."

Rhori didn't like what he was hearing. "*What* happened?" he asked. "Is Lady Dacia well?"

It disturbed him even more that Darian didn't answer him directly. Instead, he turned to Cassius and sat down right in front of the man.

"Cass," he hissed. "Look at me. Do you understand? *Look at me.*"

Cassius' head lolled in his direction. "I *am* looking at you."

"Can you understand me?"

"Of course I can understand you. I am not a dolt."

"Then understand me clearly. Dacia may be dying. You

must come back."

Cassius went from drunkenly disinterested to filled with terror all in one swift moment. He reached out, grabbing Darian by the arm and knocking his cup of ale off the table. It spilled all over the floor.

"W-*What*?" he said, his voice cracking. "What are you saying? What happened?"

Darian held on to him because, suddenly, he was quivering violently. "I had to tell you that to get your attention," he said. "Now that I have it, listen to me closely. Amata has…"

Cassius cut him off, his face contorting with rage. "Did she have something to do with this?" he boomed. "I do not care if she is a woman. I'll…"

Darian shook him to shut him up. "Nay," he said. "Cassius, *listen*. Amata's father, Sir Hugh, forced Amata to confess the lies she told about Dacia. Amata confessed it to the priests at St. George's and to most of the village when they came to mass. They all know that the rumors against Dacia are untrue. Cass, her reputation is restored. Amata confessed *everything*."

Cassius just stared at him, his sotted mind trying to process everything. That was most definitely not what he had expected to hear.

"No more rumors that she stole me away from Amata?" he asked.

"Nay."

"No rumors of a dead baby?"

"No more rumors."

"Amata told the truth?"

"She did."

Cassius blinked, appearing more sober than he had in days. "Then why did Dacia not send word to me?" he said. "I would have come back. I swear, I would have come back to her. All I want is to come back to her."

"It only happened yesterday," Darian said. "I came as soon as I could."

"But… but you said Dacia may be dying? What happened?"

Darian sighed again, this time with pain in his expression. "It was an accident," he said, squeezing Cassius' arm in sympathy. "Her maid was supposed to give her sleeping powders but accidentally gave her a poison. You must come back to Edenthorpe, Cass. Dacia needs you."

Coming from the man who had hoped to marry Dacia, once, it was a bittersweet moment for Darian as well as for Cassius. In fact, Cassius put his hand on Darian's cheek, perhaps a silent acknowledgement of Darian's selflessness in the situation. Even through his drunken haze, he knew that. He could see a brave man before him. But that was as much as Cassius could do before he was on his feet.

"I am going now," he said. "Rhori, have the tavernkeeper bring back that putrid boiled juice. Anything to help flush the ale out of my veins. And get the horses saddled."

Rhori was moving for the chamber where Bose had just finished having his way with the serving wench. He threw open the door, startling them both.

"Bose," he barked. "On your feet. We are returning to Doncaster immediately."

Bose was laying in the bed, fully dressed with the exception of his breeches being around his knees.

"Why?" he demanded. "What is happening?"

"De Lohr is here."

Bose's expression darkened. "Cass does not need to return, Rhori. He'll only find heartache there."

Rhori's gaze lingered on him. "More than you know," he said. "De Lohr says Lady Dacia may be dying. We must go."

He didn't need to say another word. Bose was already flying into action.

Within the hour, they were heading for Doncaster.

CHAPTER TWENTY

I T WAS ABOUT twenty miles from Pontefract to Doncaster, so not a terribly long distance in the grand scheme of things. But to Cassius, it seemed like a lifetime.

Time was moving so very slowly.

They'd departed Pontefract in the early afternoon, riding hard south, but not hard enough because the horses from Doncaster had already made that trek and were tired, so the men didn't push them too much.

Cassius couldn't push too much, either – Old Man was fat and lazy from having spent over a week eating and sleeping, and Argos was running alongside, which wasn't something the dog normally did. About halfway into their ride, Cassius had to stop and pick the dog up. He handed the animal over to Rhori, who kept the dog in front of him as they continued down the road.

But exhausted horses, and fat horses, made for a slower journey then Cassius had hoped for.

It was late afternoon when the lands of Doncaster began to come into view. The meadows were green, the trees tall and proud and fresh, and Cassius had a strange feeling that he was coming home again. In just the few days he had been at Doncaster, less than two weeks to be truthful, he felt something for the place because it belonged to Dacia. As she had said, she *was* Doncaster.

It was strange how he could feel her everywhere.

He wasn't feeling so drunk by the time they reached Doncaster's lands. A brisk ride for several hours had the desired effect of sobering him up. Before he'd left the tavern, however, he had spent quality time in a rain barrel in the stable yard because it was full of cold, fresh water and, at that point, he was desperate to sober up. Therefore, he had dunked his entire body into it and the brisk temperature had the desired effect. Mostly, anyway. He was a shivering drunk now, but at least not as drunk as he had been.

There was more to come.

In the preparations for leaving, Rhori had managed to obtain a pitcher of boiled cider for Cassius, which he drank until there was nothing left. He also ate more bread and meat. He did all of the things that a man is supposed to do to sober up because he desperately wanted his wits about him.

He needed them.

Once the ride to Doncaster began, as his senses returned, so did his focus and sense of dread. He tried hard not to think on *why* they were going there, but he kept hearing Darian's words over and over in his mind –

Dacia may be dying…

Dacia may be dying…

Those words were like tiny daggers tearing at him, poking holes at his composure, trying furiously to rattle him. He fought against those words more desperately then he had ever fought anything in his life. He tried to focus on the good news, the news that Amata had confessed her sins to the priests and to the villagers. He tried to focus on the fact that Dacia was no longer a target of their scorn and fear. He tried to focus on all those things, because if he thought on what he would find once he reached Edenthorpe, he was afraid he might crumble.

He had to believe it wasn't as bad as Darian said.

It was the only thing that kept him going.

Drawing closer to Doncaster, the land around them was beginning to level out and they could see the village straight ahead. The big, white walls of the city reflected the late afternoon sun, and soon they would be closing the gates for the night.

The party made it in time, rushing through the northern gate, charging through the town that was rebuilding admirably since the mercenary raid. But Cassius didn't pay any attention. He didn't even pass a glance at the goldsmith's stall where he and Dacia had selected their wedding rings. They were probably still there, waiting for them.

But they didn't matter.

Nothing mattered without Dacia.

Emerging from the gate that faced Edenthorpe Castle, Cassius suddenly felt a surge of anxiety. Gone were his attempts to keep his composure. Dacia was within those walls, and he couldn't get to her fast enough. He spurred Old Man forward, charging through the gatehouse before the gates were even fully open, dismounting his horse so swiftly that he stumbled. Soldiers were there, and stable servants, and they took his sweating, exhausted horse away as Cassius literally ran all the way to the keep.

Cassius was blind to anything else.

He was blind to his surroundings, to people or animals or

buildings. The only building for him was directly in front of him and he took the steps into the keep two at a time. He hit the entry door running, only to be blocked by the duke, who was waiting for him.

Startled by the man's abrupt appearance, Cassius came to a halt because he had to, tearing the helm from his dark, sweaty head.

"I am here," he said breathlessly. "Where is she? *How* is she?"

The duke put up his hands to ease the panicked knight. "Cassius, calm yourself," he said steadily. "Thank God you have come, but please... calm yourself. Let me tell you what you need to know before you go to her."

"Is she still alive?"

"She is."

Cassius stared at him a moment, the words confirming that Dacia had not passed away sinking into his weary, still slightly drunk mind.

And then, he burst into tears.

He hadn't realized how much he'd been holding in, terror and fear that he'd lost her for good. A big, gloved hand slapped over his mouth to prevent the sobs from emerging, but he closed his eyes tightly and the tears spilled over. The duke, seeing how distraught he was, put his hands on the man to ease him.

"Cassius," he said with surprising gentleness. "Be at ease, lad. She is still alive, though she has not yet awakened. I sent for the best physic in Sheffield and the man is with her now. His name is Whittington and he is the personal physic to the Earl of Sheffield. She has the best of care, I promise you."

Cassius was trying desperately to compose himself. "I do

not understand," he said hoarsely. "Darian said she was accidentally given poison. How could that even happen?"

Doncaster sighed faintly, with great regret. "Because her maid mixed up the phials," he said. "It was an accident. Whittington has determined that what she was given was not exactly a poison, but something used for swelling and dropsy. If the person is given too much of it, it will affect the heart and the breathing. That is what has happened to Dacia – she was given too much of it and the physic hopes that she will simply wake up without any effects, but it will take time."

Cassius was wiping at his face, gaining control of his composure now that he'd suffered his outburst. "But what if she does not wake up at all?"

Doncaster averted his gaze and dropped his hands from Cassius. "If she has been given too much, she will never awaken," he said sadly. "I pray that is not the case. Mayhap prayer is the only thing that can save her now. Did Darian tell you about Amata and her confession?"

Cassius nodded. "He did," he said, his voice husky from fatigue. "She actually confessed everything?"

Doncaster nodded. "She did," he said. "To the priests, to the entire village. Her father brought her here to apologize to Dacia."

"Did Dacia forgive her?"

"Nay," the duke said, shaking his head as if to suggest just how badly that apology went. "It was not a pretty sight, Cassius. Dacia lost her moon and her sun because of Amata. In other words, she lost *you*. There was never any chance she would forgive the woman."

Cassius seemed to look uncertain. "She has spoken those words to me before," he said. "Did... did she speak about me after I left?"

"Only when Amata came," the duke said. "When I look at you now, I know that her distress equaled your own. She had the same look in her eyes that you do. She was a shell, Cassius. A shell of who she used to be. Just like you."

Cassius knew that feeling well. The duke, a man who usually kept to himself and didn't get involved in the problems of others, seemed to be a man of understanding when he took the time to think of others.

Oddly, it gave Cassius some comfort.

"May I go to her now, please?" he asked.

Doncaster nodded, just once, stepping aside so Cassius could move past him and up the mural stairs. In the entry to the keep, Bose and Rhori and Darian stood, watching the conversation, now watching Cassius as he made his way up the stairs. Argos wriggled out from behind them and trotted after his master.

No one stopped him.

Now, the lovers would once again be united.

The rest was in God's hands.

THE DOOR TO Dacia's suite of chambers wasn't locked. Cassius didn't even knock. He simply pushed the door open.

The rich and lavish chamber opened up before him, the largest chamber in the suite. Dacia's bed was over near the far wall, positioned near windows in the spring and summer seasons, away from them in the fall and winter. Cassius could see the maid he recognized as Edie standing at the foot of her bed and a small, gray-haired man bending over something on the mattress. His back was turned to Cassius.

There were other maids moving about, silently, carrying linens or bowls of water. One was by the hearth, heating something over the flames in a heavy, iron pot. Cassius could see the steam. He came into the chamber but stopped immediately and began to remove his things. He'd no sooner pulled off his gloves than Argos darted past him, ran across the floor and hid under Dacia's bed. The swift movements of the animal startled both the physic and Edie.

"What on earth was that?" the physic asked, trying to get a look under the bed.

"That was Argos," Cassius said. "He is… Dacia's dog."

The maids gasped when they heard his voice. All of them. Edie rushed in his direction, her pale face full of exhaustion and hope.

"You came, my lord!" she said. "Sir Darian found you!"

Cassius nodded, still holding his helm. "Aye," he said, putting everything on a table that was next to the door. He began to unstrap his sword. "How is she?"

Edie watched him quickly undress. "The physic thinks she is better," she said. "But… oh, thank God you are here. Let her hear your voice and awaken, my lord. I know she will!"

Cassius pulled his tunic over his head, eyeing Edie as he put it on the table. "You are her maid," he said. "Edie, is it?"

Edie nodded quickly. "Aye, my lord."

"Were you here when she was given the poison?"

Edie's eyes immediately filled with tears. "It was me," she said. "She asked me to bring her sleeping powders and the names on the phials… I cannot read very well and I showed her the phial and she said it was the one, but it wasn't. She hasn't been sleeping, you see, and she wanted to sleep. I gave it to her, but it was an accident, my lord, I swear it. She wasn't trying to take her life and I wasn't trying to kill her."

Cassius bent over at that point to shimmy off his mail coat. Edie watched him fearfully, finally giving him some help when he couldn't get it off his wrists. He tossed the mail coat over the nearest chair.

"For being honest, I thank you," he said quietly. "You have told me what I needed to hear."

"What is that, my lord?"

"That she did not try to kill herself."

Edie shook her head, horrified at the suggestion. "Oh, *nay*, my lord," she said. "My lady would never think of such a thing."

Cassius knew that, but he still wanted to hear it. In truth, that had been at the back of his mind, something he'd refused to acknowledge until now. A horrible fear that Dacia had been so distressed by everything that she had tried to end her pain permanently. Edie had eased his mind considerably on that account. He pulled off his padded tunic, leaving a thin linen tunic underneath. He hadn't even started on his leg protection yet.

"The physic," he said. "Send him to me. I would speak with him."

Edie scurried away, over to the physic and spoke to the man as she gestured to Cassius. The physic left Dacia's side and approached Cassius as he was removing one of his *cuisses*, or leg protection. He was just slinging it onto the table when the physic spoke.

"You are the betrothed, my lord?" he asked.

Cassius turned to the man. "Aye," he said. "I am Sir Cassius de Wolfe. My father is the Earl of Berwick, Patrick de Wolfe. I am a member of the de Wolfe Pack that rules the Scottish border with Northumberland. If you've not heard of us, you should."

The physic nodded quickly. "I know of the family, my lord," he said. "I am told that you and Lady Dacia are to be wed."

Cassius didn't know who told the man that, but he was glad someone had. It made him feel as if the brutal separation from Dacia had only been a momentary nightmare. Everything was still as it should be.

He could only pray.

"We are," he said after a moment. "What can you tell me about her condition?"

The physic turned to look at Dacia, lying on the bed and buried beneath a myriad of coverlets. "She was given a large dose of purpurea, which is mostly used for swelling. It helps reduce the swelling in the hands and feet, but in larger doses, it affects the heart and the breathing. Lady Dacia was ill to begin with when she was given the dose and it is taking her body longer to overcome it."

Cassius' brow furrowed. "Ill?" he repeated. "What was the matter with her?"

The physic looked at Edie and because he turned to her, so did Cassius.

"Edie?" Cassius said imploringly. "Was she ill?"

Edie had a look of sadness about her. "She would not eat and hardly slept," she said. "I was having to amend her clothing because she could no longer fill it. She was grieved, Sir Cassius, as I have never seen anyone grieve before. Aye, she was ill. Ill and weak. That is why she wanted to sleep, so she could think clearly and send for you."

Cassius felt as if he'd been hit in the gut. "She... she was?

That was her intention?"

Edie nodded. "Aye," she said, seeing his relief and disbelief. "She loves you, my lord. Being apart from you made her ill."

Cassius didn't need to hear anything more. His gaze moved to the figure on the bed and, without another word, he made his way over to it. His first glimpse of Dacia lying pale and unconscious on the linens put his stomach in knots and a lump in his throat, but he resisted the urge to give in to the grief. He was here, with her, and that was all that mattered. Falling to his knees beside the bed, he bent over her form, hand on her head, as he kissed her forehead and cheek, gently.

"My beautiful lass," he murmured, tears forming. "I am here, Dacia. I will never leave you again, not even for a moment. I am here to stay, I swear it. But I must tell you how much I love you. I do not think I have ever told you plainly. I have let innuendos and actions speak for me and I should not have done that. I should have told you how much I love you every hour of every day. You are my moon and sun, too."

He bent over and kissed her freckled cheek, completely unaware that the physic had left the room and Edie had silently ordered the maids out. Even if Cassius had known, he wouldn't have cared, because this moment was only for him and Dacia. Just the two of them, as if no one in the world existed but them.

It was their golden hour.

A time of total truth.

Cassius placed his forehead against her face, feeling her warmth against him, one hand on her head and the other seeking out her fingers, buried beneath the coverlet. He found a soft, warm hand and brought it to his lips.

"I should not have left you," he murmured. "I am sorry that I did. I suppose I did it because I was hurt and confused, but that doesn't matter any longer. I am here and that is all that matters. Please, angel… wake up and look at me. Wake up and tell me how much you love me."

He kissed her face again, her lips, feeling more desperation that she wasn't immediately responding to him. He had hoped, foolishly, that the mere sound of his voice might bring her out of her stupor. Perhaps it still would.

Perhaps he simply wasn't talking enough.

Despair begin to feed his mood.

"Since you do not feel like talking right now, I shall talk until you feel like making this more than a one-sided conversation," he said, stroking her forehead with the hand that was on her head. "There's not much to tell about the two weeks we have spent apart. I did not get any further than Pontefract because I simply didn't want to get any further away from you. I know that sounds strange, but it's true. I couldn't bear to be further away from you than necessary. Darian found me at a tavern in Pontefract called the Barrel and Blood. He's a good man, Darian is. Not many men would go after the lover of the woman they wanted to marry. He's also a cousin to the House of de Wolfe. Did I ever tell you that?"

There was no reply, but he thought he might have seen her twitch. Her eyeballs seemed to be rolling around beneath the closed lids.

That spurred him on to continue talking.

"Darian told me about Amata," he said. "So did your grandfather. He suggested that Amata's apology to you did not go well and I must say, I support whatever you said or did. For everything she's done to you, the woman deserves worse than she received, I am certain. I saw you slap her once, and it was deserved, so can I assume that there was more of the same. Did you slap her right out of the window? I have thrown a few bodies out of the window myself, lately. But that's a story for another time. Or, mayhap I'll tell you now. It all started when four Maltravers soldiers came to the tavern for some respite. That's not what they got. One of them said that Argo should be killed and a rug made out of his hide, and that started a nasty fight. But no one says that about our dog and lives to tell the tale. He may be ugly, but he is *our* ugly."

With that, he looked under the bed, calling Argos forth, who gladly came out and jumped on the bed next to Dacia. The dog laid right next to her, licking her on her chin. Cassius snorted.

"Angel, if you do not wake up and fight off the dog, he is going to lick you to his heart's content," he said "I will not pull him off you. That is your prerogative."

He continued to chuckle as the dog licked happily, but Dacia didn't move, so he eventually called the dog off. Argos laid his head down beside her and promptly fell asleep.

"He is weary like you are," he said as the dog began to snore. "He has had an exhausting day. We both have. But I do not want to miss a moment with you, angel. Watching you sleep… there is nothing better that I could ever think of."

He kissed her cheek again, stroking her forehead tenderly. She twitched again, a little stronger this time, and his heart leapt with anticipation. Was she finally coming around? Or was it her death throes? He knew it was morbid to think such things, but in his state of despair, he couldn't help those thoughts.

To distract himself, he began to talk.

More talk.

Not knowing what else to do or say, he started from his childhood. He spoke of his birth at Berwick Castle, the second of six children. He spoke of his upbringing, how he spent one summer in Bjorgvin, the big city where his grandfather lived. He spoke of learning the Northman's language, at his grandfather's insistence, but it was a difficult language to learn. He spoke of his father actually having to sail across the sea to collect him and his older brother because Magnus had decided to keep them just a little while longer. His father and grandfather had very strong words over Magnus wanting to keep his grandchildren.

He was never allowed to visit his grandfather again after that.

The sun eventually set, casting ribbons of pink and orange light into the chamber, only to gently fade away as the veil of night fell. Edie silently entered the dark chamber, bringing tapers with her and lighting the other tapers around the chamber, filling it with a soft and golden light.

Cassius was sitting on the ground now, next to the bed, still talking about anything he could think of. Edie smiled timidly at him as she went about lighting the tapers and he smiled back, weakly, letting her know that her presence was welcome. She was just in time to experience a series of dog farts, so powerful that even Cassius' eyes watered. All of that beef he'd fed the dog back at the tavern was having an effect on the canine's guts, so Edie found a fan that Dacia sometimes used in the summertime and fanned all of that horrific smell towards the windows. Cassius ended up laughing so hard that he wept.

He was hoping the noxious fumes might stir Dacia and, indeed, she did stir a little.

That nasty but powerful smell gave him hope.

He kept talking.

The night deepened and Edie brought Cassius some stew

and bread, which he gratefully devoured as he told Dacia about his training at Kenilworth Castle and then later at Lioncross Abbey Castle, seat of the House of de Lohr. He told stories about older knights who liked to target him and his brothers because they were so tall, and it was a triumph to be able to best the massive de Wolfe brothers. He was quite proud in saying that no man had ever bested him or his older brother, though Titus and Magnus had been taken down more than once.

Towards midnight, Cassius began to grow weary. He'd talked a blue streak for hours on end and now that he was completely sober, his head was beginning to ache and his body screamed for sleep. He was just finishing a story about a wedding feast at Bamburgh Castle a few years before that included a massive tournament when there was a soft knock at the door. Cassius turned to see Father Lazarus being ushered in by Edie.

In truth, Cassius wasn't sure how he felt about the man's appearance. He knew that Father Lazarus had been Dacia's ally when the rumors were flying but, somehow, he didn't like seeing the man in the chamber. As if Dacia needed last rites or absolution. Stiffly, he moved to stand up but Father Lazarus waved him down.

"Nay, my lord, please stay where you are," he said. "The duke sent word to St. George's, telling us of Lady Dacia's illness. I have come to see how the lady is faring and pray for her full recovery. I hope you do not mind."

In truth, Cassius didn't. She needed all the prayers she could get. He motioned the man towards the bed.

"Come in, Father," he said. "Your concern, once again, is appreciated."

Father Lazarus smiled as he came near the bed, his gaze

inevitably moving to Dacia, pale and unmoving.

His smile faded.

"The poor lass," he said sadly. "I have known her for most of her life. She has suffered so much. Losing her mother and father at a young age, being cursed with people around her who did not love her like they should have. Even so, she was always good to the poor and the sick. She took care of those who needed tending. And now... this."

Cassius was looking at Dacia, feeling the impact of Father Lazarus' words. They were words one would say at a funeral and he didn't like it one bit.

"She will recover," he said firmly. "She is simply exhausted and the powder she was given has had a lasting effect. But she will awaken soon."

He sounded so positive that he was clearly in the realm of denial. Father Lazarus looked at him, hearing anguish in those words as well.

But he wasn't going to dispute Cassius.

"They say that everything happens as it should," Father Lazarus said quietly. "God has a plan for us all, my son. I think that mayhap Lady Dacia's life happened the way it should because all of it seems to point to a great reward."

Cassius looked at him, puzzled. "What do you mean?"

Father Lazarus walked to the foot of the bed, his gaze moving to Dacia. "She was born with a face that some consider less than perfect," he said. "I had a sister who had freckles like Lady Dacia, so I never saw anything strange in them. My sister was a beautiful woman, I think, and so did her husband. But she had to find the man who saw that beauty in her. It took time and tribulations for that to happen."

A thought occurred to Cassius. "Then that is why you have

been sympathetic to Dacia."

Father Lazarus shrugged. "In a way," he said. "I understand what a woman like her must suffer. I feel that it is the same with Lady Dacia as it was with my sister – she has been through tribulations. She has never had a suitor as far as I know. I heard she chased them all away, and it is a good thing, too. She would have never met you had she not, a man who sees the beauty in her. That is God's plan for her, my son – *you* are her great reward."

Cassius hadn't thought of it that way. A smile creased his lips as he turned his attention back to Dacia, his hand on her forehead.

"As I told her, she is one of God's most magnificent creatures," he said. "I suppose she wore the veils for a reason."

"She did. So she could reveal herself only to you."

Cassius continued to look at her, kissing her hand. "I am the most fortunate man in England," he said. "And you, Father... thank you for being her ally. She hasn't had many."

Father Lazarus nodded. "I know," he said. "People can be cruel... and superstitious. But Dacia never failed to rise above it. She never lost her dignity."

Cassius glanced at him. "Did Amata's confession have the desired results, then?" he asked. "Do the villagers seem forgiving? Dacia loves Doncaster, you know. Even when the villagers turned against her, she would not leave. She has more loyalty to them than they have to her."

Father Lazarus lifted his eyebrows as he averted his gaze. "I am afraid I was harsher with Lady Amata than I should have been," he said. "That young woman has been wicked since she was a girl. There are many of us who could see what she was doing, but I am sorry to say that many of the villagers are weak-willed and easily swayed. Lady Amata could be persuasive. When her father finally forced her to confess her lies, Lady Amata told those attending vespers. When she came to matins this morning, her penitence was to stand in front of the church and tell everyone who passed that she had lied about Lady Dacia. She stood out there for two hours before I allowed her father to take her home."

Cassius couldn't even muster the strength to find that humorous. He saw it as a small bit of penitence in what should be a lifetime of penitence for Amata.

"For the pain she has caused, that is little comfort, but at least it is a start," he said. "I do not think you were harsh at all, Father."

"I've told her she must do it for the next month," Father Lazarus said. "Every morning, she is to spend two hours in front of the church, telling everyone how she lied about Lady Dacia. If she does not, I will take a switch and beat her."

"That sounds much better," Cassius said firmly. "Next time, the people will not be so foolish as to believe her. *If* there is a next time."

Father Lazarus nodded. With someone like Amata de Branton, it was difficult to know what the future would bring. He almost didn't care because, at the moment, there was a sick woman in front of him that he was concerned about.

A young woman that Amata had tried to destroy.

"I would like to pray for Lady Dacia now, if you will allow it," he said. "May I?"

Cassius nodded, sitting against the bed in a way that had him leaning against the wall, but still holding Dacia's hand. He had no intention of letting her go.

"Please," he said. "But no last rites, Father. She is not dying."

"Of course not, my lord."

Cassius listened to the droning prayers for a few minutes before they lulled him into a deep, dreamless sleep.

SOMEONE WAS SNORING.

Loudly.

Dacia wasn't sure how long she had been awake. She wasn't even sure when she began to hear the snoring in her ear, louder than anything she had ever heard in her life. She lay there, eyes half-open, seeing her familiar chamber but hearing sounds that she had never heard coming from that chamber.

It took her a moment to realize there was more than one person snoring.

There were a few.

Blinking her crusty eyes, she opened them wider, turning her head slightly to look at her surroundings and immediately spied Argos sleeping next to her. In truth, he was partially sleeping on her, his legs on her torso as he burrowed against her.

The dog was snoring.

But there was more noise coming from her left side. As she slowly turned her head to see who it was, her gaze fell upon Father Lazarus at the foot of her bed, sitting in a chair but his head was lying on the bed. He was snoring, too, fast asleep. But she continued turning to her left only to catch sight of an enormous body on the ground next to her bed. She couldn't see more than part of a torso and legs, but she noticed that whoever was sitting there was holding her hand.

It was a massive hand.

She recognized it.

"Cassius?" she said weakly.

He was the one snoring loud enough to wake the dead. It was so loud it was practically rattling her teeth. He was holding on to her hand, so she squeezed his big mitt.

"Cassius," she said, her voice hoarse and faint. "Wake up, Cass."

One big snore and he felt silent. She squeezed his hand again and, suddenly, he was in her face, his sleepy eyes wide with shock.

"Dacia?" he said in disbelief. "Angel, you're awake!"

She was so glad to see him that the tears were almost instant. "Of course I'm awake," she said. "Why would I not be awake? And... and you're *here*. But why? How?"

He could see her eyes welling and it set him off. Exhaustion, relief, and genuine joy filled him and he put a big hand on her head, leaning forward to sweetly kiss her lips as tears filled his eyes.

"Aye, I'm here," he said tightly, kissing her cheeks. "I will always be here, Dacia. I will never leave you again, I swear it."

Weakly, Dacia lifted her free hand, or at least tried to. Argos was laying on it. When Cassius saw what was happening, he gently shoved the sleeping dog aside to free her trapped arm. Her hand came up to his bearded face and he kissed it reverently.

"Why did you come back?" she whispered. "I was going to write to you and tell you... tell you... God's Bones, my mind feels like mush. I do not understand why you are here, Cass. What has happened?"

Cassius could see how muddled she was. Meanwhile, their chatter had awoken Father Lazarus, who was standing at the end of the bed, beaming at the sight. Cassius turned to the man.

"Can you please send for the physic, Father?" he asked quietly. "And tell the duke that his granddaughter has awoken."

Father Lazarus nodded and hustled off, leaving Cassius alone with Dacia. At least, for a few moments until they were invaded by well-meaning people. Knowing this, Cassius put his hand to her face, gazing into her pale, bloodshot eyes.

"What do you remember last, angel?" he asked softly.

Dacia had to think hard. "Amata came," she said after a moment. "She came to apologize for telling her lies. I told her to... leave. I think I may have slapped her again. Truly, I do not remember much. Why? What is going on, Cass?"

He kissed her cheek gently. "I am here because Edie accidentally gave you a poison and not a sleeping powder," he said. "She mixed up the powders, evidently, and gave you something that has put you to sleep for two days. Darian came to find me and brought me back here because no one was sure if you would awaken."

Dacia's eyes widened. "A poison?" she gasped. "What poison?"

"Something the physic from Sheffield called purpurea," he said. "It slowed your heartbeat, your breathing. But you are awake now and you shall recover fully, thank God. But I want you to know, Dacia... I want you to know how much I love you. Until the end of all things, I will love you and only you. You told me once that your heart was mine and no longer yours to give. The same can be said for me, angel. My heart is no longer my own – it belongs to you now and always will."

The tears returned to Dacia's eyes as she cupped his big face between her two hands. "I am sorry I sent you away," she wept softly. "I truly thought it was the best thing for you, but I know now that I should not have done so. You wanted to protect me and I should have let you. But I thought I was protecting *you*."

He kissed her as she wept. "I know," he said. "I understand you thought you were doing what was best, but it is all over now. We are together again and we shall never be apart, ever."

She returned his kisses with as much strength as she could muster. "Promise me, Cass."

"I swear it upon my oath as a knight, my sweet angel."

A knock at the door interrupted them. Cassius turned to see the physic standing there with Father Lazarus. Behind them stood Doncaster. He charged into the chamber in front of the others, his gaze riveted to Dacia. When he saw that she was indeed alert and looking at him, he nearly collapsed with relief.

"Dacia," he said, putting his hand to his heart. "Thank God and the saints that you have awakened. There is something you must see!"

He seemed quite excited. "What is it, Grandfather?" Dacia asked.

The duke was quite excited, indeed. He waved his arms at Cassius. "Get her up, lad," he said. "Pick her up and bring her. There is something she must see."

"Carry her, my lord," Father Lazarus said, apparently agreeing with the duke. "You must bring her."

Cassius wasn't sure he wanted Dacia jostled about or even moved from the bed so soon after she had awakened from two days of unconsciousness. "She has only now become alert," he pointed out. "I do not want to tax her. Surely she must stay in bed."

He turned his attention to the physic, who was still standing by the door. The man didn't seem any too excited about the directives given by the duke and Father Lazarus, but he reluctantly nodded his head.

"For a short time, it will be all right," he said without any great sense of approval. "Bundle her in a coverlet and pick her up. They want her to see something."

Cassius stood up, frowning. "This is *not* a good idea," he said. "What does she need to see that is so important?"

The duke was still waving his hands, only now, he was moving back to the door. "Pick her up, Cassius," he commanded. "Bring her!"

The orders of the Duke of Doncaster weren't meant to be disobeyed, but Cassius would have done it had the physic not given his hesitant approval. He looked at Dacia.

"I do not know what is happening, but they seem to think it is important," he said. "Do you feel up to it if I carry you? If you do not, I will refuse your grandfather and lock him out of this chamber."

Dacia laughed softly. "He would be very angry."

"I do not care."

"You are my Lord Protector, too," she murmured. "Ever my champion, Cass, and I love you for it."

He smiled faintly. "And I love you," he whispered. "I told you enough while you were sleeping. Didn't you hear me?"

She grinned. "Even if I had, I would tell you that I hadn't," she said. "I want to hear it every day for the rest of my life."

"You will, I swear it."

She shifted a little in the bed. "Then help me up and do as Grandfather has asked," she said. "Old Cuffy is desperate for me to see something important."

Cassius laughed softly at the mention of the duke's nickname, but he carefully pulled her into a sitting position as the physic rushed to help. Dacia was feeling quite weak and a little dizzy, so she sat for a moment to settle her head before the physic put a soft blanket around her and Cassius lifted her into his arms. He cradled her against his broad chest, following Father Lazarus and the physic from the chamber.

The duke was down in the entry of the keep, standing with Fulco. Cassius noticed that Rhori and Bose were standing in the open doorway. They were all looking at something outside of the open entry door. The duke simply motioned Cassius forward, to the door, and once he saw what was outside in the bailey, he came to a halt.

There were people, everywhere.

It looked as if the entire village of Doncaster was crowded into the bailey, all of them looking at the keep entry as Cassius stood there with Dacia in his arms. She saw the people, too, and her head came up from his shoulder, greatly confused as to why the full population of Doncaster should be in the bailey of Edenthorpe, and more besides. The gatehouse was open and they were spilling out into the road beyond.

"Grandfather?" she said, bewildered. "Why are they all here? What has happened?"

"*You* have happened," Father Lazarus said from her other side. When they turned to look at her, he spoke softly. "While Sir Cassius and I were sleeping away at your beside, the villagers heard about your illness and began to come to Edenthorpe. They came to say prayers for you, to bring you whatever small gifts they could manage, or they came simply to show you that you are, indeed, the Lady of Doncaster, and they are sorry for their sins against you."

Dacia was looking at the sea of people. "But... but I do not understand," she said. "These are the same people who listened to Amata's lies... *aren't they?*"

"Aye," the duke said, coming to stand next to her. "But Father Lazarus has worked a miracle, evidently. He has made Amata stand in front of the church and confess her lies, and it seems that the people of Doncaster have a conscience. They realized they were wrong and have come to apologize. That is why I wanted you to come and see this, Dacia. They have been here since last night, ever since I sent word to St. George's, holding vigil for you. Hundreds of voices in prayer, lifting to God, and he has listened. You will be well, child, I know it."

As Dacia looked over the crowd with awe, she recognized Old Timeo as he and his wife made their way towards her. They came to the bottom of the steps of the keep, slowly taking the first few steps so they could get a little closer.

"My lady," the old man said. "We came as soon as we heard of your sickness. We have been praying ever since. You have always been good and kind to us, when no one else would, and we have always been grateful. I... I am sorry we ran from you in town. It was wrong and foolish. We've brought you a token of our gratitude for everything you've done for us."

His wife set something down on the steps wrapped up in burlap. After they left it there, more people began to come forward, piling things on the stairs for Dacia, until the gifts covered the stairs and spilled down into the bailey. Everyone was smiling at her, waving at her, and a few of the children put new spring flowers on the stairs, just for her.

It was a tribute to the Lady of Doncaster, both an appreciation and an apology.

And it was astonishing.

Little by little, people began to trickle out of the bailey, having left their offering, begging forgiveness from a woman they'd sinned greatly against. Snuggled in Cassius' strong arms, Dacia could hardly believe any of it.

"For so long, I hid myself away from these people," she said. "I only went into town for mass and little more. I nursed the sick and hungry when I was called upon. But I did it because it was expected of me."

The duke nodded. "You held true to your heart and to your position," he said. "They know that now. But this is more than that, Dacia. These are offerings of apologies for treating you as poorly as they have. For listening to Amata's lies for all these years and for shunning you because Mother Mary led them to think that was what they needed to do. Far be it from me to speak ill of the dead, but she is to blame almost as much as Amata is. As I am. Dacia, I am sorry I did not do more for you in that regard. I suppose... I suppose it was easier to retreat into my own world and pretend it wasn't my problem, but that was wrong. I have not been a good grandfather to you for some time and I shall do all I can to make amends to you, too. When we come close to losing something, we sometimes realize just how important that something was. In this case, it was you. Do you understand that, child?"

Dacia did, but she was still surprised. At that point, something occurred to her that hadn't before. She looked between Cassius and her grandfather.

"You thought I was going to die?" she asked.

Cassius couldn't answer the question. He couldn't even voice those fears. He hugged her to him, kissing her on the temple, as the duke answered quietly.

"It was a possibility," he said. "Thank God it did not come to pass. We all have a second chance with you, child. We shall make the most of it."

Dacia started to reply when something caught her eye. She recognized Eloise Saffron and Claudia Lockwood as they came through the departing crowd, timidly approaching. Cassius saw her expression when she saw the young women, feeling her stiffen, but he didn't say anything. He wasn't sure who the young women were, but he suspected they were part of Amata's ring. Dacia had mentioned that she'd had friends in the village, long ago, that had eventually shunned her.

That told him who the young women might be.

"G-Greetings, my lady," Eloise said hesitantly. "We came to offer prayers for your recovery and tell you... tell you that we are sorry for what happened. Years ago, Amata told us that you no longer wished to be friends with us, but considering everything that just happened, we think that it might have been another of her lies. If it wasn't, then we shall bid you a pleasant farewell, but if it was... we wanted you to know."

Dacia looked at the two young women who used to be her friends when she was younger. She had liked Eloise in particular. It had been a sad thing when Amata told her that the girls no longer wanted to be friends with her.

But now, everything made sense.

"I never said that, as you can believe," she said. "I am sorry we have been separated for so many years, Eloise. I hope we can change that."

Eloise visibly relaxed, as did Claudia. "I hope so, too, my lady," she said. Then, she lifted a pouch wrapped with a red ribbon. "I brought you something that might make your days more cheery as you recover."

"Thank you, Eloise. That is very kind of you."

"And I brought you something, too," Claudia said, picking

her way up the steps because there were so many tributes on them. "This is from my father. They are the rings you and your betrothed purchased. He wanted me to give them to you and return the money you paid for them. He says it is the least that he can do. He also says that he hopes to see more of you both at his shop."

She held out a heavy leather pouch to Dacia, who took it from her. She smiled at a woman she also considered a friend, long ago.

"That is very kind of your father," she said. "He did not have to do it."

Claudia looked between Dacia and Cassius. "I know," she said. "But he says it is the right thing to do. I… I hope that I can see more of you, too, my lady."

Dacia smiled brightly, reaching out to clutch Claudia's fingers. Claudia squeezed them tightly and then hurried back down the steps where Eloise was waiting for her. They both waved at Dacia before following the crowds out of Edenthorpe's bailey.

"What did Lockwood give you?" the duke wanted to know.

Dacia grinned at Cassius before reaching into the pouch and pulling forth two rings. The first one was the magnificent diamond ring with *Cassius* engraved in very small letters on the inside of the band. The second ring was the big gold ring Cassius had requested. It was smooth and lovely, and on the inside of the band, the inscription of *Dacia* could be seen.

"Put it on me," Cassius said softly.

But Dacia shook her head and put both rings back in the pouch. "We shall not wear them until our wedding day," she said. "But you know I would have married you without them. I would have married you in any case, Cassius de Wolfe."

He leaned in to kiss her, but the duke interrupted. "And when are we to expect the nuptials?" he demanded. "Half of England shall be invited and we shall feast for an entire week."

"Not until I am feeling better, Grandfather," Dacia said, looking at Cassius. "Besides… we shall be married at Castle Questing, in front of Cassius' grandmother, the most important woman in Northumberland."

The duke shrugged. "I look forward to a trip to Northumberland, then," he said. "But I am still inviting half of England. I will discuss this with your father, Cassius. The earl and I will do what needs to be done with the joining of two great houses."

With that, he headed down the steps to look at all of the tributes that had been brought to Dacia. Rhori and Bose, standing behind Cassius and Dacia, simply grinned as they pushed past the pair, following the duke.

"I'm going to hunt down any bottles of wine," Bose mumbled. "Surely some have been brought. I am telling you right now that I shall claim all I can carry."

As Cassius and Dacia laughed, Rhori followed Bose. "And I am going to stop him," he said. "He'll steal it all and your lady shall get nothing."

As they watched the knights descend the stairs, another one was coming in their direction. Darian had waited until the crowds mostly departed before making his way to the keep and Cassius was about to turn and take Dacia back inside when she stopped him. Together, they waited for Darian to come up the steps, but not before he picked up a big bunch of the spring wild flowers that had been left behind and brought it up to Dacia.

As he handed it to her, he smiled.

"I am very glad to see that you are feeling better, my lady," he said. "I suspected that Cassius would have that effect on you."

Dacia remembered what Cassius had said about Darian hunting him down and bringing him back. The man who had been her true friend for years, sometimes her only friend, and a man who had taken defeat in the quest for her hand more graciously than most men would have. She took the flowers from him, her expression soft.

"Thank you, Darian," she said sincerely. "For everything… you have my eternal gratitude."

There was something more to her simple words, something poignant and heartfelt, and Darian knew she meant it. He wasn't a sore loser by nature, but a man who had been truly selfless. Reaching out, he took her hand and kissed it gently.

"And you are welcome… for everything," he said. Then, he let go of her hand and gestured towards the keep. "You'd better let Cassius take you back to bed. Go, now. I will make sure all of this is cleaned up."

But Dacia stopped him. "Nay," she said. "Please… I want to look at every single gift when I am feeling stronger, right where they left it. Please do not clean it up just yet."

Darian nodded. "Very well," he said. "I suppose you've earned that right. I'll make sure de Shera doesn't steal anything, either."

He headed down the steps after Bose and Rhori, and some of the servants had wandered over to get a look at the tributes paid to their sweet, young lady. A lady who, Father Lazarus said, had never lost her dignity, no matter what.

Cassius took Dacia back into the keep where he remained with her for the next week, sleeping on the floor next to her bed, feeding her broth and stew, and retelling her all of the stories he'd told her when she had been lying unconscious. He was as devoted as any man could have been to his lady. She had never left him when he had been injured, and he wasn't going to leave her, either.

Ever.

For the Lord Protector of King Edward, it turned out that his heart was far stronger than the de Wolfe sword he carried. He was a man who had finally found his place, and his purpose, in the arms of a woman who had been made for him.

Cassius de Wolfe had found his heaven.

EPILOGUE

Berwick Castle
Autumn, 1303 A.D.

"There once was a lady fair,
With silver bells in her hair.
I knew her to have,
A luscious kiss... it drove me mad!
But she denied me... and I was so terribly sad.
Lily, my girl,
Your flower, I will unfurl
With my cock and a bit of good luck!
Your kiss divine,
I'll make you mine,
And keep you a-bed for a fuck!"

THE GREAT HALL of Berwick Castle boomed with laughter and cheers as a man with a very fine singing voice, Blayth de Wolfe and the uncle of the groom, serenaded the room with his beautiful voice and naughty song. In fact, within the de Wolfe family, this particular song was literally known as *The Naughty Wedding Song*.

Blayth was quite proud of himself. He had stolen a citole from one of the minstrels hired to entertain the guests and he'd stood on a table full of de Wolfe guests to sing his bawdy song. As Cassius had once told Dacia, sometimes one must surrender one's dignity in order to have a bit of fun. And everyone was having a ball.

Over at the dais, however, trouble was stirring in the form of his extremely old but still spry grandmother.

Jordan de Wolfe was on the move.

And the crowd knew it. The same situation played out at almost every de Wolfe wedding. Blayth would sing, usually accompanied by a loud-mouthed de Norville, and his mother would go after him to box his ears. However, this time, knowing she wasn't fast enough to catch him, she had made other arrangements. Her daughters, and Blayth's sisters, had smuggled in a switch. And when she went after Blayth, it was with a big willow switch in her hand.

The crowd loved it.

There was much yelling and cheering and laughing going on as Jordan went after Blayth, who wasn't running away from her as fast as he used to. She was slower, and he was slower, so it was like watching a slow chase. But he was still taunting her.

"You'll have to catch me if you want to beat me, old girl," he called merrily. "I'll not make an easy target."

So, she chased him around the hall, much to the delight of the crowd. At one point, she lost sight of Blayth only to have him come up behind her and kiss her on the cheek. He thought he was moving fast enough to get away from her, but like any good Scots mother, she swung that switch with lightning speed and caught him on the buttocks.

The crowd roared.

The bride and groom were part of that cheering. Cassius was yelling encouragement to his uncle while his wife was calling to Jordan, advising her of her wily son's movements.

"I think your grandmother is winning," Dacia said.

Cassius chuckled at his sly uncle. "Not if Uncle Blayth has anything to say about it," he said. "He does this at every single wedding and, every time, she takes the bait. It has become a tradition."

Dacia shook her head at the exploits going on. "I think she must enjoy this as much as he does," she said. Then, she looked out over the warm, fragrant, and crowded hall. "So many wonderful friends and family are here with us, but I am sorry that Rhori and Bose had to miss this. I feel as if they have been on this journey with us every step of the way. I'm sorry they had to miss the wedding."

Cassius sat back in his chair, cup in one hand and caressing her fingers with the other. "As am I, but Edward wanted them returned," he said. "He wants me returned, too, so when this is finished, I will go to London to formally retire my post."

"And you'll take Magnus with you?"

Cassius glanced at his younger brothers, down the table, and at one in particular. "My brother will make a wonderful Lord Protector. Not as wonderful as me, but good enough." He smiled fondly at Magnus and Titus, who lifted their cups to him. "I forgot how much I missed those dolts. And I'm quite sorry that my grandfather, Magnus, was unable to attend. The feast is not the same without him."

Dacia looked at him, giggling. "But he sent the name we are

to use for our first-born son," she said. Then, she gestured to her grandfather, in a serious conversation with Cassius' Uncle Scott, head of the de Wolfe family. "My grandfather seems to be having a wonderful time. I am so glad he was able to make the journey. But I am also sad that Darian did not."

Cassius shrugged. "I think it would be too much to expect for Darian to attend the wedding of the woman he wanted to marry," he said, noticing that Blayth and his grandmother were all the way across the hall at that point. He tugged on her arm. "Come. Let us hurry and get away from the crowd while they are distracted with my uncle and grandmother. Shall we?"

Dacia nodded quickly, gathering her beautiful pink skirts and following her husband from the hall in their quest to finally be alone and away from the hundreds of guests that had attended their wedding mass and the dozens of de Wolfe family members who were so overbearingly happy for them.

It was their break for freedom.

Unfortunately, they were seen by none other than Blayth himself as he darted away from his mother. He captured Cassius' father's attention and pointed frantically to the stairwell where the couple had disappeared. Patrick de Wolfe, or Atty as he was known to the family, was quite drunk from the fine wine his son's grandfather-in-law had supplied, but he wasn't so drunk that he didn't understand his brother's gestures.

With that in mind, he called forth the de Wolfe Pack.

They went on the hunt.

Scott de Wolfe, Earl of Warenton, was still speaking to Doncaster when he was tapped by Patrick. The eldest de Wolfe brother, he was a gregarious man when the mood struck him, and he casually excused himself from the duke. Down the table, he thumped on his twin, Troy de Wolfe, who lurched to his feet. With the twins on the move, Patrick continued down the table to brothers Edward de Wolfe and Thomas de Wolfe. Edward was the diplomat of the family and the only one who wasn't terribly drunk, and he tried to talk some sense into his older brothers to at least give the couple an hour or two alone.

But his pleas fell on deaf ears.

Thomas de Wolfe, the Earl of Northumbria and a man who liked a good party, pushed Edward aside as he followed Patrick and Blayth. Not wanting to be left behind and also thinking there needed to be one sober man in that group, Edward pursued.

So did various sons of the de Wolfe brothers, including Cassius' older brother, Markus, and younger brothers, Titus and Magnus. All of them moved after the couple, carrying pitchers of wine with them. They were prepared to take the party wherever it was necessary, even if that meant invading the marital bedchamber.

But Cassius and Dacia didn't know that. They thought they'd gotten out of the hall without being seen and only found out too late that they had a herd of stampeding cattle behind them. Cassius saw them coming and grabbed his wife, who shrieked and giggled as they ran all the way to their chamber. Cassius managed to shove her inside, but he was caught up when his father and uncles grabbed him.

"Cass!" Uncle Troy said as he threw an arm around the man's neck and pulled him close. "Cass, listen. You are a boy now, but you shall emerge from that chamber a man. A husband. It is very important that you..."

Patrick yanked his son from Troy's grasp. "My son," he said, putting his enormous hands on Cassius' face. "I knew this moment would come. I thought that your grandfather would be here, but alas, he is only here in spirit. He was very proud of you, Cass. We are all very proud of you. If your grandfather was here, he would tell you to…"

"Give her what she wants!" Blayth and Thomas finished for him, shoving Patrick out of the way. Blayth grabbed his nephew by the arm. "Papa would say to treat her like a lady, but make sure she enjoys tonight."

"And if she doesn't weep with pleasure when you take her, you're not doing it right!" Thomas elaborated loudly. "And no spanking. Women do not appreciate that!"

They were laughing, having a great time at Cassius' expense, when all the man wanted to do was get to his wife. He was pushing his uncles away, trying to get to the door.

"I will not have the chance to do anything if you lot don't leave me alone," he said. "Go back into the hall and find your wives and leave me to mine."

He was genuinely trying to move away so Patrick decided to stop tormenting his son and help him. He pushed his brothers back, helped by Markus, as Cassius finally made it to the door. He no sooner put his hand on the latch when he heard a distinct *whack* sound.

Blayth hissed.

Jordan and her willow switch had made an appearance, mostly on Blayth's backside.

"Get back, all of ye," she said. "I dunna care if ye have grandchildren of yer own. Ye're not too big for me tae take a switch tae, so leave Cass alone. Get back tae the hall."

She swatted Troy because he started to defend Blayth, which was the wrong thing to do. No man, no matter how old he was, was obliged to obey his mother instantly. Jordan didn't use the switch again, but she held it aloft in her hand for all to see so they would know she meant business.

"Atty, get them moving," she told Patrick. "Ye know better than tae harass a man on his wedding night."

Patrick came to a pause, along with Edward, and they both started to laugh. "Don't you remember what happened on Eddie's wedding night?" Patrick said, pointing at his brother. "Papa and Uncle Paris were so drunk that you could not get them out of Edward and Cassie's bedchamber. Remember? You had to drag Paris out and even then, he stood at the bedchamber door and cried."

Jordan remembered that night very well. Edward had married the daughter of William's best friend, Paris de Norville. Cassiopeia de Norville had been Paris' one living daughter and the man had turned into a mess when the time came to consummate the marriage.

She fought off a smile at the memories.

"'Tis true," she said. "But we chased him away, eventually. Just like I'm chasing ye away. Leave the happy couple alone or I'll never have any great-grandchildren."

Laughing softly, Patrick and Edward turned away, heading back down the corridor. When they had faded from view, Jordan turned to Cassius and Dacia, who had opened the door now that it was safe.

She lowered the switch.

"They dunna mean any harm, ye know that," she said, looking between the pair. "They are simply happy for ye. 'Tis how this wild bunch shows their love. And the dirty songs, too."

Cassius went to his grandmother, hugging her gently. "I know," he said. "And I love them for it. But the fact that you're here, and you were able to witness our marriage, means everything to me, Matha. I just wish that Poppy could have been here, too."

Matha was what all of the grandchildren called Jordan, and *Poppy* was their term of endearment for William. Jordan patted her enormous grandson on the cheek.

"He is," she said simply. "In fact, that's why I've come. I want tae give ye something of him."

As Cassius and Dacia watched curiously, Jordan pulled forth a delicate golden chain, dark with age. She held it up to Cassius, who took it carefully.

"When yer Poppy and I were married, it was a secret ceremony," she said. "I was supposed tae marry another man, but I married Poppy instead. I couldna wear a ring for all tae see, so he gave me a ring on that chain. Instead of putting the ring on my finger, he put the chain over my head. I've cherished it for seventy-two years and I brought it with me tonight because it's something from Poppy. In spirit, I wanted him tae be present and he is – in that chain he gave me. I want ye tae cherish it, Cassius, and give it tae Dacia. It represents a marriage that not even death can destroy."

Cassius had never heard that story about the chain before and there was a lump in his throat as he looked at it. Bringing to his lips, he kissed it. "Thank you, Poppy," he murmured, looking to his grandmother with tears in his eyes. "You could have given me all of the gold in England and it would not have been as valuable to me as this is. Thank you for this, Matha."

Jordan patted her teary-eyed grandson before looking to Dacia. Tossing the switch aside, she took Dacia's hands in her own and held them firmly. "And for ye, Lady de Wolfe, a good Scots blessing," she said. "May ye always have a roof for the rain, wood for the fire, and the love and laughter of the man ye hold dear."

Kissing Dacia sweetly on the cheek, she turned and headed back down the corridor where her sons and grandsons had gone. Cassius watched her go, his heart fuller than he could have imagined. Turning to Dacia, he carefully put the chain over her head and she took a moment to look at it.

"I will never remove this," she said seriously. "This is mayhap the most important piece of jewelry I have ever had."

Cassius smiled weakly, still quite emotional, and directed her into the chamber. Shutting the door behind them, he bolted it.

"I seem to remember my mother telling me once that she occupied this chamber when she first came to Berwick," he said. "The window overlooks the river."

Dacia went to a small table against the wall, one that held her capcase, and began to remove the ribbons in her hair.

"I find all of Berwick beautiful," she said. "How fortunate you were to grow up here."

"Fortunate, indeed. Do you want some wine?"

Dacia looked over to the table next to the bed, where someone had thoughtfully put a pitcher of wine, two cups, and several pieces of fruit.

"Nay," she said, pulling the last of the ribbons from her hair and starting in on the ties that held the dress together. "I think I have had enough wine to last me for quite some time. So have your uncles and father. Oh, and I forgot to tell you – my grandfather received a missive from Father Lazarus yesterday. You know the priest has been helping Darian keep an eye on the village. You'll never guess what Father Lazarus said."

"What?"

"Evidently, Amata's father pledged Amata to the same nunnery where her sister is serving," he said. "She's going to spend the rest of her life away from men, parties, and gossip."

Cassius grunted. "She can still talk," he said. "Where there are women, there is gossip."

"It's a silent order, Cass."

Cassius laughed softly at the fate of Amata de Branton as he removed his fine tunic, leaving his chest bare. Sitting on the bed, the boots were next followed by the breeches, made of the finest leather. It was then that he noticed two dog paws underneath the bed, reaching underneath to pet Argos, who was never far away from him or Dacia these days.

The old dog was part of their family.

Nude, Cassius sat back on the bed, throwing the coverlet over his hips, as he watched his wife slither out of her wedding dress. The pretty pink dress went up on a peg in the wardrobe. Stripped down to everything but the shift, she finally turned and faced her husband.

He smiled at her.

"Well?" he said. "Shall we spend our first few moments together as man and wife?"

She came over to the bed. "I'd like to before that mob returns and demands blood."

Cassius laughed softly. "My mother's father did that when Markus married but, alas, his wife was a widow and already had four children," he said. "But you... unless you have something to confess to me, I will go on the assumption that you are not a widow."

She giggled. "Fortunately, I am not."

"Good," he said, his smile fading. "Come to me, angel. Do not make me wait."

She didn't. Swinging his big legs over the side of the bed, he pulled her shift over her head, tossing it onto the pile of his own clothing. Grasping her by her slender waist, he flipped her onto her back.

They were nude now, facing one another in the dim light. The moon was rising, casting a silvery glow in through the partially covered windows. Dacia was looking up at him, studying him, and Cassius could see that her focus was on his chest, his waist, and finally his manhood, which was already aroused. He was quite well endowed. She simply lay there, looking at him, before finally lifting her gaze to his face.

Cassius met her eyes, a warm glimmer in his own. "Please," he said. "Look all you wish. I will not stop you."

She smiled faintly. "I like the look of you."

"Good. Any questions?"

"No questions. Let me feel you now, my husband."

Her words set him on fire. He settled down on top of her, wedging his big body in between her legs. Dacia was more curious than she was apprehensive, although the feel of his weight on her body made it all seem so very intimate and close. It was the moment they would fully commit to one another, as man and wife, and she couldn't remember when she hadn't loved him. As the ring on her finger said, she belonged to *Cassius*. He kissed her tenderly on her freckled cheek.

"Do not be afraid," he said. "You will like this, I promise."

Dacia lifted her hands to his face. "Show me."

He did.

Cassius slanted his mouth over hers, pulling her close with one arm while the other hand began to roam. Her skin was like silk, warm and beautiful, and he touched her shoulder, her arm, dragging his hand over her belly. Her breasts were full and beautiful, and he enclosed one in a big, callused hand, caressing gently, feeling the nipple harden against his palm. All the while, he rubbed her thigh with his erection, moving it ever closer to the intended target.

His mouth moved away from hers, down her neck, to capture a nipple. He suckled on it and Dacia quivered with delight. This was not any man; it was Cassius, her husband, the only man she had ever loved, and this moment was particularly poignant for her. It seemed as if it had been so hard-fought to reach it. Her hands were on his shoulders, in his hair, memorizing the feel and the smell of him.

She wanted all of him.

More than that, she wanted a piece of him.

His son.

Dacia had discovered something about herself during the few months of their betrothal. She secretly yearned for a child, a son in the image of his mighty father, because she'd spent most of her life without siblings or parents, with only her grandfather as immediate family, and it had been a lonely way to live. Coming to know the enormous de Wolfe family had made her realize that. She knew she wanted as many children from Cassius as he could give her. She wanted the man to fill her with his seed and give her his son.

The erection against her thigh moved higher and now the tip of his phallus was against the dark fluff of curls. Dacia could feel it. Instinctively, she opened her legs wide to him, feeling his manhood rub against her, feeling terrible large. She had visions of him not being able to fit inside of her. Cassius tightened his embrace around her, his mouth on her ear, and suddenly coiled his buttocks. He thrust hard.

Dacia gasped at the stinging sensation, his manhood feeling enormous within the confines of her tight body. But rather than resist, she went with her primal instinct, which was to open her legs wider and moved her hips forward, trying to capture more of him. The action drove Cassius mad and he coiled his buttocks again and drove into her again and again, driving himself all the way to the hilt as Dacia held on to him tightly. Already, he could feel her body clutching at him, demanding him.

It was too much for him to take.

Cassius began his slow and steady thrusts, listening to Dacia groan, feeling her young and nubile body rise to the challenge. She was deliciously tight and slick, her legs flung wide open to welcome him. He shifted himself so that he was on his knees, grasping her legs and holding them on either side of his body as he watched her in the weak light. Pale skinned, full-hipped and full-breasted, the sight of her fed his lust like nothing he had ever experienced.

In fact, he had lifted himself off her for a reason – he wanted to watch her as he made love to her, watching her breasts quiver every time his body came into contact with hers. It was arousal beyond anything he had ever experienced. He looked down, watching his manhood as it entered her body, seeing the faint stain of blood from her breeched maidenhood. It was the sign of his possession, the evidence that she completely belonged to him now.

His thrusts increased. He could feel his release coming and he wanted her to join him, to experience the same pleasure that he was, so he released her right leg and reached down between their bodies, rubbing her swollen bud of pleasure as he continued to thrust. As highly aroused as Dacia was, Cassius' expert fingers brought her to her first release quickly.

She started to gasp as he felt her tremors begin and he

thrust hard, releasing himself within her. Still moving, still pulsing, he lowered himself onto her again, his mouth finding hers, kissing her deeply as she experienced her first release.

It was a deeply personal, and deeply moving, experience.

As their wedding feast continued long into the night, Cassius lay with his arms around his wife, in a room he had known since childhood, listening to the nightbirds call to one another as a gentle river flowed beneath the moonlight. He was home, where he wanted to be, with the spirits of his ancestors surrounding him. For certain, he drew strength from it just as Dacia drew strength from Doncaster. As she'd told Cassius, she *was* Doncaster. Cassius might not have been Berwick or Questing, or any of the other de Wolfe land, but he was an integral part of the de Wolfe Pack. Their lives and loves were intertwined for eternity.

Their mark was all over the lands they loved and protected.

As Dacia slept peacefully in his arms, Cassius glanced down at her, catching sight of the gold chain around her neck. He smiled at the sight, knowing exactly why his grandmother had given it to them. It was a symbol of something that no man and no king could break, something forged by the gods that would keep them together until the end of time.

Like the circular chain, Dacia was his beginning and his end.

Somewhere outside the window, he thought he heard a wolf howl. With the full moon, it wasn't surprising, but Cassius took it as a sign. As Jordan had said, the great Wolfe of the Border was still with them. Perhaps not in a form they expected, but he was there just the same. He was present in Cassius, and his father and brothers, and the rest of the de Wolfe males. And he would be present in the eleven children the Duke and Duchess of Doncaster would eventually have.

The House of de Wolfe-de Ryes would continue on into legend and for Cassius de Wolfe, he would make his own mark in life.

And so would his wife.

Through witch's marks, mercenaries, wounds, wicked cousins, and accidental poisonings, they had survived and would continue to survive until the end of all things. And in the end, their legend would become one.

Just like the chain, for Cassius and Dacia, there was no beginning and no end.

Theirs was a love story for the ages.

ᘯ THE END ᘰ

Children of Cassius and Dacia, Duke and Duchess of Doncaster
Erik (courtesy of Cassius' grandfather, Magnus)
Dacian
Vincent
Bennet
Jason
Maxima
Luciana
Stellan
Amalia
Reese
Michael

AFTERWORD

I hope you loved Cassius and Dacia's tale as much as I loved telling it. Quite a roller coaster, wasn't it? Just a quick mention...

So... what was the "poison" that Dacia was accidentally given? Something that was quite available in Medieval times – powdered foxglove, essentially. The forerunner to digitalis, which is used for cardiac ailments. Too much of it causes drowsiness, unconsciousness, even seizures and possible death. Fortunately, Dacia didn't receive a fatal dose, but she received enough to knock her out for a few days. Her exhaustion, coupled with very little food and sleep, made her highly susceptible to Emmeric's powdered foxglove. We never met Emmeric, but the man had quite a stash of medicines and poisons.

There were actually a lot of plants in Medieval times that contained curative or restorative or even deadly properties, including willow bark (salicylic acid – or aspirin), the opium poppy (morphine, among others), and belladonna to name a few. They had quite a bit available to them, so it makes for interesting reading.

Check out more reading about the pharmacy garden here: www.discoveriesinmedicine.com/Com-En/Digitalis.html

As a final note of this book, I wanted to make a point of mentioning the chain that Jordan gave Cassius and Dacia. If you've read *The Wolfe*, the book that spawned all the others, there is a scene where William de Wolfe gives Jordan a golden chain with a ring on it. Because their marriage was secret (at the time) she couldn't wear the ring openly, so he gave her the ring on a chain so she could wear it next to her heart. It was a particularly meaningful and powerful moment in the book, so the fact that Jordan parted with that chain really did mean a lot to her – and to Cassius. It's kind of like passing the torch from one generation to the next. I think Cassius is one of the more sentimental and emotional heroes I've ever written about and, as I said, he's quickly become one of my favorites.

I hope he has become one of yours.

And the de Wolfe Pack lives on…

THE PARENTS, CHILDREN, AND GRANDCHILDREN OF DE WOLFE

(Note: Don't be intimidated by these family trees – refer to them if you need clarification on a relationship)

William (deceased 1296 A.D.) and Jordan Scott de Wolfe

Total children: 10

Total grandchildren: 75 (including 4 deceased, 7 adopted, 3 step-grandchildren)

Scott (Troy's twin) – (Wife #1 Lady Athena de Norville, has issue. Wife #2, Lady Avrielle Huntley du Rennic, has issue)

With Athena

- William (married Lily de Lohr, has issue.)
- Thomas "Tor"
- Andrew (deceased)
- Beatrice (deceased)

With Avrielle

- Sophia (with Nathaniel du Rennic)
- Stephen (with Nathaniel du Rennic)
- Sorcha (with Nathaniel du Rennic)
- Jeremy
- Nathaniel

- Alexander
- Seraphina
- Jordan

Troy (Scott's twin) – (Wife #1 Lady Helene de Norville, has issue. Wife #2 Lady Rhoswyn Kerr, has issue)

With Helene
- Andreas
- Acacia (deceased)
- Arista (deceased)

With Rhoswyn
- Gareth
- Corey
- Reed
- Tavin
- Tristan
- Elsbeth
- Madeleine

Patrick – (Married to Lady Brighton de Favereux, has issue)
- Markus
- Cassius
- Magnus
- Titus
- Thora
- Kristiana

James – (Wife #1 Lady Rose Hage, has issue. Wife #2, Asmara

ap Cader, has issue)

With Rose
- Ronan
- Isabella

With Asmara (as Blayth)
- Maddoc
- Bowen
- Caius
- Garreth (known as Garr)

Katheryn (James' twin) – (Married to Sir Alec Hage, has issue)
- Edward
- Axel
- Christoph
- Kieran
- Christian

Evelyn – (Married to Sir Hector de Norville, has issue)
- Atreus
- Hermes
- Lisbet
- Adele
- Aline
- Lesander (goes by Zander)

Baby de Wolfe – (Died same day. Christened Madeleine)

Edward – (Married to Lady Cassiopeia de Norville, has issue)

- Helene
- Phoebe
- Hestia
- Asteria
- Leonidas
- Dorian
- Dayne
- Stephan
- Pallas

Thomas – (Married Lady Maitland "Mae" de Ryes Bowlin, has issue)

- Artus (adopted)
- Nora (adopted)
- Phin (adopted)
- Marybelle (adopted)
- Renard & Roland (adopted)
- Dyana (adopted)
- Alexander
- Cabot
- Matthew
- Wade
- Tacey
- Morgan

Penelope – (Married to Bhrodi de Shera, Earl of Coventry, hereditary King of Anglesey)

- William
- Perri
- Bowen
- Dai
- Catrin
- Morgana
- Maddock
- Anthea
- Talan

HOLDINGS AND TITLES OF THE HOUSE OF DE WOLFE AND CLOSE ALLIES AS OF 1300 A.D.

Scott de Wolfe – Earl of Warenton (Heir: William "Will" de Wolfe, Lord Killham)

Troy de Wolfe – Lord Braemoor (Heir: Andreas de Wolfe)

Patrick de Wolfe – Earl of Berwick (Heir: Markus de Wolfe, Lord Ravensdowne. Second son, Cassius de Wolfe, married the heiress to the Dukedom of Doncaster)

Blayth (James) de Wolfe – Baron Sydenham (Heir: Ronan de Wolfe)

Edward de Wolfe – Baron Kentmere (Heir: Leonidas de Wolfe)

Thomas de Wolfe – Earl of Northumbria (Heir: Alexander de Wolfe, Lord Easington)

Wark Castle (Wolfe's Eye):
Larger outpost for the Earl of Warenton. Literally sits on the border between England and Scotland.
- Titus de Wolfe (son of Patrick de Wolfe), commander
- Ronan de Wolfe (son of Blayth/James de Wolfe)

Berwick Castle (Wolfe's Teeth):
Massive border castle, strategically important, de Wolfe holding and seat of the Earl of Berwick, Patrick de Wolfe
- Alec Hage, commander

- Edward "Eddie" Hage, commander
- Hermes de Norville, second

Castle Questing (Wolfe's Heart):
Massive fortress, seat of the Earl of Warenton, Scott de Wolfe.
- Apollo de Norville, second
- Nathaniel Hage
- Owen le Mon

Rule Water Castle (Wolfe's Lair):
The largest outpost in the de Wolfe empire, known as The Lair. Seat of William "Will" de Wolfe, Viscount Kilham, heir apparent to the Earldom of Warenton.
- Magnus de Wolfe, second
- Adonis de Norville, second
- Perri de Shera, son of the Earl of Coventry and Penelope de Wolfe de Shera (squire)

Monteviot Tower (Wolfe's Shield):
Smaller outpost in Scotland, strategic. Holding of Troy de Wolfe.
- Andreas de Wolfe, commander

Kale Water Castle (Wolfe's Den):
Larger outpost on the England side of the border, strategic.
- Troy de Wolfe, Lord Braemoor, commander
- Troy also commands Sibbald's Hold, former home of Red Keith Kerr (his wife's father). A minor property commanded by son Garreth de Wolfe.

Kyloe Castle (Wolfe's Howl):
Seat of the Earl of Northumbria, Thomas de Wolfe

- Christoph Hage, second

Roxburgh Castle (Wolfe's Claw – unofficially)*
Large royal-held castle near Kelso, formerly manned by knights from Northwood, but awarded to the House of de Wolfe by royal decree for meritorious service to the crown. Volatile location, often attacked by Scots, and is manned by both royal and de Wolfe troops.

- Blayth (James) de Wolfe, Lord Sydenham, commander
- Axel Hage, second

*Note: Because of the extreme volatile location and nature of this garrison, Blayth (James) de Wolfe was given the title Lord Sydenham and the Sydenham Barony, a small but strategic barony between Wark Castle and the town of Kelso.

Blackpool Castle (acquired by Scott de Wolfe around 1300 A.D.) known as Wolfe's Strike:

- Thomas "Tor" de Wolfe, commander
- Christian Hage, second

Northwood Castle:
Massive border castle, very important and strategic. Belonging to the Earls of Teviot. Not part of the de Wolfe empire, but strongly allied to de Wolfe by marriage and blood. The Earl of Teviot is John Adrian de Longley, Adam de Longley's eldest son. Adrian's mother is Cayetana Fernanda Teresita Silva y Fausto de Longley, Princess of Aragon.

- Hector de Norville, captain of the guard (also Lord Bowmont)
- Atreus de Norville, second

- Tobias de Bocage, second

Penton Castle (property of the Duke of Doncaster, Cassius de Wolfe. Also titled Lord Westdale) Known as Wolfe's Sword:
- Commanded by Adonis de Norville and Gethin Ellsrod

Edenthorpe Castle (Seat of the Duke of Doncaster, Cassius de Wolfe, as of 1305 A.D.):
- Darian de Lohr
- Rhori du Bois

Edenburn Tower (House of de Norville):
Smaller tower on the southern end of de Wolfe properties belonging to the House of de Norville. Owned and commanded by Alec Hage

Castle Canaan (Kendal) Wolfe's Bite:
The Earl of Warenton's southernmost holding, not directly related to the Scottish border but a source of additional troops if needed. Inherited the property when he married the widow of Castle Canaan.
- Stephan du Rennic, commander

Seven Gates Castle (Kendal):
- Seat of Edward de Wolfe's Barony – Kentmere in Kendal that adjoins brother Scott's lands at Castle Canaan
- Isleworth House, Surrey

Cheswick Castle (Northumberland) Wolfe's Roar:
- Seat of Markus de Wolfe, Lord Ravensdowne, heir to Berwick earldom

- Also included in this alliance is Trastamara Castle, home of Markus' stepson, Atlas Abril (formerly Atlas de Sauque) and wife Caria de Wolfe Abril.

Kathryn Le Veque Novels

Medieval Romance:

De Wolfe Pack Series:
Warwolfe
The Wolfe
Nighthawk
ShadowWolfe
DarkWolfe
A Joyous de Wolfe Christmas
BlackWolfe
Serpent
A Wolfe Among Dragons
Scorpion
StormWolfe
Dark Destroyer
The Lion of the North
Walls of Babylon
The Best Is Yet To Be

De Wolfe Pack Generations:
WolfeHeart
WolfeStrike
WolfeSword

The de Russe Legacy:
The Falls of Erith
Lord of War: Black Angel
The Iron Knight
Beast
The Dark One: Dark Knight
The White Lord of Wellesbourne
Dark Moon
Dark Steel
A de Russe Christmas Miracle
Dark Warrior

The de Lohr Dynasty:

While Angels Slept
Rise of the Defender
Steelheart
Shadowmoor
Silversword
Spectre of the Sword
Unending Love
Archangel
A Blessed de Lohr Christmas

The Brothers de Lohr:
The Earl in Winter

Lords of East Anglia:
While Angels Slept
Godspeed

Great Lords of le Bec:
Great Protector

House of de Royans:
Lord of Winter
To the Lady Born
The Centurion

Lords of Eire:
Echoes of Ancient Dreams
Blacksword
The Darkland

Ancient Kings of Anglecynn:
The Whispering Night
Netherworld

Battle Lords of de Velt:
The Dark Lord
Devil's Dominion
Bay of Fear
The Dark Lord's First Christmas

The Executioner Knights:
By the Unholy Hand
The Mountain Dark
Starless
The Promise (also Noble Knights of
de Nerra)
A Time of End
Winter of Solace
Lord of the Shadows
Lord of the Sky

Contemporary Romance:

**Kathlyn Trent/Marcus Burton
Series:**
Valley of the Shadow
The Eden Factor
Canyon of the Sphinx

**The American Heroes Anthology
Series:**
The Lucius Robe
Fires of Autumn
Evenshade

Sea of Dreams
Purgatory

**Other non-connected
Contemporary Romance:**
Lady of Heaven
Darkling, I Listen
In the Dreaming Hour
River's End
The Fountain

Sons of Poseidon:
The Immortal Sea

**Pirates of Britannia Series (with
Eliza Knight):**
Savage of the Sea by Eliza Knight
Leader of Titans by Kathryn Le
Veque
The Sea Devil by Eliza Knight
Sea Wolfe by Kathryn Le Veque

Note: All Kathryn's novels are designed to be read as stand-alones, although many have cross-over characters or cross-over family groups. Novels that are grouped together have related characters or family groups. You will notice that some series have the same books; that is because they are cross-overs. A hero in one book may be the secondary character in another.

There is NO reading order except by chronology, but even in that case, you can still read the books as stand-alones. No novel is connected to another by a cliff hanger, and every book has an HEA.

Series are clearly marked. All series contain the same characters or family groups except the American Heroes Series, which is an anthology with unrelated characters.

For more information, find it in **A Reader's Guide to the Medieval World of Le Veque.**

ABOUT KATHRYN LE VEQUE

Medieval Just Got Real.

KATHRYN LE VEQUE is a USA TODAY Bestselling author, an Amazon All-Star author, and a #1 bestselling, award-winning, multi-published author in Medieval Historical Romance and Historical Fiction. She has been featured in the NEW YORK TIMES and on USA TODAY's HEA blog. In March 2015, Kathryn was the featured cover story for the March issue of InD'Tale Magazine, the premier Indie author magazine. She was also a quadruple nominee (a record!) for the prestigious RONE awards for 2015.

Kathryn's Medieval Romance novels have been called 'detailed', 'highly romantic', and 'character-rich'. She crafts great adventures of love, battles, passion, and romance in the High Middle Ages. More than that, she writes for both women AND men – an unusual crossover for a romance author – and

Kathryn has many male readers who enjoy her stories because of the male perspective, the action, and the adventure.

Kathryn loves to hear from her readers. Please find Kathryn on Facebook at Kathryn Le Veque, Author, or join her on Twitter @kathrynleveque, and don't forget to visit her website and sign up for her blog at www.kathrynleveque.com.

Please follow Kathryn on Bookbub for the latest releases and sales: bookbub.com/authors/kathryn-le-veque.